This was going to be b . . .
not turn away.

Marcos smiled at the cops around him, pointed the gun at the back of Uni's shiny bald head . . . and pulled the trigger.

The sound of the gunshot exploded throughout the cavernous hangar . . . and it really did seem like the round hit Uni's skull. But whether the gun misfired, or it was divine intervention . . . the bullet ricocheted backwards . . . and hit Marcos right between the eyes.

Silence. Marcos stood there for the longest time, absolute bewilderment in his eyes. He even reached up and felt the hole in his skull. In an eerie moment, Marcos turned to Hunn and said one word: "How?"

Hunn was so shocked by what he'd just seen, he couldn't speak. He could only shrug.

Marcos went over in a heap a second later.

This was a little too freaky . . .

"Mack Maloney has created a team of realistic characters that pulse with patriotic fervor. With intense military action, twists and turns that keep you turning the pages well into the night and a collection of the most evil bad guys you will ever come across, Mack Maloney hasn't just crafted a great war story, he has set a new standard for action-packed thrillers."

—**Robert Doherty**, bestselling author of the *AREA 51* series

St. Martin's Paperbacks Titles
by Mack Maloney

Superhawks: Strike Force Alpha
Superhawks: Strike Force Bravo

SUPERHAWKS

★ ★ ★

STRIKE FORCE BRAVO

Mack Maloney

St. Martin's Paperbacks

SUPERHAWKS: STRIKE FORCE BRAVO

Copyright © 2004 by Mack Maloney.
Excerpt from *Superhawks: Strike Force Charlie* copyright © 2004 by Mack Maloney.

ISBN: 0-312-98606-8
EAN: 80312-98606-3

Printed in the United States of America

St. Martin's Paperbacks edition / August 2004

St. Martin's Paperbacks are published by St. Martin's Press, 175 Fifth Avenue, New York, NY 10010.

10 9 8 7 6 5 4 3 2 1

In memory of those U.S. soldiers lost in the War Against Terrorism

PART ONE
One Crazy Night

Chapter 1

Singapore

The terrorists came dressed as waiters.

They arrived at the rear service entrance to the Tonka Tower Hotel at precisely 10:00 A.M. There were eight of them. They unloaded six food carts from their two vehicles. There was no security in this part of the building and the rear door had been left open for them. They rolled the carts up onto the kitchen's loading platform and simply walked inside.

It was checkout time and the lobby of the enormous hotel was packed. Hundreds were waiting in line; hundreds more were picking up luggage or trying to find cabs. The routine chaos gave the eight terrorists all the cover they would need. They walked right through the lobby, heads down, pushing their carts, and made for the service elevators. Once there, they pushed the button to call the largest of the hotel's 16 service lifts. It arrived a few seconds later. Loading the carts and themselves aboard, they quickly closed the doors and hit the button to go up.

The Tonka hotel was one of the tallest structures in the

world. It was shaped like a futuristic pagoda, with a tower that soared 1,200 feet in the air. There were more than 3,000 rooms here, most of them expensive suites, plus many function areas, shops, and trendy restaurants. The hotel's grand style and downtown location made it a popular place for foreign businesses, especially American companies, to hold meetings and corporate events. The Singapore government encouraged such things and frequently picked up the tab.

The hotel was especially crowded with American citizens today, as it had been declared America Day by the city government, a fete for the families of U.S. business and foreign service people living in Singapore. Several gala events were being held at the Tonka. A huge breakfast for the American consulate was in progress on the sixteenth floor. A reception for U.S. Embassy employees was about to begin on the forty-fourth. Another for the Ford Motor Company was scheduled for 10:30 on the ninety-sixth.

But the disguised terrorists in the elevator passed all these floors. They were heading directly for the top.

They were members of Qeza al-Habu, a terrorist cell linked directly to Al Qaeda. Their destination was the building's penthouse, up on the one hundred and fortieth floor. There was an expansive banquet hall here known, simply enough, as the Top Room. A party for children of U.S. diplomats serving in Singapore had started in the hall around nine. There were 300 kids on hand, most under the age of 12, some as young as just a few months old. There were 22 adults watching over them.

The eight terrorists arrived on the top floor and unloaded their carts. Two stayed in the hallway and, using tools hidden in a steaming dish, disabled the hotel's elevator system by short-circuiting its main and auxiliary power panels, all of which were located here at the building's peak. This jammed more than 50 passenger lifts in place, trapping hundreds and making access to the top floor nearly impossible. It also knocked out every light in the hotel from the ninety-ninth floor down.

The six remaining terrorists proceeded to the Top Room function hall. They reached its one and only door and wheeled the food carts in. The large triangular room had a long dining table set up in the center. On it sat four gigantic chocolate cakes. Huge lime-tinted windows made up the three walls of the room; balconies went all around the outside. The Top Room was so high, wisps of clouds could be seen passing the windows.

The terrorists were met by several adults who greeted them quizzically. The children's party had already received their cake order from the kitchens downstairs. Why were these men here?

The terrorists didn't reply. They simply locked the door behind them, then uncovered their food carts. There were eight AK-47 assault rifles hidden inside. The terrorists pushed seven of the adults against the nearest wall and calmly shot each one in the head. Panic erupted. Children began screaming; some of the other adults tried to hide. The terrorists fanned out around the room, hunting down five more adults and killing them, including two shot at point-blank range found cowering under the banquet table. This thoroughly terrorized everyone in the room. The remaining adults froze in place. Many of the children went numb with fear. A few, however, did not.

Some began crying. The terrorists walked around the room and shot each one. Soon enough, the room was deathly quiet.

The terrorists made their captives lie facedown on the floor. Some muffled cries could still be heard as the young hostages and the adults complied. Those terrorists charged with disabling the elevators joined their colleagues in the function room. Besides their tools and more weapons, their food carts were full of *plastique*, the highly volatile plastic explosive, nearly 60 pounds of it in all.

The leader of the terrorist group was a man known only as Moka. He was a tall, skinny Syrian Arab. He began shouting orders. While four terrorists watched over the hostages, three others began setting up the explosives. The Top Room had three immense pillars, one in each corner of the triangular hall. They were painted pearl white, with gold leafing. Exotic vines and flowers grew up their sides, and at night, under low light, these flowers became translucent. But the three pillars served a purpose beyond ornamental. Soaring right through the glass ceiling 35 feet above, they held the roof of the immense tower in place. The terrorists knew this because they had taken a complete set of building plans for the Tonka off the Internet. They also knew if the pillars were severed with enough force, the concussion of the blast and the weight of the debris would send the entire tower crashing to the ground.

The terrorists attached explosive charges to the three pillars 20 pounds each. Plastique was very pliable and the individual 2-pound packets stuck to the pillars like glue. Plastique was also easy to detonate. Two wires from a 20-

volt motorbike battery would provide the spark for each pillar; a simple kitchen timer would throw the switch. The terrorists worked quickly, as they had been trained to do. This operation had been planned for six months. The participants had practiced for it every day for the past eight weeks.

Once the explosives were in place, the terrorists took out their third arsenal of weapons: cell phones. Each man had three, except the leader, Moka, who had five. Each cell had a set of phone numbers preprogrammed inside it, each number connected to a large news organization somewhere around the world. The terrorists began activating these numbers. In seconds, phones were ringing at the news desks of CNN, Fox, the U.S. broadcast TV networks, the BBC, the Associated Press, Reuters, and more. The message transmitted by the terrorists was short and grim: they had taken over the world-famous Tonka Tower and were planning to destroy it, with thousands trapped inside, in 15 minutes.

Moka's last call was to a local Singapore TV news station, Sing-One TV. It was the largest of the four news stations in the city. Moka was soon talking to an individual identified as Sing-One's executive manager. The man believed Moka right away, as reports that something was wrong at the Tonka Tower had already reached the TV station.

Moka made himself very clear to the TV executive. This was not a situation for negotiations or ransoms or diplomacy. This was an unfolding act of war. He and his men were dedicated to publicizing the plight of Muslim peoples everywhere. To this end, they were going to blow up the Tonka and kill everyone in it. Why was Moka per-

sonally calling Sing-One TV? Because he wanted the entire incident broadcast live around the world.

Sing-One's manager called Moka a bastard and a religious devil but then quickly complied with his wishes.
Moka would allow only one news chopper to come close
to the building. A camera onboard would be able to
record everything happening inside the function hall.
When the station manager pointed out there were other
TV copters in the city and that a number of police and
military helicopters would soon be heading for the tower
as well, Moka assured him that only the Sing-One chopper would be allowed to approach.

The rest would have to stay at least 1,000 feet away, or
Moka's men would start killing hostages.

In the next 10 minutes, the situation around the tower
changed dramatically.

The city police cordoned off the entire downtown area,
20 blocks in every direction. Military police were flood-
ing onto the scene. The government's Rapid Response
Team arrived in six armed helicopters, landing just three
blocks from the besieged tower. These special operations
soldiers dispersed to buildings closest to the hotel, setting
up weapons' positions and listening posts. The U.S. Embassy had also been alerted. Despite Moka's warning, an
emergency diplomatic team was on its way.

Meanwhile thousands of citizens were streaming out
of the area. They included the hundred or so guests who'd
managed to get out of the tower simply by not being on an
elevator when the terrorists first struck. Many more
frightened guests were flowing down the stairwells of the
hotel; most had a long, slow trip ahead of them, espe-

cially in the darkened stairwells. And hundreds were still trapped inside the building's fifty stalled elevators.

The sky above downtown Singapore had changed, too. As predicted, a small fleet of military aircraft, police copters, and TV news choppers had arrived. Thirteen in total, they were all orbiting the tower, except one: the bright yellow Bell Textron belonging to Sing-One TV.

So far the other helicopters had grudgingly obeyed Moka's orders, staying out at least 1,000 feet. The yellow Sing-One copter, however, was allowed to hover just 15 feet away from the Top Room's grand balcony, located on the east side of the building. This was a huge parapet, enclosed in glass except for a plant-filled open-air terrace. By floating just off its railing, the people inside the Sing-One chopper were indeed able to capture just about everything going on inside the function room, thanks to their computer-stabilized Steadicam. Inside two minutes of the copter's arrival, the horrifying images at the Tonka Tower were being broadcast around the world.

And it was all very clear for billions around the world to see: the hostages, the explosives, the terrorists, and the dead. It was early evening in the United States; the attack had been planned precisely for this hour so that it would be watched by a prime-time audience back in the states. A few minutes into the drama, Moka and three terrorists came out onto the terrace. Normally this would have been a very windy place, but glass valances installed around the balcony blocked most of the wind. Moka's men held up a banner. Scrawled in both Arabic and crude English letters, it declared the cell's intentions for all the world to see. At the same time, a phone connection was made between the Sing-One news copter and Moka. The conversation was conducted in Arabic, a common language between the head terrorist and at least one person inside the copter.

Moka reiterated his group's plans, and to prove his point, he signaled that four bodies be brought out to the terrace. Two children and two adults. They were unceremoniously thrown over the side of the balcony, twisting, turning, the smallest caught by the wind, all to plunge nearly a quarter of a mile to the ground below. It was a horrifying sight to see on camera and in person.

Then Moka read a statement, saying again that he had no demands, that he intended to destroy the tower at exactly 10:30 A.M. and that the timers to do this had already been set. This was going to happen, he said, and the world could only sit and watch. If anyone tried to interfere, Moka's men would start shooting hostages, children first.

A tiny clock popped up in the lower right-hand corner of Sing-One's broadcast screen.

Catastrophe was five minutes away.

More than two thousand people were still trapped inside the tower. To make matters worse, all of the lights had gone out in the building by this time, even inside the Top Room. Somehow a small fire had started on the thirty-first floor, filling the stairwells with acrid smoke. As the power continued to fail, many of the sinks and toilets began to overflow, too.

The people in the Sing-One news chopper asked Moka if he had any last statement to make. Moka responded that he'd already spoken his last word, as had his men. The people in the copter asked Moka if he wanted them to get final shots of the faces of his martyrs on TV, before the blast went off. To this Moka agreed.

He called all but three of his men to the balcony. Each man took out photos of loved ones he'd carried with him on the mission; they held the photos up to the copter's Steadicam. By the time the four terrorists got into camera position, the deadline for the explosives to go off was just 60 seconds away. Each man shouted a short prayer, then raised his right arm above his head, with two fingers extended. Oddly, a peace sign.

Moka then signaled the copter that the explosives were about to go off. Sing-One TV had to back away. But the copter remained where it was, just 15 feet off the balcony. Moka signaled again. But the copter came in even closer. Moka became furious. He began shouting into the phone that the aircraft had to get away; it was important to him that the copter crew live to tell their tale. But with the explosives just seconds from going off, the helo kept coming in.

Now Moka was confused. He squinted his eyes, trying to see into the copter's open bay. *What was this?* The man who had been holding the Steadicam just moments ago was now holding a rather large gun. Men on either side of him were holding guns, too. Moka saw the muzzle flashes but never heard the shots that killed him. Six rounds, in rapid succession, went right through his head.

The same barrage killed the other four terrorists on the balcony, this while the copter's TV camera, now relocated to its cockpit, kept rolling for all the world to see. Then incredibly, and still on live TV, the helicopter touched down on the balcony's railing, an amazing feat of piloting. Six men burst from the copter's open bay. They were not TV reporters or cameramen. They were wearing combat suits—*American* combat suits. All black with armor plating, ammo belts, side arms, and helmets that looked like props from a fifties sci-fi movie. All with stars-and-stripes patches on their shoulders.

At the same moment, two of the Top Room's great plate glass windows came crashing in. Men swinging on ropes flew through the openings. The sudden change in air pressure created a minitornado inside the room. Some of the adult hostages screamed, kids began crying, but it was the remaining terrorists who panicked. They were stationed next to the explosive-packed pillars, but now the noise was tremendous, the wind like the devil. And suddenly a small army of armed men was coming at them.

Each terrorist backed up to guard his assigned pillar, but for what? The explosives were set to go off in 30 seconds. One terrorist boldly stood in front of his plastique charges, intent on protecting them with his body. He was shot five times in the head and there is where he died. His killers vaulted over the hostages and disconnected the explosive packs on the first pillar. But two remained, and only 20 seconds were left.

The terrorist in the northeast corner took cover behind his pillar and started firing at the soldiers in black. Everyone, hostages and soldiers alike, hit the floor. The men who had crashed through the window returned fire; a vicious gunfight erupted. The terrorist returned fire in three short bursts but turned too late to see the six men who'd just landed on the balcony. He was caught in their combined fusillade, taking more than 40 rounds to the stomach alone. He fell over in slow motion, his insides hitting the floor before the rest of him. His charges were quickly disconnected.

Now just one terrorist remained, with one pack of explosives—and 10 seconds before detonation.

Suddenly alone, this terrorist grabbed two small children and pulled them back against the pillar with him. The kids began screaming. Shrieks of horror went through the hall. *"Don't shoot!"* some of the adults started screaming.

Nine seconds.

The terrorist fired in the direction of his attackers. He was sure the soldiers would not shoot him, not as long as he was holding the two terrified children.

Eight seconds.

The soldiers kept advancing, moving quickly, but in a crouch. Their weapons were raised, but they were not firing.

Seven seconds.

The terrorist fired again, hitting the soldier closest to him, but still about twenty-five feet away. He watched in astonishment as his bullets staggered the man but then bounced off his armor plating.

"You cannot all be supermen!" the terrorist cried out.

Six seconds.

Most of the adult hostages were crying now; they knew the explosives were about to go off. One pack, 20 pounds, was more than enough to kill everyone in the room.

Five seconds.

The soldiers continued advancing toward the last terrorist. But would they sacrifice two children in order to save many?

Four seconds.

As it turned out, they wouldn't have to. . . .

Three seconds.

One armed man, undetected in the distractions around him, came up behind the terrorist and put a pistol to his head. He pulled the trigger and the terrorist's skull was blown apart. He never knew what hit him, dead before he hit the floor.

Two seconds. . . .

The man with the pistol hastily reached down and began pulling wires out of the block of *plastique*.

One second.

Zero. . . .

There was one loud *pop!* as the last electrical wire was yanked from the explosive pack. The noise scared the hell out of everyone . . . but nothing happened except one long fizzle.

The bomb did not go off. The hostages were safe.

The crisis was over.

The Pentagon, Washington, D.C.

The Situation Room was overflowing with brass.

Four-star generals, full admirals, a few colonels—this was the top of the Pentagon's food chain. The bunkerlike room, buried deep inside the venerable building, was used only in emergencies. A long conference table dominated its center. A huge wide-screen TV hung on one wall. The lighting was subdued. The room was built to hold about thirty people at the most. Twice that number were crowded inside now.

All eyes were transfixed by the images on the big-screen TV. Like the rest of the world, the Pentagon officers were watching the astonishing events in Singapore unfold, stunned by what they were seeing. After the terrorists' sudden demise, all of the TV news copters circling the Tonka Tower had moved in closer. The drama was now being shot from four different angles.

The soldiers in the black uniforms came back out onto the hotel balcony where the bright yellow copter was still balancing itself on the edge of the narrow railing. Seconds before, the rescue team had been seen ushering the children and the surviving adults away from the broken windows in the Top Room and into the hallway, where they would be safer. Then the soldiers collected all the terrorists' unused explosive packs and loaded them onto their helicopter. They took all of the terrorists' weapons, too.

As this booty was being lifted onto the copter, one of the soldiers took down the terrorists' banner and ripped it in two; both pieces were taken away by the high wind. The soldier then took out a banner of his own. It was red, white, and blue. A rather crude but unmistakable American flag. He hung it where the terrorists' pennant had been, leaving no doubt what country the rescuers hailed from. Then with no further ceremony, the rest of the rescue force climbed into the yellow chopper and flew away.

A hush came over the Situation Room. Someone turned down the volume on the TV set. The roomful of military officers remained still, amazed and speechless.

Finally, one spoke up. *"Who the hell were those guys?"*

The admirals, generals, and colonels all looked at one another but received nothing but shrugs and blank faces in reply.

Standing at the back of the room, apart from the rest, were four officers. All captains, one each from the United States' four military services, they were intelligence officers. All eyes in the room now turned to them.

The officer who had first spoken up now elaborated his own question. "Those troopers," he said, nodding back toward the TV. "They were obviously Americans. And obviously very highly trained. But who are they? What special ops group do they belong to?"

The intelligence officers had a quick, hushed conversation. They'd been asking that same question since the drama began.

Finally, one stepped forward. He was Army DIA.

"I'm sorry, sir," he said. "But we have no idea. . . ."

Chapter 2

The Pentagon, subbasement level

Lieutenant Mikael Ozzi did not see the miraculous rescue at the Tonka Tower.

Stuck in one of the most remote sections of the Pentagon, his office was not wired for cable. It was big enough to accommodate his desk, a chair, and his PC and little else. In fact, before he arrived here, the space had been used to store cleaning supplies, this only because by the Pentagon building codes it wasn't big enough to be considered a broom closet. Ozzi was sure it was the smallest office in the massive building.

But if the first rule of military intelligence was to stay out of sight, then this tiny room was the ideal place for Ozzi to do his thing. He was part of one of the most secret units in the history of the U.S. military. It was called the Defense Security Agency.

Created by executive order in the wake of September 11th, the DSA's mission seemed simple enough. It was to "maintain security within the ranks of the U.S. military." This was a deliberately open-ended phrase, though. The DSA actually played several roles in the post-9/11 world.

First, it rooted out any U.S. military personnel who might be terrorist agents in disguise. (It sounded improbable, but the DSA had already caught five such sleeper agents, all of them Saudis, one serving as an instructor at West Point.) The DSA investigated any unresolved disappearances of U.S. military weapons, from bullets to bombers, another growing problem. The agency also watched over the Pentagon's on-line security systems, its communications networks, even its bank accounts. Any irregularities there might indicate foreign intrigue.

The DSA was so secret, many of the highest officers in the Pentagon had no idea of its existence. Its members wore Army uniforms, but even this was a misdirection. Ozzi was a Navy man, others in the DSA were Air Force, and Marines; only a few were true Army. The agency was practically unknown to the CIA, the DIA, the NSA, and the rest of the United States' intelligence services. It was a secret unit hidden in a sea of secret units.

It was a small operation by necessity. Just a dozen people, three staffed here, in offices found at opposite ends of the Pentagon, the rest undercover overseas. But in this case, size really *didn't* matter: small or not, the DSA was really wired in, and when needed, it could get some juice. It could call on any number of U.S. special ops units to do its bidding; it also had access to all intelligence gathered by any other U.S. spy agency. It took its orders directly from the National Security Council and operated under its cover. When the DSA got a mission, they were allowed carte blanche to see it through. Their unofficial motto: "Go Anywhere. Do Anything. Just Don't Tell Anybody."

Ozzi was just 25 years old, a graduate of Annapolis near top in his class. He was barely five-five, diminutive in size and frame, with pale skin and premature baldness already setting in. He was a hard worker, frequently staying at his desk past midnight and sometimes not leaving until dawn or later. Service to the country was the hallmark of his well-to-do Baltimore family, descendants of czarist royalty. His father had been CIA for 35 years. His grandfather had served in the OSS. The spy business was in Ozzi's blood.

He was not exactly a cloak-and-dagger guy, though. His specialty was advanced systems analysis. Most of his work was done poring over data flowing into the Pentagon's massive computer networks, again looking for anything out of the ordinary. He enjoyed his job, here on the front line of the battle for cyberspace. But often he yearned to leave his four small walls and actually get his hands dirty for a change.

Soon enough, he would have his chance.

It was shortly after 9:00 P.M. when Major Carlson Fox walked into Ozzi's office. He was carrying a DVD player and portable TV.

Tall, handsome, rugged—three things Ozzi was not— Fox was Ozzi's boss and a top operational guy in the DSA. He was in his early fifties, a CIA veteran who'd been lured back to service after the attacks of 9/11. He was married, again unlike Ozzi, had two kids and a nice house in nearby Silver Springs. His wife was gorgeous, a former model. Trouble was, they saw each other only a few minutes a day, so crazy was his work schedule. It was a rare evening that Fox was home before midnight.

He and Ozzi were opposite sides of the same coin. They worked well together because they were both easy-going and were good at keeping secrets. Fox was a down-and-dirty type guy. He had a mind like Sherlock Holmes, was more detective than military officer, which was practically a requirement in the DSA. He was from Alabama and spoke in a drawl.

"Get your nose out of your computer for a moment," he said to Ozzi. "There's something you've got to see."

Fox cleared a spot on Ozzi's desk for the DVD player and TV. The events at the Tonka Tower had already been burned onto a disk and he was here to play that disk for Ozzi. In seconds they were watching a replay of the takeover of the tower and the dramatic rescue of the young hostages. Ozzi was as astonished as the top brass had been just an hour ago, especially by the bravery and cunning of the rescuers.

And he asked the same question everyone asked: "Who are those guys?"

Fox just shrugged. "No one knows."

Ozzi was confused. "No one knows? How can that be? They're obviously Americans, obviously some kind of special ops team. They looked like Delta guys to me."

Fox shook his head. "Sure, they looked good," he said. "And they're already heroes around the world. But I checked the special operations active file myself, twice in fact. Then I ran a search through the NSC's database. Then I checked back with every contact we have here in town. No one knows who this outfit is or who they are working for."

Ozzi just stared back at the screen. It was playing the events in Singapore again.

"Fascinating," he murmured. "A special ops unit *so* secret, no one knows it exists?"

Fox smiled. "I knew you'd like it. The DoD is holding a press conference upstairs in about thirty minutes. They are going to announce that this unit cannot be identified for security reasons. That will sound good, but the truth is, they don't have a clue who they were, where they came from, where they went."

"Wild," Ozzi said, starting the DVD a third time.

"It gets better," Fox said. "This is actually the second time these guys have shown up."

Ozzi finally took his eyes from the TV screen. "I think I missed that," he said.

Fox got up, closed the door, then returned to his seat on the edge of the desk.

"What's your security clearance these days?" he asked Ozzi.

"Red-Eight," Ozzi replied. "Same as yours."

But Fox was shaking his head. "Sorry, I was bumped up to Red-Nine months ago," he said.

Ozzi was surprised and a little hurt. "And you didn't tell me?" he asked Fox.

The senior officer just shrugged. "I couldn't," he replied. "But it's a moot point now."

He reached into his pocket and came out with a DSA security badge. It consisted only of a bar code.

"Congrats," Fox said. "You're now a Nine, too."

Ozzi studied the ID card for a moment. "To what do I owe this honor?"

"To the fact that what I'm about to tell you is one of the most closely guarded secrets of the past one hundred years."

"That these guys have shown up before?" Ozzi guessed.

Fox just nodded.

"Recently?" Ozzi asked.

Fox nodded again.

Ozzi sat straight up in his seat. "When?" he asked. "Where?"

"They were at Hormuz," was all Fox had to say.

What happened in the Strait of Hormuz a little more than a month ago had been nothing less than Islamic terrorists trying to pull off an attack to rival the destruction of 9/11.

Al Qaeda–funded terrorists had hijacked 10 airliners and two military planes and attempted to crash them into the Navy's supercarrier USS *Abraham Lincoln* as the ship was making the narrow transit through the Strait of Hormuz, the waterway that led into the turbulent waters of the Persian Gulf. The attack, well planned and hyper-violent, ended in failure for the terrorists, though, dealing a major blow to Al Qaeda's network. Every airliner was either forced to land before it reached the carrier or shot down by the Navy. A bloody day certainly, as the hijacked airliners were all local Arab carriers, carrying hundreds of local Muslims. But the carrier made it through virtually untouched—and the 5,500 U.S. sailors aboard were saved.

The Navy had been heaped in glory with its valiant defense of one of its prized warships, but as was usually the case in great battles, there was more to the story.

"The reason the Navy was so successful in saving their precious carrier," Fox told Ozzi, "was not entirely due to their defensive procedures or the skill of their pilots. They had some unexpected help. A last-minute piece of intelligence, delivered to them in a very unconventional

way, allowed the Navy to know where and when the hijacked Arab airliners were coming, what their flight paths
were, and their estimated time of arrival over the carrier.
It was really just an aerial massacre after that."

Ozzi pointed to the screen. "You think these are the
guys who tipped them off?" he asked.

Fox nodded. "Not only that," he said. "But two of them
were flying around in Harrier jump jets that day—
stealthy Harrier jump jets. Even after all the airliners
were shot down, they knew two more planes were out
there somewhere. Turned out that two of our own air refueling tankers were taken over by Bahrani fanatics posing
as copilots. They came real close to banging both of those
planes into the *Lincoln*. It was only because these two
guys in the Harriers brought them down that the *Lincoln*
isn't sitting at the bottom of Hormuz right now, instead of
floating off Iraq."

Ozzi was stunned. The public knew none of this. And
judging by the security level attached to it, few people in
the U.S. government or the military knew it, either.

"What does all this mean for us?" he asked Fox.

Fox lowered his voice even further. In this business,
you never really knew who might be listening, no matter
where you were.

"You know that asshole Rushton?"

Ozzi nodded. General Jim Rushton. Assistant to the
President on military special ops. A disturbingly incom-
petent human being, somehow left over from the Clinton
administration, Rushton knew almost nothing about special ops despite his rank, yet was in a position to run
roughshod over it.

"While the boys upstairs were watching all this," Fox

explained, "the White House was watching it, too. Rushton was paging me before CNN took its first commercial break. He wants to know the same as everyone else: who *are* these people, who do they belong to, and how are they able to do these things."

Fox paused for a moment. The DSA was already running on eight cylinders, juggling many assignments. Another mission would only add to the burden. But Rushton was attached at the hip to the National Security Council. When he spoke, he was acting on the NSC's behalf. Sort of . . .

"And he wants to know *before* anyone else in this building knows," Fox added. "So, bottom line, it's up to us to find out who these guys are. Or more specifically, *you* have to find out. . . ."

Ozzi fought off a smile. Was he really going to get out of his rabbit box?

"A field op, for me? Really?"

"Think you can handle it?"

Now Ozzi just laughed. "You know I can. Where do I start?"

His boss replied: "Go home and pack a bag. I've already booked you passage to Gitmo."

Two hours later, Ozzi was climbing onto a USAF C-12 aircraft at Andrews Air Force base, just outside Washington.

It was the beginning of a scary, roundabout night for him. The plane took off just before midnight. It flew him south, to Jacksonville Naval Air Station in Florida, a two-hour journey plagued by heavy turbulence and rain the whole way. Once down at Jax, he was put aboard a Navy

C-2 Greyhound transit plane and flown out to the aircraft carrier USS *George Washington*, lying 200 miles off Miami. This was another bumpy, white-knuckle flight. It ended by banging down on the carrier's deck just after 3:00 A.M. Ozzi was immediately transferred to an SH-53, the giant naval version of the Army's CH-53. Ozzi hated helicopters, simply because the first workable one had been designed by a Russian and he didn't trust any Russian, even though he was a Russian himself. This helo especially looked too big, too old, too clumsy to fly.

The SH-53 took him to a spot about twenty-five miles off the southeast coast of Cuba. There it entered the strict air corridor allowed by the Cuban government for the United States to travel to Guantánomo Bay, the unlikely, oddly placed American base found hanging by a nub off the eastern end of the communist island. This flight took about thirty minutes, ending as the chopper set down in the middle of a severe, if local, thunderstorm. This while the sun was just peeking over the horizon.

Ozzi practically fell out of the old copter, the rain lingering just long enough to soak him to the skin. A Navy ensign was waiting for him. There was a flurry of ID checking, which ended with the scanning of the bar code on Ozzi's new security pass. Then he was put in a Hummer; it left the airstrip with a screech.

They drove up and over a hill or two and through several security checkpoints. Soon enough, up ahead Ozzi could see the detention camp set up for Al Qaeda fighters captured during American combat operations in Afghanistan after 9/11, and more recently other places. Though it was considered bad taste locally to call this place a prison, it was nothing but. A fortress of razor wire

and wooden buildings, it looked surreal in the damp
early-morning sun.

His vehicle roared past the line of simple plywood barracks, all of them skewered by miles of electrical chain
link and barbed wire. He spotted a few small figures
wearing bright orange jumpsuits kneeling in a holding
pen. Handcuffed and shackled around the ankles, they
were no doubt Al Qaeda prisoners. Ozzi could see their
faces as they drove by. None looked happy.

He was heading for a barracks built separately from
this main compound; indeed, it was nearly a half-mile
farther down the road. It was a slightly smaller building,
with its own half-dozen rings of razor wire encircling it.
While Ozzi had seen small armies of guards watching
over the Islamic detainees back at the main compound,
the road leading to this barracks was being guarded by
three Bradley Fighting Vehicles, each sporting a huge
cannon and several machine guns onboard.

His Hummer reached the barracks' main gate and a
squad of Army Rangers appeared. Ozzi had his ID card
scanned once, twice, three times. Finally the Hummer
was allowed in.

Inside the front door of the building he was met by another squad of Army troops. Green Berets, no less. The
Army is all over this place, he thought. Two were guarding a door at the far end of the room; three others were
manning a check-in station. Once again Ozzi's bar code
was triple-scanned. Then he was frisked. He was beginning to think there were little green men from Mars behind the next door.

He was finally led into the room, escorted by two
Green Berets. Four men in prison garb were sitting

around a crude metal table. Two were sporting bandages on their heads and hands. They were not Arabs. All four were white, obviously Americans, obviously military. The oldest was in his early forties and had bright red hair. He was one of the bandaged. Ozzi pegged him as the officer in the group. The other three were just kids, like him, in their early twenties. All three were the size of linebackers, though, with WWF muscles straining the upper sleeves of their bright orange detainee clothes.

Definitely Delta Force . . . Ozzi thought.

The men barely looked up when Ozzi walked in. They were not handcuffed or in leg restraints, as the Al Qaeda prisoners up the road had been. But they were so rough-looking, it seemed like they should have been. Ozzi's Green Beret escort surprised him by turning on their heels and leaving without a word.

Suddenly it was just him and the four strange men.

He introduced himself as a member of the President's National Security Council, a lie. He asked if each man was comfortable, if they needed coffee or a cold drink. All four declined with a shake of the head. Ozzi got down to business. He told the men of the startling events at the Tonka Tower now just 12 hours old. He explained in detail the actions of the special ops force that, at the very last second, managed to save the lives of hundreds of American children. As he spun his tale, Ozzi watched each man's reaction, hoping a facial expression could provide him a clue. A raised eyebrow or a slightly dropped jaw could speak volumes about a person, depending on what he was hearing when his guard was let down.

But these men were very odd. They were interested in

hearing what had happened—and were obviously learning about it for the first time. Yet they didn't seem especially surprised by the dramatic events.

At the end of it there was a long silence. Finally the guy with the red hair spoke. His name tag identified him as CURRY, R.

"The world is rid of eight more mooks—and that's a good thing," he said. "But why are you telling us this?"

"Because of what happened at the Strait of Hormuz last month," Ozzi replied sternly. "We thought you guys might know the people who were involved in this latest incident, seeing as you were involved in the last. . . ."

What did these four men have to do with Hormuz? A lot. On that day, the crucial information regarding the oncoming hijacked airliners had been delivered to the *Lincoln* by an unauthorized helicopter—actually a Stealth version of a Blackhawk helicopter. It had been chased by two F-14 Tomcats, then battered by anti aircraft fire from the carrier's escort ships, and finally flew through a massive barrage from the *Lincoln's* own close-in guns, which caused it to crash onto the deck of the carrier just as the ship was halfway through the strait. This guy, *Curry, R.*, was the man who'd piloted that helicopter and somehow lived to tell about it.

And the other three? Their story was just as unlikely. Four of the ten airliners seized that day had been diverted by various means from slamming into the carrier. One crashed. The three others had been saved, in midair, by the three muscle men. In each case acting alone, they'd overcome the hijackers and helped set the planes down safely, saving all onboard. The grateful Muslim passengers knew these people as "the Crazy Americans."

Though they were heroes, they'd been detained by the U.S. military once the planes were secured. When they refused to answer any questions about the events over Hormuz or what they were doing in the weeks before, the military, thinking they were rogue mercenaries at best, locked them up here in Gitmo, hoping they'd eventually crack. That's how the DSA learned about them.

Ozzi took some photos from his briefcase. Two showed the pair of Harrier jump jets that had appeared at the tail end of the battle over the *Lincoln*. Another showed a very unusual Blackhawk helicopter. Bigger, longer, more bulked-up—like a gunship on steroids—it had all kinds of weapons hanging off of it. This was believed to be Curry's mysterious helicopter, outfitted like the Harriers as radar-evading Stealth aircraft. Ozzi showed them surveillance photos of shadowy soldiers in black uniforms, very similar to the battle suits these four men had been wearing the day of the Hormuz attack. But these visual aids did little to shake the four men. They hadn't spoken a word about their identities since being taken into custody by the U.S. military, and it didn't appear that was going to change now. But Ozzi had to try. After all, that was the purpose of his trip down here.

"So?" he prompted them after making the case that they were obviously involved in defeating the Al Qaeda attacks that day at Hormuz. "Anyone want to 'fess up?"

The four men just looked at the floor. Their body language said it all. No way they were talking to anyone, about anything.

"You're not prisoners," Ozzi told them. "Not officially, anyway. It's not a name, rank, and serial number sort of thing."

Still, nothing.

"I don't understand," Ozzi said, betraying some frustration. "We're all *Americans* here."

The men shifted uncomfortably in their seats. Ozzi thought he might have hit the mark.

He said to them: "The involvement of these strange people and the strange aircraft at Hormuz is one of the most closely guarded secrets in history. Secret because, despite their valor, their cunning, their bravado, no one in Washington knows who the hell they are."

He paused for a moment.

"So just help me out here," he started again. "These guys who pulled off the rescue in Singapore *must* be friends of yours—buddies from your old unit. How did they do it? How did they know the mooks were going to blow up that tower? How could they *be in* that TV helicopter?"

Silence from the four men.

"Do they have ESP?" Ozzi asked them facetiously. "Are they psychic?"

The men looked at one another. Finally the biggest of the lot, a guy named Hunn, just shrugged. Like Curry, he was bandaged up. "Maybe they were stealing the copter when the shit went down."

Ozzi laughed—but then realized the man was serious.

"But . . ." he began stumbling over his words. "Why would they be stealing a helicopter in Singapore?"

"You'll have to ask them that," Hunn said.

Ozzi was perplexed. "And while they are stealing this copter," he asked the men, "this international incident goes down, and they just happened to be in the right place, at the right time, to save the day—in front of billions?"

"Well, that's just something else about them," Hunn said. "They're *really* lucky."

Hunn thought a moment, then added, "Or at least they think they are."

Silence. The men clammed up again.

Ozzi said: "This is a very important thing, to a lot of very important people. Heroes or not, there is no way of knowing what's going to happen to your friends if they remain off the reservation like this. These things make people in Washington nervous—and no one needs that these days. So, what do you say? Can you throw me a bone here?"

More silence. But then the guy named Curry shifted in his seat again.

"What's in it for us?" he finally asked Ozzi.

At last. . . .

"I can get you out of here, for starters," Ozzi replied. He wasn't telling them they'd have to sign a loyalty pledge and would be kept under surveillance for many years to come.

But to Ozzi's surprise, the four men didn't seem impressed. Not enough to crack.

"There might also be a bit of mon-e-tary re-mu-ner-a-tion," Ozzi added, stretching out those last two words to almost comic proportions. He was authorized to offer each man up to $250,000 for any jackpot information.

Still, the mention of money seemed to have zero effect on them.

Finally, Ozzi just blurted out: "OK—what *do* you want?"

The four men all sat up.

Curry spoke. "We want two things," he said. "Those guys—our friends out there, the ones who survived—have to be pardoned."

"Pardoned?" Ozzi interrupted him. "For what?"

"For everything," Curry replied sternly. "If there are any federal or military charges against them, for things done before or after Hormuz, they have to be dropped."

Ozzi had no idea what Curry was talking about, but he indicated it would be no problem. "What else?" he asked.

Curry took a deep breath. "For all the guys who didn't make it that day, and there were a bunch of them, they have to be posthumously awarded the Medal of Honor. For bravery. Above and beyond."

Ozzi was startled by the request. These guys didn't want their freedom; they didn't want money. They just wanted their friends, both alive and otherwise, to be done right.

"Now can you do that?" Curry asked him, leaning far across the table. "Or are you just a messenger boy? A small fish?"

Ozzi was insulted, but only for a moment. These guys had a story, and he knew he had to hear it.

"Tell me everything," he said, finally sitting down at the table. "And we'll go from there."

Ozzi emerged from the special barracks three hours later. He climbed into the back of the waiting Hummer and told the driver to get him back to the airstrip immediately.

It was now close to noon, but Ozzi had lost all track of time. His head was spinning, his hands shaking. He'd been in the DSA since its existence. He'd heard some crazy stuff in that time, but never anything like this.

Ozzi had been taught from his first days in the intelligence game that after leaving an interrogation he should write down his first impressions immediately. Key words, bits of phrases, body language. Inevitably, these notations would prove invaluable when it came time to compose a formal report.

But now, bouncing down the dusty Cuban road, his pen hovering over his notebook, he was suddenly at a loss for words. He didn't know what to say. How could he start writing anything about what he'd just heard and the people he'd just met?

But he felt compelled to write something down. So he scribbled just one word: *Patriots*.

Chapter 3

Alexandria, Virginia

Fox found Ozzi in the bar at the Holiday Inn down near Reagan Airport.

The bar was on the fifteenth floor of the hotel; it was a rotating, flying saucer–shaped affair that gave patrons alternating views of the airport, Washington, D.C., and the deceptively peaceful waters of the Potomac.

It was now midnight, the end of one long day for Fox and the beginning of another. His wife had dinner on the table for him when he finally got home around 11.00 P.M., but a pink Post-it note with Ozzi's cell number was also waiting on his plate. He and Ozzi had a quick phone conversation, and 10 minutes later Fox was back in his car, speeding down Interstate 95, eating a hastily made peanut butter sandwich and working his own Nokia. Fox knew his deputy had arrived back in the D.C. area at noon that day and yet he never contacted the office. This was unusual behavior for Ozzi, usually a slave to the rules. It was also unusual for him to want to meet Fox in such an out-of-the-way place at so late an hour.

The bartender was clearing away three empty glasses in front of Ozzi when Fox walked in. There was no one else at the bar. Fox smelled bourbon. Cheap stuff, mixed with Coke. He never knew Ozzi to drink much or drink alone. Yet here he was, in the middle of the night, doing both.

Fox took the seat next to him. Ozzi thanked him for driving so far and apologized for the late hour, but both were necessary, he said. The story he'd heard from the "Gitmo Four" was still spinning around his head, just as the bar was spinning around D.C. Indeed, he'd been going in circles up here most of the day. In that time, he'd concluded it might be wise to brief Fox somewhere out of the Pentagon's immediate neighborhood. Fox told him he understood.

Ozzi ordered another drink.

"I know this will sound like a bad Clancy novel," he began. "But what I just heard from those guys down there *has* to be the truth, only because I don't think anyone could have made it up."

Fox tried not to roll his eyes. Ozzi was bright and dedicated but still somewhat new to the spy game. Fox ordered a drink for himself and lit up a Marlboro.

"OK, Lieutenant," he said. "Let's hear your report. . . ."

The story the four men had told Ozzi *was* incredible:

Six months before, they'd been asked to join a supersecret special ops team being put together by a shadowy figure known only as "Bobby Murphy." No one knew who Murphy was or who he worked for. The team was given the latest in weapons and NSA eavesdropping equipment, put on a spy ship disguised to look like a container vessel, and then set loose in the Middle East. Their mission: to track down and eliminate anyone they could find who was connected to the attacks of September 11th. Whether you were one of the terrorist masterminds or just some mook who bought the tickets for the hijackers, you were on this team's hit list and they were coming to get you. Operating in the deepest secrecy, not only had they assassinated a number of the 9/11 culprits, but they'd done so with such speed and brutality, they'd managed to strike terror themselves into the hearts of many Muslims in the Persian Gulf region, guilty or not.

Then Ozzi delivered a real bombshell: the four men also told him that they'd been involved in a bioterror attack on the Gulf's food supply and the aerial bombing of a bank building in downtown Abu Dhabi. Fox was jolted by this news. About two months earlier someone had poisoned a large shipment of fruit just before it left port in Libya. The fruit was being sold by a company owned by Al Qaeda. Hundreds died from the tainted citrus all over the Arab Middle East. The fruit company, a $44-million-a-year operation, was out of business in a week.

Just days before that, a bank in Abu Dhabi had been bombed by two mysterious aircraft, at noon, while the streets around it were filled with people attending a government festival. The bank had held $12 million in cash belonging to Al Qaeda, money used to finance their army of *jihad* fighters. The bombing attack burned this money to a crisp. It also toppled the 16-story building and killed more than a thousand people on the ground.

That these two events happened was public knowledge, of course. The twin attacks had been headlines until the gigantic assault on the USS *Lincoln* knocked them off the front page. Though Fox was aware of a CIA disinformation campaign blaming these attacks on the Israelis, to his knowledge no one had ever claimed responsibility for them. Until now.

They both ordered another drink. Fox asked for a double. Ozzi continued with his report. Yes, it was them at Hormuz, this after they broke the terrorists' code at the last moment. But then Ozzi told Fox of other bloody missions the supersecret team had run. They added up to a string of seemingly unrelated incidents that had baffled intelligence services around the world for months. The rescue of a passenger liner near the Aegean Sea, an air strike on a notorious terrorist camp in Algeria. The terror bombing of a wedding hall in Beirut. The brutal executions of several high-ranking Al Qaeda operatives all caught on videotape.

Fox began gulping his drink. Ozzi's tales conjured up images of futuristic commandos who flew Stealth helicopters and invisible Harriers and who operated off a ghost ship. It *did* seem like pulp fiction, but there was no doubt that some kind of supersecret team existed. *Someone* had created all this havoc. And the people Ozzi had just talked to were living proof of it.

"But who the hell prepped them?" Fox wanted to know. One of the DSA's jobs was to keep an eye on the military's special operations forces, their weaponry, their missions. "We should have heard about these guys before they got through their first day."

"That's just it," Ozzi said. "The team members weren't recruited in any normal fashion. They were all called in the middle of the night by this mystery man, Bobby Murphy, or his confederates, of which he must have a few. They convinced these people that this was a happening thing, and somehow this Murphy guy was able to get them just about everything they needed—with absolutely no one knowing about it. A double squad from Delta Force, some Air Force special ops guys to drive the choppers, some Navy guys to run the boat, and a couple top-notch pilots all signed on. Murphy even got ahold of two Harrier jump jets—and stealthy ones no less! He arranged for unlimited air refuelings, weapons resupply, the works. And the Gitmo guys insist Murphy was running the whole show, no oversight, no nothing. That is, until he got arrested. Now, I've never heard of him—have you?"

Fox shook his head no. He knew every important special ops player in the U.S. military as well as those in the intelligence community. None of them was named Bobby Murphy. He pulled out his Palm Pilot and accessed his computer back at the Pentagon. He ran the name "Robert Murphy" through the employment files of the Defense Department, the CIA, the NSA, and every other U.S. intelligence agency. He came up with 13 hits, but all of them were low-level bureaucrats and enlisted men.

Fox showed the results to Ozzi. "I'll have one of our people check out all of these guys," he said. "Although, the 'Bobby Murphy' name is probably just a cover."

Ozzi agreed with a tip of his glass. Fox lit another Marlboro.

"How did you get these guys at Gitmo to open up to you?" he asked Ozzi. "They've been sitting down there for more than a month and no one has got a peep out of them. Everyone thought they were Israelis or mercs of some kind and that's why they were keeping their mouths shut. I'm surprised they gave you the time of day."

"Well, they're a strange crew," Ozzi replied. "They're not like the hard-ass operators we usually deal with. They're . . . well, *different*."

"Different, how?"

Ozzi drained his drink, then signaled for another.

"I can't explain it any more than to say these guys are authentic heroes. I mean *real* patriots," he told Fox emphatically. "They bleed the flag, Major. Remember the stories about the New York firefighters and cops who saved people on nine-eleven? Ordinary people doing extraordinary things? That describes these guys to a T. You see, they all have something in common, something the regular special op guy might not have. Every one of them lost someone on September eleventh or to some other terrorist attack. So it was personal, you know? They were so focused, their unit patch showed the Twin Towers for God's sake. And what they went through for this Murphy guy was unbelievable. They almost had me in tears."

Fox sipped his drink. It sounded a lot like what Israel did after the terrorist attack at the Munich Olympics in 1972. When a number of their Olympic athletes were taken hostage and eventually murdered by Palestinian gunmen, the Israelis secretly sought revenge. They identified about two dozen PLO members who'd been connected to the massacre and quietly, over the course of the next decade, hunted each one down and put a bullet through his head. What Ozzi was telling him mirrored the Israeli model yet was pumped to the max with stealthy

Harriers, Delta guys, and an enormous undercover spy ship.

Fox asked his question again: "Those guys have been locked up down there for a month. Why would they spill now? Did you make them any promises?"

Ozzi shrugged. "Nothing we can't deliver. I just assured them nothing would happen to their friends. That we'd either just let them fade away or wait until they reveal themselves. The Gitmo guys think they're trying to get back here anyhow, to get back home on their own, and I say more power to them. They did some questionable things over there, but the good far outweighs the bad, in my opinion.

"I also told them I'd do everything in my power to make sure that what they did was officially recognized somehow—especially for the guys they lost while they were carrying out their missions. They say their buddies who got killed deserve Medals of Honor. I tend to agree with them."

But Fox frowned mightily at this, though Ozzi was too busy sipping his drink to notice. As a senior man in the DSA, Fox knew a bit more about the politics of special operations. Rule One: No matter how brave the participants might be, they had to be tightly controlled, as exposure—of them or their mission—might lead to anything from national embarrassment to all-out war. It was a different world from what went on aboveground. And that world was no place for spies who liked staying out in the cold.

Fox was also somewhat surprised at Ozzi's reaction to the Gitmo Four. The young lieutenant was as loyal as the next man and still impressionable to some degree. But never had Fox seen him like this, with so many stars in his eyes.

Fox asked him: "So, there's no doubt in your mind that the guys who did the Tonka rescue are the same guys who showed up the day the *Lincoln* was attacked?"

"No doubt at all," Ozzi replied. "It's the same MO—fly by the seat of your pants, show a lot of balls, but be damn lucky at the same time."

"Well, that might have been their thing before," Fox said, slowly. "Poisoning fruit, bombing banks, and so on. But this last time, they did it for all the world to see. They're all over the news channels, with this Singapore thing and not just in this country, either. They're celebrities. And frankly, that's making some people nervous."

"So?" Ozzi asked.

"So they just can't be allowed to 'fade away,'" Fox said, "someone has to find these guys and bring them in—"

"Bring them in?" Ozzi asked, incredulous. He was drunk and suddenly getting pissed off at his boss, which was rare. Usually he and Fox agreed on everything. "Listen, Major," Ozzi said, words slurring but sincere. "I'm not such a pup here. Especially after what I just heard down in Gitmo. And I know those guys are not a bunch of angels. But going after them, in any way, shape, or form, questioning them about what they did, it would be like going after all those firemen and cops at the World Trade Center that day. Few of them were angels, either, I suspect. But look what they became. Same thing for the people on that plane that went down in Pennsylvania. The people at the Pentagon. Our first boots on the ground in Afghanistan. God damn it, these guys are just like all of

them. And they've gone through a lot. Why can't we just leave them alone?"

"Because we have to follow orders, *Lieutenant,*" Fox said. with heavy emphasis on the last word.

Ozzi just stared back at him. It was clear Fox didn't like this any more than he did. Someone must have been pressing him from above.

"That asshole, Rushton?" Ozzi asked him. "He's behind this?"

Fox just nodded and sipped his drink. "He wants to send Team ninety-nine out after them. He's logging it in as a rescue mission."

Ozzi couldn't believe his ears. In the special ops biz, Team 99 was known as the "Super-SEALs," though some suspected it was a self-designation. In any case, they weren't ordinary fish. They were hunter-killers, a particularly cunning and vicious SEAL element that was sent on only the toughest missions, usually to track down the most notorious bad guys. They, too, were a very secret unit.

"I had to call Rushton after we talked," Fox revealed to Ozzi. "I had no choice. He'd been burning up my line all day—meanwhile I'm stalling for time until I hear from you. He told me, in no uncertain terms, that if you got a lead on the Tonka Tower guys, he was unleashing T Ninety-Nine."

Ozzi continued staring at his boss in boozy disbelief. "But those assholes will more likely kill them than rescue them," he argued, but weakly, as if all the air had gone out of him. "And those people out there are heroes, sir. They don't deserve that. . . ."

Fox's eyes were downcast. "I know," he said. "But heroes or not, we just can't have a rogue team like them operating beyond the realm. No control? No oversight? No accountability? They might be right out of the movies, but this is the real world. And in the real world, these things cannot be allowed to exist."

Ozzi's eyes went black. His face turned uncharacteristically stern. He began to say something but stopped. To cause a scene here would be highly unprofessional, especially with the subject they were discussing. He finished his drink. The bar seemed to be spinning a little faster. He had to change tactics.

"But how are they going to go about finding them?" he said finally. "They're floating around out there somewhere on a containership. And there's got to be hundreds, if not thousands, of containerships in the world. How do you find just the right one? That's even if they are still on the ship. They're experts in avoiding contact. I mean look how they've managed to stay invisible so far."

Fox finished his drink. "I know that, and so does Rushton," he said. "But that doesn't mean he's not going to try. Besides, you know how it is these days. No one can hide for very long anymore."

He signaled for the check. Ozzi could barely move at this point. Fox was torn between duty to follow orders and compassion for his junior officer. The bar spun so that they were looking at the nighttime skyline of Washington.

"Look, Oz-man," Fox said, giving him a fatherly pat on the back. "If there's some way I can derail this, I promise you, I'll give it a shot."

"And if not?" Ozzi asked him point-blank.

Fox put on his hat and zipped his jacket. "If not," he said, soberly, "you'd better hope those guys out there choose not to resist."

Chapter 4

Oki Jima

The stars always seemed extra bright above the secret air base known as XH-2.

On clear nights, with no moon, it was like you could reach up and touch them, the sky out here was so crystal clear.

The base was located on the southern tip of the small jungle island of Oki Jima, which itself was just three miles off the coast of the island of Guam. XH-2 was old. Originally built by the Japanese Army as a radio listening post in the mid-1930s, it served as an intelligence base during World War II and was one of the first places to fall after the battle for Guam. The U.S. Air Force built two runways here during the Vietnam War from which to launch U-2 spy planes. The base had remained open, at various levels of readiness, ever since.

There were three hangars here. They looked like very, *very* expensive warehouses. They were painted with a coating of charcoal black paint that turned two shades of green during the day. This chameleon act was in place to baffle any photo-satellites going over the highly classified place, unfriendly or not.

It was almost 10:00 P.M., the hangars were charcoal now, and the stars above were dazzling, making the buildings look bejeweled. There was a distinct, if muffled, sound coming from each building. These were very elaborate air-conditioning units working overtime. It was a pleasant tropical Pacific night, low seventies and low humidity. But what lay within each structure worked best at temperatures of 55 degrees or below. For them, being chilled meant being invisible.

They were B-2Fs, a top-secret variation of the famous B-2 bat-winged Stealth bomber. They were bigger, stealthier, and more expensive than their $1 billion cousins. The stock-version B-2 had a large bomb bay where a mix of bombs weighing many tons could be carried, dispensed by a rotary launcher. The B-2Fs were equipped with these bomb launchers, too, but they were portable and could be quickly changed out, opening up a large area of the spy bomber to carry . . . well, just about anything. Photo recon packages. Jumbo jamming pods. Radiation detectors. Even black-ops eavesdropping gear. These exotic cargoes were called NLPs—for non-lethal payloads. Things that either the military or the intelligence services needed to be put over a target low and fast, without anyone knowing about it.

These three B-2Fs had been in existence since the late 1990s. They'd flown missions all over the world but had been home-based here on Oki Jima since the latest war in Iraq. Their mission was to help U.S. assets in and out of the Pacific Rim get whatever they needed whenever they needed it. And the B-2Fs could fly to the northern tip of

North Korea and all the way to the last hill in Syria in order to get it.

Major John Atels, code-named Atlas, had been flying B-2Fs for two years. He was early forties, divorced, no kids. He was known as one of the best B-2 frame pilots around, which was actually a backhanded compliment, as the B-2 was the only plane in the U.S. inventory where the pilot was the crew member and the mission commander was the captain of the plane. Still it took great skill to jockey the big black bomber around, especially into and out of the nutty places Higher Authority wanted the B-2Fs to go.

The plane could fly anywhere in the world on auto pilot; its almost roboticlike flight system was called Hal by many of its crews. It was that sophisticated. But once the B-2F had to go in on its target—or, in its non-lethal mode, its "target sweep"—human hands were needed on the controls.

For those few sometimes scary moments, Atlas was indeed one of the best.

He'd been told to report to the flight line at 2200 hours, not an unusual time, as the B-2Fs always flew their missions at night. He was to meet his flight partner here. He, too, was an Air Force major, Ted Ballgaite. To just about everyone who knew him, though, he was "Teddy Ballgame."

The B-2F needed someone other than the pilot to be in charge because there was a huge defensive systems suite onboard the ship; sometimes running it was more labor-intensive than flying the damn airplane. The Stealth bomber was not invisible just because of its shape, low temperature, and paint alone. It was filled with electronic countermeasures, jammers, and other secret gadgets that had to work together if the plane wanted to stay a ghost. All this hardware needed to have a good eye and a quick hand to keep running smoothly. Teddy was a good guy, in the air and to have a few drinks with. He also had a mind like a Cray supercomputer.

Teddy was speaking with two men when Atlas arrived on the flight line. He did not recognize either one. Guam was out in the middle of nowhere; Oki Jima was even farther off the map. It was a very small base and everyone knew one another. So these two had to be visitors. And because this was such a secret place, they had to be top-heavy, security-wise.

They were dressed in what Atlas liked to call "casual spy." Jeans, denim shirts, expensive sneakers, and sunglasses, even at night. These guys were from one of the United States' intelligence agencies. Atlas could spot them a mile away.

He'd been dealing with Intelligence types for years. These days many were from the NRO, the National Reconnaissance Office, a strange collection of individuals with the nonthreatening name. Reconnaissance to most people meant taking pictures at high altitudes by either fast-flying aircraft or satellites. But that was just a small bit of it. The NRO guys reconned *everything* and had the stuff to do it with. When a story came out years before that the United States had a satellite that, from 180 miles up, could zoom in so close to an individual on the ground it could read the label of the cigarette pack in his pocket, the NRO guys were pissed. That was *their* satellite—but they weren't upset by the security leak. They were mad that their eye in the sky, code-named Dressing Mirror, wasn't given its props. Reading the name of a person's cigarette pack had been achieved approximately around the same time as *Saturday Night Fever*. These days, the NRO could count the number of threads holding on the top button of the smoker's shirt. And if that button popped off, they would be able to listen in on his cell phone conversation telling his wife that she had some mending to do tonight. Then they could track the wife as she went to the sewing shop to buy thread to do the repair and hear just about every conversation she had along the way. And then they could find out what TV shows the lovebirds watched that night, what radio stations they listened to. What time they went to bed. Even what they did when the lights went out. . . .

Cigarette label? It was an insult. . . .

But these guys talking to Teddy were not NRO, Atlas surmised. The NROs tended to be younger, more wide-eyed, than other U.S. spy types. These two seemed old at 30; both were smoking, supposedly verboten on a flight line. Both were also carrying side arms, sometimes a mark of the CIA.

They were gone by the time Atlas walked up to the plane. He didn't see them leave; they just weren't there when he arrived. He and Teddy had their traditional handshake, even though they'd seen each other just a few minutes before. The ground crew was working feverishly on their aircraft's hollowed-out bomb bay. Although the vast majority of maintenance on the spy bomber had to be done inside its million-dollar hangar, last-minute stuff could be done out in the open. It just couldn't take very long.

Atlas looked back and saw the ground guys loading not a "weather package" or an exhaust detector system into the open bay but . . . suitcases. Or what appeared to be suitcases anyway. There had to be at least thirty of them, either already up inside the spy bomber or on the ground waiting to be put on. A closer look revealed that they may have been made of some kind of composite fiber; some were black, some brown. Yet they looked like nothing more unusual than what could be seen twirling around a baggage carousel at a typical airport.

"What the hell are those things?" he asked Teddy straightaway.

A very practiced shrug was Teddy's reply. "Beats me," he said. "All I know is that we're flying them in somewhere."

Atlas thought he was joking. "*Flying* them in?" he asked. "As in delivering them?"

Teddy nodded. "Dat's the plan."

Atlas just laughed. He and Teddy had flown some freaky missions since joining the Fs, but never had they *delivered* something to anyone before. But a bigger surprise was yet to come. These cases were obviously going to someone who would not normally have access to whatever was inside them. A typical shipment of anything hush-hush, to a U.S. ally or customer, would be done by a slow, inexpensive cargo plane, not a billion-dollar spy bomber. So Atlas just assumed they were moving the bags from one secret U.S. location to another, for later shipment to a third party somewhere. That would have made *some* sense at least.

But he was wrong. According to Teddy they'd be delivering them—whatever they were—to their new owners directly.

"Jessuzz . . . where?" Atlas asked him.

Teddy was no fool. He would never actually speak the name—there was no way of knowing who might be listening in. Instead he simply held up the cloth map just given to him by the Spooks. There were only numbers on this map, no names, no cities marked. But Atlas looked at the coordinates and knew immediately where they were going.

"Really . . . ?"

Teddy just shrugged and rolled his eyes.

Their orders were to fly the suitcases to Hanoi. A luggage delivery to the communist government of Vietnam.

It took them a half hour to do their preflight before they were ready to fly.

Despite the highly unusual nature of their mission tonight, from the moving-through-air point of view, it was really just another milk run. Once aloft, they would fly a course due south, avoiding anything coming within 20 miles of them. They had an in-flight refueling scheduled for 0100 hours, somewhere over the northern tip of the Philippines, then a landing at Pha Dong Airfield, a secret base 20 miles northwest of Hanoi. Vietnamese soldiers would be on hand to unload the strange cargo. They knew how to unlock the lashing mechanisms on the bottom of the plane. Atlas and Teddy would not even have to shut down the engines. Departure would be no later than 15 minutes after landing.

Then after another refuel over the 'Peens, they'd be back on Oki for breakfast.

. . .

Takeoff was normal. They climbed to 20,000 feet, steering south. The clear skies, the blazing stars, good weather was predicted both down and back. These were perfect conditions for the invisible airplane.

Atlas and Teddy had done so many highly classified flights, very little impressed them now. But this one was very different.

What if these guys come out with their Nikons and start shooting pictures? Atlas wondered as soon as they reached altitude and leveled off. There were a lot of things about the Stealth plane that were still top-secret. Now they were going to fly not just a B-2 bomber but this highly classified version of the bomber into a place where, a generation before, U.S. pilots just like them had fought hard, dropped bombs, and, in many cases, tumbled to their deaths, trying to destroy.

Teddy Ballgame knew just what he was thinking.

"Things change," he said simply.

The flight along the Pacific Rim was sweet.

Had this been a combat mission, say to Afghanistan or above some pesky target in Iraq (or even Iran), Atlas would not have to touch the main controls of the B-2F at all, through the approach, through the target run, through the exit, so computer-driven the bomber was. For the most part, this flight was no different. They were caretakers, watching over the controls certainly, but leaving it up to Hal to actually run things. The designers of the plane knew this; they factored in the crew's comfort and attention levels when designing the flight compartment—this would be the last manned bomber of this size ever built for the U.S. military, and to some degree Atlas and Teddy were just along for the ride. Teddy brought along a book, a biography of FDR. Atlas brought his *Sports Illustrateds,* three months' worth; they'd arrived from his father the day before, an accumulation that would do perfectly for the projected 12-hour flight.

They passed Taiwan, after seeing the lights of Hong Kong off to the west. Even at night, the first islands of the Philippines appeared almost emerald. They were still at 20,000 feet, still invisible. Then their communications suite came alive. It was a beacon being sent out by their refueling plane. They had arrived at precisely the moment they should have. And so had the refueler.

It was a KC-10 Extender, a reconfigured DC-10 airliner used by the U.S. Air Force to carry and transfer thousands of gallons of highly volatile JP-8 aviation fuel, the lifeblood of the B-2F and every other warplane in the U.S. arsenal. Literally, it was a flying gas station.

The refueler was out of Diego Garcia, another out-of-the-way place, this one located in the middle of the Indian Ocean. It was not unusual for tankers to fly many hours in one direction to meet a plane needing to refuel coming in the other direction. Atlas and Teddy were talking on the radio with the KC-10 within minutes of getting a clear visual. Aerial refuelings were usually done entirely over water. This one would take place mostly over water, specifically the Bangtang Channel, a narrow strip of ocean just off the mainland of Luzon. But once they reached the channel, they would pick up the small islands of Calayan, Fuggu and Dalu Pree below. Combined they did not equal the square footage of downtown Dallas. They served well as navigation guides, though, friendly reminders that Atlas and Teddy were on-course.

The Bangtang Channel was the most advantageous place for both planes to meet. In fact, it was a favorite refueling spot for the United States' aerial black ops. Isolated yet easy to find, dark except for the stars, with very few eyes on the ground looking up. Thousands of gallons of aviation fuel would be transferred up here tonight, between two planes worth about a billion and ten, all without the knowledge—or permission—of the Filipino government.

The B-2 was hands-off, but the computer couldn't fly the refueling session. Atlas would have to make sure the plane was riding right, and when it came time to fuck the duck it would be his eyes, his hands, his brain. Teddy, by procedure, would be constantly monitoring the plane's survival systems during fuel transfer. The computer quickly pulled the plane up to the long fuel boom extended out of the rear of the KC-10 and then switched the flight over to Atlas. He eased the big bat up toward the boom. The KC guys were good; they were holding their Johnson pipe steady. Atlas caught a little wind at the last moment but then pushed the throttle forward just a bit and the two planes connected without so much as a bump. In seconds, hundreds of gallons of fuel was rushing into the spy bomber's tanks.

Atlas and Teddy relaxed a little. It wasn't exactly the time to go back to their reading, but they could have. The plane was flying that perfectly.

That's why the threat-warning buzzer startled them so. One moment everything was going swimmingly; the next, chaos in the cockpit. Both assumed, in the first half-second of panic, that something was wrong with the refueling. But the warning buzzer was not emanating from anything connected with the aerial fuel hookup. Instead it was coming from the plane's air defense suite.

The first thing Teddy said was, "This has got to be a glitch." But they both knew it could not be. The B-2 was virtually glitch-proof. Especially in its defensive systems.

"Shit, we've got a launch," was what Teddy said next. "A hot home. . . ."

Atlas was astonished. They were flying above the island of Fuggu. If what Teddy was reading could be believed, someone below, in the dense jungle, had just fired a radar-guided surface-to-air missile at them.

The pilots glared at each other—just for a second. They had identical looks: *What the hell do we do now?*

Finally they went into action, but time was not on their side. Teddy frantically called the guys in the tanker, this while Atlas began to manually unhook from the tanker. But it was too late; this was a monster missile coming up at them and it was traveling very fast. Atlas tore his eyes off his controls, just for a second, to look out the window into the night—just to see if this was real. He saw a huge fireball climbing toward them. It was barely 500 feet away.

Could anyone be this unlucky? Even with the missile, just seconds before impact, the irony was as bright as its exhaust plume. Atlas and Teddy knew the SAM wasn't going to hit them. Their radar signature was less than a marble. The KC-10, however, was like a huge bull's-eye flying in the sky.

Atlas finally got the B-2F to unhook from the fuel spout. The missile hit the big refueler two seconds later. It exploded in violent slow motion not 30 feet in front of them. The missile had impacted square on the Extender's belly. There was a white flash, so bright, it blinded Atlas and Teddy. Then the concussion hit. Their control panel's TV screens blew out, showering both pilots in shards of glass. All of their primary electrical systems shorted out at the same moment. Suddenly the cockpit was filled with sparks. Then came a noise so intense, the headphones inside their crash helmets blew outward. The result was simply deafening.

Through all this, Atlas managed to yank the flying wing to the left, this as the conflagration that was the tanker slid off to the right.

The B-2F went right over onto its back, not something allowed by the flight envelope of the bat wing. Going inverted added to the confusion of the moment, but again Atlas came through. With great strength, he slowly turned the plane back over again. The strain on the engines proved too much, though. They began coughing. Atlas applied power but then looked down at his flight screen and saw through it that their third crew member—Hal the computer—was dead, killed by the concussion of the KC-10's explosion.

Atlas now fought with the controls, at the same time aware that pieces of the bomber's wing were coming off. The engines coughed again. Then the plane began spinning.

Atlas was thrown to the back of his seat. His *Sports Illustrateds* were flying all over the flight compartment.

Teddy had his nose pressed up against the cockpit window; he couldn't move. They were falling like a rock

"Do you see anything flat down there?" Atlas somehow yelled through the smoke and sparks.

But Teddy never replied.

Chapter 5

It was another rainy day in Go Dong.

The monsoon season was here, so it rained most every day. This particular morning, it was coming down in waves.

The weather wasn't bothering the residents of this small village, located on the lower fringes of the Mekong Delta, near the convergence of two bodies of water. The climate here was never very pleasant, either hot and unbearably humid or besieged by downpours like today. The locals took the bad atmospherics in stride.

The village marketplace was crowded as always. Plastic tarps and tent covers protected the merchandise from the rain. Vegetables, pots of rice, and tong sticks were the most popular items. However, anything from American-made sneakers to small TVs and radios could also be had for the right price. The same with rice wine, Australian whiskey, and even opium-laced cigarettes. One just had to know how to ask.

These exotic items came to the small village by way of the tiny port of Cong Ha, 13 miles to the south. Saigon was more than 100 miles to the north.

Most of the people in the village were wearing long rain ponchos that covered from head to toe. This helped SEAL Team 99 blend right in.

There were six of them. One man was watching each end of the tiny waterlogged village. Two more were sitting on the porch of the village exchange building, an old stucco structure left over from French occupation a half-century before. Two others were lingering on the periphery of the marketplace itself. Each man was covered with an innocuous poncho; each was carrying a small submachine gun beneath.

They were all watching a small woman in her twenties named Li Ky. She was the daughter of a farmer who raised ducks and grew rice down by the Da Thong river two miles south of the village. Li was pretty, and recognizable by the streak of premature gray that ran down the center of her long otherwise jet-black hair.

Li had arrived at the marketplace early. She'd been observed by the SEALs purchasing items that might have seemed typical for a peasant's daughter: dried fish, some candles, a roll of baling wire. But Li was also buying some unusual items: rice wine, opium blunts, cigarettes, and some decidedly American food, like canned spaghetti and soup. These were considered luxury items in this part of Vietnam, and normally well beyond the means of a simple farm girl.

Li was carrying two canvas bags; in itself this was a tip that her shopping was not typical. Most people in the area could afford only about as much as they could carry with two hands or in a pot on their heads.

Li paid for her last purchase and then climbed on her bicycle and pedaled away. Subtle hand gestures were exchanged among the SEAL team members. They moved out of the village with great stealth, climbed aboard a Toyota truck hidden in the brush nearby, and began following her.

It was raining so hard now the SEALs could barely keep her in sight. Their training told them to stay at least 500 feet behind. Li pedaled for two miles before reaching a rickety bridge that spanned the Da Thong river. A crossroads lay on the other side. Taking a right at the crossroads would lead her back to her family's hooch. Taking a left would not.

She started across the bridge but paused for a moment halfway across. Was it the weather or a sudden change of heart or just a moment to catch her breath? There was no way to tell. She began pedaling again. When she got to the other side of the bridge, she turned left.

The jungle soon became very thick. So much so, the woman abandoned her bicycle and continued on foot. Likewise the SEALs had to leave their truck and doubletime it to catch up to her. When they got her in sight again, they saw she was moving through the jungle with ease—she'd come this way many times before. But the undergrowth was so dense and the road, which was now down to a path, was so craggy, the hard-nosed SEALs were soon having trouble keeping up.

Then the rain stopped. This would have seemed like good news for the SEALs; now they could keep the woman in sight by pure eyeball. But this was Vietnam. Nothing was ever as it appeared here. With the disappearance of the rain, the brutal heat of the Mekong fell on them like a bomb. Uniforms that were a minute before soaked through with water were now soaked through again, with perspiration. Suddenly their weapons felt heavy; their equipment, cumbersome.

The woman was still moving quickly, almost delicately, through the jungle. If she was aware the SEALs were tracking her, she made no indication of it. It went on like this for more than five klicks. By the time the jungle cleared and the woman made her way down to a riverbank, the six SEALs were winded, covered in sweat— and totally lost.

They were still near the Da Thong; it split into dozens of tiny rivulets here. But they were also near the coast. The South China Sea lay beyond. This was not the way the SEALs expected the woman to go.

They still had her in sight, though. She'd crossed a stream by an ancient bamboo bridge. She ran by the rusting wreckage of a U.S. fighter jet shot down here 40 years before and up and over a dune, finally dropping out of sight. The SEALs splashed across the stream, paused just for a moment before the F-105's wreckage, then ran up the opposite bank. Getting down on their stomachs, they crawled to the crest of the dune.

On the other side was another rivulet and beyond, the vast expanse of the South China Sea. Across the stream was an island, separated from the land by just a few feet of slow-moving water.

But something wasn't right here—and the SEALs knew it.

The topography in this part of Nam featured the sea, river streams, and heavily jungled islands close to shore. This particular island was about a quarter-mile long, maybe a third of that wide. It was shaped like a finger. The small channel that separated it from the mainland was 20 feet at its widest with the water growing very deep quickly from there. Or at least that's how it appeared.

The SEALs were able to access a file in their Palm Pilots that held a GPS photo image taken of this area several months before. It showed the beach, the dune, the rivulets—and the island. But the island was significantly smaller a few months ago, and it was significantly farther offshore.

Though there was bright sun now and the heat was coming off the land in sheets, the SEALs took out their low-light infrared (IR) scope. What they saw through their distorted lens looked like a vision of hell. The island appeared as if on fire. So did the sky. But organics give off different heat signatures from the nonliving, and on the shore side of the heavily forested island they were getting a very strange indication.

Something was hidden there. Something huge.

"Just what we were looking for," the SEAL squad leader told his men.

It was a ship. A huge container-type ship. Close to 800 feet long, it fit in nicely on the backside of the island. It had been camouflaged so completely that even now, looking at it without their heat goggles, the SEALs could not see it. Somehow, someone had managed to make the huge cargo vessel disappear.

The woman had forded the shallow channel and had disappeared up under the growth the SEALs now knew to be fake.

They waited for five minutes, then scrambled over the dune.

The SEALs were climbing onto the deck of the heavily camouflaged container vessel five minutes later.

The veteran Navy operators were highly trained in taking over offshore targets, such as ships and oil platforms. But this boat was different, and it wasn't just the size of it that they found daunting. It was the eeriness—they'd just never seen anything like it before. The camouflage was so expertly put in place, they could no longer see the blazing blue sky above them. In fact, it was so dim on the deck, it was as if night had suddenly fallen.

They'd climbed up onto the bridge level and it was truly a weird scene from here. The main deck of the vast ship stretching before them, dozens of railroad car–size containers stacked neatly in rows from bow to stern. The amazingly intricate camouflage roof of branches, vines, and in some cases entire trees serving as a canopy overhead. None of it seemed real.

The six SEALs stayed together, each man with his hand on the shoulder of the man in front of him. They were not risk takers. They had no idea what might be awaiting them below the decks of the ghost ship. Nor did they know very much about why they'd been sent on this very strange mission. Some very big wigs in Washington wanted to talk to people who might be aboard this vessel—that was just about the extent of it. The problem was, these people could be armed and there was a good chance they might not be in the mood to talk.

The SEALs moved slowly across the bridge level, weapons pointing this way and that. Up ahead, the main hatchway that led into the ship's aft end bridge house. This was their first goal. But just as they turned toward this hatch, suddenly came the most god-awful groaning sound. It shook the ship for 10 long seconds before fading away. The squad members froze in place.

"What *the fuck* was that?" one whispered.

"It's just the ship moving in the water," the squad leader barked under his breath, but really he had no idea what the noise was. They moved 10 feet forward—and the noise came again. Twice as long and twice as loud. The SEALS froze a second time. The deck was vibrating under their feet.

"Is someone messing with our heads?" one man wondered aloud. "That almost seems like a psy-ops effect."

No one answered him.

They reached the main hatch and started climbing up to the next level. It was pitch-black in here. Each man lowered his IR goggles, but this just gave the place an even spookier look. The sound of their boots on the ladder seemed extremely loud, this even though the SEALs were experts in stealth. Reaching the first passageway, they heard more strange noises around them: machinery turning on and off; a woman crying. Even the rattling of chains. Yet as soon as the squad leader took two steps into the next passageway, all the noise suddenly stopped. One step forward, the noise started again. Another step, it stopped. The squad froze again.

"This is like a bad ride at Disneyland," one member said.

They started moving again and finally reached the ship's bridge. It was empty. They climbed up to the next deck, to the captain's quarters. It was surprisingly ornate, but it, too, was vacant.

They went back down the ladder, moving very carefully in the dark. They heard the eerie groaning noise again. But this time, no one wanted to stop and wonder what the hell it was. They just kept on moving. Down another series of ladders, they found themselves one level below the cargo deck. Here they stumbled into a cabin that in normal circumstances might have acted as the ship's bursar office. But the cabin was not filled with file cabinets and adding machines. Rather, it was stuffed with surface combat equipment that looked as sophisticated as any found on the U.S. Navy's most advanced warships. Air defense radar, high-end communications sets, a huge 3-D combat display. There was at least a quarter-billion dollars' worth of high-tech gear down here. What was it doing on this very old, very rusty containership?

They went down to the next level. The noises started up all around them again. The clanging of chains became almost deafening. They came upon a very dark, very dour, very dirty mess hall. Its walls were painted black; its portholes had been covered over with tarpaulin also painted black. The ship groaned again. The SEALs stopped in their tracks again; this time they couldn't help it. The noise was very unnerving.

They slowly moved into the mess hall. One man unlashed his combat light and played it around the darkened room. They were startled to see the Vietnamese woman again. She was sitting at a table at the far end of the room, up in its darkest corner. There was a plate of food in front of her. She was calmly eating a steak.

Sitting next to her were four men, all Caucasian. They looked ghostly in the very dim light. They were looking back at the SEALs without the slightest bit of surprise. The SEAL squad leader pulled out his Palm Pilot. It flashed four pictures for him. They were the service-record mug shots of the four men. A Navy officer named Bingham, an Army colonel named Martinez, an Air Force chopper pilot named Gallant, and another USAF officer, a colonel named Ryder Long.

These were four of the people the SEALs had been sent here to find.

Without lowering his weapon, the SEAL squad leader addressed them: "Gentlemen, it is my duty to inform you that you are wanted for questioning by U.S. military author-ities. It is in your best interests to come with us peacefully."

The men just stared back at him. The Vietnamese woman continued eating her steak.

The SEAL team leader took a step closer; his team did as well. He repeated his message. The men still seemed unfazed.

Then the ship groaned again. The SEALs jumped in unison. The four men almost laughed.

The SEAL squad leader was growing both anxious and angry. He raised his weapon to eye level. His men did as well.

"Look . . ." he said forcefully. "I'm not in the business of shooting other Americans, but you've got to know who we are and why they sent us to get you. If you resist in any way, I can't guarantee your safety."

Finally one of the men spoke. It was the Navy officer. He said: "Nor can we yours. . . ."

At that moment, the huge hatch leading into the mess slammed shut, sealing them in. Now dark figures began to emerge from the gloom. They were more heavily armed than the SEALs and they, too, had their weapons raised. And there were at least eight of them.

Team 99 was trapped. That had never happened before.

Their captors were wearing uniforms, *special ops* uniforms. Black, not camos, like them. Their weapons were M16/15s, the specialized variation of the M16 combat rifle. Their helmets were oversize and came with night-vision goggles already attached. Every guy seemed enormous in size and breadth.

The SEAL squad leader was the first to realize just who these people were.

"Delta Force . . ." he breathed. The words had trouble coming off his tongue.

Dead silence. No one moved. The SEALs were still holding their guns on the men sitting at the table; the Delta guys had their guns on the SEALs. Blue-on-blue. That's what they called it when different Americans units wound up firing on each other. But these were always friendly-fire accidents, mistakes made in the heat of combat. This was a little different.

Keeping one eye on the four men at the table, the SEAL squad leader took a closer look at the uniforms on the Delta guys. They were very unusually decorated. Their shoulder patches showed the silhouettes of the New York City Twin Towers backed by the Stars and Stripes, with the acronyms NYPD and FDNY floating on either side.

They hardly seemed military-issue. The four men at the table were wearing them, too.

The SEAL squad leader finally started talking: "OK, everyone stay cool. We're all brothers here." He glanced at the woman who was still calmly eating her steak dinner. "Or at least most of us are."

"You can be as cool as you want," Bingham the Navy officer, told him. "Just turn your asses around and go back to where you came from."

Some of the Delta guys laughed.

"But we can't do that," the SEAL leader said. "They're expecting us to bring you back."

Bingham leaned forward, allowing the captain's bars on his shoulder to glint in the bare light. "What's your name, son?" he asked the squad leader.

The SEAL stumbled a bit. "Lieutenant Barney. First name Charles, sir. . . ."

"From where, Charlie?"

"Philadelphia, sir. . . ."

Bingham sat back again. "Well, when you get back home, you can grab a cheese steak sandwich on me. OK? Bye. . . ."

"But, sir . . . we have our orders," the squad leader told him.

"We have our orders, too," Bingham said. "Want to know what they are?"

"Sure. . . ."

"That no one knows who we are, or where we are—at all costs."

As he was saying this, each of the Delta guys took a step forward, tightening the ring around the SEALs.

"You guys are nuts," the squad leader replied harshly, breaking the protocol. "You really think *I think* you'll shoot us?"

"*You* were going to shoot *us,*" Bingham reminded him.

The Delta guys came in closer. The SEALs cocked their weapons and the tension ratcheted up another notch. One wrong move now and a lot of the people in the room would be dead.

"We have our orders," Barney, the squad leader, said again. A bead of sweat was making its way down his nose. His arms and back were soaked with perspiration. He looked at the Delta guy closest to him again. The man wasn't sweating at all.

"And we have ours," Bingham repeated, his voice very low. "And you've got five seconds, starting now, to lower your weapons. Four seconds . . . three . . ."

Each SEAL remained in place. They had to. They were Team 99; there was no way they could back down to these freaks.

"Two . . ."

The Delta guys flicked on their laser aiming devices. Now each SEAL had a tiny red dot dancing between his eyes.

"One."

There was a loud *pop!* An instant later, a great white flash filled the hall. Its light was blinding. An instant after that, the huge door that had been slammed shut behind the SEALs was blown into a million pieces. The flames and smoke were intense, just for a moment. Then, *more* armed men began streaming into the room. They were not military, or at least they were not in uniforms. They were all wearing flak vests, sunglasses, ball caps, and jeans. They moved with frightening swiftness, taking up positions around the Delta guys.

Just like that, the circumstances inside the mess hall had changed again.

The new arrivals aimed their weapons at the Delta soldiers, who still had their guns trained on the SEALs, who had never taken *their* guns off the four men sitting at the table. The four looked more than mildly surprised at the sudden appearance of the civilian gunmen.

Finally, someone yelled: "Who the fuck are *you* guys?"

That's when one more person walked into the mess hall. He took off his helmet and calmly brushed back his unruly hair.

It was Major Fox of the DSA. A long way from home.

He waved his red ID badge over his head.

"I am from the Defense Security Agency," he announced to the mystified crowd of soldiers. "Anyone here ever heard of us?"

His question was met with blank stares all round.

"I didn't think so. OK, all you have to know for now is that I'm in charge here. And as my first order, I want everyone to lower his weapon."

Fox put his helmet back on and took a paper bag from his pocket.

Then he collapsed into the nearest chair and said: "There's something very important we've *all* got to talk about."

Fox was exhausted.

The last time his feet had stayed on the ground was 20 hours ago, back at Andrews, in the middle of a downpour, another of his wife's peanut butter sandwiches packed inside a tiny brown bag.

From there an aerial odyssey began, carrying him, in the back of a C-17 Globemaster cargo jet, to Luke Air Force Base in Utah, where he was transferred to an S-3 Viking naval bomber, which brought him to Guam, with three aerial refuelings to kill the boredom over the Pacific. From Guam it was a chopper trip over to Oki Jima, for a quick walk around, then back by chopper to Guam, then back on the S-3 for a flight down to the carrier *USS Roosevelt*. From there, another copter, a bigger one, an elderly Sea Knight, brought him to an isolated island a hundred miles off the eastern coast of Taiwan. It was an old CIA base. Here he met for the first time the small army of gunmen who broke in with him. They were SDS—State Department Security. Usually charged with protecting U.S. officials both at home and abroad, they did side missions as well at the bequest of the NSC. Fox had worked with them before. They were arguably the toughest if least-known special ops force around. From this little island they were all put aboard the ugliest airplane ever built—and now he was here. In Vietnam.

And he was very tired.

And very hungry.

So Fox unwrapped his wife's sandwich and finally took a monstrous bite. It was strange: Despite his initial command, no one had lowered his weapon. But upon seeing him take that first bite of his sandwich, it was like a spell was broken. All rifles went down a notch. Another bite, as Fox was ravenous, and people seemed to relax a little more. Bite three, weapons were lowered all the way to the deck. Bite four, and the sandwich was gone—and everyone was breathing normally again. Fox laughed. His wife *did* make a great Skippy sandwich.

Of course, it was the SEALs who began squawking first. Squad Leader Barney took two giant steps forward and lined himself up in front of Fox.

"I beg your pardon, sir," he began, still with a sweaty nose and upper lip. "But I believe my orders supersede yours. . . ."

Fox took a long swig from his field canteen, stood up, and stretched. Then he addressed the SEAL.

"You want to make trouble here, Mr. Barney?"

"No, sir. . . ."

"Then why are you standing in front of me?"

Barney cleared his throat and said again: "I believe my orders supersede yours, sir."

"You do? Well, I have two words for you, Mister Barney. . . ."

"Sir?"

" 'General Rushton.' "

Barney began to respond but stopped himself. He and Fox inhabited the same underworld of Washington and spies. Barney knew who General Rushton was. He was the man who'd sent Team 99 on this mission. But even though they were out here doing his bidding, Barney would never utter his name lightly. That would be sinful. In fact, few people would speak his name unless they were authorized to do so.

"And, Mr. Barney, General Rushton says you and your men now belong to me," Fox went on, each word hitting Barney like a body blow. *"Capeesh?"*

To his credit, Barney handled it with grace. He knew when he was being outjuiced. He saluted sharply and said: "*Capeesh,* sir . . . yes, sir. . . ." Then he took two giant steps backward and returned to his original position.

Fox scanned the rest of the room, palms up, arms outstretched, as if to say, *Anyone else want to bitch to me?* There were no takers.

"OK then," he said. "Let's get jiggy with this thing."

He directed the SDS men to arrange the mess tables into a semicircle. All the SEALs, all the Delta guys, and most of the SDS guards sat down. The four men sitting in the back didn't move, though. Neither did Ky Li. They remained where they were.

Fox had a laptop that could project images onto the wall. Even against the black paint, these pictures were crisp and clear. There was no need to douse the lights in the mess; it was already dark as a dungeon. Fox activated his remote and put up the first image.

It showed a typical B-2 Stealth bomber.

"I don't have to tell anyone what this is," he began.

He showed a second image. It was of a B-2F spy bomber. It looked a little bigger, a little newer. The image had the word CLASSIFIED stamped across it.

"This is just another version of the B-2, except it's a spy plane and, as you can see, highly classified," Fox went on. "They call it a B-2F."

His next graphic was a satellite image of Oki Jima, the secret base off Guam.

"That B-2F took off from here on a 'routine' flight just over twenty-four hours ago. A training mission was how it was logged. This plane is now missing."

He let that information sink in a moment, then put up the next image. It showed a sat photo of the Bangtang Channel, with its three tiny islands.

"The aircraft's last known position was on a refueling track above these three specks, north of the Philippines' big island of Luzon. For those of you who flunked geography, that's about 1000 miles east of here. Communications were lost with the B-2 soon after it hooked up for the refueling. The KC-10 Extender never came back, either. Because they were flying the mission mostly in radio silence, it took a while to determine that both were missing."

The next image showed a close-up of the Bangtang Channel.

"These are the islands of Calayan, Fuggu and Dalu Pree. If the B-2 went down, in one piece or not, over dry land, it is probably on one of these postage stamps. If not, it's under the water nearby. But the Navy has had two subs combing the channel's seabed for the past twelve hours or so. They've found nothing so far."

Next image. A split screen showing both the B-2 spy bomber and the KC-10 refueler in better days.

"Higher Authority has no idea what happened to either of these planes," Fox went on. "An accident of some kind? A midair collision? No one knows. However, it is very important that these planes are found and the fate of their crews determined quickly. That goes especially for the B-2, for a variety of reasons but mostly because it's an advanced model that's not suppose to exist.

"The problem is, no one in that part of the world knows what's going on—and it has to stay that way. I'm talking specifically about the Philippine government. Don't get me wrong. They are still allies of our country— or at least they were this morning. But the current Filipino administration and especially the national police add up to a security nightmare. Nothing can be kept a secret for more than two hours inside the presidential palace, and the national cops just cannot be trusted. They'll have every mook within five thousand miles looking in on us if they find out. So, any search and rescue has to be done not just quickly, but very quietly."

Fox paused a moment. He wished he had another sandwich.

"Now how we all wound up here like this is a moot point," he began again. "But it's also serendipity. Look around. Can you see what we've got here? Delta, SEALs, SDS guys, plus two pilots, a ship's captain. We all know our business. But more importantly, we are now the closest special ops force of any kind to the crash zone. We can be on the job in a matter of hours. It will take another team at least a day to get up to speed."

He let those words hang in the air for a moment. He'd been on some screwy missions before, but this one was already the screwiest.

Finally someone in the mess said: "So?"

"So," Fox replied. "The President's men want us—*all* of us—to go find those two planes."

At 46, Ryder Long was nearly the elder statesman of this group.

He was sitting next to the girl eating the steak, but at the moment he was craving a peanut butter sandwich. He suspected most of the people in the mess hall were.

Technically Ryder was a colonel in the USAF Reserves, but that was just a formality. He'd spent the last 20 years flying secret aircraft for people like Boeing and Northrup while doing the occasional black op for the

Pentagon. It was not just a good life; it was *a great* one. Then came September 11th—and that's when everything changed. Returning from a job assignment in Boston, his wife was on one of the planes that hit the World Trade Center towers. No last second phone calls, no chance to say good-bye. In an instant, his world turned upside down.

Weeks of black hell followed, caused by crushing sadness, whiskey anger, and the psychic need for closure that he knew would never come. Holed up in a crappy Las Vegas motel, he was one breath away from eating his gun.

But then his telephone rang. Salvation was on the other end. Like the others in Bobby Murphy's mystery unit, he'd been given the opportunity to hit back at the people responsible for what happened that day. Like everyone else, he jumped at the chance. That's what they'd been doing in the Persian Gulf the day the carrier *Lincoln* was attacked. That's why their unit patch showed the silhouette of the Twin Towers. No matter what else happened in that crazy part of the world—the war in Iraq, the death or capture of the top mutts of Al Qaeda—the unit had the job of hunting down every last mook connected with 9/11 and whacking him.

Or at least that was the case until about a month ago.

Sitting to his right was the Navy officer Wayne Bingham. Everyone called him Captain Bingo. He was nearly as old as Ryder, with a graying beard and enormous eyeglasses. Bingo had a dry wit about him, a window to his street smarts. He'd commanded cruisers, destroyers, and even some small secret ships during his Navy career. These days he was the captain of this, the unit's spy ship, the *Ocean Voyager.* He'd shown great skill in the six weeks the team secretly operated in and out of the Persian Gulf.

Sitting next to Bingo was Ron Gallant, the Air Force Special Operations chopper pilot. It had been his partner, Red Curry, who'd crashed his beefed-up Blackhawk aboard the *Lincoln,* the tide-turning act that led to the successful defense of the carrier. Gallant looked exactly like Clark Kent right down to the specs. He was a sort of brilliant muscle man who was also a great helo driver.

Next to him was the Delta CO, Martinez. Those were his guys who'd so expertly got the drop on the Team 99 SEALs. But he didn't even look in the game at this point. Martinez had been the most emotionally damaged from the events in the Persian Gulf, and especially during the battle of Hormuz. Just why was a long story. The short version was this: the terrorists who hijacked the planes meant to be used against the *Lincoln* had been under surveillance by Martinez's guys earlier on the morning of the attack. In fact, one Delta guy trailed each pair of hijackers, thinking they were on their way to hijack American planes in Europe. That's why there was a Delta guy on each of the hijacked planes when they took off that fateful morning. But at the time, no one ever dreamed the hijackers would use Arab airlines filled with Arab citizens in their bid to sink the carrier.

Had Martinez ordered his men to take down the mooks before they ever got on those airplanes, the nightmarish events later in the day might have been avoided. Hundreds would still be alive; there was no question about that. So now Martinez was faced with a life of "If only." If only he'd stopped the hijackers before they got on those planes. If only he'd listened to some of the others, who'd advocated shooting the hijackers as soon as they'd been spotted at the airport.

If only . . .

Never very talkative anyway, the Delta officer with the Latino movie star looks had barely spoken a word since the events in Hormuz. He'd withdrawn, become vacant. A victim of combat stress.

Despite their show of bravura, Ryder, Bingo, and Gallant were in almost as bad shape as Martinez. This last month had not been a pleasant one, floating around out on the sea, living on rationed food and water. No money, no cigarettes, no beer. They were trying to get back to the states, quietly. But the unexpected and very impromptu rescue mission in Singapore had kicked the shit out of that plan. And them . . .

With all this in mind, and after listening to Fox describe the highly unusual circumstances as to why he was here, Ryder raised his hand like a kid in school. Fox finally saw him, waving from the back of the room.

"Yes, a question?"

Ryder stood up and half-shouted: "What does this have to do with us, Major? Personally, I'd rather be arrested. . . ."

Laughter went through the room. Fox indicated that everyone could relax; then he walked to the back of the hall and casually took a seat across from the four rogue officers. He produced a fresh pack of Marlboros and offered them around. By time he got the pack back, it was empty.

As the four men and the Vietnamese girl lit up, Fox remembered the bio on Ryder. Test pilot. Black ops veteran. Did some time inside the military's top-secret Nevada Special Weapons Testing Range, the place known in the biz as War Heaven. That gave them at least one thing in common.

"I understand you've been to 'the desert'?" Fox asked him, his voice low, using the unofficial name for the ultra-high-tech weapons range. "What did you think of the place?"

"It was like a bad episode of *The X-Files*," Ryder replied.

Fox chuckled. "Exactly. . . ." War Heaven specialized in advanced psychological warfare training as well.

He pulled out a small loose-leaf binder. Inside were the notes Ozzi had taken down at Gitmo. Fox had read them over many times in the past 48 hours. He could almost recite them by heart.

He looked up at the four men and then just told them bluntly: "Unlike Lt. Barney and his friends, I *know* who you people are. And I know what you've been up to out here. I know about the food poisoning. I know about the bank you bombed. I know what you did over Hormuz."

Ryder, Gallant, and Bingo shifted uncomfortably in their seats. Only Martinez remained still.

"Now, I came out here for a reason," Fox went on. "But it's probably not the reason you think. I don't expect you to answer any questions that might compromise national security. What you were all doing to a month ago . . . well, by some people's clocks, that's already ancient history. It is by mine. What we have to talk about is this thing that's happening right now, just a few hundred miles away."

But the four men just weren't interested. Especially Ryder.

Still, Fox went on: "Look, we obviously have a big security problem here. And if it isn't attended to quickly, it's gonna unravel and then all hell breaks loose, guaranteed. It's a situation where the insertion of veteran special ops people is vital."

"But if you arrest us first," Ryder told him, "you have to fly us right home. We couldn't get involved in this little sideshow of yours if we were in custody, right?"

Fox did not reply. Unlike the SEALs, he wasn't here to arrest Ryder or any of the other members of the secret unit. Just the opposite.

"Let me show you something," he said. He pointed back to the laptop map still projecting on the wall, indicating the larger landmass of Luzon, just south of the three islands. "Much of the uninhabited real estate north of Manila is controlled by Abu Sabas, a new Philippine chapter of Al Qaeda. Bin Laden's guys have been pumping money, intelligence, and know-how into this part of the world for the past several years. And it's been getting results. Now here's where it might become a little more interesting for you."

Remote click to the next image. It was a photograph of a very ugly *jihad* terrorist. Pop eye, scarred face, bad teeth, and crooked turban.

Ryder, Bingham, and Gallant sat straight up in their seats. Only Martinez remained as he was. A picture of this man was probably the only thing that could have got their attention like this.

The picture was of Sheikh Abdul al-Ahari Kazeel. He was not only one of the top planners of 9/11; he was the chief architect of the attack on the *Lincoln*, as well. He was also one of the last big Al Qaeda types the mystery unit had been seeking to whack.

"I understand this guy is a friend of yours," Fox said to them dryly.

"He's the number-one mook we want pushing up daises, if that's what you mean," Gallant replied.

"Did you know they're calling him a 'superterrorist' these days?" Fox went on.

"Who is?" Ryder wanted to know.

Fox shrugged. "*Time*? *Newsweek*? The *Washington Post*? CNN. . . ."

"He fucks up the *Lincoln* attack," Gallant said testily. "He fucks up in Singapore. And they christen him a 'superterrorist'?"

"The *world's first* superterrorist," Fox added casually. "Crazy, isn't it?"

"That's what the kids call 'failing up,'" Bingham said in disgust. "The guy's a mass murderer and what happens? They turn him into a celebrity."

Fox almost smiled. "Well, now that I've caught your attention," he said. "I have another news flash for you. The CIA says Kazeel arrived in the Philippines forty-eight hours ago. And they think he might have been near the crash zone shortly before the B-2 went down. Maybe it's a coincidence; maybe it's not."

All four men were sitting up straight now, even Martinez. It sounded corny, but Fox was cleverly making them an offer they couldn't refuse.

"Interested now?" Fox asked them.

Gallant power-puffed his Marlboro and crushed it out on the table. "We might be," he said.

"Well, let me sweeten the pot just a bit more," Fox went on. "Off-the-record, I appreciate what you guys did, in Singapore, at Hormuz, and before. If I had had the chance, I would have been right there with you."

He nodded back toward the SEALs. "But obviously, some people aren't such big fans of yours. The guy who sent those fish heads after you, especially. He'd like to see you in jail—or worse. Now, he happens to be my boss, too. So when this B-2 thing came up, I convinced him to send me out here, carrying an offer for you.

"This is both a search *and* a rescue mission. I want to find those planes and their crews and the reason they went down. Trouble is, these Abu Sabas characters can be very tough customers if you catch them on a bad day. Bottom line: You guys are good at rescues. You know how to get your hands dirty. And obviously, you know how to keep your mouths shut. Help us out here and maybe you find your guy Kazeel in the bargain."

The four men stared back at him. There would be a lot of satisfaction in catching Kazeel. Many in the mystery team held him directly responsible for the deaths of their loved ones. Wheels were turning now. . . .

"But what about when it's over?" Gallant finally asked him. "What about us getting back to the states in one piece?"

Fox was a bit more careful here. "When it's over," he said, "we can see about getting you all back home again—with no questions asked."

"All of us?" Ryder asked him. "Bingo's crew? And our guys you already have in custody?"

"I'll give you my word that I'll do my best," Fox replied sincerely. "But I'll tell you this: If we turn up aces on this B-2 thing, it will go a long way in convincing my boss to give you a pass."

A few moments of silence went by. Finally Bingham just mumbled, "That's all we really want. To get home, without someone trying to send us to Leavenworth."

Fox smiled wearily. "That's just what I needed to hear. In fact, that's the best thing I've heard in the past two days."

But then he checked his notes again and saw there was one more item he had to discuss. He turned to Ryder and Gallant, the two pilots. "I've got to make sure of just one more thing—and it will sound strange," he said.

"Stranger than all this?" Ryder asked him.

"Maybe," Fox replied. "I've been led to believe you two guys can fly just about anything with wings; is that true?"

Ryder and Gallant just nodded.

Fox then asked: "Would that include a seaplane?"

Minutes later, Ryder, Gallant, and Fox climbed up to the deck of the creaking spy ship and headed for the bow.

The air tasted fresh; the ocean sounds were close by. It was Ryder's first time up from below in a while and he couldn't stop taking in deep breaths. Even the unbearable heat seemed soothing somehow.

They had to maneuver themselves around the web of steel cable and lashing bars that kept the dozens of railroad car-size containers in place. Walking around the loading deck had never been a favorite of Ryder's; there were many things on which to crack a kneecap up here. He wasn't big on ships anyway. He was an Air Force guy and felt if you're not flying, your boots should be firmly on the ground. Even now, in the relatively shallow water, he could feel the deck rolling beneath his feet.

About halfway to the bow, they came upon a container

whose front doors were wide open. A six-foot piece of something was sticking out between them. It was as heavily camouflaged as the green ceiling above covered with nets and pieces of fauna. Ryder and Gallant tried to steer Fox away from the container, but there was nothing doing there. The DSA officer practically ran up to it.

He peeled away the camo to find something metallic beneath. Metallic—and yellow. He pulled back another clump of palm fronds and discovered that what he was looking at was the tail of a helicopter. A very, *very* yellow helicopter.

The Sing-One News helicopter.

"So it *was* you guys," Fox said, as if he'd finally become convinced of the team's alleged exploits. "Damn, I'm impressed."

"We can't answer any questions about that, either, Major," Gallant quickly told him, pushing his Metropolis-issue glasses back up on his nose not once but twice in the course of the sentence.

"And I'm not asking you any," Fox said. He really *was* impressed. Again, it was his business to know the bible on every U.S. special operations group in existence, both past and present. They were all good, and indeed, they were all special. But he didn't know of one who could have pulled off what the supersecret team did at the Tonka Tower, never mind over Hormuz.

Fox ran his hand along the length of the hidden helicopter. "Or maybe I could ask just a few?" he quickly amended himself.

Ryder and Gallant began to walk away. "I know how you did the rescue mission!" Fox called after them. "The whole world does. It was on TV. But my question is, *Why* did you do it? How did you know it was going to happen? What gave you the wherewithal to get the chopper and arrive there so quickly?"

But the two pilots never replied. They just kept on walking.

When Fox reached the bow, Ryder and Gallant were hanging over the front railing, mouths agog.

This was pretty much the reaction Fox had been expecting.

"Well?" he asked them dryly. "What do you think of her?"

Floating on the calm sea about two hundred feet off the bow was one of the ugliest airplanes Ryder had ever seen. It looked about a mile long and a mile wide. In reality it was roughly the size of a 727 airliner. It had a high wing sitting atop its fuselage. Its cockpit windows looked like a pair of yellow eyes staring out from the plane's long, bulbous black nose. It had four huge engines, arrayed across the wing, with a small pontoon at each end. The tail sat unnaturally high, not unlike that of a C-5 Galaxy.

Ryder heard himself groan. This was no seaplane. It was a boat—a *flying* boat.

"This is the pooch you were asking us about?" he said to Fox.

" 'Pooch'?" Fox replied with feigned insult. "Colonel, this airplane features the best in Japanese engineering and manufacturing. The Japanese Self-Defense Forces have been flying these things for more than fifteen years. It's also just about the only flying boat operating today. It can fly almost anywhere in the Pacific, get to islands that have no runways, pick up people who are sick or whose ships are sinking. Hundreds owe their lives to this aircraft."

Ryder just shook his head. "And *this* is how we're going where we're going?"

Fox nodded.

"And you expect us to fly it?"

"Can you?" Fox asked them.

Ryder and Gallant contemplated the huge aerial boat again. There was an old saying in aeronautics: If it looks good, it flies good. But the reverse was also true. Just looking at the airplane, Ryder knew it would be a bitch to fly.

"Fifteen years old, you say?" he asked Fox. "Does it have flight computers onboard? Pilot assistance? Fly-by-wire, things like that?"

"You bet," was the reply. "The guys who flew it here tell me it handles like a dream."

Ryder and Gallant just looked at each other. *The guys who flew it here?*

"If they loved it so much, where are they now?" Ryder asked Fox looking around. "And why can't they be the drivers?"

Fox readjusted his wraparound sunglasses. "Number one, even though they are on the CIA's payroll, they don't have the security clearances that you guys do," he said. "Number two, they have an idea where we are going . . . and, well, they wanted no part of it. So they're on their way up to Saigon as we speak."

Sure enough, Ryder and Gallant could see a small motor launch north of them, two people onboard, waving furiously but moving away from them as fast as they could.

In the movies, this was the part where one of the men on the boat would yell out: "So long, suckers!"

"So you really *were* counting on us to get everyone out of here in this thing?" Ryder asked him. "That was a leap of faith."

"Your friends in Gitmo assured us you could do it," Fox told him. "So did your service résumé."

Ryder threw his expended cigarette over the side. He could fly anything; he knew that. Ditto for Gallant. Though he was a chopper pilot, he knew his way around big planes, too. But this monster?

"You say this thing is Japanese military?" he asked Fox.

The man nodded. "Self-Defense Forces, right. It's called a 'Kai.'"

The plane was unmarked—or more accurately, the huge red ball of the Japanese national insignia had been painted over, hastily.

"If this belongs to the Japanese Navy, what are you guys doing with it?"

Without missing a beat, Fox replied: "We stole it. . . ."

Ryder and Gallant looked at each other again and did a simultaneous eye roll. "Stole it?" Ryder asked.

"Well, it's a game we play," Fox said, as if these things were routine. "They know we've got it. They're just not trying too hard to find it."

It took just 10 minutes to get the composite team loaded aboard the enormous Kai flying boat.

The eight Delta guys sat up front, just behind the crew compartment. The half-dozen Team 99 SEALs, still sulking, were huddled at the opposite end of the compartment.

In between were the State Department Security guards, 10 in all, yet to be seen without their sunglasses. These guys were as top-secret as the DSA itself. Tough and very, very quiet. Facing straight ahead, they resembled automatons.

Ryder and Gallant settled into the pilots' seats. Fox hadn't misled them here at least; the control panel was highly automated, just the way they liked it. There were extensive microprocessing assist units and everything was indeed fly-by-wire. This meant tiny computers actually flew the airplane by responding to the movements of the pilots on the controls and not through cables or wires. The flight panel looked as good as anything found inside a modern airliner.

They ran down a checklist. Ryder recited from a document crudely translated from Japanese, as Gallant tried to pick out the corresponding control system. They started the engines; the four huge turboprops coughed to life in sequence, like clockwork. They were big, noisy, powerful, with tons of horsepower in each. And yet the torque barely rocked the flying boat as it floated in the calm inlet water.

Fox took up the seat behind Ryder and Gallant. Martinez was installed in a jump seat located on the far edge of the cockpit, silently looking on.

It took about twenty minutes to check and recheck everything. Finally they were ready for takeoff. The people in the back sat stoically. Fox, however, wasn't so calm. Convincing Higher Authority that including the rogue team was a good idea had taken some doing. It was only the passion displayed by Ozzi after he spoke with the Gitmo Four that gave Fox the gumption to even suggest it to General Rushton and the NSC. In the end they agreed only because not doing so would have wasted precious time. That clock was still ticking, and Fox knew with each passing moment their window of opportunity was getting smaller.

Finally Ryder just looked over at Gallant, who gave him a mock thumbs-up. Could a jet test pilot and a special ops chopper driver really get the huge flying tub into the air?

They would soon find out.

Bingo and most of the remaining occupants were now on the bow of the huge hidden containership. Only here was there a respite from the heavy camouflaged top; about two dozen people were crowded on the deck now, including the Vietnamese woman, Ky Li.

They watched as the flying boat's four huge engines whipped themselves into a frenzy, gaining more power by the second. The air around the ship seemed to be vibrating, so powerful were the propellers, just 200 feet away.

At last the Kai started moving. The calm waters of the small bay suddenly began to roll. Pushed by the strong props, the big plane did a 180-degree turn, its huge snout for a moment turned right at the front of the secret boat. Many on the ship's deck waved as the airplane bobbed on by.

Flying boats had gone out of style, at least in U.S. forces, just about the time Captain Bingham was graduating kindergarten. He'd never seen one this big before. As it slowly gained speed, plowing through the waves first like a yacht and then like a speedboat, it seemed too large to get into the air, never mind having to rise up from the water to do so. Its takeoff run could stretch on to infinity, though, Bingham thought, and indeed, the plane was now skimming very fast along the inlet's surface. There came another huge roar from the airplane—it was now about a quarter-mile away from the ship. The water around it began spraying up fiercely. The engines roared again. More water, more spray. One last scream from the engines and the huge airplane leaped into the air.

A spontaneous cheer rose from those on the ship. The Kai went up grudgingly, though. At just 50 feet or so, it began a wide shaky turn, its engines now crying and billowing smoke. For one frightening moment it appeared to be in trouble.

But it climbed a little more and then leveled off. It was also heading right for the ship again. More cheers, more waving. Another roar from the engines. The big plane was coming on full guns—but it was not climbing anymore; in fact, it had dipped a little. The noise of those four engines, a moment before so powerful, now became frightening as the plane seemed way too low to clear the top of the ship. Everyone on the deck stopped waving and started ducking. The big Kai went over the *Ocean Voyager* a second later. It clipped the main antenna off the top of the ship's forward mast, sending a rain of parts down past the camouflage canopy and onto those below.

"Jesuzz!" Bingham cried. "Those bozos are trying to kill us!"

The plane somehow cleared the rest of the ship and finally got a little more air under its ass. Flying it was obviously a work in progress for Ryder and Gallant, but at last it began to gain significant altitude. It managed to wag its wings back at those on the ship before taking another long slow turn, this one to the east.

That's when a separate hatch on the deck popped open

and a handful of people climbed out. They mixed freely with Bingham's crew. They were a ragged lot. Uncut hair, overgrown goatees, tarnished earrings, thread bare Hawaiian shirts. All were in their early twenties; they looked like a bunch of hip Wall Street investment bankers who'd been shipwrecked for a month or so.

In reality, these were the Spooks, the contingent of computer geniuses that had run the eavesdropping devices aboard the *Ocean Voyager* during its short heyday. They weren't CIA and resented any suggestion that they were. They were, in fact, employees of the National Security Agency, the NSA, America's biggest and probably by size its most secret spy works.

The Head Spook was a guy named Gil Bates. He was just 20 years old. He'd been a key figure in the events leading up to Hormuz—and a controversial one. Not only had he been in charge of the ship's high-tech listening station (still buried at the bottom of the boat); he'd also fathered the plan to attack downtown Abu Dhabi in broad daylight, an act that killed more than a thousand innocent civilians. In many ways, his heart should have been weighed down just as much as Martinez's. But Bates had had a reprieve: he was the one who cracked the terrorists' code at the last possible moment, just before the *Lincoln* was attacked. It was only by his warning, carried to the carrier by Red Curry in his crash landing, that the big carrier had been saved.

Incredibly though, despite all the special ops activity on the boat in the past two hours, no one—not the State Department guards, not the SEALs, not Fox himself— ever asked about the NSA Spooks. And no one onboard the ship was about to volunteer the information.

After all, they had to keep *some thing*s secret.

The Spooks had to allow their eyes to adjust to the sunlight. They didn't come up from the bottom of the boat too often, and today was now an intensely bright day.

"Anyone mention us?" Bates asked Bingham as the Navy captain lit a cigarette for him.

Bingham just shook his head. "All clear as far as I'm concerned."

But Bates had already started back down the hatch, heading to the bottom of the ship again. His eyes were starting to hurt.

"That's good," he said over his shoulder. "Though I'd prefer it if they thought we were *all* dead."

Bingham watched the flying boat disappear over the horizon.

"You never know," he said. "We might still get that wish."

Chapter 6

The cage was made of bamboo.

It was four feet square and just 18 inches high. Forty-seven bamboo sticks held up the top, each one precisely 4 inches from the next. The sticks served as bars. The tiny cage was a jail cell.

This was where the B-2F pilot code-named Atlas found himself when he came to.

His last conscious memory from the night before was of the big bomber falling out of the sky. His engines were barely turning, they'd sucked up so many pieces of the doomed KC-10 tanker. They were heading straight down, the three tiny islands and a lot of dark water rushing toward him. It was an image burned onto his retinas forever. Sitting next to him, Teddy Ballgame was not talking. His nose was pressed against the cockpit window, while Atlas tried to get some control over the wounded bomber.

Then a miracle, it seemed. Suddenly Teddy was shouting: "There! Down there! See it?"

Atlas saw only a strip of pearl white—almost phosfluorescent in the dark night—cutting through the jungle on one of the islands. He really didn't have much time to think about it, for in the next instant they were at treetop level, and the next he was heading for a very hard landing on that strip of pearl, which turned out to be a beach of sand and white coral. Not a runway, just a flat piece of ground in the midst of the thick jungle.

A hard landing, of course, was just another way of saying a crash landing. But the B-2 was a bat-wing design, and this helped in the last few moments before they hit. Atlas had had the presence of mind to pull the bombers' drag chute just seconds before impact. The combination of the drag chute and the bat wing pulled the front of the airplane up, just for a second, but enough to allow it to glide in, as opposed to going down nose-first.

Still, when it came, the impact was violent. It split Atlas's helmet in two and sent chunks of flight panel flying off in every direction. The windshield gave in, showering him with shards of glass. Fire burst forth. Smoke filled his lungs. It seemed to go on forever, but finally they came to a halt. He recalled looking around the remains of the cockpit and thinking that while he'd survived the crash, he'd also managed to total a $1.5 billion bomber. He lost consciousness soon after that.

When he awoke again, he was inside this box.

He was a prisoner of the Abu Sabas terrorist group. They were the Filipino affiliate of Al Qaeda and had been operating in the islands around the northern and central parts of the Philippines for at least a couple years. Their aim was to create a radical Islamic state in this part of southeast Asia—and kill as many nonbelievers as possible in the process.

Known locally as the "Aboos," the Muslim terror group was vicious even by Al Qaeda standards. They had a penchant for kidnapping American tourists and making long lists of impossible demands for their safe return. When those demands were not met, the group would make good on its threat to execute their hostages. Their favorite means of dispatch: decapitation.

As with all the pilots at the secret base on Oki Jima, Atlas had been briefed on the Aboos, because sometimes their classified missions brought them over territory held by the terror group, just like the mission the night before. But never did Atlas ever think it would amount to anything like this.

It was now about noon. Atlas had been awake for a few hours. Though he was in pain, he was nevertheless coherent and luckily not in shock. He was in a small camp dug into the side of a heavily forested hill. His cage was last in a line of at least a half-dozen. There might have been more, but movement was difficult inside the bamboo box so his vision was limited. As it was, he was forced to lie on his side, with his arms and legs drawn up into a fetal position and his head hard against one corner. He was so scrunched up, he couldn't even tell if he had any broken bones.

He was sure his mission commander, Teddy Ballgame, was in the next box down. His back was to him, but Atlas could see his flight suit and someone had put his boots on top of his cell.

But Teddy wasn't moving; he hadn't moved all day. There were many guards prowling around, easy to spot in their black pajamas and red bandanna ensemble. The small camp was so well guarded, Atlas had not been able to call out to his colleague.

Atlas could see people in the next five boxes down, but again it was hard to get a good read on them. It was also dark in the camp, even though it was the middle of the day. However he thought he could see a woman in the box next to Teddy, a man with a gray beard next to her, and a younger female next to him.

The camp was not only frightening for its gloom; it was putrid as well. There was a stream running next to Atlas's box. Even though he was very thirsty and parched—his guards had given him neither food nor water—he would not have wanted to even dip his fingernail into this slowly trickling water. It looked like an open sewer. There was the smell of body odor, burned rubber, and fetid jungle around the camp.

The stink of death was here as well.

Atlas knew he was in trouble. But he also knew that if somehow he was able to live through this, he would have a lot of valuable intelligence to pass along to somebody. Convincing himself that he was actually doing some good here helped keep his anxiety from getting out of control. As it was, though, it was right on the edge.

Many of the Aboos were gathered in a hut in the middle of the camp. Though the living conditions were crude, the hut was equipped with a number of modern devices, including a satellite dish, color TVs, a satellite phone receiver, a GPS device, and many, many weapons. The terrorists also had cell phones capable of taking and transmitting pictures, which they treated like toys.

There was much coming and going around this command hut. The camp would go into lockdown anytime an aircraft was heard; this happened about once an hour. At-

las was keeping a mental list of each one. Some of the aircraft had to be U.S. planes looking for his B-2 and the
missing tanker—or so he thought. But most of those he
heard were way off in the distance. None had flown directly over the camp.

One problem: Atlas had no idea where he was or how
far away he was from his own crash site. He'd been un-
conscious at least 12 hours and maybe a lot more. His
flight uniform was torn and bloodied, especially on the
knees and elbows. He believed he'd been dragged for
some distance. He also detected the odor of chloroform
around him, another tactic known to be used by the Filipino guerrillas for subduing their hostages.

For all he knew, he could have been a hundred miles
away from his crash site by now.

The heat inside the box became unbearable as the day
wore on. An early-afternoon rainstorm saved him. Only a
few drops made it down through the jungle canopy, but
they were enough to cut the brutal heat a bit.

Once the rain passed, the jungle seemed cooler. The
terrorists became more active, leaving the hut and loung-
ing about the garbage-strewn camp. At midafternoon or
so, Atlas saw the leader of the group have an animated
conversation with two men who appeared to be his officers. A round of orders was given, and soon three underlings were opening up one of the tiger cages. It was the
box three down from him, the man with a beard. He was
in his fifties and it took a while for the terrorists to untan-
gle him from his cramped position. Even when they finally extracted him, he had trouble standing. The woman
in the box next to him was his wife. She began crying out

for him. Judging from his emaciated body, Atlas guessed he'd been here at least a couple months.

They took the man to a bench set up next to the main command hut. The man's clothes told Atlas that he was a minister, perhaps a missionary of some kind. A guard approached him with a cup of water but instead of giving it to him to drink threw it in his face. His wife cried out again. One of the Aboo officers arrived with a super-eight video camera. He turned the camera on the dazed man, and the other officers started interrogating him.

Atlas could not hear what was being said exactly, but he could tell the poor man was trying his best to both answer the terrorists' questions and steal glances at his wife, back in her box. By giving her brief smiles and on occasion a wave of his hand he was trying to indicate to her that he was all right.

The taping went on for an hour. The man grew weaker as the terrorists grew angrier. Finally the bench was removed and the man made to stand up. An ancient Willys Jeep appeared from somewhere in the jungle. It stopped in front of the prisoner and his guards. At first Atlas thought the terrorists were moving the minister to a different location. But the man's wife began wailing at the first appearance of the jeep. Whatever was about to happen, she'd obviously seen it before.

Atlas contorted his body, hoping to get a better view. The back panel of the jeep was lowered. A large piece of wood had been bolted to this panel, with belt buckles for straps located at either end.

The man was made to lay his head on this block of wood, his hands put into the buckle restraints. He looked over at his wife; his face was pure white. He knew what was about to happen. She did too. He mouthed some words of comfort to her; Atlas tried to lip-read them. That's how he failed to see the terrorist who walked out from behind the Jeep with the huge ax in his hand.

The terrorist set himself over the man, made sure the camera was running, then raised the ax over his head.

Atlas was able to close his eyes just a second before the blade came down on the minister's neck.

Chapter 7

Fuggu Island.

It was but a grain of sand when viewed from space. It was shaped roughly like a fist, one with an extended middle finger sticking out of it. The natural formation perfectly fit its obscene-sounding name. Of the three islands inhabiting the Bangtang Channel, Fuggu was the smallest. It was the first destination of the hastily assembled American team.

The trip of eleven hundred miles aboard the Kai had been fairly uneventful. There were a lot of different airplanes flying around this part of the world; many were old, prop-driven, and carrying a pair of sea floats underneath. A big Japanese-made flying boat was not so out of place.

But for security reasons, the fewer eyes that saw them, the better. So Ryder and Gallant had made the dash across the South China Sea at wave-top level. This involved a bit of work. Planes liked flying high, especially big ones, because there is less resistance where the air is thinner. Flying the giant Kai below 50 feet was dangerous. One slip and that 50 feet would be gone in a snap and they'd go in nose-first. Few people survived a crash at sea like that, even if the plane was a flying boat.

The Kai had a terrific communications set in its cockpit. Because its primary mission was long maritime patrols, flown over vast areas of water, for long periods of time, a powerful and reliable radio suite was essential. Fox had put the plane's radio receiver to its "monitor-all" setting shortly after leaving Vietnam. They'd heard a cacophony of radio squawk the whole trip, very little of it in English. Most was commercial air traffic, small island airlines flying around 10,000 feet, the bigger carriers sailing up near 35,000. They heard a few stray U.S. military conversations, too, but these went to white noise a second or so after being picked up.

They'd also been monitoring the weather channels closely. A massive bank of clouds to the north had been trailing them for most of the journey. Building up over the course of the afternoon, those clouds were heading in roughly the same direction as the Kai. So far Ryder and Gallant had managed to outrun the atmospheric disturbance. Even way down low, the Kai could fly at 250 knots. But the weather in this region was famous for its unpredictability. Some of South Asia's largest typhoons were born here.

And it was very hard to outrun a typhoon.

It was late afternoon when they spotted the Bangtang Channel. The lights were already on throughout Luzon to the south. The streetlights of Manila were coloring the horizon in an odd pinkish glow.

No light was coming from their destination, though.

The Bangtang Channel ran deep red in the rays of the departing sun. The swift waters were giving off a glow that was strangely phosphorescent. Lots of coral lying beneath, no doubt. But Fuggu itself was absolutely dark.

That this was would be their first landfall was not due to anything any search planes had found. In fact, there were no U.S. search planes looking for the missing spy bomber. The number of people in the world who even knew of the B-2F's existence could fit inside a small room. Fewer than one-third of them knew it had gone down. To mount a huge air-sea search effort would have set off alarms that the deep operations command at the Pentagon did not want set off, for many reasons. That's why this thing had to be done quickly.

They were about ten miles out from Fuggu when the weather suddenly changed. The dark clouds to their north began blowing south. Black and churning mightily, they'd been whipped up by heat from the Chinese mainland and the energy of moving over the open water. At that moment reaching critical mass, the bank of clouds turned into a huge storm right before their eyes. High winds began to swirl; rain, torrential in sheets, exploded from its inner regions. A waterspout began forming below. And this hellish mix was now heading right for the Kai.

Ryder and Gallant stayed cool. They'd seen worse. They started climbing, quickly, to 2,500 feet. Using hand gestures, they indicated to Fox what was happening. Fox went pale; he couldn't believe a storm could build that fast. Martinez, too, stood briefly at his seat, just long enough to see the gigantic plume of clouds coming at them.

"Damn, we don't need this!" someone cried. No sooner were the words out than the Kai was hit by the concussion wave traveling before the storm. The big plane was pushed violently to the left and then to the right. The nose suddenly dropped. Ryder and Gallant fought to get it level again. They succeeded, but then the nose started to wildly go up. They fought mightily to bring it back down.

The rain came next. Very quick, very heavy. Soon they could not see out the cockpit's windshield. Ryder and Gallant remained calm; they worked together to keep the airplane straight. The people in back weren't so cool. The sudden departure from level flight knocked many to the floor of the cabin. Now that the plane was bouncing all over the sky, both Delta guys and SEALs were being tossed about like rag dolls. Their equipment was flying around, too, unguided missiles ricocheting off the un-padded walls. Only the SDS guards were able to stay in their seats; in fact, their hair was barely mussed. They'd thought to tie their gear down before takeoff and had their seat belts fastened throughout the flight.

The plane's nose dropped again. Suddenly they were heading straight for the drink. Yelps from the back, cursing from Fox. A voice-activated warning signal began addressing them in Japanese. Slowly, though, Ryder and Gallant pulled the plane back level again. They stayed this way . . . for about three seconds. Then they were hit with a massive blow of turbulence on their port side. The plane almost went completely over; only because Ryder quickly applied more power did they gain control of it again. The center of the birthing storm was just a mile away and they were being sucked right into it. Ryder and

Gallant immediately put the plane halfway up on its left wing. They had to try to skim the edge of the gigantic front. The people in back didn't appreciate it, as they continued being pummeled. But the two pilots had saved their lives at least twice already.

They collided with the worst part of the storm a moment later; it was all the pilots could do to keep the wings tipped up. The smell of burnt plastic flooded into the cockpit. All those microprocessors were overheating as the two pilots struggled to keep the big flying boat in the air. It was black as night all around them now. The wind was screaming and the rain so heavy, it was like they were flying through a car wash. Everyone finally got tied down in back, but the sheer horror of being thrown all over the sky in such a huge airplane was something even the battle-hardened spy teams had trouble containing.

But then, suddenly, they broke through. One moment it felt like the plane would finally come apart at the seams; the next, they were looking down on the strangely colored water of the Bangtang Channel.

Directly below, enshrouded in rain and fog, was Fuggu Island.

It took them five minutes to turn the big plane back to the west, the direction they had to land in.

They slowly brought the Kai back down to the wave tops again, this time at full flaps and with the engines backing off on the power.

There was a tiny inlet right in the knuckle of the island's crook finger. This was where Fox wanted them to go. The waters around the island had been churned up by the locomotive that had just swept through. Instead of landing atop of glasslike surface, as would normally have been the case, they were about to set down in eight-to-ten-foot waves.

Ryder and Gallant didn't care. They hit the water hard and fast. The huge flying boat went straight up into the air, only to be slammed back down again and again. This seemed like it would go on for an eternity, but gradually the flying boat settled down. They made the outer reaches of the inlet, and here the water did indeed turn to glass. Suddenly they were riding smooth. There was practically a prayer meeting going on in the back, so many people were whispering thanks to the Lord. The Nipponese engineering had come through. The Kai looked ugly, but it was tough as well.

The flying boat slowed, and a calm came over the airplane. It had been one of the roughest 10 minutes Ryder had ever been through—and he tested experimental planes for a living. He looked over his shoulder to see many ashen faces staring back at him. Half the Delta guys looked like they wanted to hug him for getting them down safely; the other half wanted to kill him for putting them through such an ordeal. At the far end of the cabin, the SEALs were still in their duck and cover positions. Only the SDS guys still looked composed.

Fox, too, was just recovering his equilibrium. He came up on Ryder's shoulder as the pilot shut down the plane's outer engines.

"Please tell me we are where we are supposed to be. . . ." He was holding a GPS readout of Fuggu Island.

"Close enough," Gallant said.

All Ryder could see was jungle, and it was getting closer. He checked his depth gauge. They were quickly being drawn into shallow water. He searched the control panel, looking for the land-gear set-down switch. He was sure it was here someplace. The Kai was a true amphibian; it had the ability to come out of the water and roll onto land. But they would have to put the wheels down quick for that to happen.

Gallant joined the search for the magic button even as the big plane drifted dangerously close to shore. Finally they found a control just below the throttles. Gallant gave it a push. The plane shuddered as a set of tricycle wheels came out from the bottom. Wielding more control now, Ryder eased the big plane toward the shore. Small waves helped carry them in even closer. Finally came a huge *thump!* The Kai's wheels had met the sand. Ryder gave the throttles another goose and the plane crawled up out of the sea and onto the land.

"Thank you, Mr. Darwin," Gallant deadpanned.

There was a grove of overgrown rubber trees just twenty feet off the beach. Ryder headed straight for it. The hanging branches parted ways and allowed them to hide the Kai beneath. Ryder and Gallant quickly shut down everything; they even killed all power from the generators. Then came the silence. They all just sat there, for more than a minute, catching their breath, collecting their thoughts. Becoming one with their stomachs again.

Then Fox bellowed, "Time to rock! We've only got a few hours to do what we have to do—so let's get to it. . . ."

He gathered the team around him in the hold of the plane for one last briefing before they set out. Standing on an ammunition box, he looked like a college football coach addressing his players minutes before the big game. The Pentagon had precious few clues as to where the secret bomber may have gone down, he told them. No one was even sure it went down in the Bangtang Channel. However, he did have an image from an NSA Keyhole satellite, an orbital package that was designed to look for nuclear explosions, as in nuclear testing, or nuclear missile launchings. The satellite's imagers were light-sensitive. One of them picked up a speck of light in this area just about the time the B-2 went missing. That speck of light occurred just a mile east of here. Maybe it was the B-2, maybe it wasn't, Fox said. But if it was, the telemetry indicated something might be sitting right about the center of Fuggu's middle knuckle. Even though subsequent satellite images had shown nothing, this was where they would look first.

Fox asked if there were any questions. Barney, the chief SEAL, raised his hand.

"Any chance this bomber was carrying a nuclear weapon?" he asked.

The usually unflappable Fox hesitated a moment. Did spy bombers carry nukes? It was a good question but it was never addressed before Fox's hasty departure for the Pacific. The DSA officer really didn't know and said as much to those assembled.

From that moment on, though, most of the team members were convinced they were out here looking for a nuke.

They climbed out of the flying boat and onto the tiny beach. It was past dusk and the last light was fading fast. They contemplated the jungle before them.

It was heavily overgrown and looked antediluvian, prehistoric even. The trees seemed much taller than what would be expected in a tropical jungle, much thicker and darker, too. Running throughout them were vines upon vines, covered in green moss, a massive spiderweb that looked like thousands of years in the making.

"Jesuzz Christmas," Fox said, startled by the forbidding jungle up close. "Haven't I seen this in a movie before?"

The sun had disappeared for good by now, just as they were standing there. Not two seconds after the last ray faded into darkness, a symphony of strange and disturbing noises erupted from the thick Asian forest. Hoots, cries, caws. Roars. *Screams.* . . . Not all of them were coming from birds.

"Yeah, I saw that movie, too," Ryder finally replied. "This place looks like Kong Island. All we need now is the big monkey."

Two of the SDS guys would stay with the Kai; they were equipped with a .50-caliber machine gun and a cell phone. This was such a remote location, it seemed impossible for another human to be anywhere close by. But no one on the team was naive enough to believe that.

"I think I might even smell him," Gallant said to Ryder as they checked their weapons. He was talking not about King Kong but Kazeel, the man they'd been enticed out here to capture—and kill. According to Fox, the terrorist mastermind was in the Philippines and might have even been spotted in this area just a couple days ago. Though the thickly jungled island seemed a long way from the sands of the Middle East, Ryder replied: "If he's out here, we'll find him."

Like the Delta guys, Ryder and Gallant were carrying M16/15s, the special ops version of the famous M16 combat rifle. This model had a shortened stock, an oversized bullet clip, and extra gear that allowed its user to fire grenades, flares, and even shotgun shells. Most had laser-aiming devices on their muzzles; a thin line of red light would tell the bullets where to go. The Delta guys were all wearing night-vision goggles as well. The SEALs were carrying their standard assortment of weapons, waterproof M16s mostly, with a couple shotguns as backups. The SDS guys were all sporting Uzis, including Fox. Only Martinez was unarmed.

Fox also had an unusual communication device connected to his Fritz helmet. About the size of a Nokia cell phone, with tiny headphones and a microphone built in right above his chin strap, it was called a UPX, for a universal personal communicator. The UPX was a highly classified piece of equipment. It could contact anyone, anytime, anywhere on the planet by either phone, highband radio, E-mail, or even instant messaging. It could send and receive digital photo images. It could send and receive voice mail. It also served as a GPS device. It was obvious to the team that Fox was the type of guy who had to be plugged in at all times. His UPX would see plenty of action in the hours to come.

Ryder and Gallant found a narrow pathway leading into the jungle. Putting down their night-vision goggles, they plunged right in. This was very thick undergrowth around them: bean leaf plants, *azore* vines, and *kantaki*, a small thorn-covered bush that grew just about everywhere in the Philippines. Martinez and Fox went in right behind them. The Delta operators came next. Behind them the SDS guards, still a little too well dressed for the terrain but plowing forward, jaws tight, shades in place, even at night. Bringing up the rear were the half-dozen SEALs. Soon enough they found themselves having trouble keeping up.

The team moved swiftly, Ryder and Gallant setting the pace. The prospect of finding Kazeel *and* getting home was too much for them to go anything but full-out. The island was about six miles long but just three miles wide. It was about two miles to the center of the knuckle, their first and they hoped, only destination. The jungle was exactly the green hell it appeared to be from the beach, though. The terrain was a nightmare; nothing was flat or straight. The path, centuries old perhaps, turned into an obstacle course of fallen trees, sinkholes, and narrow but rapidly rushing rivers. The jungle canopy overhead was as thick as anything they put on top of their container-ship, the *Ocean Voyager;* it was a true horror as viewed through the night scopes. Every once in a while they would see birds the size of pterodactyls glide over their heads. Screeches that seemed to be coming from other Jurassic-type creatures also shook the night.

It took them all of an hour, but finally they reached a small clearing just about in the center of the island. The team finally stopped and caught its collective breath, all except Fox, who was talking into his UPX device. He'd been using it continually throughout the dash to this place, keeping those on the other end apprised of the team's progress, though always doing so out of earshot. Even now, Fox moved a good distance away from the others to have his hushed conversation.

Ryder and Gallant finally stepped into the clearing, Martinez a few paces behind. They began sniffing the air.

They got a noseful of jungle stink in return but detected something else, too. Burnt rubber, seared metal, the unmistakable odor of aviation fuel. It told them one thing: an airplane had crashed nearby.

A thick ring of dwarfed rubber trees lay beyond the clearing. Behind them was a ridgeline, which in turn led to the base of a thickly covered mountain. Mist was spouting from its peak; it almost looked like a volcano.

Ryder and Gallant followed their noses, Martinez and now Fox were close behind. They made their way across the clearing, through the stunted rubber trees, down into a shallow gully, and then up the side of the ridge. It was maybe 50 feet high. Ryder and Gallant were the first to reach the top. They crawled up to its peak and looked over the other side.

The first thing they saw was a large black metal wing, horribly twisted and sticking nearly straight up in the air. There was a long thin stream of black smoke rising above it. Directly below the wing were the guts of a cockpit, turned inside out and smashed almost beyond recognition. Nearby, was another twisted, misshapen wing. More smoke was rising above it.

"We're not this lucky, are we?" Gallant asked.

"Why not?" Ryder replied. The site seemed to match exactly the telemetry followed from the location of the bright flash on Fox's satellite photo. But as soon as Ryder said those words, he knew he was wrong. Adjusting his night-vision goggles, he saw large pieces of external-style jet engines, two good-sized cargo doors, and the remains of a very large tail section. Much of this was covered in charred white paint.

"Damn . . ." Ryder whispered.

This was not the B-2. It was the wreckage of the KC-10 tanker.

Even its refueling probe was still intact, though it was melted into the shape of a pretzel. But something was strange here. While the wreckage was strewn over an area the size of a football field, with most of it scattered haphazardly amid a grove of ink-plant trees, some of the pieces were stacked neatly in piles around the periphery of the crash site.

Fox finally joined them up on the ridgeline. He quickly realized that this was not their primary prize—but declared it a valuable discovery nonetheless. Without another word, the DSA officer went over the top and started scrambling down the other side of the slope, sliding toward the wreckage.

But at the same moment, Ryder noticed something moving in the rubble. Just beyond the smashed cockpit, a glint of metal against the dark sky. A man stood up, alerted by the sound of Fox dropping down the hill. This man was dressed in a black uniform, with a red bandanna wrapped around his head. He was holding an AK-47 assault rifle.

"It's one of those Aboo assholes," Gallant whispered urgently to Ryder. "The Filipino Al Qaeda. . . ."

No sooner had this man stood up, than another, dressed the same way, emerged from under the bent right wing. Then another appeared near the tail. Then another, and another. And another. Many gunmen were popping up at the bottom of the ridge itself. So the Americans were not the first to discover the tanker's crash site. The terrorists had made it here before them.

If these gunmen had been sleeping when the team came upon them, they were quick to break out of their stupor. All of them turned their guns on Fox, who was just now reaching the bottom of the slope. Ryder raised his weapon; Gallant did, too. But it was too late. The Aboos had spotted Fox and were taking aim at him. Ryder couldn't believe he was about to see the peanut butter sandwich guy get killed. Yet there wasn't even time to shout out a warning to the unsuspecting DSA officer. Disaster seemed inevitable.

But then came an explosion of gunfire from somewhere over Ryder's head. A dozen streams of green tracers combined to hit the terrorists like a tidal wave. The gunmen danced in grotesque slow motion as they were unmercifully riddled with bullets. No sooner had it begun than it was over. Ten Aboos were dead, and Fox was scared shitless. But he was still alive.

Ryder and Gallant looked behind them. It wasn't the Delta guys who'd saved the DSA officer. Not the SEALs, either. It was the SDS guards. Still looking natty in their Banana Republic combat wear, they'd quickly formed a firing line along the ridge and disposed of the Aboos in frighteningly efficient fashion. Ryder and Gallant were astonished by their coolness and accuracy.

Gallant leaned over to Ryder and whispered: "These dudes are beginning to scare me."

As the rest of the team set up a defense perimeter around the crash site, Ryder and Gallant joined Fox at the bottom of the ridge. They searched the Aboo dead, but none was carrying anything more than a gun and some ammo. One man had been found wearing a *kufi*, head garb more at home in the Middle East. But he was small, very dark, and certainly Asian in his appearance. In other words, it was not Kazeel.

The wreckage was eerie up close and personal. Much of it was still smoking, and here and there they could detect the crackle of flames. With the perpetual fog and the heavy overgrowth, though, the site would have been very difficult to see from the air.

Fox was crawling under a piece of torn fuselage, snapping pictures with his UPX.

"Lucky for us this thing was low on fuel when it came down!" he called over his shoulder to the pilots. "Usually when these refuelers crash, there's nothing left but a big hole in the ground."

They found five charred corpses near the head of the wreckage. This was the plane's crew. The terrorists had recovered their bodies, or what remained of them. Fox scooped up a handful of ash from each and deposited it in its own separate plastic bag. "We'll have to give these guys a decent burial when we have a chance," he said.

Even after 10 minutes of poking through it, Ryder and Gallant were overwhelmed by the sight of the huge wreck. No pilot wanted to see anything like this.

"What the hell happened to it?" Gallant asked. "I mean, are we saying that on the same night, in the same area, at the same time, two of our airplanes both crashed, accidentally?"

"Damn—this was no accident," Fox said. He'd climbed up on top of the twisted wreck by now. "Come up and look at this."

Ryder and Gallant scaled the wall of shredded metal.

They found the DSA officer examining a large hole under the tail section of the KC-10 that was now twisted upright. The hole looked like a human puncture wound. The metal was bent in a circular fashion and gallons of red hydraulic fluid had splashed all over it. It looked very much like blood.

"You know what this is, don't you?" Fox asked the pilots, pointing to the hole. "It's an impact point, caused by a significant external explosion. This means the plane didn't go down by accident, nor did it collide with the B-2.

"It was shot down. By a surface-to-air missile. . . ."

They climbed back up to the ridge. The rest of the composite team had reassembled here. Fox separated himself from the group, then activated his UPX communication device again. He was soon talking to someone on the other end.

The conversation was brief. Fox hung up and informed the team that they had to move off the ridge and all the way back to the edge of the clearing. This took about ten minutes. Once there, Fox had these words of advice for those present: "Get down and hold on to something," adding, almost as an afterthought: "I hope we're far enough away."

Ryder heard it coming seconds later. A deep rushing sound at first, getting louder and louder until suddenly there was no noise at all. He looked up just in time to see the Tomahawk cruise missile flash over his head. It nicked the top of the ridge and detonated right above the KC-10's wreckage.

The explosion was tremendous. The shock wave felt

like an earthquake. It sent a shower of hot mud and debris on top of the team members. A fiery cloud rose into the night, but Ryder never saw it.

He was down in the muck, holding on to something, just like everyone else.

Chapter 8

There was a small Aboo camp dug into the summit of a mountain about a half-mile from the KC-10 crash site.

It was a strange place for a terrorist camp to be. Very little tree cover to hide it from the air. Very little but rocks and shrubs to hide it from below. More than two dozen Aboo fighters were stationed up here, but they were in the process of making a hast exit.

They'd heard clearly the sounds of gunfire coming from the next mountain over; then they'd seen the Tomahawk destroy the wrecked airplane. The Aboos knew these things could only mean one thing: The Americans were coming. To find their missing aircraft, to retrieve their dead. And that meant it was time for the Aboos to *vamoose*.

Most had faced aerial attacks before, very halfhearted ones, launched by the Filipino Air Force. But no one wanted to be on the receiving end of a Tomahawk missile. This encampment had been established by the Aboos just three days ago. They'd been told to watch over something up here and if necessary defend it with their lives. But those orders were forgotten now. They were *jihad* fighters, not soldiers. No one had told them they had to face the might of the U.S. military.

They were about halfway through bugging out when suddenly one of their comrades appeared at the edge of the camp. He was one of four men stationed between the plane wreck and the Aboo mountain camp, a trip-wire squad of sorts. The man was out of breath and in shock. He'd climbed out of the bare jungle, his uniform torn and bloody, with no weapon, no boots, no bandanna. It was obvious someone was chasing him; indeed, someone was right on his tail.

The man raised his arms in small triumph upon making the camp, but in the next instant a combined fusillade of M16 tracer fire nearly severed him in two. What was left of him hit the ground and slid back down the mountain. His fellow Aboos were horrified. Their decision to withdraw had come too late. Their aerie camp was already under attack.

A small army of men in black uniforms was advancing rapidly up toward them. Streams of tracers were suddenly coming at the Aboos from all directions. Panic ensued; men began dropping, screaming, dying. Those fighters getting hit were all being shot in the head. Red laser horror, in the middle of night.

Twenty-six terrorists were caught in this crossfire. It took less than a half minute to kill them all.

The combined American assault team streamed into the camp seconds later. Ryder was at the head of the column, Gallant and the others close behind. They'd come upon the trip-wire squad, killed three of them, then followed the fourth one here. Now Ryder scanned the compound with his night-vision goggles. Why had the Aboos built a camp way up here? So out in the open, with very little cover? This wasn't a permanent base, he surmised. The Aboos were up here guarding something.

The SEALs ransacked the place, turning over anything that was covered, tearing down a handful of small huts in the process. They found nothing out of the ordinary, though. Just food, weapons, and mats to sleep on. One SEAL did come up with a pair of sandals. They were dusty and well worn, of a style more ready for the desert, not the mountains of the Philippines. Did Kazeel wear such sandals? Had he been here?

Ryder examined the footwear and put the question to Gallant. The chopper pilot looked around and sniffed the air for effect. "Hard to tell," he said, only half-kidding. "Lots of things stink up here."

They heard one of the Delta guys call out. He'd spotted something. It was a tent, hidden under a crude stick and dirt camouflage net, set off about fifty feet from the camp. Once noticed, it stood out like a sore thumb.

The team converged on it. "What the hell is this?" Gallant asked.

Ryder tore off the top piece of the netting. What lay beneath looked like a prop from a bad sci-fi movie. It was a big piece of machinery, painted bright silver and sitting on a trolley with ten huge rubber tires. A control column that looked like it was run by old-fashioned radio tubes was hanging off one side. Both Chinese and Cyrillic writing could be seen all over it.

It was an SA-4 missile launcher—a very big Soviet era

antiaircraft weapon that harkened back to the sixties. Its one and only missile had already been fired.

"Damn . . . *here's* what killed the tanker," Fox said, spitting on the launcher's tracks. "One missile, set up for one shot."

He pulled out his UPX phone and used it as a GPS plotter. He punched in the coordinates of this camp, then matched them with those of the KC-10 crash site and the brief flash of light picked up by the spy satellite.

"See? The telemetry all fits," he declared. "Someone fired a missile from here; it reached its altitude quickly, and nailed the tanker—and probably the B-2 as well."

Fox put the UPX away and looked up into the night sky. "They were probably going after an airliner," he said wearily. "We've seen more than a few fly over since we've been in the area."

But did that really make any sense? Ryder looked around the camp again. They were about as far from nowhere as they could get. "So someone hauled this monster all the way up here," he asked, "just to try for a shot at an airliner? You would think there's got to be better places than this to attempt something like that. At least under busier air lanes."

But Fox just shrugged. "Well, they would have wasted their time if they were gunning for the bomber," he said. "Besides not being able to know when it was flying overhead, a missile like that couldn't down a B-2. It's a radar-guided weapon and the B-2 is a Stealth."

Ryder looked at Gallant, who just shook his head. At that moment all he wanted to do was find the damn B-2 so they could all get their ticket punched for home.

They scanned the nearby terrain with their night goggles. It was nothing but mountains and jungle all around them.

"The question is," Fox said, "where the hell did the bomber wind up?"

At that moment, his UPX started beeping. Another call was coming in. He answered, had a short conversation with someone during which he passed on news about finding the launcher, then said: "Really? Intact? OK—patch me in."

In a rare moment, he held up the small UPX screen for everyone to see. The rest of the team crowded around him. It was all static at first. But then an image started to form.

"This was shot by a Predator drone just a few hours ago," Fox explained. "It's only about a mile from here."

The tiny screen displayed a river, a small beach, and thick jungle all around it.

Sitting on the beach was the unmistakable outline of a B-2 bomber.

The quick march through the jungle now became a sprint. Running down trails, over dead trees, across streams. The terrain was continuous in its changes. Jungle paths, ridges, gullies, and hills, all connected by an endless series of hollows and valleys. Through it all, Fox was yelling into his UPX communicator, asking which way they should go next. North? South? Over the next hill or around it?

Someone was directing them, maybe from a Predator, maybe from a satellite, maybe from some piece of gear

Fox was carrying. Ryder and the others didn't really know and, at this point, really didn't care. They were too busy running.

It seemed almost impossible, considering the rugged terrain and the darkness of night, but they were nearing their destination in under a half hour. A few more instructions from the UPX phone and they soon broke through a line of undergrowth—at the exact spot they were told to be.

Problem was, there was no beach here, no river. No clearing. And definitely no B-2.

What they found instead was a black lake.

"What the fuck is this?" Fox cursed. He studied his UPX readout, matching their GPS position with the coordinates that had just been provided by the Predator.

Everything checked out. They were where they were supposed to be. It was the lake that was out of place.

The team collapsed at the water's edge, exhausted from their grueling, breathless trek. This didn't make any sense. Fox rechecked his data over and over again. He gave it over to Ryder and Gallant. They did the math. It still came out right. Everything matched—except the lake.

"Are we on the right island?" Gallant wondered.

Just then Martinez, who'd been sitting quietly a few feet away from them, suddenly got up, took off all his clothes—dived into the dark water.

"What the hell is he doing?" Gallant yelled.

He and Ryder were both up on their feet in an instant; the whole team was.

"Not the time for your guy to go for a swim!" Fox yelled.

They all watched the surface of the water, black and treacherous. The seconds ticked by. Five. Ten. *Fifteen*. . . . Martinez never came back up. Ryder and Gallant began ripping off their boots, intent on jumping in to save their colleague. But just as they were about to dive in, Martinez came back up. He looked half-drowned. He could not swim. He was struggling to catch his breath. Ryder and Gallant jumped in, pulled him to the water's edge, then dragged him up to land. Only then did they realize he had something in his hand. It was a long, thin piece of metal, with several tiny protrusions on the tip. Fox took it from him, though for a few seconds Martinez was reluctant to let it go.

"This is a high-gain UHF antenna," Fox said, examining the object through his night-vision goggles. "It's right off the front of a B-2 bomber."

They all turned back to the lake.

"Son of a bitch," Ryder said. *"It's under the water?"*

"Damn," Fox said over and over again. "Damn . . . it *must* be down here."

"But how?" Gallant asked. "The photo shows it on *dry land*."

They stood in silence for a long time, trying to solve the puzzle. It was Barney, the chief SEAL, who figured it out first.

"They dammed a river," he blurted out. "They raised the water level in this area somehow . . . and covered the bomber over."

He and his SEALs were off like a shot. They began running along the south bank of the lake. Just as quickly, the Delta guys headed north. In two minutes, the Delta squad called Fox's cell phone. They'd found an ancient water gate 500 feet up from the team's location. It was in the open position. Then the SEALs called in. They'd discovered a temporary earthen dam about the same distance to the south. This barrier was keeping the water in. Fox gave two quick orders: he told Delta to close the water gate; then he told the SEALs to blow the temporary dam.

Then everyone else just sat down on the edge of the small lake and watched the water go down.

It only took about ten minutes before the top of the B-2 came into view. The moon had risen by this time and it was actually easier to see without their night goggles. The water drained out quicker by the second, revealing the huge bomber a few inches at a time.

Fox was on his UPX again, repeating over and over, "We've found it. That's affirmative. . . . We found it." He was giving someone a blow-by-blow description of what was happening, this as the water continued to drain from around the large, bat-wing shape.

The more the water went down, though, the more obvious it became that this billion-dollar bomber had not been shot down, as had the KC-10. Rather, it had crash-landed and had somehow stayed in one piece, more or less. It was also clear that the Stealth plane would never fly again. Its nose was crushed, its cockpit windows were blown out, and its bat shape was twisted and torn. There was a lot of debris surfacing on the water all around it.

Gallant lit up a soggy cigarette. "Who's going to pay for this?" he asked snidely.

Fox meanwhile was becoming especially anxious. He was pacing the water's shrinking edge, the UPX burning his ear, continuously checking his watch, and talking to his mysterious friends, always out of earshot of the others. He seemed to grow more uncharacteristically agitated as the minutes ticked by.

Ryder and Gallant tried their best to listen in on Fox's conversation. He was raising his voice, but his words were mostly garbled . . . except for one last sentence Fox half-bellowed into his UPX. They heard it very clearly. He said: *"It was carrying what?"*

Ryder and Gallant exchanged worried looks. They turned back to the bomber, now about halfway revealed.

"I knew it," Gallant whispered. "That fucking thing has a nuke in it."

Ryder, too, was concerned. "I don't think they carry just one nuke," he said. "I think these things carry many, many nukes."

At that moment, they saw Fox hastily end his conversation and toss his UPX to the ground. He looked extremely pissed off. Then he suddenly plunged into the shrinking lake, clothes and all, its water now just four feet deep. He waded over to the waterlogged bomber and boosted himself up on its crumpled wing. Ryder and Gallant followed him in. By the time they got to the wing, Fox was already inside the bomber, having gone in through the cockpit's broken windshield.

Ryder reached the top of the plane, walked out onto its very blunt nose, and nearly slipped. Black Stealth paint was coming off on his hands and feet. He dropped down through the open window, hitting the pilot's seat with a thump. The water had drained out of here by now, leaving behind a major soggy mess.

Gallant came down almost on top of him. He was

jarred by the battered cockpit, too. "Got to be at least fifty mil down the drain just in here," he said.

"Maybe twice that," Ryder told him.

They moved aft, finding the bomber was not so gigantic on the inside. It was actually rather cramped.

They could hear Fox down below. He'd quickly slipped through an access panel leading directly into the bomb bay, as if he'd been prepped ahead of time on just how to do this.

By the time Ryder and Gallant reached Fox's location, the DSA officer was standing in knee-deep water, his flashlight shooting beams madly about the bomb bay. But the bomb bay was empty. No bombs. No bomb racks. No nothing. Just an empty chamber.

And Fox seemed very upset by this.

"Time to come clean!" Ryder yelled down to him. "What was *supposed* to be in there? A bunch of nuclear bombs?"

Fox glanced up at him. He looked very dejected.

"We should be so lucky," he said.

Chapter 9

The explosion went off just 10 feet from where Atlas was sleeping.

The concussion slammed him against the bars of his cage. A wave of flame and sparks washed over him. This was how he woke up—his head bleeding, the hair on his arms afire.

Still, the first thought that came to him was: *How the hell did I ever fall asleep?*

The horror he'd witnessed in the camp over the past few hours seemed to be enough to guarantee that he would never sleep again. The Aboos had executed three more people since the man with the beard was so cruelly murdered. His wife had been brought out next. She was too hysterical to go through the Aboos' videotaped interrogation routine. They roughly put her head on the chopping block and decapitated her just minutes after she was taken from her box.

A younger man went next, this just as the sun had gone down and the terrorists had started drinking what appeared to be homemade beer. The Aboos tortured the young man—he looked Hawaiian—burning him with cig-arette butts and candles and making him sing a song be-fore they cut off his head. The Aboos then urinated on his body.

The fourth victim was taken at the height of the drunken rage. She was a young overweight teen, probably 15 or so. The terrorists tried to sexually assault her, but they were too intoxicated and she fought them to the end. They decapitated her, but because the executioner was drunk, it was messy and she went very badly. Her killing disgusted even the drunken terrorists, and the blood lust ended abruptly. In a way then, the poor girl saved Atlas's life, as he was certain he would have been next.

Somewhere after that, exhausted and depleted of adrenaline, Atlas fell asleep.

It was the sound of one of the terrorists getting blown to pieces that had woke him up. It took him a few seconds to get his bearings. Then he saw that the guy who had been guarding his box was now lying in pieces on the ground right next to him. Strangely, Atlas thought the man had blown himself up with his own grenade. Atlas had seen him tossing it around the day before. . . .

Blam! Blam! Blam!

Suddenly another terrorist fell next to Atlas's cage. He was practically face-to-face with him. It was his other guard. The man had taken a bullet between the eyes, an-other in the mouth, another in the neck. Three bullets all in a line.

Tap shots . . . Atlas thought. Well aimed. Quick. Deadly.

That's when it finally hit him: the terrorists' camp was under attack.

Atlas tried to move away from the two ghastly bodies, but of course this was impossible inside his tiny cell. Another explosion went off right next to him. It lifted his box up a few inches before slamming it back down to the ground again, nearly crushing him. Then came more machine-gun fire. Rocket grenades were exploding all over. The camp's guards had all been shot instantaneously. The rest of the Aboos were in their cots either asleep or still passed out. They were being riddled with bullets before their feet could hit the ground. More explosions, more heavy firing. An earsplitting scream shook the area. And what the hell was that going over his head?

Atlas had prayed to be rescued, prayed harder than he had ever prayed before. But never did he think the cavalry would arrive not knowing there were still hostages alive here. He was convinced he'd be killed right along with his tormentors. But then this thought was cut short by another explosion—the biggest one yet. It was so powerful it ripped the top off Atlas's box. Suddenly he could see the trees and the vines overhead and even a few stars—things he'd thought he'd never see again. He tried to get up, tried to get out before someone came along and put the roof back on. But then came another blast. This one knocked the rest of the cage right over. Atlas landed facedown in the mud and the blood and the homemade beer. When he cleared the crap from his eyes, he saw a pair of boots in front of him. A heavily armed man in a black uniform was standing over him. He knew he was some kind of special operations soldier. Except he was very unkempt.

He roughly pulled Atlas to his feet kicking away the last remains of the cage. Atlas saw the strange patch on the man's shoulder. The Stars and Stripes with the outline of the Twin Towers and the letters NYPD and FDNY on either side.

Atlas couldn't help it. He had to ask the man: "Who the hell are you?"

"That's a good question," the soldier replied.

Explosions were still going off all over the camp. The sky was filled with flares, suspended in air, turning the night into weirdly twisting shadows. Atlas and his rescuer raced through the compound trying to avoid being hit by all the ordnance coming from just about every direction.

They ran by two more black-uniformed soldiers who were brutally beating one of the Aboos to death with their rifle butts. Atlas saw another terrorist get shot first in the nose, then twice in the neck. Two more were burned alive in their hut as the raiders threw incendiary grenades into its opening. It was bloody and shocking, even after what Atlas had seen the terrorists do to their hostages. There was no mercy here, no quarter given—and certainly no prisoners.

Again, the questions came to him: *Who are these guys? Are they really Americans?*

Suddenly the bullets stopped flying. The sky was empty and everything had gone dark again. Still on the tail of the man who had helped free him, Atlas tried to make some sense of the smoke and flames. The raiders had left one hut standing. It was the terrorists' HQ, their commander's hut. Atlas crowded inside with the rest of the rescue team. Each soldier seemed bigger than the next, and many were wearing the same stars-and-stripes-and-Twin-Towers patch as the guy who'd pulled him from his box. But others were clearly SEALs. And others seemed to belong to an army of male models. But at the same time they *all* seemed so unusual. So different. . . .

They had the Aboo commander bound to his bamboo chair in the middle of the hut. His elaborate array of video paraphernalia had been smashed to pieces all around him. One man not wearing the stars-and-stripes patch was interrogating the terrorist commander, speaking to him in a combination of Portuguese, English, and Tagalog. Four other soldiers were standing right over him. Whenever the Aboo CO would refuse to answer or gave an answer they didn't want to hear, he got a rifle butt across the face or a boot in the nuts. Atlas never thought he could feel bad for the Aboo CO. He'd seen the guy brutally murder four hostages in just one night and would have killed him as well, had it not been for this strangely divine intervention. But he felt a pang of grief for this man now, because the raiders were beating him so.

Atlas was on the verge of shock and disoriented from his own ordeal. And he didn't speak Portuguese or the local Filipino tongue. But suddenly came one sentence in bits of English he *could* understand: the interrogator asked the terrorist leader where the cargo from the B-2 was. Atlas froze when he heard this. The cargo? Why was he asking about the cargo and not the B-2 itself? Strange as it was, what they'd been carrying in the belly of the beast was a very top secret. Yet these unusual rescuers knew about it—or at least the cracker asking the questions did. It was unclear if the rest of them even heard the question, so intent were they on beating the Aboo.

That's when it dawned on Atlas: These soldiers weren't so much here to rescue him and the other surviving hostages, as they were to recover what he'd been carrying inside the B-2.

This is very weird . . . he thought.

At that moment, he vowed not to tell anybody anything about what happened the night before, at least not until he had a chance to speak with his superiors.

The terrorist commander was white with fear by now. He could barely speak, his lips were so bloody. The soldiers brought in one of the CO's underlings; he was the only other Aboo member left alive in the camp. Atlas recognized him as the guy who drove the execution truck. They put a gun in this man's mouth and then made it clear to the Aboo CO that if he didn't start answering their questions, he would suffer the same fate as was about to befall his hapless colleague. The soldiers then made the underling pull his own trigger. His skull exploded and he went over like a lead weight.

The Aboo commander threw up all over himself. He was pleading with the raiders for mercy. In bits of English now, he went into detail about people coming to him with a plan to shoot something down, on a certain night and in a certain place, and saying that he and his men would be paid to provide men and guns for the operation, but that their involvement ended there. He knew nothing about any cargo. In between all this, the Aboo commander was asking the soldiers over and over: *"How did you find me? We were supposed to be hidden. . . ."*

Suddenly one of the men wearing the strange stars-and-stripes patch got right in the terrorist's face. "We *smelled* you, asshole!" he roared furiously before being led away.

Another man in a black uniform appeared and shoved

a digital photo of someone in the Aboo CO's face. Atlas caught a glimpse of the man in the photo. He was an Arab, in full turban and robe. He had a pop eye, bad skin, and terrible teeth.

"You know him?" the man was screaming at the Aboo CO. "Has he been here?"

The Aboo shook his head violently no, but Atlas thought he might be lying. He was beaten again, this time savagely about the face and stomach. He started crying and threw up again. He looked up at Atlas, as if he was the only sane one in the room—and maybe he was right. But Atlas turned his back on him. He was not in the business of helping murderers, even if it was at the hand of other, if friendlier, murderers.

This went on for what seemed like forever. The last Aboo was beaten to a pulp. Finally the terrorist uttered his last two words: "Dirty Arabs. . . ." It was clear he was unable to say any more. The soldiers put a gun in his mouth a moment later. Someone pulled the trigger and his head was blown away.

Atlas felt all the energy drain out of him at that point. The raiders decided it was time to go. Atlas stumbled outside just ahead of them, looking about the camp. The place was in flames. Bodies were everywhere. Atlas was a jet pilot; he'd never been this close to combat. It was making him sick. One of the raiders asked him if he could walk. Atlas told him he'd crawl if it meant getting out of this place. The raiders and the rescued hostages began moving out. The three others freed were missionaries, like the ones Atlas had seen killed. They were Americans, and they were now in tears that they had been saved. Atlas had never seen their faces until now.

The rescuers were hustling them out of the camp faster than the hostages could walk. Atlas lingered behind for a moment, looking over the camp, looking over the dead. Each body was wearing black pajamas and a red bandanna—no one else had been killed. Each tiger cage had been overturned and was now empty. Everyone had been freed.

But this didn't make sense.

If all the terrorists were dead and all the hostages had been released, then what the hell happened to Teddy Ballgame?

The American team made its way to a mountain called Wabala Tang.

It was located a mile east of the Aboos' main camp, near the tip of Fuggu's extended middle finger. It took the team about an hour to scale the 2,500-foot rise, the strongest of the Delta soldiers assisting the four surviving hostages. Wabala Tang's flattened top would give the team a good vantage point. Plus, as the summit was thick with vegetation, they would have a place to rest and hide from the heat of the coming day.

It had been one crazy night. Weird, full of twists and turns. And very bloody. But they'd accomplished what they'd been sent here to do: They'd found the KC-10. They'd found the Aboos. And most important, they'd found the B-2—the prize they'd been told would get them back to America.

But now what?

The view from atop the mountain was spectacular. Dawn was coming and the waters of the Pacific off to the east looked jewel-like in the early light. A ferry was crossing the Bangtang Channel about a mile offshore. It was painted bright green, heading south, no doubt to Luzon, its passengers most probably unaware that a small war had just been fought overnight on this lost little island. Overhead, contrails of commercial airliners reflected the coming sunrise, their silver fuselages gleaming as the stars began fading away. It all seemed so peaceful.

Most of the team had retreated under the rubber trees. They would provide surprisingly cool shade and enough room for the hostages and the team members to stretch out. Those rescued feasted on MREs brought along by the assault team. Reconstituted spaghetti and meatballs, under the rising Filipino sun.

Ryder and Gallant sat out on the edge of the mountain's cliff, awaiting the sunlight. They'd spent enough time in the dark, nearly a full month belowdecks of the *Ocean Voyager* after the events at Hormuz. They had to grab the rays anytime they could. When it came the warmth would feel good. And they could easily see the rest of the island from here. It looked like a paradise.

"Isn't this the part where we meet some native girls and all get laid?" Gallant asked Ryder with a straight face.

"And *then* we all go back home again?" Ryder replied. "Yes, I think that's coming right up."

They relaxed and smoked cigarettes, buoyed by the knowledge that upon their keeping half of the bargain, Fox would now keep his and that they would indeed all be heading home very soon.

Wabala Tang overlooked another beach, and another inlet, farther up Fuggu's short coastline. To their left, at the base of the next mountain over, was the terrorists' main camp, still smoldering. To their right, the other mountain where the Aboos had been guarding the SAM launcher. In front of them, the river that had fed the lake where the B-2F went down and was so unusually hidden. Even now, with the ever-brightening sky, they could see the outline of the doomed bomber.

Fox had stationed himself atop a pile of rocks nearby, about fifty feet away from the two pilots. He hadn't said anything to anybody since interrogating the Aboo commander. It was now about 0500 hours and the DSA officer was again whispering into his communicator. A few minutes later, Ryder and Gallant heard a somewhat familiar whooshing sound. Off to their right, a couple miles south of them, a Tomahawk missile was approaching, flying very low over the jungle. Ryder and Gallant watched the weapon streak by and explode directly above the remains of the Aboo main camp. The detonation was so bright and so symmetrical, it looked like a movie special effect. The camp had been in bad shape when the team left it. It was just a black scar on the side of the mountain now.

No sooner had the flames from this explosion dissipated than they heard Fox whispering into his phone again. Sure enough, a few moments later another Tomahawk arrived.

"There must be a sub laying offshore," Gallant reasoned. "Judging by the time it takes for him to make the call and then for them to show up."

Ryder touched fists with him. "Yeah, good guess," he said.

The second Tomahawk streaked by, headed for the Aboos' other mountain base, the place where the SAM had been launched. It plowed into the hilltop, exploding with such power, the resulting landslide buried the remains of the SAM camp forever. Two more Tommies showed up right on its tail. They were headed for the ghost beach where the spy bomber lay. They circled the area once, then peeled off and dived into the B-2.

One would have probably sufficed. A ton of high explosives tended to punch a pretty big hole in the ground. Two of them had the ability to create a small moonscape. Sure enough, when the flames and smoke lifted, Ryder and Gallant could see there was nothing left inside the impact area. No plant life. No water.

And of course, no sign remaining of the top-secret bomber.

An hour went by. Dawn came and the heat of the day arrived. The team stayed up on the summit, under the rubber trees, so cool and giving with their shade. Ryder and Gallant remained out on the ledge, though, smoking cigarettes. Everyone was waiting for Fox to tell them what to do next.

But the DSA officer had moved even farther away from them by now. In fact, he was standing on top of the highest rock at the highest point of the mountain. A very exposed position, but as it turned out, he was up there more as an antenna than an unintentional target.

Something was wrong. Fox had been trying to raise somebody, anybody, on his UPX device ever since the last two Tomahawks creamed the B-2F. But strangely, none of his calls were going through. Or if they were, he was not getting any bounce-backs. It wasn't a problem with the UPX; it was working fine. The problem was on the other end. Fox had been yapping into the device almost nonstop the whole night, keeping those listening informed on practically every step the team had made.

But now, ever since all the evidence of the small war had been wiped out by the Tomahawk missiles, no one was returning his calls.

Noon came and went.

The heat grew. Fox had still yet to hear from anyone and was getting increasingly agitated as the hours passed. A call to the two SDS men left with the Kai two miles down the coast confirmed that the airplane was all right, but that no orders or any messages at all had come through the flying boat's communications suite. Everyone on top of the mountain thought that once they'd rested they'd simply march back down the beach to where the Kai lay hidden, get onboard, and take off. But Fox was still in charge. And while he was waiting for someone to contact him the others had no choice but to wait as well.

The DSA officer remained up on the high rocks, in the blistering heat, throughout the early afternoon. He was no longer standing, though, and he was no longer on the phone. He was just sitting up there and staring out at the water. He didn't say anything to the pilots sitting nearby in all that time. In fact, the only person he'd talked to was the guy named Atlas, who they now knew had been the pilot of the B-2. Their conversation, held atop the burning summit, had been brief, sharp almost, with Atlas saying very little and answering most of Fox's questions by emphatically shaking his head.

Ryder and Gallant stayed on the edge of the cliff, watching all this happen even as they were beginning to finally mind the heat. The afternoon wore on; the weather cooled. Fox stayed in place, though, his UPX maddeningly silent. Just as Ryder and Gallant were lighting up their last cigarettes, a very unexpected visitor came up behind them. He fell to the seat of his pants next to Ryder.

It was Martinez, their troubled colleague. He sat there for a long time, silently looking out on the black spot of ground where the B-2F had met its end—twice.

Finally he turned to Ryder and Gallant and for what seemed like the first time since the events back in the Strait of Hormuz actually spoke to them.

"All is not right here," he told them, his eyes reviving a bit of their former fire. "You guys know that, don't you?"

"What do you mean?" Ryder finally replied, shocked to hear his voice again.

"Just think about it," Martinez said, keeping his words low. "This whole thing started when someone sent that B-2 someplace, right? A training mission, did they say?"

Ryder and Gallant both nodded.

"Well, if that was true," Martinez said, "why the hell were they doing an aerial refueling in sight of land? And in someone else's airspace at that? Some 'training mission.' Don't you think?"

Ryder shrugged. It was true, most refuelings were done way out over water if possible, especially training missions. It was just safer that way. But this did not mean some weren't done over land as well. Plus . . .

" 'Training missions' are always a cover for covert stuff," Ryder said. "It's the most convenient lie."

"*Exactly,*" Martinez said, with a slightly disturbing smile. "So, let's assume it wasn't a real training mission."

He looked back to where the SAM site had been. A thin pall of smoke was still rising above it.

"OK now, what about these Aboo guys?" Martinez went on. "*They* were in the right neighborhood, weren't they? Shooting wildly up into the sky, just as our planes were going overhead. And do you really believe they got that old SAM on their own?"

Then he turned back to where the B-2 had been.

"And why didn't the people who sent us here just bomb that thing when they first spotted it? If they were going to destroy it anyway, why did they have us go through all this first? Why wait? I'll tell you why: because they had to find out something first. You saw how Fox acted when he finally made it to the bomb bay. What the hell was he looking for if it wasn't a nuclear bomb? And besides, that bomb bay, it had been cored out—I saw it myself. There was no way that plane could have been carrying a bomb anyway! It had to be carrying something else."

Ryder and Gallant puffed their Marlboros and thought about what Martinez had to say. Having the SAM on the island. Having the Aboos looking after it. Having someone fire it at just the right time to knock down the KC-10 *and* force the B-2F to crash-land. Maybe they had all seemed like unlucky accidents before, coincidental in the middle of this crazy night. But strung all together like this, in the light of day, maybe coincidence wasn't the only explanation.

Maybe the SAM had been meant to down the B-2 after all.

"But how could the Aboos know the B-2 was coming?" Ryder asked him. "That plane was so special, any mission it was flying would have to be highly classified. They're out here eating bugs and pissing in the stream, for God's sake. They're the bottom of the food chain. Even Kazeel couldn't get information like that."

"It *had* to be a lucky shot," Gallant said. "They were going for an airliner and missed . . . big-time."

But Martinez just shook his head. "It was no lucky shot," he insisted. "I don't know how, but they *knew* what they were shooting at. And they must of known it would be the two planes hooked up. Sure, a SAM like that couldn't take down a B-2, because it runs on radar and the bomber is a stealth. But if they knew the B-2 would be hooked up when it was going overhead, then if you hit the tanker . . ."

He let his words trail off. He was almost ranting, yet he was also making some sense, in a disturbing kind of way.

He turned and pointed up to Fox, still stationed atop the pile of rocks, still staring out to sea, still waiting for a callback.

"And I'll tell you one more thing," Martinez said grimly. "See that guy up there, waiting for his phone to ring? Well, it ain't going to ring. Take it from me: A very dirty job has just been done and now someone is seriously messing with his head. And now he's stuck out here, too. Just like the rest of us. . . ."

PART TWO
Off to the Pushi

Chapter 10

Sheik Kazeel had never laughed so hard in his life. Tears were rolling down his face. His sides ached. He could barely catch his breath. He was usually as joyless as a man could be, an occupational hazard of being the world's first "superterrorist." But at the moment, he could hardly contain himself.

He was sitting in the back room of the Impatient Parrot brothel in downtown Manila. This part of the Philippine capital was known as the Combat Zone. A throwback to the days of the Vietnam War, it was a six-block area heavily populated with strip clubs, saloons, dance halls, and whorehouses. These days the streets were crowded not with US soldiers on R and R but sex tourists, from Europe and Japan, who were looking for a little bit of the strange. They'd come to the right place. It was a Saturday night and the Zone was rocking. There was plenty of strange going around.

The Impatient Parrot would have seemed an unlikely place to find the shadowy Kazeel. He was a devout Mus-

lim. He prayed the required five times a day and never
went anywhere without his copy of the Koran. Alcohol,
drugs, slatternly women, young girls? Just about everything the Prophet Muhammad had warned all Islam to
avoid was on display at the Parrot. Kazeel was then sitting in a defiled place, and to do so was considered unholy. He was also a senior member of Al Qaeda. Being
spotted in a whorehouse might not please the Saudi fun-
damentalist *mullahs* who were still the backbone of Al
Qaeda's financial network.

So why was he here then?

And why was he laughing?

That Kazeel planned the attack on the USS *Abraham Lincoln* was known around the world. That he also helped
plan the attacks of 9/11 was also common knowledge. It
was for these reasons that the Department of Homeland
Security, imprudently, as it turned out, proclaimed him
the world's first superterrorist. That's how Kazeel's
blurred photo wound up on the cover of *Time*.

That the plan to sink the *Lincoln* had failed miser-
ably was also known to the world, of course. But in the
twin Byzantine cultures of *jihad* terrorism and international notoriety, Kazeel's standing had not diminished a
bit, despite handing the Americans a huge victory that
day. That he even attempted the attack was enough to
please his fans in the Saudi palaces, the casbah, and the
Islamic religious schools through the Middle East
where hatred of all things American made for most of
the curriculum.

Kazeel's street rep aside, though, the failure of the

Lincoln attack, as well as the events at the Tonka Tower, were hardly good news for worldwide Islamic terrorism. Both had succeeded only in draining away much of the momentum Al Qaeda had generated after the attacks of September 11th and since. And this holy war against the United States was all about momentum. Al Qaeda's aim was to put fear into the hearts of all Americans and keep it there, permanently. They did this by being brutal, unrelenting, and evasive. But in less than 40 days the terrorist network had been thrown on the defensive, not once but twice. It had been made to look inept. Funds flowing into Islamic charities, Al Qaeda's lifeblood, were slowing. Huge chunks of money from the House of Saud or Syria or Iran were not so forthcoming as they had been. Many of Al Qaeda's members were still on the run, trying to stay one step ahead of the 82nd Airborne in Afghanistan. Many were in jail. Many more had been killed. Despite Kazeel's newfound celebrity, the Al Qaeda movement itself seemed in danger of running out of gas.

For these reasons, the next attack against America *had* to be big and it *had* to be a success.

That's why Kazeel was in Manila.

In his own toothless, pop-eyed way, Kazeel loved irony.

The United States was now sitting in Iraq. The oil was finally beginning to flow and at least some of the Iraqi people were beginning to get happy. In many ways, the American dream was coming true half a world away. Plus, the military victory against Baghdad, for all its faults, had made the United States more *respected* in the Arab world, whether through fear or admiration.

But while Gulf War II had turned some old adversaries into friends, it had also produced the reverse effect. It had created some new, unexpected enemies for America. Friends who were now foes. One of them, the most powerful, had decided it was in their country's interests to take the United States down a peg or two.

To say this new enemy was well-placed in the global community was a huge understatement. Indeed, they were entrenched in both world history and current affairs, in diplomatic parlance, a "real player."

And now, for reasons that were beyond Kazeel's reckoning, they were willing to help Al Qaeda in operations against the United States. Very secretly, of course.

War made strange bedfellows; politics did too. And, frankly, Kazeel's new *ashaab judus*, his "newfound friends," were only a little less repugnant than the Americans themselves. But he was in no position to be choosy. After the events at Hormuz and in Singapore, he would take all the help he could get. And he was already getting a lot of it.

Because of this strange new alliance, Kazeel now owned the contents of the downed B-2F's cargo bay—and it was hardly a shipment of American Tourister luggage. The thirty-six cases contained launchers for Stinger missiles, the ubiquitous shoulder-fired, American-made anti-aircraft weapon favored by armies and insurgents alike.

Stingers were one of Al Qaeda's most cherished weapons, almost custom-made for their needs. When matched with their missiles, they were light to carry, just 22 pounds, and compact, at five feet and change. They were simple to operate: just aim, fire, and forget. The heat-seeking missile carried a two-pound fused warhead designed to explode on contact. It could fly as high as 2 miles, and had a range of five. It also hit its target going 1,500 miles per hour. Put it all together and it was more than powerful enough to bring down a helicopter. Or a jet fighter.

Or even an airliner.

Just how his *judus* was able to get the launchers into the belly of the B-2F, and then arrange for the spy bomber to crash-land on Fuggu Island, Kazeel had no idea. In many ways, he didn't want to know. When he and the *judus* agreed, quoting an old Arabic phrase, "to get their hands dirty together," it was also understood that for security reasons, both sides would only know what they had to know, and nothing more. The Aboos were involved, as was an almost-antique Soviet-made SAM—but beyond that, Kazeel was blissful in his ignorance of how his new friends came by the precious launchers.

"High-level connections," was how he reasoned it out.

There really was no other explanation.

Kazeel was a dark-skinned Arab. He was thin and perpetually dirty. However, if he dressed in jeans, sneakers, and a Hawaiian shirt, he became indistinguishable from the thousands of Filipino men walking around Manila. Not that it made any difference. He'd been assured by his new patrons that he could also move around the city with virtual impunity, that the local authorities had been paid off to leave him alone. Another indication how powerful the *judus* could be.

Kazeel had flown in three nights before, using a fake

Egyptian passport again supplied by the *judus*. He was met at the airport by the *judus'* Manila contact, a balding, rotund, 50-ish Filipino hoodlum named Marcos. They left the airport in a limousine; they even did lunch. On the third day, Kazeel was taken to see the launchers; they were hidden in a bunker on a small island outside Manila Bay. Kazeel had been whisked there in a multimillion-dollar yacht. The bunker was in a deep chamber bored into the side of a small mountain. It was guarded by uniformed members of the Philippine national police. The launchers, still sealed in their carrying cases, were piled in three stacks inside. The cases were muddied and some were dented, but all had survived the impact of the B-2F's crash landing, as they had been made of a material similar to that used in commerical aircraft crash-proof black boxes.

Marcos told him the cache of missile launchers was still "very hot" though, and could not stay in the bunker for very long. The plan would be to move them around continuously until they could be shipped to their final destination.

Visiting the bunker was like walking into a bank vault for Kazeel. In the past, Al Qaeda had been hard-pressed to find even a handful of Stinger launchers at any one time. Now that he was working with the *judus*, these kinds of weapons could be had almost readily.

All Kazeel had to do now was get three dozen missiles to mate with the launchers and the next big assault on America would be one step closer to reality.

The viewing in the bunker had been complete by early afternoon. When the yacht docked back in Manila, Marcos asked if he could join Kazeel for dinner. Normally Kazeel would have told him a flat no. But in this new world of his, he surmised the contact wasn't doing this because he longed for Kazeel's company, but rather that his *judus* wanted someone to keep an eye on him while he was in town. And Kazeel *was* learning to become flexible. So he accepted Marcos' request.

Kazeel spent the rest of the day holed up in his five-star hotel. Around 6 P.M., Kazeel received a message from Marcos. He was on his way up. Dinner was eaten in Kazeel's suite, during which Kazeel lectured the hoodlum on the fruits of Islam, his one condition for agreeing to meet. The conversation after that was trite. Marcos quickly grew bored. It was so obvious he was here just to keep tabs on Kazeel, it was almost painful.

But then room service arrived and a bottle of post meal wine was offered, courtesy of the house. Kazeel rarely drank alcohol, as it ran counter to Muhammad's laws. But for whatever reason, he didn't feel very Muslim tonight. He'd had a very stressful past couple months, trying to get the world to stand on its head for Allah. He deserved a little respite. So he agreed to just one.

That one glass quickly led to another however; Marcos fancied himself a wine connoisseur and he was also a lush. Soon the first bottle of wine was gone, and room service brought two more. They were drained as well. Then Marcos ordered some liquor Kazeel had never heard of. They drank it in little glasses poured right from the bottle. Kazeel was soon very drunk. That's when Marcos revealed that in addition to working for the *judus*, he was also the owner of a brothel, downtown. In the Combat Zone.

That was how Kazeel found himself here now, in the back room of the Impatient Parrot, cackling hysterically, not unlike a jackal.

What was making Kazeel laugh so hard was the two girls sloshing around in the mud pit in front of him.

They were young and topless and they were wrestling each other ferociously. A dozen well-heeled Filipino businessmen were sitting around the pit. They'd made a corral of metal folding chairs and were occasionally flipping U.S. half-dollar coins into the mud as tips for the two young combatants. Kazeel and the Parrot's owner sat in padded seats at either end of the squared ring. The back room was small and grimy. A giant plate glass window, covered in thick black paint and pictures of some rather sick pornography, made up one of its walls. Brick and perforated bamboo sticks made up the other three. The room was filled with tobacco, marijuana, and opium smoke. The floor was a half-inch deep with spilled beer. The stink of sweat was almost overwhelming.

For the most part, the other men sitting around the pit were silent, intense. Not unlike a pride of lions getting ready for the kill. The two girls would be made available to all after this slop match. If the crude pictures on the black wall were any indication, a rough outing was guaranteed for both.

But Kazeel's delight was not coming from anticipation of sex. Having been taught from an early age to hate women, he was virtually sexless. Yet he was finding it highly amusing to watch the two girls roll around in mud, slapping each other, pulling hair, ripping off what was left of their clothes, groping at their privates.

The others in the room saw the mud fight as a prelude to nocturnal depravity. Kazeel saw it as slapstick.

There were four security men watching over him; they'd been supplied by Marcos. Kazeel's *shuka*—Arabic slang for assistant or companion—was standing close by as well. He was Abdul Abu Uni, a nickname, of course, and a cruel one. Abdul was a eunuch, mutilated by an uncle at the age of two. Keeping such a thing hidden in an Arab community was impossible. People had been calling him Uni most of his life.

A dead ringer for the American ad icon Mr. Clean, right down to the huge gold ring in his left earlobe, Uni was six-foot-two, wide and strong, with a powerful face and gigantic hands. He was fanatically loyal to Kazeel. He was also a functional idiot, with an IQ of less than 75. They'd been a couple for nearly 10 years. While the superterrorist had traveled alone in the weeks before the *Lincoln* attack, back when he was less well known, these days Uni went everywhere with him. He could usually be found standing at Kazeel's left shoulder, arms folded, a perpetual scowl in place.

But even Uni was laughing now. The two girls rolling around in the mud, the hair pulling, the ripped clothes. He shared the same humor as his boss. He thought the whole thing was hilarious.

Until the bullets started flying.

The brothel's four security men had been arrayed around the room in a protective box, one for each corner. Standing back in the shadows, they couldn't see anything but the back of a lot of heads.

Kazeel had just downed another glass of Stoli when he noticed one of these guards suddenly disappear behind the row of Filipino businessmen. One second the man was there; the next he was gone.

As this was registering in Kazeel's woozy brain, another of the bodyguards went down, the one directly off to his left. But this time, before he fell forward, Kazeel saw a button of blood appear on the man's forehead. A bullet, shot through a silencer and passing through the bamboo, had cracked the man's skull in two.

Kazeel's mind began racing. Then a third guard, the one right in front of him, got a bullet between the eyes. His head, too, split open like an egg. Everyone noticed it this time. Someone killed the music. One of the mud girls screamed. Then came another loud *pop!* and the fourth guard went down, another bullet to the brain.

Kazeel froze with drunken fear. Each of the bodyguards had been killed by a tap shot, a single round to the skull. This was a favorite means of dispatch by many of the world's more notorious special ops teams.

"Praise Allah!" Kazeel screamed.

An instant later, Sergeant Dave Hunn came crashing through the window.

He was 20 pounds heavier since the last time he'd done something like this. His forty days at Guantánomo Bay as both a prisoner and someone recovering from wounds received above Hormuz had done a job on his waistline. If anything he and his three associates had been fed *too* well in captivity. But if he was just a bit older and fatter, he was also a bit wiser. And as fired up as ever to grease some mooks.

He'd come through the room's plate-glass window, feetfirst. The crash alone was deafening. This was Hunn's specialty back in Delta Force—he was a door kicker, the guy who went in first. He was armed with a shotgun, two pistols, and butcher's cleaver. Landing in a crouch, he fired his 12-gauge at one of the room's two lightbulbs. It exploded in a storm of sparks. Two more men came crashing through the window. These were Puglisi and McMahon, the other two Delta Force guys who'd shared Hunn's prison down in Gitmo. Unlike Hunn, they came in headfirst, like two guided missiles, taking down the line of Filipino businessmen and firing into the ceiling as well, adding to the confusion.

A fourth and fifth quickly followed behind. One was Red Curry, the heroic special ops helicopter pilot who'd also taken the unexpected vacation in Gitmo.

The other was Lieutenant Mikael Ozzi, he of the DSA.

Paper cuts. Falling on a slippery floor. Bad coffee in the cafeteria. These were the most dangerous things Ozzi had faced flying a desk back at the Pentagon. *This?* He'd never done *anything* like this. But he was different man these days. He was pumped to the point of feeling stoned. The excitement and terror were exhilarating.

The epiphany he'd experienced after meeting the strange prisoners down in Gitmo had not faded a bit. In fact, it had grown. Why was he so enamored? He'd been able to boil it down to one simple fact: the Gitmo guys were different. Certainly Ozzi had known many fine soldiers in his career. Men who'd served their country with both intellect and brawn and who would lay down their lives for America in a heartbeat. But that was their job. They were professional warriors. Combat was a vocation, what they got paid to do.

The Gitmo Four were different. None of the mysterious special ops unit had ever received a paycheck. Ozzi knew this because he asked them. Neither had they been given a promise of promotions or stellar duty in the future. What they'd done in the Persian Gulf and at Hormuz had come from the gut. And from the heart. Ozzi's theology professor back at Yale would have said they were following their souls. After sitting in the Pentagon basement for most of the past three years, Ozzi wanted nothing more than to be like them.

He got his chance when a secret communiqué forwarded to the NSC from the CIA crossed his desk by mistake. It had been intended for Fox, a follow-up to a previous report. It had been marked for his eyes only, but Ozzi read it anyway. The agency report said that Abdul Kazeel, the mastermind of the *Lincoln* attack and an architect of 9/11, was in Manila. The CIA even knew the five-star hotel he was staying in. This was the good news. The bad news was the Philippines Intelligence Service had forbidden the CIA to do anything about it. Not a big surprise. That higher-ups in the PIS were in the pay of the Aboo guerrillas was an open secret around the Pacific Rim. Diplomatic niceties prevented the United States from publicly accusing them of such. The 'Peens were still considered a strategic asset to the United States, a dictate larger than the lust for intelligence gathering. Because of this, the CIA had to live with Manila's ban on anything but surveillance of Kazeel.

But this didn't mean the DSA had to. It seemed to fit right into their "Go Anywhere, Do Anything, Just Don't Get Caught," dictum. And being that they ran a very small shop, and with his boss, Major Fox, away, that left Ozzi the top DSA officer in Washington. And of course he knew all about Kazeel and what he had done and how much the guys in Bobby Murphy's supersecret special ops team hated him. Yet here he was, right out in the open, walking the streets of a country the United States considered, on paper at least, to be a friend.

But could Ozzi go after the superterrorist without running it by Higher Authority? He took a long walk along the Potomac that day, trying to figure out a way he could capitalize on this piece of information. He thought of every trick in the book, but nothing applied. The memo had been meant for Fox and as a follow-up; this meant Ozzi's boss already knew that Kazeel was in Manila— and he'd certainly not left any orders for Ozzi to do something about it. Plus, it would be very out of character for Ozzi to do anything without running it by his boss. To do so was probably a court-martial offense as well.

The first 10 minutes of Ozzi's walk, then, were fairly glum. The banks of the Potomac were crowded with tourists and government workers, tens of thousands of them, as it was such a pleasant day. That's when Ozzi finally felt something in *his* gut. A guy who would just love to drop a dirty bomb on these people was running around Manila, untouchable by the big boys of America's intelligence agencies. If Ozzi did nothing and disaster struck,

two months or two years from now, how could he live
with himself knowing he could have saved all of these
fellow Americans? How could he sleep? Eat? Breathe? It
would have been impossible.

So he returned to his subterranean office and simply
wrote a bunch of orders to himself. Again, it was something he would never have done just a few weeks before.
But now it came to him as easily as signing his name. It
took him nearly an hour to fill out the correct paperwork.
But when it was over, Ozzi had essentially authorized
himself to go after the superterrorist.

But Ozzi knew he still had to be careful. Anything he
did would be beyond classified. Causing a rift between
the United States and the Philippines would not be good
for job advancement. In fact, going against State Department orders was career suicide. This meant he had to be
superquiet. He needed some muscle, but using regular
special ops troops would not make it the seamless mission he knew it had to be. It was a Catch-22. How could
he pull off a top-secret operation without *anyone* knowing it?

Then, a brilliant idea. A simple one, too. Ozzi knew
Major Fox was tracking down the larger group of the
mysterious special ops team to help in the emergency up
near Fuggu Island. Why couldn't Ozzi take a page from
the same book? Work another supersecret operation with
guys from a special ops team that didn't exist. Incredibly,
with one terse fax forged in Fox's name, he got the Gitmo
Four released to his custody. They were immediately
flown to Mexico City, where in a cheap hotel room Ozzi
told them what he knew of Abdul Kazeel's whereabouts
and the diplomatic impasse that allowed him to roam free.

Ozzi wanted to go get the bastard. Could the Gitmo Four help him out?

The reply was unanimous. "Superterrorist? Super-mook is more like it. Screw the PIS. Screw the Philippines. We'll go in and get Kazeel before he knows what hit him." They would do their thing and be out of the country before anyone—the PIS, the CIA, anyone—knew better. It was exactly what Ozzi wanted to hear.

They flew coach to Manila and bought four shotguns in a back alley behind a police station. Then a hunting rifle was found at an open-air market nearby. Puglisi fashioned a silencer out of a stolen motorbike muffler. They took a room across from Kazeel's hotel and settled in to wait. It didn't take long for the snake to show his tail. They saw him leave with Marcos and followed both to the Impatient Parrot. After that, the crash and smash had been routine.

At least, so far.

The Filipino businessmen dived for the floor at first sight of the Americans. The mud girls went down, too. Only one lightbulb had been spared in the barrage. It was swinging wildly back and forth, casting strange shadows across the crowded, smelly room.

The businessmen were quickly frisked; each had been carrying a pistol. The two girls were obviously clean, but Puglisi frisked them anyway. Red Curry frisked Marcos and found a list of all the underage girls who worked in his establishment. Curry hit the guy on the jaw with the butt of his shotgun. The man went over with a thud.

All this happened in just seconds. With the room secured, Hunn walked over to Kazeel sitting petrified in his fancy padded chair and put the muzzle of his shotgun against the terrorist's substantial nose. Meanwhile, McMahon's gun was resting on the back of Uni's neck. Hunn got up in Kazeel's face. Hunn's young sister had been in the World Trade Center the day the towers were hit. At 18 years old, she was among the youngest victims. That's what gave Hunn the bones to be in the secret unit, and now here was a dream come true. His sister's murderer just the length of a gun barrel away. One pull of the trigger, sweet vengeance would be at hand—and lights out for the world's first superterrorist.

There was no mistaking that now. Executing Kazeel was why the American team was here. There was no other reason. There would be no need for impossible sacrifice on Hunn's part. He would not have to reel in his emotions and spare this puke for some trial at the World Court or somewhere. The Americans were executioners. Hit men. That's what made them so scary, so off the reservation. Their target was anyone connected with the 9/11 attacks.

And now, they had the top guy himself. Hunn looked to Ozzi. The DSA officer steeled himself, ready to see Kazeel's skull blown apart. The room tensed. Kazeel had turned absolutely white. Hunn moved the double-barreled gun muzzle off Kazeel's nose and put it square against his forehead.

That's when the cops arrived.

Or more precisely, the Philippine national police.

This was how things worked in Asia—and maybe America needed a few more lessons in it. The double cross was not enough in this part of the world, not when a triple cross was much more fashionable. What happened? It was hard to say. Word of Ozzi's plan must have leaked back to the PIS. But how, when no one even knew he was here?

Whatever happened, he and the others were now reaping the price. More than two dozen heavily armed Filipino cops were suddenly in the room. They were all holding their weapons up, a bad sign. The American team immediately took a defensive posture, their weapons raised, too, poised for a fatal shoot-out.

That's when Ozzi just laughed out loud. He couldn't help it.

"We drop in on them, they drop in on us . . ." he said, looking at the small army of policemen. "Wait till my boss hears about this. He won't believe it. . . ."

But not everyone was listening, and especially not Hunn. He still had his 12-gauge on Kazeel's brow, fighting an almost impossible urge to just pull the trigger and kill the monster anyway. The only reason Hunn hesitated was because otherwise his comrades would all get killed in the process. If it had just been him, he would have done it in a second. But he couldn't die with the murder of his buddies on his soul. So while he kept his gun on the terrorist's head, he eased his finger off the trigger.

A man in the crowd of green faces stepped forward. His name tag IDed him as Captain Ramosa, a chief of the National District Police. He looked like he'd walked right out of Central Casting: oily hair, oily skin, a bad complexion, and very beady eyes. Oddly, he was wearing a cheap paper armband with the letters *UN* printed on it in blue ink.

"What the fuck is this?" Hunn screamed. "The UN has no jurisdiction here!"

"Well, they do now," the officer, Ramosa, told them as

another dozen or so policemen squeezed into the room, making it almost comically crowded. "This is an action taken on behalf of the UN Subcommittee on Refugees. I am here at their request. This man is a foreign national. We are here to protect him."

Hunn was furious. "You're a fucking cop!" he screamed at Ramosa. "Don't you recognize this guy? He's the mook of mooks. The top guy. . . ."

Ramosa just laughed. "I'm sorry," he said with a fake bow. "I am not so up on current events as you."

Hunn looked to Ozzi, who was just as perplexed. It was like they were suddenly in a bad kung fu movie.

"How could you possibly know we were here?" Ozzi railed at Ramosa. "This thing was tighter than a drum."

"Apparently not tight enough," the police chief replied. He nudged Hunn's weapon away from Kazeel's head, much to the relief of the Arab terrorist. "Better luck next time."

"You bastard," Hunn said to Ramosa. "Whose side are you on?"

The Filipino officer just smiled. He had a mouthful of gold teeth. "On the side of peace, of course," he said.

Hunn scanned the room. His comrades would never know just how close he came to pulling the trigger and greasing the supermook—and getting them all killed.

But if the situation was now impossible, that didn't mean Hunn was going quietly. He got right back in Kazeel's face. He screamed at him: "Look at me, asshole! I'm from Queens, New York! My name is Dave Hunn! Remember me. Next time you see me, I'll be chopping you to pieces!"

At that point, the mighty Kazeel, superterrorist, wet his pants.

On a curt nod from Ramosa, two of the policemen lifted Kazeel to his feet and quickly carried him out of the room. Uni followed close behind. Ramosa turned back to the five Americans. "I assume everyone here has a valid passport?"

Hunn spit in his face. Ramosa wiped it off with a neatly folded handkerchief. He never lost his snide grin.

"I'll take that as a 'no,'" he said.

He gave a quick *"hup-to!"* to the rest of his men. They began filing out, but with their weapons still up, still ready for anything.

Ramosa went out last, walking backward, protecting his tail.

"My condolences on Nine-Eleven, gentlemen," he said, flashing his seedy gold smile again. "My prayers were with you that day. . . ."

Manila International Airport was a typical Third World mess.

Dirty, dark, chaotic, dangerous. It was all breakdowns and plastic baggage and noise, filthy windows, and broken doors. Tens of thousands of people, running, walking, staggering, sleeping, many wearing SARS masks, many carrying knives. It was Saturday morning, an insanely busy time. The line of passengers waiting to depart stretched through the main terminal, out the main doors, and all the way to the curb. Nearly every scheduled flight coming in was at least an hour late. Those going out were even further behind.

It was even worse out on the runways. Air traffic control at Manila International was more rumor than fact. Planes were taxiing everywhere with no reason to their movements. A major accident seemed likely at any moment. A bottleneck of airliners was jammed up at the end of the airport's main runway; all were waiting for some kind of signal to take off and get out of this place. Some of these planes had been waiting here since before sunrise—and that was three hours ago.

A dirty white cargo plane suddenly appeared in the middle of all this. It rolled onto the tarmac from a part of the airport off-limits to commercial aircraft. It was an Airbus A321, the smallest version of the cookie-cutter European airliner. Two large letters, *UN,* had been hastily applied to its fuselage behind the wing; streaks of blue paint were already running off them. A small drama played out on the field. The airplane suddenly stopped. A police Jeep drove up to it. The plane's cockpit door opened and a boarding ramp appeared. Two men were led out of the Jeep and sent up the steps. They were both draped in long, hooded robes. Once they were inside, the door was quickly closed, the ramp was pulled away, and the plane started moving again.

The Airbus rolled right past the traffic jam of commercial airliners, taking a place at the head of the line. This infuriated passengers and pilots alike on the waiting airplanes. But no measure of outrage directed toward the airport's control tower would change anything. The top three people at Manila International—the airport chief administrator, the traffic captain, the security chief—had all been paid off. The UN airplane had priority over every other aircraft.

It waited at the head of the line for just a half-minute. Then it revved up its engines, covering the rest of the planes in dirty exhaust, and went screaming down the runway.

Past the airport's fences, over the highway, over the dump, over the shantytowns, the shacks, and up on a hill overlooking the southern end of Manila International a battered rented Ford Taurus was parked, engine running, AC blowing, all four doors wide open.

Ozzi was sitting on the hood, shoulders drooped, ball cap pulled low. He watched the UN plane a half-mile away pull up its gear and start to climb.

In the backseat of the Ford were Puglisi and McMahon. Both were trying to sleep. Red Curry was sitting behind the wheel, chain-smoking. They were all exhausted, except Hunn. He was stalking around the car like a madman, talking to himself and swearing mightily.

"Jesus Christmas!" he screamed, shaking his fist as the airplane carrying Kazeel went right over their heads. The noise was tremendous. "I just can't believe these Zips let that asshole go! Didn't we free these people from the Japs a while back?"

"Gratitude isn't in much supply these days," Curry said over the roar of the departing jet's engines. "Not for guys like us."

"Then how about we just nuke this shitty little place?" Puglisi asked with a yawn from the backseat, eyes still closed. "You can get a nuke, can't you, Lieutenant?"

Ozzi took the question half-seriously. "It might take a few weeks. But . . ."

He looked out on the mountainside slums. They

stretched for miles. "I'm not sure it would make much of a difference here," he added.

A brutal, smelly wind blew by them. They were quiet for a long time.

Then Ozzi let out a moan. "Well, this is just great," he said. "We're at the end of the world here—and damn it, now we've got to fly back. I'm not looking forward to the ride home, boys. I don't even know if I still have a job."

Suddenly Hunn stopped pacing. He looked at Ozzi strangely. Hunn was a huge individual, perpetually unnerved and like a time bomb ready to go off at any moment. But for a few seconds he turned pro.

"Wait a minute," he said to Ozzi. "Why are you getting us all bummed out?"

Ozzi just looked up at him. "Did you just say 'bummed out'?"

"Yes . . . sir. You're bumming us out."

Ozzi was confused. "Don't I have a good reason to?" he asked sincerely. "We just went through a major-league Chinese fire drill, and I'm sure, with the UN involved, we lit up every phone between here and D.C. I'll be lucky if they let me sweep my office when I get back."

"Get back?" Hunn asked him. "You keep saying that. Get back where?"

"To the states. To Washington. And for you guys, probably back to Gitmo."

All four men started laughing and couldn't stop. Hunn was almost in tears.

"Oh man, Lieutenant," he told Ozzi, "I understand you're the new guy around here. But, sir . . . you got to get a four-one-one on this. We ain't going back." He turned toward the spot where the "UN" plane was now just disappearing into the west. "And believe me, that guy ain't getting away this easy. . . ."

Chapter 11

On the Pakistan-Afghan border

The three SUVs arrived at the abandoned air base just after midnight.

This place was called Bakrit. Built by the CIA for the resupply of Afghanistan resistance fighters during their war against the Soviet Union twenty-five years before, the base was surrounded by snowcapped mountains and high, barren plains. The runways had been made long enough back then to support all kinds of aircraft, from large cargo jets to U-2 spy planes. The main strip was more than three miles long. It could handle anything flying these days.

The small A321 200 Airbus arrived five minutes later. It touched down in the dark aided only by the pilot's night-vision goggles. Blowing up a small storm of snow and dust, it taxied to where the three SUVs were waiting. The men in the SUVs were high officers in the Intelligence Service of Pakistan, an organization that, despite its name, was closely aligned with Al Qaeda. Each SUV was carrying two officers; each was heavily armed.

The plane stopped and its cockpit door opened. A ladder folded out and Kazeel and Uni climbed down. Kazeel was immediately whisked into the second-in-line SUV; Uni took a seat in the third. Their separation was a matter of security procedure. Though joined at the hip, Kazeel and Uni almost never traveled together, especially on the ground, because, simply by osmosis, Uni knew almost as much about the next big attack on America as Kazeel. Furthermore, Uni held on his person, at all the times, a piece of information that, when implemented, would activate Kazeel's sleeper agents who were waiting to carry out the big attack. This was known as the *sharfa*—loosely Arabic for "The Key."

Only Kazeel and Uni knew the *sharfa* and it would be acted on only when it was confirmed that the weapons for the big attack were safely in place. Crude and hardly perfect, it was the terrorist version of a fail-safe. If the worst ever happened to Kazeel, Uni would still be around to activate The Key, and the plan could still move forward.

So for them to be killed by the same bomb, rocket, or land mine would not be wise. An entire brain and a half would be lost.

Thus the separate cars.

The small caravan screeched away and drove north, toward the section of northwest Pakistan known as the Pushi.

Their destination was even more remote than Bakrit. It was so isolated, in fact, and wild in its terrain that in better days NASA sent its lunar astronauts to the Pushi so they could train in the most moonlike conditions possible without actually leaving the Earth.

The trip would take four hours. The three SUVs passed several military checkpoints along the way. In each case they were simply waved on through by Pakistani troops, even though it was an open secret that Sheikh Kazeel himself might be riding in one of the three trucks.

Around two in the morning they reached the Krutuk mountain range. The Pushi lay beyond. This was where the terrain became particularly rugged and as unearthly as advertised. The three trucks began climbing. They easily went over a series of small mountains; *boodis,* the locals called them. But soon enough the mountains became larger and the roads became steeper. The going became very slippery as some of the higher peaks were encased in thick, icy clouds. After another 90 minutes, they'd reached the Pushi, a hidden valley surrounded by Himalayan-like summits. The village of Ubusk sat in its center. For the past 10 years, this was what Kazeel had called home.

The three SUVs roared through the village at high speed, waking many of its 400 villagers. Then the vehicles began climbing the *boodi* on Ubusk's north side. This small mountain was known as Pushi-pu. Kazeel lived at the top.

His house was square, two stories, with a flat roof and many windows. It had four rooms in all, a palace by this region's standards. The largest room was the master sleeping quarters. It was all windows, including six in the ceiling. Kazeel had a monstrous water bed in here, but he never used it. Most nights he spent here, he slept in a blanket on the floor.

The rest of the house was spare of furniture. However, there were many high-tech media devices about. Large-

screen TVs, radio receivers, video recorders, CD players—all American-made. There was also an extensive
videotape and DVD collection on hand. All of these were
American as well.

The house had a grand view of the ring of barren
mountains surrounding it. It looked out over the valley
and gave an impressive panorama of the night sky as well.
The view from the bedroom was the best. Both the sunrise and sunset could be seen from here. In the morning,
the mountains turned a weird orange; in the late afternoon, they took on a shade of blue.

But the house's location had nothing to do with aes-
thetics. Kazeel, being joyless and sexless, saw nothing of
the beauty in nature. Why he lived at the top of this
mountain was all about his security.

There was only one road up to the top. A small army of
security guards watched this entrance, located at the
southern base of the *boodi*. These guards were Ubusks,
men from the village; they were also distant cousins of
Kazeel. They kept an eye on things while he was away,
guarded him when he was home, and provided protection
for him whenever he moved about Pakistan or
Afghanistan. They were very loyal and fierce fighters.
Kazeel trusted them highly.

Their checkpoint was heavily fortified. Not only were
they armed with machine guns and rocket-propelled
grenades; they also had an old T-72 Russian-made tank
hidden inside a rock shed next to the entrance to the access road. The tank could hit a target just about anywhere
in the valley below, including the village, as well as the
road leading up to Kazeel's mountain.

• • •

Seven men were waiting inside Kazeel's house. They were the people who'd helped him plan the attack on the *USS Lincoln*. They'd all had a hand in 9/11, too. Once Kazeel was airborne out of Manila, he'd used a secure in-flight phone on the Airbus to call a meeting of these men. Without a doubt his closest advisors, all of them were made men in Al Qaeda as well. They all lived in caves nearby, which was no surprise. After the United States landed in Afghanistan and tore up the Taliban, the Pushi was where this pack of rats came to hide.

Kazeel's small convoy arrived at the base of his mountain just before 4:00 A.M. The horizon was just beginning to brighten, the start of a cold and windy day. They drove up to the main checkpoint, the place where the tank was hidden. But no one came out to meet them. Kazeel was puzzled. The guards were supposed to be on alert 24/7. He had his driver beep the horn. Nothing. The driver beeped again. Finally, four sleepy gunmen emerged from the tank house.

They went pale when they saw Kazeel through the back window. They'd taken a vow to lay down their lives for him. But he'd caught them napping.

Kazeel got out of the SUV and greeted the men warmly nevertheless. This surprised them, but they recovered quickly. The hugs and double-cheek kissing went on for nearly a minute.

Then Kazeel climbed back into the SUV and proceeded up the hill.

• • •

His compatriots had been waiting since midnight. They knew all about his brief capture—they thought, by a CIA team—and subsequent quick release. His safe return was a great relief for them. He was the alpha dog here, the godfather of the clan. Without him, the rest would be nothing. Kazeel rarely let them forget it.

He walked through his front door with no fanfare. The Pakistani Intell men were nowhere in sight. The seven friends greeted Kazeel with exaggerated warmth, sloppy kisses on both cheeks, four, five, six times. Kazeel finally had to put an end to it. He threw up his hands and then Uni ushered him away.

Kazeel didn't bother to wash up after his long ordeal, nor did he change out of his Western-style clothes. Rather, he commenced the meeting immediately. He and the seven men sat on the floor in the main room of the house. The windows were blacked out with cardboard and curtains, shutting off that grand view of the universe. Candles were lit. Uni dispensed bowls of yogurt and lamb's guts and cups of tepid tea.

Kazeel did not eat or drink. He got right down to business.

"Brothers, we are in possession of the launchers," he said, his tired voice betraying no hint of triumph.

There was applause from the others.

Kazeel went on: "And I have secured the means to get them into the United States—thanks to our new *judus*."

More applause. Several men shouted: "Praise Allah!"

"Now, all we need are the missiles themselves," Kazeel said. The other men quickly settled down. They looked at each other worriedly. Kazeel was surprised by their unease. Something was wrong.

"Brothers, you have known of this need all along," he began lecturing them. "This was the agreement with our New Friends. They would get us the launchers. They would get us the funding. They would get the weapons into the United States. But we had to 'get our hands dirty together'—and that meant our providing the missiles. And I assured them that this we could do."

The seven men looked at their dirty feet for a very long time. Finally one man spoke up. He was Abu al-Saki el-Saud, a minor Saudi prince.

"But just as with the launchers, the missiles too are a very hard item to get these days," he said nervously as Kazeel was known to have a volatile temper. "Supply was never very good anyway. And now, our friends in the Afghan are all gone. Our friends in Iraq, gone as well and our brothers in Syria have become women since the Americans landed next door. And Brother Ghadafi—well, as we all know he *is* a woman. So, my sheikh, it has become very hard for us to . . ."

"Are you saying you could find *no one* who would want to make a deal with us?" Kazeel cut him off tersely. "With all our contacts? Are our old friends deserting us?"

"It is the quantity, brother," El-Saki told him bravely. "We could probably get one or two missiles from the Yemenis. A couple more from the Egyptians. One or two from the Irish. Maybe even our friends inside the Pakistani military could find two or three. But you require at least thirty-six. A very large number all at once. Why?"

Kazeel paused for a long moment. Outside, the wind began to howl.

"Brothers, we have been in this *jihad* together for a very long time now," he began, fingering his crusty beard. "We have had our highs and lows. We have been praised by Allah and cursed by him. But you must believe me, we are now in a new chapter, thanks to our newfound friends. And along with this new alliance comes the greater need for security, even amongst ourselves."

Kazeel took a deep breath. He was trying his best to sound sincere, but the truth was, he didn't trust any of the seven men, even though they were his closest friends. He barely trusted Uni.

"This is why you must believe in me now," he began again. "And believe that the plan I have in mind, with the blessings of our *judus,* will make the events of September 11, and anything since, look like child's play. But as for the kernel of the plan itself, I have to keep it close to my heart and no one else's."

The seven men shifted uneasily on the floor. They did not like being left out of the loop. But this was one of the things that had changed since Kazeel hooked up with the *judus*. The risks they took had not decreased, as even now, sitting here like this with Kazeel, was enough to get them all shot on sight by any of their various enemies. But access to what was going on inside Kazeel's head was quickly becoming a thing of the past.

"It's a security issue," Kazeel told them, quite aware of their concerned looks. "In this case, and for what is at stake, some things are best not known, even by myself. But again, be reassured, that this is a massive assault we are talking about—one that will attack the very fabric of the Americans' way of life, praise Allah, in ways they can never dream of. *That* is why so many weapons will be needed."

Kazeel had actually expected some applause at this point. Some praise, even if it was perfunctory and rote. But all he got from his associates were more nervous stares. There was still doubt in the room, Kazeel could taste it.

He took another deep, troubled breath. Suddenly he felt old and tired. But he pressed on: "Now, I'm sure I can read your minds. You are asking: 'Remember our snipers in Washington? Remember how they met their end?' Yes, brothers, I do. But that was just a drill. That taught what to do as well as what not. With this new assault, the Americans will be stung for a very, very long time. The confusion we will sow, the chaos we will create, it will rock them to their foundations. Indeed, they may never recover, not fully anyway. And isn't that what our ultimate goal is? To get a knife right into their heart and give it a twist?"

Kazeel paused again, caught his breath, and then continued: "We have so many people standing by, sleepers, in their cities, in their suburbs, just waiting for our call. So many martyrs, it will be impossible to subdue them all. And even if half or two-thirds were somehow caught before they acted, that would still mean plenty will be free to carry out the big plan."

He looked each man in the eye now. "So we are so very close, my friends," he said slowly. "And so many things are already in place. We have the launchers. We have the funding from our *judus*. We have their guidance. Their expertise. And we have God's blessing. What more do we need?"

He looked around the room again.

"Just one more thing, brothers," he answered his own question. "We need the missiles."

But the seven men never did look up at him. Kazeel repeated his earlier question: "You have found *nobody* to deal?"

A long silence. The wind blew again outside. Al-Saki finally spoke up: "We have, brother. Just one. . . ."

Kazeel's eyes lit up a bit. "Praise Allah. Now that's better. Why would you withhold such positive information from me for so long?"

"Because of who he is," al-Saki said.

Kazeel seemed confused. "Tell me his name."

Al-Saki finally looked Kazeel in the eye. "It is Bahzi. He will deal."

This took Kazeel by surprise, but in the same moment he knew why his friends had been so reluctant to speak the name.

Usay Bahzi was scum. He was an Iraqi, strike one in Kazeel's book. He was a Ba'ath Party member and one of Saddam's former legion of black-market arms dealers. Bahzi fled to Pakistan just hours before the U.S. troops rolled into Baghdad and transitted through Iran and Afghanistan on a diplomatic pass and a suitcase full of money. He now lived under an assumed name in Karachi, Pakistan.

Kazeel intensely disliked the Iraqi. He was well known as a sneak, a liar, and a cheat. But he also had extensive contacts in arms markets, both legal and not. He had access to everything, including anthrax, biotoxins, radioactives. But his customers sometimes wound up dead—always after money had already changed hands. He was a dangerous person and dealing with him would be a dangerous undertaking.

But time was running out. Kazeel's *judus* were impatient types, and the pressure was on him to perform unlike ever before. How he wished for the old days, before the Americans finally woke up.

He snapped his fingers and Uni was there with a cup of hot water.

"No one at Pan Arabic ever rose to the top?" Kazeel asked the seven glumly.

They all shook their heads no. This was a cut that went deep. Prior to the failed attack on the *USS Lincoln,* Kazeel and his cohorts had been financed in large part by a Saudi prince who owned the Pan Arabic Oil Exchange, a huge company that controlled nearly a fifth of the oil leaving the Persian Gulf. By siphoning money from their oil profits, this Prince—His Royal Highness Prince Ali Abu Abdul Hamini el-Saud Muhammad—had supported many of Kazeel's terrorist activities, including his role in 9/11.

But on the same day as the attack on the *Lincoln,* not an hour after the carrier had been saved, a chartered airliner crashed into the headquarters of Pan Arabic in downtown Riyadh. Everyone inside the multistory building was killed, as was everyone on the plane. The crash was somewhat lost in the headlines surrounding the *Lincoln*'s near-miraculous escape. But the startling fact was this: onboard this charter plane was none other than the man who ran the company itself, Prince Ali. Why would Ali—along with several of his closest friends—want to die by plunging their charter plane into his own building? The assumption was that it was a bizarre mass suicide, as Ali and his band had been very involved in the *Lincoln* attack. But other reports said the pilot of the plane was actually an American agent and that he'd *intentionally* carried the Prince and the others to their deaths. An

American dying as a martyr? This did not make sense to anyone. But neither did the mysterious circumstances surrounding the crash.

The loss of Prince Ali and his money had forced Kazeel to deal with people he would not have normally even spoken to. His *judus* were some of them. And Bahzi was certainly another. But Kazeel knew he had to adapt to survive, even if it meant dealing with the devil.

Kazeel remained quiet for a very long time. Finally he asked: "You can set up a meeting with Bahzi?"

His friends nodded yes. "We can," al-Saki replied. "You say where. You say when. Just tell us . . . and it will be done."

Kazeel's reply was interrupted by four gunshots—distinct, sharp, in the brisk mountain wind. Kazeel winced when he heard them but quickly carried on.

"Tell Bahzi the place will be Sat Put," he said.

"And the time, brother?"

They heard four more gunshots; they came quicker than the first, but Kazeel hardly moved this time.

"I will inform the snake of the time and date later," he said. "Carry this news to him, and make it clear I am plumbing the depths even talking about him. . . ."

With that, Kazeel abruptly dismissed his guests with the wave of his hand. The men rose to their feet. Uni brought them their various outer garments. Woolen robes, bedsheets, in one man's case house curtains.

As they started for the door, Kazeel grabbed the man he considered his closest associate, Ali Hassan Wabi, a small elderly Kuwaiti with snow-white hair. Out of earshot of the others, Kazeel indicated to Wabi he had one more piece of business to conduct.

"I have a favor I must ask of you especially," he said to Wabi.

"Anything, brother . . ." Wabi replied.

Kazeel lowered his voice. "I need new bodyguards. Can you help?"

Wabi paused a moment. "You mean, you want *additional* bodyguards, my brother?"

But Kazeel shook his head. "No—I must replace the ones I have now."

Wabi was very surprised to hear this. Kazeel's Ubusk security people had been with him for years. They were considered the best in the business. It seemed like a strange time to change them out.

But Wabi knew better than to ask Kazeel why. "I will talk to my contacts," he said instead. "And I will let you know."

"Make it fast, my brother," Kazeel told him before showing him out the door. "We have many challenging days ahead. Whoever you get for me will have to be the very best."

Wabi didn't like the sound of that. He'd never seen Kazeel this nervous.

"Can you confide in me?" Wabi asked him. "What is the problem, brother?"

Kazeel paused a moment. He did not open up to people so quickly. But . . .

"Let's just say my escape from Manila was not as clean as it might have seemed," he told Wabi. "I was a breath away from Paradise, and pray, brother, I do not want to go there so soon."

"But you are now *here,* my brother," Wabi said, trying to provide comfort. "And Allah be praised you are still in one piece."

Kazeel just shook his head. He was suddenly on the verge of tears. "Brother, you don't understand. For the first time in my life I am looking over my shoulder. These people who almost had me in Manila. They weren't just some CIA group. They were the *Am'reekan Maganeen*. I'm sure of it."

Am'reekan Maganeen, the infamous Crazy Americans. The words sent a chill down Wabi's spine. The Crazy Americans were the secret special ops unit that had been sent against them—the 9/11 plotters—even before the attack on the *Lincoln* took shape. It was widely believed in the Islamic underworld that these special U.S. soldiers had been the reason the carrier survived that day. There was even talk that they had foiled the big attack in Singapore as well.

Unlike most U.S. special ops troops the *jihad* organizations had come up against, the Crazy Americans held to none of the conventions that other American units did. No Geneva rules of war for them, the Crazy Americans were terrorists themselves. They rarely spared anybody who crossed their path, especially anyone who was in on the planning of the 9/11 attacks. Their means of extracting information from those they collared was already legendary for its sheer brutality.

Wabi could not shake off the chill. This was not good news. With what they were about to do they certainly did not need this interference from these very dangerous, very brutal American troops. But he also felt sorry for Kazeel. The Crazy Americans' reputation certainly preceded them. They *always* got their man. If you were on their hit list, you were as good as gone. All this finally explained Kazeel's queer tension.

"I will make my inquiries immediately," Wabi told him. "I have heard of a protection outfit recently relocated to this area. Highly trained. Highly disciplined."

He lowered his voice. "Blue-eyed Muslims," he said. "Do you know the type?"

Kazeel's face lit up. *Blue-eyed Muslim* was a code. And upon hearing it, for the first time since arriving home, Kazeel actually relaxed a little. But then came the apprehension.

"You are talking about . . . ?" Kazeel started to say.

"I am, my brother," Wabi confirmed. "But I do not want to even say the name, as I don't want your hopes to soar, and then have it not come through."

"But you must try to arrange for that!" Kazeel told Wabi anxiously. His voice became so loud Uni heard him from the kitchen.

"I will certainly try," Wabi replied, now just in a whisper. "But as they are skilled, and loyal and disciplined and fearless, they, too, will have to be very well paid—"

"And they will be," Kazeel said quickly. "Our new friends will pay the bill. Just talk to them for me, brother. Promise them heaven and earth. And please do so with haste. . . ."

Wabi kissed him good-bye and climbed into his own armored SUV. His driver proceeded slowly down the steep hill.

The conversation with Kazeel had made Wabi nervous. Kazeel's escape in Manila had been harrowing. So why was he so suddenly in need of new bodyguards? Why would he not keep his own guys on and hire some more?

Only when he reached the bottom of the *boodi* did Wabi get his answer.

Out in the field next to the tank house he saw four figures lying motionless, facedown, in the short grass. They were Kazeel's bodyguards, the Ubusks who'd manned the tank house. Standing over them, smoking cigarettes, were the Pakistani intelligence agents, the men who had driven Kazeel here. They looked menacingly at Wabi and his driver as they rolled by.

But Wabi passed close enough to the field to see that each bodyguard had two bullets in the back of his head.

The price these days for falling asleep while working for Sheikh Kazeel.

Five days went by.

In that time, Kazeel ate little and slept less. He'd also installed a Roland antiaircraft launcher near the front door of his house. It was a leftover from Gulf War I, a present given to him by Saddam Hussein himself, back in friendlier times. Kazeel had been keeping it in storage in a cave nearby; the original idea was to sell it someday. But his second day back he sent to the village for its two engineers. They pulled it out of its hiding place and checked its systems, with a manual in hand. It was a little out of their league, but eventually they got it to turn on and come on-line.

Did it work? No one knew. Kazeel kept it up anyway, not so much for his own protection but just for the peace of mind he thought it would bring.

It was a stupid thing to do, because if a U.S. satellite spotted the missile battery an American bomber would soon be circling his house. But Kazeel didn't care. He was never so in fear for his life as these past few days. That's what the Crazy Americans did to you. They got inside your head. They got you thinking what they would do to you, the horrendous torture they inflicted on their victims before finally putting them to death. They were rumored never to sleep, hopped up on drugs, endlessly stalking their victims. Kazeel knew they had been haunting Prince Ali and his syndicate—and look what happened to them. In some really dark moments, Kazeel believed Prince Ali *did* kill himself simply because he knew the Crazy Americans would get to him eventually. The man was a multibillionaire, yet he could not outrun his ghosts.

Praise Allah, the Paki agents were still watching the road below. He'd asked them to stay on, as his temporary security force, until he could make his other arrangements. They'd graciously agreed, after a nod from the top in Islamabad. But the Pakis could not stay forever. They were not professional bodyguards; they were intelligence men. They had other things to do.

It was just another example of the turmoil in Kazeel's life. He did not want to deal with Bahzi but knew he would have to. Yet he couldn't go to Sat Put to see the Iraqi until he had some reliable protection. But time was running out. His *judus* were not the most patient souls. They had their own agenda and they didn't like things to go slow. The longer the plan dragged out, the better their chances of it being discovered. So it was always chop-chop, *toot-sweet*, hurry the hell up with them.

That's why Kazeel felt paralyzed, a prisoner in his own house. Unable to move.

. . .

It was now the beginning of the sixth day. Midnight had arrived and the wind was howling again.

Kazeel was lying not on his water bed but on his prayer mat, looking through the room's ceiling window. The stars were out and the moon had risen over the eastern peaks, but these celestial events were lost on him.

He was not counting stars overhead but rather the number of insects crawling on his ceiling. It was a rare night when he couldn't get to sleep. But this had been going on for five nights now. More than 100 hours with little more than a doze or two. It was a new and very unpleasant condition for Kazeel. He'd personally murdered more than three dozen people in his lifetime, many of them brutally, many with his bare hands. He'd been responsible for the deaths of thousands more in the terrorist acts he'd planned and executed. Yet none of this had ever disturbed his sleep. He had no conscience, so there was nothing that could keep him awake.

But these days anytime he closed his eyes the ghosts of those he'd killed would flash before him, some as corpses, some not. And mixed in, always, was the scowling red face of the American soldier who'd laid his gun muzzle briefly on his nose back in Manila. *Dave Hunn!* . . . *Queens, New York!* . . . *Remember me.* . . . This was a vision Kazeel could not shake. There was hate inside this American. Real hate and real emotion, which was strange, because Kazeel never believed Americans *had* any emotions. Then again, that had been the closest he'd ever been to a real-live American. This man Hunn scared him deeply and Kazeel knew he would never give up in his pursuit of him.

Again, that was how the Crazy Americans worked. They hunted you, they found you, and then they killed you, very painfully. Simple as that.

Kazeel checked his Rolex watch. It wasn't even one in the morning yet. . . .

He started counting bugs again. He had six more hours of this hell to endure.

But suddenly came redemption from the darkness. It arrived with the sound of his cell phone ringing.

The voice on the other end was distant and distorted.

"Hoozan!" it was calling to him, using his boyhood name. "Wake up! I have good news!"

"Who is this?" Kazeel asked.

"It is Wabi, your white-haired friend and brother."

Kazeel cleaned out his ear. Wabi's voice sounded different.

"Good news, my friend," Wabi said. "You'll soon have new eyes watching over you."

Kazeel shot straight up on his prayer mat. "Is it how we had spoken?" he asked anxiously.

"They have blue eyes," Wabi replied, his voice smug but still distorted. "Though friend and enemy alike will be hard pressed to see them."

"And they have no qualms about who they may have to fight?"

"I've been told these people were in Kosovo, Bosnia, and Serbia and became millionaires for it," was the reply. "You know recent history, my friend. Do you not think that surviving, indeed *thriving,* in those places would give them the mettle to keep you safe?"

"Certainly better than most," Kazeel replied. "But where do these men call home exactly?"

"Let me put it this way," Wabi replied. "These men are the best because they are from a place that has been called the worst. . . ."

Kazeel did not have to hear anything more after that. He thanked Wabi and said good-bye.

Then he settled back down and finally drifted to sleep, knowing that starting tomorrow he would be well protected again.

It was just before noon the next day when the three black Range Rovers climbed up the mountain road, heading for Kazeel's compound.

The trucks' windows were tinted to opaque and each had a small forest of cell antennas poking up from the roof. They arrived and parked three abreast. They turned off their engines in unison; then every door on each of the three vehicles opened, again in unison. Five men stepped out.

Four were huge, towering over Kazeel's five-seven frame. They were wearing identical black combat uniforms, with plenty of ammo belts, utility packs, and night-fighting gear but no insignia. Each man was carrying an AK-47 assault rifle, a Magnum pistol in a shoulder holster, and a gigantic knife in his boot.

All five were also wearing black ski masks, with holes cut out for their eyes and nothing else. Kazeel met them by his back door. They formed a line in front of him, and each snapped off a smart salute, his first and last for the new boss.

Kazeel didn't even have to say a word. He already felt psychically connected to them. Their body language said it all: they were ruthless, unwavering. Their regimentation was hugely impressive, yet they didn't seem real somehow. They were more like Robocops, characters from one of Kazeel's favorite American movies. Having them watch his back was a fond wish come true.

His new bodyguard detail hailed from what many thought was the worst place on earth: a place called Chechnya. How fanatical were the Chechyans? There was a slang term going around the Gulf these days, being called Chechnya meant you were a "totally crazy person." According to Wabi, in addition to their mercenary work these blood-and-guts fighters had been battling the Russians for nearly 10 years in their own country. For the most part, they'd embarrassed the old Soviet empire almost as badly as it had been in Afghanistan twenty years before. What made them even more different was that these blue-eyed Chechyans were also Muslim fundamentalists, some of them even more radical than Kazeel and his Al Qaeda cohorts.

This particular group was known as the Dragos. They were famous for two things: their masks, which were for intimidation purposes but also so the men could never be identified even by the one they were protecting (*You don't want to see our faces* was a favorite Drago phrase), and, more important, their uncanny ability to extract those they were protecting from some of the tightest, most dangerous predicaments. Assassination attempts. Predator drone strikes. Carpet bombings. The Dragos always managed to pull their client through.

Kazeel was smiling so wide now his cheeks hurt. These men would make a great match for the Crazy Americans, he thought. If the two teams were to ever meet up, it would be the battle of the century, at the very least.

One Drago finally stepped forward and bowed a bit. He addressed Kazeel in perfect Arabic. He introduced himself simply as Alexi.

"I understand you want to travel soon?" he asked.

"I should be in Sat Put tomorrow at dawn," Kazeel replied. He'd called Bahzi that morning.

"Who knows you are coming?"

"The people I have to meet," Kazeel told him. "And their security people."

The man looked over his shoulder at the Roland missile launcher. Then he turned back to Kazeel, who suddenly felt very embarrassed.

"Did you make any of your arrangements on a cell phone?"

Kazeel was taken back by the question. He rarely kept a cell phone longer than 24 hours these days. This procedure had been drummed into all the Al Qaeda hierarchy from the very beginning. Simply put, the United States could intercept cell phone calls and track their user. That was a quick way to get a Hellfire missile dropped on one's head.

But Kazeel hadn't dumped his phone now in nearly a month. He couldn't. Just about everything having to do with the next big attack on America was locked into the photofone's extended memory. Kazeel had nowhere else to put it.

"I'm sorry, but yes, I did use my cell," Kazeel finally admitted. "But it was a necessity. Time was running while I was waiting to hear from you. I had to set up the meeting quickly."

"It's fine," the bodyguard replied with a touch of good nature, a big surprise. "No problem at all. Can you leave in two hours? It's a fourteen-hour drive to Sat Put and it's best that we sleep along the way."

Chapter 12

Early the next morning, Kazeel was standing on a small mountain overlooking the village of Sat Put.

He'd spent the night up in these hills, sleeping soundly again as the Dragos kept watch over him. He awoke with the sun, refreshed despite the grueling drive to get here the night before. He shunned any morning hygiene and told the Dragos that they should proceed into town immediately.

Alexi, the lead Drago, had accompanied Kazeel on the trip down from the Pushi, riding with him in the backseat of the middle Range Rover. (Uni rode in the car behind.) Kazeel and Alexi discussed many things on the way. The success of 9/11. The failure of Hormuz. The embarrassment of Tonka Tower, which Kazeel claimed to have no hand in. But most of all, they talked about Bahzi. Kazeel told the Drago leader about Bahzi's habit of staging ambushes near the site of his business dealings, sometimes absconding with the money if the person who'd just paid him happened to get iced. Yet when he did make a legitimate deal, the Iraqi's prices were usually fair and the merchandise always top quality. You just never knew which Bahzi you were going to sit down with.

For reasons like this, the Dragos insisted on taking all three vehicles to the meeting; in case one or two broke down or were damaged, they would have an option for escape. Kazeel liked that kind of thinking. He also liked the transportation. These weren't ordinary Range Rovers, Alexi had revealed to him along the way. They were actually Italian Fiat armored cars with Range Rover bodies *fitted over* them. They were moving arsenals as well. The Dragos carried everything from shotguns, to grenade launchers, to antiaircraft guns inside them and more. The trucks' armored siding could take a .50-caliber round fired less than 25 yards away. Their windows were made of glass and epoxy 17 layers thick. The tires weren't tires at all. They were steel wheels.

The streets of Sat Put were empty as the three Range Rovers pulled into town.

It was a very small, very desolate place, surrounded by sawtooth peaks covered permanently in dirty snow. In anticipation of this meeting, the local warlords had ordered everyone into their houses at sunset the night before, telling them not to come out, open a shutter, or even light a candle until noon. No one in the town would dare defy such a decree.

There were only a few streets here, all unpaved and muddy from the hooves of many horses. There was just a dozen buildings in all. These, with a few tents on the periphery, made up almost the entirety of Sat Put.

Of course, the place had a mosque, a rather grand one. Located near the center of town, just off the small avenue heading south, it was the Mosque of Ali Nasra, named after Muhammad's favorite son no less. It was overly huge and ornate and looked very out of place among the frozen squalor. Yet the temple was perfect for Kazeel's purposes. He'd been in the terror business for 12 years, and yes, it *was* a business. Whenever a really big deal had to go down, such as for arms or bioweapons, there was no better place to do the transaction than inside a mosque.

The first Range Rover screeched to a halt in front of the Ali Nasra.

Two armed men were peeking out of the mosque's front door. These were Bahzi's men; both looked unkempt and unfed. Kazeel's bodyguards smartly deployed themselves around his Range Rover, as always, the middle vehicle. Their eyes were moving, looking out from behind their masks, trying to see everything at once. It was cold and some snow was blowing around. And it was very quiet. Kazeel wanted to get inside fast.

But when he tried to open his door he realized one of the Dragos was holding it shut. Kazeel pushed harder, but the man stayed firm. Then he held up his hand, indicating Kazeel should not move.

"Why? What's the problem?" Kazeel yelled at him through the 17-layer glass.

The bomb went off a second later.

It was in the building across the street, an abandoned grain silo. The blast was so powerful it nearly tipped Kazeel's car over. Every window in every building on the street was blown out. The sound of the blast reverberated through the small town like a roll of thunder.

Kazeel was thrown across the backseat by the concussion, smashing his head on the truck's rear window. Suddenly the back door opened and one of the bodyguards jumped on top of him. Gunfire rang out. Two Dragos ran by the rear of the truck, firing their weapons into the burning building across the street. Ignoring the danger, they poured it on with AK-47s, and grenade-throwing rifles. Suddenly the snowy street was awash in tracer fire. Kazeel was astonished. *Where have such brave men been all my life?* he found himself thinking anxiously.

The gunfire lasted for nearly a minute; then it died away. The bodyguard waited about ten more seconds, then finally climbed off Kazeel and allowed him to sit up. Kazeel saw three things at once: the building across the street from him was gone, his bodyguards were ringing his truck with their bodies, forming a human barrier between Kazeel and further mayhem, and Bahzi's men, cowering behind the doors of the mosque.

Another Drago yanked Kazeel out of the vehicle.

"Inside!" the man growled at him. "Now!"

He was hustled up the stairs and through the mosque's door, two more Dragos practically carrying the enormous Uni right behind him. The Dragos pushed Bahzi's men aside and led Kazeel and his *shuka* down into the basement to a safe room located in the center of the structure. It had 12-foot-thick walls and 15 feet of concrete for a ceiling. It also had seven separate exits, a labyrinth of escape tunnels should the occupant get advance word that something really bad—like a U.S. air strike—was on the way. Around the Middle East, these places were known as Saddam Rooms. Just about every grand mosque had one.

Kazeel was visibly shaken but not hurt. Only dumb luck was keeping him from going into shock. Was that bomb meant for him? Or Bahzi? Or both of them? Or neither? Why would Bahzi try to kill him *before* the transaction was made?

At the moment, it really didn't matter. Had the Dragos not acted the way they did, Kazeel knew he'd be dead right now.

Just before entering the safe room—this was the prearranged site of their meeting—Kazeel asked the Chechyans to stop for a moment, so he could catch his breath. Uni, too, was trying to regain his composure. Per their custom, the *shuka* would wait outside while the quick business was conducted. His role in the deal was yet to come.

Kazeel calmed himself down; Alexi was right beside him, giving him strength. The Drago assured Kazeel that they would be safe here for about fifteen minutes. Then, by security procedure, it would be time to leave. Kazeel pushed his robes back up on his shoulders and kicked off his filthy sandals. "This will be complete in half that time," he said. "I promise. . . ."

Then he walked into the room.

Bahzi was already there. He was sitting at a table in the middle of the room. Spread out in front of him were cups of tea and copies of *Time, Newsweek,* and *Mad,* all adorned with Kazeel's image. As usual, Bahzi looked as big and ugly as something from a *Star Wars* movie. He'd been curiously safe here, inside the huge bombproof basement, when the blast went off. Kazeel walked over to him, helped him up, and kissed him twice on each cheek, mumbling: "Allah be praised. . . ."

"Brother—*are you hurt?*" Bahzi asked him with feigned concern, still holding him in a bear hug.

"I am here, aren't I?" Kazeel snapped back.

"What happened? I heard this terrific noise and—"

"Relax, brother," Kazeel told him, disentangling himself from Bahzi. "Nothing happened. Unexploded ordnance going off. Something like that. I am still alive and my men have scattered anyone who might have been lurking about. I've been through worse."

Bahzi shrugged, a little nervously. "Perhaps you've become too famous, my brother," he told Kazeel, eyeing the magazines. He'd placed them there as a way of needling the Al Qaeda operative, but Kazeel wasn't biting. He put the magazines together, stacking them in a neat pile, then pushed them aside. He indicated to Bahzi that they should sit and talk business. It took Bahzi several long seconds to squeeze back into his seat.

"You have your launchers I hear?" he asked Kazeel, once he was settled. He took out a notebook full of information on weapons systems and their price quotes.

"I do," Kazeel replied. He displayed a few digital photos stored in his photofone for Bahzi. They were images of the muddy launchers still in their protective suitcases. Bahzi's eyes lit up when he saw them. For an arms dealer, seeing so many Stinger launchers was like seeing a gold mine. He immediately coveted them.

"Brother, this is a very formidable cache," Bahzi sighed. "Now I see why you need some missiles."

"Which is why we are here," Kazeel replied, impatiently.

Bahzi shifted in his seat. Kazeel didn't like his body language all of a sudden. "How many do you want?" the Iraqi asked.

"I have thirty-six launchers," was Kazeel's reply. He

continued showing Bahzi the 'fone photos of the stash of dented suitcases; he was like a mother showing off baby pictures.

"Thirty-six in all, you say?" Bahzi wheezed. "Why so many?"

Kazeel resisted the urge to reach across the table and slap Bahzi. *Why must I always explain this. . . .* he **thought**.

"I need thirty-six missiles," he said firmly. "Because I am going after thirty-six different targets."

Bahzi's eyebrows shot up. This sounded interesting.

"Tell me, brother," Bahzi said. "Tell me your plan."

Kazeel laughed in his face. "You should know better than to ask that, my friend."

Bahzi shrugged. He was so fat, his robes were ripping under his armpits. "Just from what little I know now, I could get twenty-five million dollars from the Americans for turning you in."

"But why would you bother doing that, brother?" Kazeel volleyed back at him. "You wouldn't have a moment of peace to spend such a windfall."

Bahzi laughed, a little testily. "But why not, my brother? *You* would be in America's hands. And I would enjoy their money to my heart's content. Only your ghost would haunt me."

Kazeel looked Bahzi right in his blubbery eyes. "My men," he said, indicating the Dragos. They'd taken up positions all around the room, including one who had moved directly behind Bahzi and, without the Iraqi knowing it, was taking pictures through a helmet cam of the pricing notebook Bahzi had on the table before him. "My men would hunt you down and feed you to the dogs, while you were still alive."

The two Dragos nearest Bahzi took one step forward. Suddenly they were towering over him.

Bahzi laughed nervously. The time for jokes had clearly passed.

"I'd prefer to die of old age," he said. He reached into his bulky *mufti* and came out with his own photofone. It was slightly bigger than Kazeel's. He began displaying images of Stinger missiles. They were in a warehouse somewhere; that's all Kazeel had to know about them now. Each one of Bahzi's photos, which showed stacks of missiles in long metal tubes, also showed one of his men holding up a recent newspaper front page, proof that they were in possession of these missiles as late as yesterday.

"Half are leftovers from our victory against the Russians," Bahzi said, as if he himself had been in the mountains of Kabul fighting off Soviet Hinds—and nothing could have been further from the truth. "Half are new."

"A motherlode," Kazeel said, with some surprise. "But how do I know they work?"

"Why wouldn't they?" Bahzi replied, looking authentically offended. "If I sold you bad merchandise then your men would have another reason to come and get me, and their dogs would get their dinner yet."

"You've tested some from this batch?"

"Some were tested in Kenya." Bahzi began ticking off his fingers. "At Basra. Above Baghdad. They were battle-tested because we live in a world of conflict, my friend. Those that remain have been recalibrated, recharged. Ready to go."

Kazeel sighed heavily. He could smell Bahzi from across the table. "Then just give me your price."

Bahzi wrote down a figure in his notebook, tore the page out, and pushed it in Kazeel's direction. Kazeel picked it up, read it, then neatly tore the page in half and passed both back pieces to Bahzi. Bahzi smiled, picked up both halves, and halved one again and pushed both back to Kazeel.

Kazeel picked up the smallest piece and removed just a corner of it. Then he looked back at Bahzi. "Deal?"

"Deal . . ." Bahzi replied.

Kazeel wrote a bank account number on another piece of paper, along with the time and place he wanted the missiles delivered. He passed the page to Bahzi. Once Kazeel was sure the missiles had arrived at that location, he would contact his bank in Switzerland and have them release the funds being held in the box Bahzi now had the account number for. On that day, $17 million American, all of it provided by Kazeel's *judus,* would go into Bahzi's pockets. Uni would stay with Bahzi until he saw the missiles and then follow them to where they were being shipped. Thus the deal was concluded.

No cash. No computers. Not even a calculator.

This was how business was done in the Middle East.

The ride back to the Pushi started out well enough.

They left the small village ahead of Bahzi's men. One of the Dragos' Range Rovers stayed behind to cover the other two. If Bahzi was known to kill his business partners shortly after striking a deal, then the Dragos were taking no chances. Only when the first two Range Rovers were out of range of anything fired from the village, did they consider themselves safe. The third vehicle immediately joined the first two. Turning north, all three began the ascent into the mountains.

They were going back the long way, this again for security reasons. As secretive about his movements as Kazeel liked to be, anytime he was in the region word of his presence usually spread quickly. The route taken on the way to Sat Put had been grueling, but it had passed mostly through the high plains of northwest Pakistan, going around the mountains instead of over them. But these days, only a fool would take the same way twice. Of such things were successful ambushes made. That's why on the return trip to the Pushi the Dragos would be taking Kazeel over the mountains instead of around them.

It started raining about an hour into the trip; the temperature quickly dropped toward freezing. The mountains were getting progressively higher; indeed, this way back to the Pushi would take them over some of the highest peaks in southwest Asia. The roads up here were built in the early 1800s. At times the Rovers had to slow to less than five miles per hour. By the second hour of travel, they were so high up in the mountains, they were driving through the clouds formed around the peaks. It became difficult for Kazeel, sitting alone in the back of the middle vehicle, to see the armored truck in front or behind him. The rain and fog were that thick.

The rolling gloom gave him time to think, which was not a good thing. He tried to console himself that the bomb and gunplay back in the village either had been intended for Bahzi or were just the norm these days in this very lawless part of Pakistan. He just didn't want to believe he'd been the target. He already had too much to think about.

But as the miles wore on, that one thought began gnawing at him and would not let go.

By the fourth hour, the rain had turned to snow and the travel became even slower. Kazeel was constantly on the verge of having an anxiety attack. He didn't like going slow because, as his *judus* liked to say, slow meant being a better target. Even though there was practically a blizzard going on around him, Kazeel was still concerned. And he didn't like going over mountains anymore because mountains tended to be slippery and wet and icy and dangerous, especially on the way down.

Most of all, he cursed those bastard Crazy Americans for putting these thoughts in his head; he'd considered himself practically invulnerable before coming face-to-face with them. Now he was turning into a woman. Finally he knew what old Prince Ali must have been going through. No wonder he crashed his own plane!

Thankfully they passed out of some bad weather by going down the side of yet another steep mountain. But no sooner were they at the bottom than they started climbing yet another steep incline. Kazeel felt the panic rising in his chest again. Another mountain! Another slippery way up, another very slippery way down. He tried to look for a silver lining and came up with one after a few moments. This mountain wasn't as steep as the last few. This calmed him. After those last few monsters, this one would be a piece of cake, right? He leaned forward and tapped his Chechyan driver on the shoulder, indicating the man was doing a good job. The bodyguard simply grunted in reply.

Then Kazeel lay back and closed his eyes for the first time in a long time. They only had about seven more hours to go. Perhaps he could sleep some of the way home.

No such luck. . . .

The instant he closed his eyes, his vehicle was rocked by an enormous explosion. Kazeel was thrown to the floor, violently gashing his head on the way down. Smoke suddenly filled the truck's interior. His masked driver began swerving madly, back and forth, steel wheels screeching on gravel. It was so wild, Kazeel didn't know if the man was really in control of the truck or if he'd been shot or even killed. The smoke was that thick inside. Kazeel tried to pull himself off the floor but found this nearly impossible. They were moving that crazily.

All this happened in a matter of seconds. Somehow Kazeel finally found the strength to crawl back up onto the seat. It was then the truck crashed through a wall of fire; it was so intense, Kazeel could see his reflection in the raw flames outside the window. *"What is happening!?"* he finally yelled.

The guard just gave him a quick grunt—at least he was still alive. But he was driving so intently Kazeel knew it was best that he shut up. Another explosion went off not 10 feet in front of them. Then another, on the left shoulder of the road. Another, off to their right.

"Big bombs . . . from air . . ." was what the driver finally yelled back to him in very broken English. Kazeel got the message. The little convoy was under air attack.

The driver never lost his cool. He was steering frantically with one hand and talking very loudly in some Slavic language into his cell phone in the other. Presumably he was communicating with his colleagues in the other two vehicles. More explosions were going off all around them, but Kazeel's driver managed to anticipate them all. He swerved just in time to miss an explosion right in front of them. Another blast went off to the right; the man went left. Another explosion in front of them. The man coolly steered right. It was almost as if he knew where the bombs were going to land.

Kazeel was pinned against the backseat during all this, stuck there like glue. What was attacking them exactly? An American B-52 letting out a string of satellite-guided bombs? Or a smaller U.S. fighter aircraft—an F-15 or F-16—dropping HARM missiles or cluster bombs? Or even an A-10 Thunderbolt firing its huge cannon *and* dropping bombs on them? These kinds of planes were known to roam over Afghanistan, and over Pakistan, too. Their aim was to look for people just like him. Had his cellphone finally done him in?

They turned a sharp corner about twelve hundred feet up the side of the mountain and found a huge outcrop of rock sticking out of its side. It seemed almost big enough to shield them from their aerial attacker. Here they sat for an agonizingly long minute. Then two. Then three. If the pilot couldn't see them, would the attacking plane just go away? Or would it drop more bombs in hope of bringing the whole mountain down on top of them?

Four minutes passed. Then five. Finally the driver had another phone conversation, then put the truck back in gear.

"Gone . . . fly away . . . bye, bye," he called over his

shoulder with a muffled laugh. "Up ahead . . . more snow. Help us to hide you. . . ."

Kazeel couldn't believe it. He was simply astonished that he was still alive. Praise Allah, his faith had not been misplaced.

The Dragos had driven him through an air strike and not a single hair on his head had been harmed.

Afternoon turned to night, night into morning.

The three Range Rovers picked their way up and down many more scary, slippery mountains. The hours went agonizingly slowly throughout the stormy night, but as Kazeel was somewhat buoyed by their narrow, brilliant escape from the air strike, the rest of the ride was passable. Except for the loneliness; it became crushing about halfway through. He wasn't sure why the Dragos had put him alone in this car for the ride back. His driver could barely speak, never mind converse with him in Arabic. Uni of course was with Bahzi. Even if he was not, he and Kazeel never traveled together on land. But at the moment, in that darkest hour before dawn, climbing over yet another slippery, icy mountain, Kazeel wished his *shuka* were here, if just to keep him company.

He never did get to sleep. But as they finally ground into the last hour of their journey, Kazeel's demeanor had settled down considerably. He'd cheated death twice just today: in the ambush at Sat Put and during the air attack. Maybe he wouldn't have to worry about meeting his Maker again anytime soon.

They came over the top of a mountain named the Meshpi. The Pushi finally lay before them. But the Dragos in the

first truck apparently noticed something was wrong and
screeched to a halt. They could see the center of the Pushi
from here. Indeed, they could see Kazeel's house.

It was in flames.

The second and third Drago trucks stopped with a
screech as well. His driver stood on the brakes so
abruptly, Kazeel nearly went through the windshield.
Then he saw the flames for the first time and nearly threw
up. Not until that moment did he realize how much his
home meant to him.

What had happened? Another air attack? His driver's
phone buzzed.

"Your friends' friends burn down your house," the
driver tried to tell him.

Kazeel just shook his head. Who were his friends'
friends? And why would they want to destroy his home?

"Your old bodyguards," the driver crudely clarified.
"These are their friends. They are mad at you. For termi-
nating them."

Kazeel tried to sort out the man's verbal puzzle. His
old bodyguards, the four men he'd taken out. They'd been
residents of Ubusk, the village nearby. Was it their
"friends" who'd stormed his mountain fortress and were
now destroying it?

The driver came up with a pair of very powerful binoculars and handed them back to Kazeel. Once they were
adjusted to his teary eyes, Kazeel could see dozens of
armed men rampaging through his compound, burning
and looting. They were carrying everything but torches
and pitchforks. Kazeel was astonished. He couldn't believe the villagers would want to harm him. Not because

they loved him—quite the opposite, because they feared him.

Or at least he thought they did.

Suddenly there was a great crash against the passenger side door. Kazeel turned to see the face of a very bloody man pressed up against the window. He looked like something from a horror movie, screaming and bleeding from hundreds of wounds. But it was his eyes that were the most frightening. They were positively bugging out. The man began saying something—but he suddenly disappeared, only to be replaced by another face, this one bloodier.

Now came the crash of explosions—not aerial bombs this time. Kazeel could hear sprays of shrapnel hitting the side of his vehicle; RPGs were landing all around them. Their sound was unmistakable. Then came the gunfire. Torrents of it. Again unmistakable, it was large-caliber and vicious.

Only then did it dawn on Kazeel what was happening. Despite their best efforts, they'd driven right into an ambush.

This is not a very good day, Kazeel thought. And quite possibly, his last. He knew these armed men on the outside of the car, knew whose dirty hands were trying to get him. They were also Ubusks, people from the village near his mountain. A trademark red cloth worn to keep their hoods on was a dead giveaway. Erasing his former bodyguards so close to home was going to be the end of him, Kazeel was sure. He should have carried his former guards up into the hills and disposed of them quietly. It would have avoided the catastrophe he found himself in now.

Dozens of these people were swarming over his Range Rover. The vehicle ahead of him suddenly exploded in flames. The two Drago bodyguards tumbled out just a second before the truck was blown apart.

Kazeel's driver stood on the brakes again. He shifted the truck into neutral, but he was racing the engine madly. The way in front of them was now blocked. Kazeel frantically turned to see the vehicle behind them explode into flames as well. The crowd of furious villagers began swarming over it, even though many were catching their clothes on fire.

Kazeel turned forward again.

They were trapped.

The next thing he knew, the door closest to him flew open. The sounds of the ambush flooded in. Gunfire, RPGs going off, louder, more intense explosions. Above it all, the screams of those attacking his convoy.

Kazeel expected hundreds of hands to reach in, to grab him, to tear him limb from limb, then pull him in pieces into hell with them. He was surprised then when two black gloves reached in and clamped down on his shoulders and an instant later he was literally dragged out of the backseat. It was one of the Dragos. The biggest one of all. There was a tremendous explosion close by. The concussion was enormous. Yet Kazeel could feel himself being whisked away. Indeed, his feet never touched the ground. Bullets were zinging all around him. Explosions were going off everywhere. This was combat—madness and fire. It was the closest that Kazeel the superterrorist had ever come to it. Still the Dragos were carrying him through it.

Another huge blast went off. Kazeel was unable to see,

unable to breathe. He felt another pair of hands on him, and together two Dragos ran him off the road and threw him down the side of the mountain. Kazeel went tumbling head over heels. There were many boulders and trees on the way down; how he wasn't killed by colliding with one of them he would never know. It seemed like he was falling forever.

Finally he stopped tumbling and hit something soft, sparing him any broken bones. He'd landed in a pool of mud, moss, and snow hard by a raging mountain stream. Kazeel had lifted his head from the muck, amazed at the luck of his soft landing, when one of the Dragos slammed into him. He, too, had rolled down the hill. Then another Chechyan came down on top of them. Then another. And another.

By the time Kazeel lifted his face from the muck a second time, the Dragos had formed a defensive perimeter around him. He was pummeled and bleeding and was now soaked to the skin. Yet somehow Kazeel was *still* alive.

But for how long? Hundreds of armed men were rushing down the slope toward them. Many more were converging on them from the north and south. Apparently the entire village of Ubusk had turned out for this massacre. The Dragos were scanning the terrain immediately around them, looking for a way out. But there was none. They were surrounded.

Kazeel collapsed back into the cold stream. The Dragos . . . Praise Allah, their bravery and fighting skills were beyond compare. But to what end? Their valor and courage were simply putting off the inevitable. Cruel death, for all of them, was just seconds away.

"We will never get out of this, my brothers," Kazeel told them in despair.

But one replied gruffly: "We have a way. . . ."

Then this man slammed him to the cold mud again. "Just stay down!"

Kazeel obeyed. The gunfire became more intense, the explosions closer and more frequent. But in among it all, he heard another sound. Mechanical. Whirring, blades turning. A helicopter! Its noise soon drowned out everything else. A great downwash splattered him with more crud in his face. Once again, he couldn't see. He could hardly breathe. Suddenly a metal ladder was in front of him. Unseen hands hoisted him to it. He was sternly ordered to hang on.

Kazeel could feel himself being lifted up, bullets passing so close to him they singed his beard as they went by.

He was quickly hauled into the open bay of the helicopter. The remaining Dragos piled in after him. The aircraft began moving away even as tracer fire was bouncing off it. Kazeel was simply astounded. He was close to going into shock again, but the exhilaration of still being alive was overwhelming. He just couldn't believe what was happening. The ferocity displayed by the Dragos in protecting him was astonishing. But to have the foresight to have a helicopter near the site of the ambush? That went so above and beyond . . . The Chechyans had saved his life so many times over the past 24 hours, he'd lost count.

But there *was* something strange here, at least to Kazeel's battered mind. It was the helicopter itself. It wasn't really a military aircraft. It was roomy inside, but he saw no weapons. And to his amazement, the Dragos knew how to fly it. Two of his sterling bodyguards were behind the controls. Or at least men that looked like them.

But the really odd thing was the helicopter's color. It didn't seem appropriate somehow for a battle zone. Not green or black or a camouflage combination of both.

Instead, it was painted very bright yellow.

And on its tail were the words: Sing-One TV.

PART THREE
The 2000 Buddhas

Chapter 13

Her name was Tiffany, and she was quite possibly the only Tiffany in all of Manila.

She was the assistant day manager of the Xagat Pacific Hotel, by far the most expensive place to stay in the Philippine capital. Tiffany was an American, but on duty she spoke English with a vague European accent. She was just 22, attractive, and stranded in the Philippines by a failed romance. She hated her job. Hated her boss. Hated the hotel's well-heeled customers. She was also in charge of the Xagat's public relations.

She arrived at her office this Saturday morning, 20 minutes late to begin her shift. No sooner had she sat down with her first coffee of the day than she got a call from the front desk. There was a strange man in the lobby. He was claiming he had to pick up a very important message from his boss, yet no message had come in for anyone under his name. He was causing a bit of a ruckus and would not leave.

"Is his boss a guest here?" Tiffany asked the front desk. "He was about a couple weeks ago," came the reply, or at least that's what the strange man was saying. But he refused to give his boss's name, so there was no way to check. Hotel security had the man under surveillance, but no one working the floor knew what to do. Tiffany gulped the rest of her coffee and charged down to the lobby. This was not the way to start her day.

Her elevator arrived, and she marched past the front desk to a cluster of couches near the main door. The disruptive individual was now sitting here quietly. Tiffany approached the lobby matron, the person who'd first flagged the problem. She was standing about ten feet away from the strange man, giving him his space.

He wasn't really being difficult, the matron explained to Tiffany in a whisper. He was just slow on the uptake. If the message from his boss hadn't arrived yet, he would just wait here until it did. That sort of thing.

Tiffany walked around the couch and finally got a look at him. Bald head. Big muscles. Gold hoop ring in left earlobe. He *was* odd-looking. And his scowl was frightening. But Tiffany noticed he had the eyes, and the eyelashes, of a woman. Six security men were watching him from afar, but Tiffany could tell the guy was making them nervous. She couldn't blame them; he looked like he ate children for breakfast.

He reeked, though, and was dirty and was wearing filthy Middle Eastern–type clothes. He would have to go.

It took all the security people, two bellhops, plus the concierge to finally get the man out. He was half-dragged, half-pushed through the huge revolving door and deposited, butt-first, on the sidewalk outside. Yet no sooner was he on his feet than he was up against the plate-glass window looking back in. He was crying.

Tiffany went over to shoo him away. He pressed an index card up against the window for her to read. It contained just one sentence, written in several different languages. She recognized only two of them: Arabic, which she couldn't read, and English, which she could.

The card said: *My name is Abdul Abu Uni. Can you direct me to the nearest bathroom or airport?*

He was lost.

In a strange country, filled with strange people, with no money, no luggage. Nowhere to go. Uni, the *shuka,* was lost.

What went wrong? The plan had been so simple up to this point. By Kazeel's wishes, he'd accompanied Bahzi and his men down from Sat Put to see the stash of missiles, which turned out to be stored in the basement of Bahzi's house in Karachi. Uni counted them, which was all Kazeel ever wanted him to do. Eventually reaching the correct number of 36, he okayed the missiles' shipping to their next destination, somewhere in the Philippines. They would make the trip, by cargo air, in crates marked: UNITED NATIONS—DECONTAMINATED HAZARDOUS WASTE.

This done, Bahzi's men put Uni himself on an airplane and essentially pointed him east. He was in Manila just a few hours later, again all according to plan. But stepping off the plane at Manila Airport this time was like stepping into another world. Although it was his second trip here in little more than a week, he'd never traveled this far

alone before. Through the eyes of someone no brighter
than an eight-year-old child, the airport and its chaotic
environs were frightening for him.

From there, the plan called for Uni to go to the Xagat
Pacific, the same place Kazeel had stayed earlier that
month. Here a message from Kazeel would be waiting for
him. It would tell Uni what to do next, most probably to
wait in place until Kazeel himself returned to Manila,
something he'd intended to do all along. But even though
it should have arrived more than 48 hours before,
Kazeel's message was not there.

Something was not right, and even a half-wit like Uni
knew it. He wasn't totally cut off. He did have a cell
phone with him. It was a clean Nokia, given to him by
Kazeel at Sat Put, to be used only if something went
wrong once the two had parted. But only one number was
programmed into it: that of Kazeel's cell phone. Uni had
been pushing that button madly since discovering there
was no message for him at the hotel. But his boss never
picked up. Instead, the *shuka* kept getting Kazeel's answering service, a French-speaking woman who was so
cold and emotionless, she could even infuriate a dolt like
him.

Once tossed from the Xagat, Uni was at a loss as to
what to do. Although he'd stayed in a very seedy hostel
around the corner from the grand hotel during his first
trip here, he'd accompanied Kazeel everywhere he went
in those few days. They'd toured the Bangtang Channel
together on a private yacht. They'd met the *judus*'s contact. They'd seen the mud fight in the brothel.

Desperate, Uni began searching for familiar places
now, just as a child would do. He wandered the streets of

Manila, a big ugly stranger in a strange and frequently ugly land. The slums were horrific; they overwhelmed Uni, who'd grown up in the isolated high desert of northwest Pakistan. Somehow he found the waterfront and from there the marina from which they'd embarked on their yacht trip. The yacht itself would be easy to find, even for him. It was painted in blue, white, and red, and it was so clean, so smooth, so sleek, it seemed to glisten. But though he searched the marina several times, all he saw were fishing boats and junks. The yacht, which in his mind was the size of a battleship, was no longer there. He was crushed. He'd loved riding on the expensive vessel. It was big and fast and protected him from falling into the water. He'd actually dreamed of riding on it again someday.

He drifted for several more hours, going back through the shantytowns, stumbling his way through the crowds, pushing away the beggars who seemed to be everywhere. By dumb luck he found the fancy restaurant where Kazeel and Marcos had had lunch. It was called the Luzon Cricket Club. Uni stationed himself outside its front door, closely examining anyone going in or out, hoping to see a familiar face, but scaring many. A small army of security men showed up, and just like at the Xagat, he was told to move on.

More hours of confused meandering followed. Night fell, and it began to rain. By the glow alone Uni found the section of downtown Manila called the War Zone, the neighborhood where young girls fought in the mud. He stumbled from saloon to dance hall to strip club, looking for the one sign he thought he would recognize in the neon watercolors of the night.

But though he searched for it until way past midnight, he couldn't find the place called the Impatient Parrot.

Cold, wet, tired, and not knowing what else to do, Uni returned to the Xagat.

It was now two in the morning and the rain had turned into a monsoon. The streets around the hotel were empty. Uni avoided passing directly in the front of the place; instead, he crawled up under a low-hanging palm tree next to the hotel's entrance.

He lay there crying, pounding his head on the ground, wondering why Allah was doing this to him. He prayed for forgiveness, prayed for advice. Prayed for good luck. Eyes closed tight, he asked God to send him a sign. When he opened them again, he saw a woman's face staring in at him under the palm fronds. It was Tiffany, the nasty woman who'd ejected him from the hotel earlier. She was leaving work after a long day and had spotted his huge bare feet sticking out from under the branches.

"You . . ." she was saying, an odd inflection in her voice.

Uni stayed frozen. He was sure the woman would call her friends and have him removed again.

But she had a surprise for him. "You . . . your message," she began stuttering. "It came. I mean, it didn't come. But *something* came for you."

Uni didn't understand her. But she motioned for him to come out from under the tree. The rain had stopped and the sky above was filled with stars. She led him back into the hotel, not through the front door but via the service entrance. They walked through the empty kitchen, where she passed him some dish towels to help dry off. She brought him to a small employee break room near the food storage bin. The tiny room had vending machines, a coffeemaker, a pot of tea on a warmer, some couches, a TV, and a VCR. She left Uni here, sniffing around the teapot, but returned shortly with a small package.

"I saw your name on your card," she tried to tell him. "And it looked very much like the one on this address. It was delivered here today. In fact, it arrived right after you left."

Again Uni didn't understand, but he recognized his name on the package and took it from her. He was confused, though. He'd been expecting a simple letter from Kazeel, a love letter in fact, with coded messages within containing his instructions. Why then would Kazeel send him a package?

He opened it with the woman's help; his hands were still stiff from being so wet and cold. She finally tore away the thick paper envelope to find not a letter, but a videotape inside.

Uni was even more baffled now. He equated videotapes with movies, American movies, of which Kazeel had dozens back home in Ubusk. Why would the boss send him a movie?

And was this package even from Kazeel? There was no return address, no paperwork for its delivery. But then again, who else but Kazeel would know he was here?

The woman turned on the TV for him and pushed the tape into the VCR. Then she smiled, briefly, muttered her apologies, and left, her PR work done for the day.

"Show yourself out when you're done," she told him. "And please, use the back door."

• • •

Uni took off his soaking wet robe and dried off.

He placed his Nokia phone atop the TV set, hoping the water in his pockets had not damaged it. It took him a while to find the VCR's play button. In between, he nearly scalded himself while stealing a cup of tea.

Finally the tape began. At first it showed a bare piece of snowy ground, the camera work very shaky. Then Uni heard a voice. A man said, in Arabic: "Recognize your friends?"

The camera panned over to three dead bodies lying next to a mound of bloody snow. Uni almost dropped his cup of tea. This wasn't a Hollywood movie. This was real. Even he could tell . . .

The bodies were lying faceup; one of them was huge. The camera zoomed in on the face. It was Bahzi. Shot twice in the head. Next to him, his two oily bodyguards. Their throats had been slashed.

Uni stared unblinking at the screen, not quite sure what was going on. There was a burst of static and an edit to another piece of video. "How about these guys, *shuka?*" the voice asked again. "They were friends of yours, too, weren't they?"

The video focused now on a room full of bodies, the floor beneath them splattered with blood. Uni's stomach turned inside out. He recognized the bloody rug as the one in the main room of Kazeel's mountain home. The bodies were those of the council of seven, Kazeel's closest advisors, the men who lived in the caves around the Pushi. All of them had been shot in the head, right in Kazeel's living room.

Another burst of static, another edit. Uni remained numb. He saw six more men, all bound to chairs in a filthy house somewhere. They, too, were all dead, garrotes around their necks. Uni recognized them as well: they were the Pakistani intelligence agents, the men who'd served as Kazeel's temporary bodyguards.

Still, none of this was making any sense to Uni. But then more static came and went and suddenly he was staring into the face of Kazeel himself. . . .

Uni did drop the hot tea this time, right in his lap, but he didn't feel a thing. He was stunned, reality slowly sinking in. Here was Kazeel, in the middle of the high desert somewhere, clothes torn away, hands bloody, on his knees, begging for his life.

Four masked men appeared behind him; each was carrying a small hand ax. It was early morning, and the sun was coming up. Kazeel saw the men, saw the axes, and commenced wailing even louder. He began pleading with the man operating the camera, begging him to spare his life, that he was sorry, that he would make restitution. It did him no good. The men with the axes converged on him and began chopping him up. His screams were hellish. It took a long time for Kazeel to die. Uni threw up on himself.

But still, one part of this didn't make sense. The people doing all this were the Dragos. Uni knew because they were wearing the Dragos' jet-black battle garb, including their trademark black masks. But why would they kill Kazeel?

The answer came when one of the men turned toward the camera and slowly took off his mask. Uni threw up again. This man was not a Chechyan. He was an American. The face he would never forget. The man smiled and said: "Remember me? Dave Hunn, Queens, New York."

He continued staring into the camera, cruel smile glued to his face, as if he was waiting for Uni to put it all together. This he did in a surprisingly few seconds. The Chechyans were never Chechyans at all! They were Americans. The *Crazy Americans*. And they'd somehow fooled Kazeel—and everybody else.

Suddenly Hunn was holding up Kazeel's photofone. His smile had turned demonic.

"And look what I found," he said into the camera as it was turning to show a bright yellow helicopter in the background. "That's right; we got the whole plan right here. And now we know where you are and what you are doing. And so we're coming to get you. You got that, Cue Ball? *You're next*. See you soon. . . ."

The tape ended. Ten minutes went by.

Uni was cowering in the corner of the room, shaking uncontrollably. He was no longer sure where he was or how he got there or why he was soaking wet. But Kazeel was dead. He was sure of that. Sure enough that he wasn't going to watch the horrible video again.

Even his dull brain knew this meant *very* big trouble. The attack on America was certainly canceled. The seven men from the Pushi were gone. The Paki bodyguards as well. The real Dragos themselves—where were they? No one who had knowledge of the big plan was left. Except himself, of course. But Uni was not Kazeel or a martyr or a soldier of fortune. He was a *shuka*. A pair of eyes, a pair of hands, those were the extent of his abilities. Even in the best of circumstances.

An overwhelming dread was running through him. It felt like cement in his veins. Kazeel was gone and the plan broken—that was painful enough. But Uni had another problem: the *Crazy Americans* were now coming after *him*.

He sat on the floor like this, crying for a very long time. God had fooled him, he thought. All that praying and sacrifice, and for what? His life would soon be over; sure enough, his end would be painful as Kazeel's. Or even worse.

But then he heard an odd electronic sound. It took him a moment to realize the source. Over on top of the TV. It was his cell phone, the one Kazeel had given him to use for outgoing calls only.

It was ringing.

But who would be calling *this* phone? Only Kazeel knew the number.

Uni picked himself up, walked slowly to the TV, took the phone into his shaking hands, and pushed the receive button. He heard a man's voice, speaking in Arabic but with a very strange accent, certainly not American. "Thank you for answering, my friend. And we are friends; let me first assure you of that. And we are friends of your friends. We are all one together. We are aware of what has happened to your colleague Kazeel. We grieve his loss along with you. But don't worry. We are here to help you. You must not be afraid."

Uni was dumbstruck. At first, the voice sounded like Kazeel, talking to him from beyond the grave. But of course that accent—there was no mistaking that.

"Though we've had this setback, we can still proceed with the big plan. It is very important that we do. You just have to do exactly what we tell you and the attack will go off as scheduled. The people who will use the weapons are in place. As you know, they've been in place for years. Kazeel worked hard, and he put everything together. The weapons just have to get to their destination and our brother Kazeel can enjoy Paradise knowing his dream will be fulfilled."

There was a short pause.

"We know you can do this because we have faith in you. In fact, my friend, the truth is, you are probably the most important person in the world right now. A true maker of history. As only you hold the *sharfa*."

There was a longer pause.

"Now, I realize this might be a shock to you, but you must relax, as it is totally under control. I understand that by holding the *sharfa* you alone control the means to activate those agents hiding in America. And I realize, my friend, that your vow to our departed Kazeel was to never tell anyone that piece of information. . . ."

A very long pause. "But, good sir, should you ever choose to unburden yourself of that weight, please let me be the one to lend you an ear. Do we understand each other?"

Uni was simply stunned by all this. Was he hearing right? Someone wanted the plan to proceed—without Kazeel? Who was crazy enough to want that?

The person on the other end of the phone anticipated the question. So he answered it before it was even asked.

"Who am I?" the voice said. "I am the *judus,* the new-found friend. But from now on, you'll know me as 'Palm Tree.'"

Chapter 14

Uni had no idea who Georgio Armani was or why he was wearing one of his suits.

Yet here he was, in a light gold pants and jacket ensemble, white Lord & Taylor shirt, red Savoy silk tie—and Gucci shoes, of course.

He was standing on the concourse of the Luzon Cricket Club, the exclusive resort on Manila Bay. This place had been built by the British a hundred years before, its snotty appeal surviving World War II and many periods of internal unrest in the Philippines. The club was palatial, white and silver and surrounded by a small forest of palm trees and tropical plants. Their colors were dazzling; they were reflecting wildly off Uni's mirrored aviator sunglasses. Less than 48 hours ago he'd been chased from this very same place. Now he was a guest for lunch.

He nodded to his limo driver; the car had been provided to him by the Xagat hotel, the same one he'd been tossed from, again just two days ago. The driver bowed deeply, lit up a cigarette, and settled down to wait.

. . .

Many things had changed for Uni ever since he made the connection with Palm Tree.

Once a derelict, Uni was now being treated like royalty at the Xagat Pacific. All it took was a phone call from Palm Tree to the hotel's owner, an old Arab friend, and Uni was given the Xagat's top suite, four rooms, two baths, much nicer than the room where Kazeel had stayed. The expensive clothes Uni found waiting for him in the suite's master closet. Unlike Kazeel, Uni could not pass for Asian. Therefore, he would have to pass for a gangster.

For the first few hours inside the huge suite he sat in the smallest chair, wrapped in towels, not moving, not touching anything. Just sitting there, so certain a mistake had been made. Frequent visits from hotel staff, including a very contrite Tiffany, finally convinced him it was not so. They taught him how to turn on the TV, how to order dirty movies, how to start the Jacuzzi. He soon made himself at home, cleaning out every Coke and nut in the minibar and even ordering room service. Somehow, though, they never did manage to bring him his extra towels.

Palm Tree called him frequently over the next two days, always via his special cell phone. He stayed of the attitude that the big plan could continue. Much had already been invested in this thing: time, money, risks of being caught, found out. For the collusion to be revealed now would drop such a bombshell in the world community, Palm Tree's government would most likely not survive. A war might even result. Still, the plan had to move forward, or at the very least the weapons had to make it to America.

This could be done, Palm Tree said, by Uni simply walking the steps that Kazeel himself would have walked had he not flown off to Paradise. It might not be as impossible as it seemed. Anyone who knew Kazeel knew Uni. He was, in effect, Kazeel's perfect substitute. Uni was so unique, such an unmistakable character, no one—inside Al Qaeda or out—would question his authority to act for Kazeel. In the meantime they would keep it a close secret that the superterrorist was now in heaven. The first order Uni carried out was to destroy the hideous videotape.

During these phone chats, some of which Uni took in the Jacuzzi, Palm Tree talked about what had to be done. It boiled down to three things: getting the missiles and the launchers in the same place, making arrangements for their packing and shipment, and being on hand when the weapons were actually shipped. It sounded easy, at least to Uni.

Palm Tree laid out for him a number of simple instructions, which Uni put down on index cards, telling him where he had to go and what he should do once he got there. (These notes included the magic words: "Palm Tree sent me.") If they were able to do all these things together, then Uni could activate the *sharfa* and the big attack would come off—and Uni would be the new hero of the Muslim world.

This was heady stuff for the *shuka*. The excitement. The phone calls. The macadamia nuts.

It was almost enough to make Uni forget that Kazeel was really gone.

• • •

One thing Palm Tree emphasized, though, was Uni not lingering too long in the hotel room, caught up in the evils of bathing, TV, and the minibar. Time was short, and it was important that he properly attend to details. That's what he was doing now. That's why he was at the Luzon Cricket Club.

First on his to-do list was meeting Palm Tree's prime contact in Manila. Uni knew only that the person would be a "friendly face." He entered the club's lobby and was immediately spellbound by its grandeur. This certainly wasn't the Impatient Parrot. He was approached by a gorgeous Filipino girl. She was dressed in a short, tight miniskirt and blouse, the servants' uniform of the club. She seemed to know who Uni was right away.

She took him lightly by his arm and led him out to the veranda. This place was *beaucoup* beautiful. More palms, more incredibly bright flowers and plants, with much glass and stone and peacocks in vivid feathers, strutting about with authority. The shade from many willow trees cut down on the brutal noontime heat.

The girl led him to a table tucked away in the corner of the patio. Three men were sitting here. One was dressed in a black suit, black shirt, black tie. He rose to shake Uni's hand. Uni didn't recognize him at first.

"Captain Ramosa," the man finally said, reminding him. "We meet again."

Now Uni remembered. This was the police officer who'd saved them from the Crazy Americans in the back room of the brothel. All that seemed like it had happened years ago and not just a matter of a week or so. Besides,

Ramosa looked different. His hair was a lighter color and no longer greasy. His mustache was gone and he looked like he'd had a skin peel. He appeared, for want of a better word, to be more sophisticated, and not the rat with a badge they'd met in the Impatient Parrot.

The two other men were his personal bodyguards. They weren't as nattily dressed as Ramosa. On the table in front of them were three tiny coconut shells, cut in half and lined up in a row. The men had been playing a game when Uni arrived. Ramosa saw Uni's curiosity and smiled again. He lifted up the first half-shell to reveal a large yellow poker chip underneath. He lifted the second shell to reveal a red poker chip of the same size. Under the third shell was a sparkling gold coin. Ramosa tugged at his shirt sleeves like a magician, then began moving the shells this way and that, over, under, and around. After a few seconds, he stopped, then looked up at Uni.

"Where is the gold coin, my friend?"

Uni pointed to the first shell. Ramosa lifted it: the red poker chip was beneath. He lifted the middle shell to reveal the gold coin.

"Watch closely this time," Ramosa told Uni, moving the shells again. Uni kept his eye on the shell he knew held the coin beneath, but when Ramosa stopped and it was time for him to pick again, the shell he selected held the yellow poker chip instead. Ramosa's men laughed as their boss lifted the shell next to the one Uni had picked to show it was covering the gold coin.

"Try again," Ramosa told Uni—and he did, a dozen more times. But no matter how hard he tried to keep track of the gold piece, Uni never managed to pick the correct shell. Ramosa's men were in hysterics by this time. The *shuka* was an easy mark for the shell game. Ramosa ended the episode with a flourish, moving the three shells with even quicker motions and then, even before asking Uni to select, turning over all three himself to reveal that nothing remained under any of them.

Uni was clearly fascinated—and very confused.

"It's a game of misdirection," Ramosa told him. "Something you should remember for the future."

He gave a nod to his men, and they quickly departed, taking the shells with them. Uni finally sat down, selecting the seat directly across from Ramosa.

"I have heard about our setback," Ramosa said to him, once Uni was settled. "I liked Kazeel. I really did. But can you carry on?" Uni indicated he could, but Ramosa's expression revealed he wasn't so sure.

A waiter approached, and suddenly a watercress salad and a bottle of mineral water appeared in front of Uni. He'd never had either. He sniffed the greens and sampled the water with his finger. Then he looked across at Ramosa, who nodded in a friendly manner. Only then did Uni begin to eat.

The back lawn of the club was bright green and well manicured. The water of Manila Bay lay beyond, sparkling, alive with junks, fishing boats, and ferries, many, many ferries, brightly colored; one moving at top speed close to the beach was painted in vivid, glaring green. Ramosa spoke amiably, about Manila Bay, about the salad, about the peacocks. Uni was certain the birds were being kept and fattened for the menu someday. Ramosa had to ask him to stop throwing morsels of food to them.

Finally, he got down to business. Ramosa said to him: "We can secure both the missiles and the launchers tonight. We can put them together by early morning. Pack them correctly and they'll be on their way by tomorrow night. There are many people in this city who will help us to this end."

He took out a matchbook and wrote an address on the back.

"But first, you have things to do, and so do I," he said, passing the matchbook to Uni. "Meet me at this place, tonight, at ten. And we will begin the final leg."

Uni took the matchbook. A silence passed between them. Ramosa sipped his mineral water.

"I understand you are carrying a key piece of information regarding the implementation of this attack," Ramosa finally said to him. "Something referred to as the *sharfa*. This must be quite a burden for you, holding the key to putting the plan in motion. If so, I am here to tell you, should you ever want to share that information, please be my guest." He smiled, but this time not so flashy. "I mean, if recent history is our guide, should anything happen *to you*, my friend . . . well then, all would be lost, wouldn't it?"

But Uni wasn't really listening. He'd finished his salad and was now using one of the five spoons next to his plate to scoop up the remains of the dressing. This done, he began to lick the plate clean, as he usually did at mealtime. Only the appearance of a bowl of sherbet stopped him. Ramosa took a call on his cell phone, and this signaled the end of their meeting.

They shook hands and Uni left. He was intercepted

again by the girl in her tight club uniform. This time she took his hand tightly in hers and walked him to the front door. As she bid him good-bye, she pressed a card into his hand. It was her private phone number.

Uni picked his teeth with the card, then threw it away.

His next destination was a section of Manila called Makak.

It was a strip of beach near the poorest section of the capital city. The structures here were built on stilts, as high tide and sewage frequently ran in the streets. There were many drug addicts and hookers and street beggars down here. There were also many small-time export shops in the area. Housed in tiny huts clustered together into a dreary marketplace, they were known to deal in everything from the cheapest trinket to HD TVs, much of it stolen or illegal knockoffs of expensive items, much of it destined for the United States.

Uni's limo looked very out of place here. His Armani suit did, too. His Guccis became muddied as he stepped out onto the street. He had to push a few little beggars away; the limo driver beeping the horn got rid of most of them. This time the limo driver remained in the car, though, with the windows up and doors locked. He kept the engine running, too.

Uni found the address he was looking for. It was a small, dilapidated hut down a very dark, very busy back alley. The front door was open; Uni walked right in. Here he found boxes stacked to the ceiling, all containing the same item: a plastic Buddha. They were all of the same design, the tubby deity sitting cross-legged, bemused smile, flowing robes, a tiny 10-watt bulb inside to illuminate the illuminated. Like the poker chips, they came in either red or yellow. There were easily hundreds of them here, thousands perhaps.

A Chinese man was sitting behind an ancient cash register. Uni took out the script Palm Tree had prepared for him, selected the correct color-coded index card, and handed it to the man. "It say here you want two thousand Buddhas?" he asked Uni in broken English, his tone displaying some disbelief.

Uni nodded, pointing to the place on the script that instructed that 1,000 Buddhas should be the red version and the other 1,000 should be yellow.

The man was still uncertain. "This big order," he tried to say. "Not sure I can do." Uni then handed him an index card with the words: *Palm Tree sent me.* The man immediately smiled, his lips seemingly going ear to ear. Suddenly he was bowing and trying to kiss Uni's hand.

"Palm Tree is a dear friend," he said. "He is one of my *best* friends. And for my friends, I move anything. Explosives. Drugs. We send crack directly to the barrios of Los Angeles for him. We can hide anything, anywhere."

He waved his arm to indicate the hundreds of chubby statues he had on display. Then he smiled. "So, tell me, what are you going to hide under them?" he asked Uni.

Uni smiled back, then put his finger to his lips.

The man understood with a laugh.

"I get it," he said. "Top-secret."

Uni's next stop was in a part of South Manila called the Ghost Town.

It was a section of the city that was dedicated to cemeteries. There were dozens of them, each with its own enclosure, its own main gate, its own name. They were all dreary, creepy, with shabby crucifixes and ancient wooden tomb markers. Rolling hills filled with the dead.

The limo arrived at an ancient barn that nevertheless had a Jaguar coupe parked out front. It made the limo look shabby. Uni rechecked his index cards, making sure he had the right place. Apparently, he did. He took off his mirrored shades and walked in. The barn was old and run-down and smelled of teak and bananas. The floor was covered with straw. There were huge power saws hanging on the walls and much wood lying about, waiting to be cut. A small window in the roof provided the only light.

A Filipino man was stooped over a large rectangular wooden box, nailing it together. He paid no attention when Uni came in. Uni walked over to him, but still the man did not acknowledge him. The *shuka* was prepared for this. He took out the index card, the one with the magical words on it: *Palm Tree sent me,* and put it in front of the man's eyes.

The guy almost went over. Suddenly he was bowing and scraping, groveling with much more zeal than the Buddha salesman. Uni was beginning to like this. He handed him another index card. It told the man that Uni needed three large crates. They had to be built to the exact specifications written on the card.

The man indicated this would be no problem, then motioned for Uni to come into his back office. They sat down and the man poured them some tea. He explained that he was by trade a coffin maker, but he could build special shipping crates to order for the right people. The back room was indeed filled with coffins.

The man saw Uni's interest in his handiwork.

"At times, the police need to clean up the city's streets," he tried to explain. "Not of litter, but of the homeless, the addicts, all the panhandling kids. There's no place for them, so the police murder them. Then they dump them here. They give me fifty dollars for each . . ."

Uni picked up a piece of wood. The man knew what he was thinking. "No—my friend," he said. "The fifty dollars is not just for the casket. *That* is cheap. The fifty is for me to get rid of them. So I put them in a box and hide them by burying them in the cemetery. Who would ever think to look there?"

The coffin maker took out a blue velvet case from his desk drawer. He opened it to reveal a diamond necklace. The light reflected off Uni's face. The jewels were that brilliant.

"They are for my wife," the man explained proudly. He nodded at the stack of coffins behind him, some of them very small. "You see, it's turning out to be a very good year."

Chapter 15

Uni tasted whiskey for the first time that night.

A bottle had been placed in the back of the limo the hotel was providing for transportation to his meeting with Ramosa.

Uni found the fifth of Jack Daniel's as soon as he climbed in; on hand as well were five chilled glasses, a bucket of ice, and three varieties of mixers: ginger ale, soda water, and seltzer. Four beautiful women had delivered these things to the limo. Uni knew this because all four were sitting in front of him right now, each holding a glass with whiskey and some mix in it. The women were here for instruction purposes, he believed, on the proper way to put alcohol and non-alcohol together. That the hotel thought to send four women to teach him these things, though, seemed like overkill to Uni. One female would have been sufficient to explain it to him, and he would have got it, after a while. There was no reason to send four, each with a sample drink in her hand. And what was with their clothes? They were barely wearing anything.

It had already been a whirlwind day for him. Lunch,

the meetings with the exporter and the woodworker, it had run Uni ragged. He wasn't used to this hustle and bustle. Luckily, he'd found a few hours to relax.

He'd returned to the Xagat after visiting Ghost Town, did a Jacuzzi, and then emptied out the minibar again. He'd developed a passion for the Pepsi, saving the bottle-cap for each one he drank. He washed his Armani suit in the bathtub, using the hotel-supplied shampoo for soap. A room service meal followed. Uni sat on the bed, licked his plates, and channel-surfed for the next two hours.

A phone call from Palm Tree got him in gear again. He climbed back into his clothes (the Armani was still a bit damp), went downstairs, and found the limo waiting as usual. He and the doorman continued their strange rit-ual—every time Uni saw him, the man had his hand out, so Uni would shake it. This time he did so quickly, before disappearing into the back of the stretch. And here he found the whiskey and the mixers and the girls to tell him how it all worked.

The girls mixed several drinks while still parked in front of the hotel, laughing and making odd cooing sounds as they did so. Uni just sat back, patiently, trying to make some sense of it. Finally he raised his hand, took a glass, put in some ice, some whiskey, some ginger ale, stirred it, and sipped it. The girls all clapped, and then laughed when he began staring intently into the clear bot-tle of ginger ale. That's when Uni waved all four out of the car; their work here was done. They were very sur-prised and seemed reluctant to go. One tried to explain to him that friends of his had made sure they could stay with him the *whole* night, but again Uni just indicated good-bye. He wasn't so much of an idiot that he couldn't mix

his own beverages. There was another, brief protest, but
then the girls just gave up.

They left him in the backseat of the limo, staring into
the ginger ale bottle, clearly fascinated by the bubbles.

The trip through the muddy slums of the city's east side
took twice as long as it should have. The limo had to
make its way through streets jammed with hookers and
beggars. In some places, traffic was slowed to a crawl, so
many of these people were about. They were attracted to
the limo like flies.

Finally, Uni's driver pulled up to the main gate of the
east side docks. It was now about 10:00 P.M. A deep mist
was rolling into the area. Foghorns moaned; bells
clanged. The stink of exhaust, marine oil, and dead fish
mixed with the salty air. Uni, though, loved the smell.

He stepped out of the limo and had a short, fractured
communication with the driver. Uni wanted the limo to
wait for him and very unwisely stuck a fistful of money in
the driver's face as incentive. But the driver never gave
the money a second glance. Some places in Manila you
just don't hang around—and this was one of them.

So he just rolled up the window and drove away.

Uni found himself alone in the fog. He started walking.
He was looking for Pier 55; the driver had dropped him at
Pier 7. There were many old boats, fishing shacks, and
loading areas down here, but just about no lighting. Uni
could see faces in the shadows, though, some illuminated
by the glow of cigarettes, the glint coming from a knife
blade, or the barrel of a gun. None of this bothered him.
He just kept walking.

He heard gunfire just as he was passing Pier 13, off in the distance, piercing the encroaching fog. Uni was not armed; in fact, he'd never even *fired* a gun, let alone owned one. Strange, here he was doing the work of both Al Qaeda and the *judus,* and yet he was not carrying a weapon of any kind.

He passed Pier 26, nearly halfway to his goal. Suddenly a figure stumbled out of the darkness, falling from a doorway next to a dilapidated warehouse. The man was bleeding heavily. Indeed, he still had a knife sticking out of his ribs.

He staggered up to Uni, mumbled something, but then kept right on going.

And so did Uni.

He finally reached Pier 55.

It was at the far end of the dock, and down here the piers were so old they were literally falling into the water. Uni stood on the edge for a moment, trying to get his bearings. Then another figure came out of the fog walking toward him. This one was not bleeding. Uni saw the eyes before he saw the face. It was Ramosa.

They shook hands. The foghorn moaned again.

Ramosa smiled pure gold. "Let's get down to the boat," he said. "We have a bit of a journey to make."

Uni thought, *Boat? What boat?*

He followed Ramosa down the gangplank to find sitting at the end of the dock the blue, white, and red yacht.

Uni was thrilled. He'd been told nothing about a trip out to sea. He'd just assumed the weapons were in hiding inside a building along the waterfront. Now he was overjoyed about going on the yacht again. Before this, Uni had always hated the water. Hated being above it, hated being in it. Even hated drinking it. But the yacht was so big and so unlike anything he'd ever experienced. He felt safe on it. And at top speed, it seemed like the water was moving for him.

Ramosa saw his delight as they were climbing aboard. "This should be a very pleasant trip," he said.

The vessel was 75 feet long, made of both teakwood and fiberglass, with accommodations for up to 20 and a crew of 12. When Uni had taken the ride with Kazeel earlier, the yacht's crew were wearing white shirts and shorts. Now they were each dressed in a black combat suit with a shoulder patch identifying them as members of Ramosa's secret police. There were several females onboard this time too, working as servants of course.

The yacht slowly moved out of the harbor, leaving the fog bank behind. Uni was ushered to a seat on the stern—the view from here was spectacular. The water was calm; the stars were sparkling; a full moon was on the rise. Over his shoulder, the city of Manila, lights ablaze but receding. The water ahead was deep coral blue in the starshine. The ocean breeze felt good blowing across his bald head. Uni lay back in his seat and smiled.

He was in Paradise, so to speak.

They arrived at their first destination just before midnight. It was the island of Gugu. Just a spit of volcanic rock among the hundreds, located about twenty miles outside Manila Bay. It featured a small mountain on one side, a tiny beach on the other, and a lot of jungle in between.

There was an elaborate pier hidden beneath some

overhanging *azure* trees. Four men were waiting here to help them dock the boat. The lights of Luzon were way behind them now, but the moon was rising and it was surprisingly bright. It cast elegant shadows everywhere.

Uni recognized this place, of course. He'd been here before—the first time he and Kazeel had been in town. But on that occasion, Uni had been left at the dock while everyone else had disappeared into the jungle. That would not be the case tonight though. This time, he was the guest of honor.

They climbed off the yacht and made their way inland with no problems. Ramosa was in the lead, Uni and six of the yacht's crew trailing behind. They walked along a well-established path for about five minutes before coming to a high chain-link fence bordering a patch of ground at the foot of the mountain. Here they found two heavily armed men, sitting in the darkness.

It was hard for Uni to tell if these guys were Aboo guerrillas or more of Ramosa's secret policemen. Actually there was little difference between the two. The gunmen jumped to attention at the first sight of Ramosa. They opened the chain gate and escorted the small party through the hidden compound. Beyond lay a man-made tunnel that had been drilled into the side of the mountain. Uni was fascinated by it. It would have seemed to be a monstrous undertaking, to smash one's way into God's earth like this. Back in Pakistan, they just crawled in and out of the holes. Reading his thoughts, Ramosa said to him: "This was built during World War Two. By the Americans. . . ."

They went through the entrance to find a large artificial cavern within. Its ceiling was at least 50 feet high and was as wide as a soccer field. Again Uni was wide-eyed, enchanted. This place looked right out of a James Bond movie. It was as bright as day inside, its walls lined with high-tech equipment and flashing lights, with many guards walking gangplanks up near the ceiling and looking down on everything from above.

This was a very elaborate weapons bunker. Pallets of rifles, machine guns, rocket launchers, were stacked everywhere. Many of them were packed in crates that looked like miniature coffins. Uni recognized the handiwork.

There were also several unexploded cruise missiles on display, along with a handful of JDAMs and other American smart bombs.

"Left over from Afghanistan and Iraq," Ramosa told Uni as they passed this cache. "Sometimes they come down where the Americans don't expect them to. And sometimes, they just don't explode."

They reached an inner chamber. It, too, was well lit and watched over by armed men. Ramosa led Uni to what looked like a small mountain of suitcases. They were made of black leather, long and thin, but would not have looked out of place on a baggage rack at any airport. They were stacked in pyramid fashion.

Ramosa smiled; his gold teeth flashed in the overhead lighting.

"My friend, your launchers . . ." he said.

Two guards stepped forward, retrieved one of the cases, and opened it for Uni's inspection. Inside was the five-foot-long rail-like launcher, with an IR aiming device attached that looked like a flattened soup can. And while it was obvious even to Uni that the suitcases were made to look nothing but ordinary, each one had a small battery-operated cooling unit built inside. This device kept the key components of the launcher's aiming system at the correct temperature during transport and storage.

Uni contemplated the hill of launchers now. They all seemed in good shape, which was a great relief. He bowed simply to Ramosa. The policemen immediately began shouting orders. A squad of armed men appeared, and began carrying the launchers out of the bunker, two at a time.

Uni smiled broadly now. So did Ramosa. This part of the plan at least was done.

The launchers had all been loaded aboard the yacht by the time Ramosa and Uni returned. They shoved off from the hidden pier and once clear of the island's shoals turned not south, back to Manila, but west, toward deeper water.

Uni was delighted by this. They were going someplace else! The night was still very warm and the moon was shining close to full glory. He took his seat at the back of the yacht again. One of the female servants brought him a glass of champagne—those bubbles again!—and of all things, a large bowl filled with cherries.

Uni stared at the bowl for the longest time, crimson fruit glistening in the moonlight. As a child taking a trip to Islamabad, he'd seen a billboard that featured just a bowl of cherries like this one sitting alone on a table. Essentially the wording on the billboard said: If you have a bowl of cherries then your life has become happy and complete. Uni laughed out loud, a rare occasion. That had been so many years ago, yet now here it was, happening to him.

They glided along for another hour. The stars grew more brilliant; the moon was like a minor sun. Uni ate his cherries, watched his bubbles, and wondered, deeply at times, if Ramosa would ever let him drive the boat.

Then he heard voices coming from the control bridge. Something had been spotted off their port bow. A light flashing in sequences of three was out on the horizon.

Uni saw Ramosa take over the yacht's wheel. He turned the boat 40 degrees, pushed the throttles forward, and headed right for the blinking light. It grew dramatically in size as they quickly converged on it, yet it would take Uni a while before he realized the blinking light was actually attached to another boat. A ferry, painted very bright green.

Ramosa killed the engine and was soon right alongside the 200-foot vessel. A rope ladder came over, and Uni and Ramosa started up. Uni had some trouble keeping his feet on the rungs, though, as the two vessels bobbed in the three-foot waves. Finally the men on the ferry had to reach down, grab him by his Armani pants, and drag him over the side. Ramosa made a much more graceful arrival.

Ramosa's secret operations involved moving men, money, and weapons around, whether it be for Al Qaeda, Palm Tree, or the Aboos. He did this in two ways: by burying the contraband deep underground until it was ready to change hands or by, in effect, hiding it in plain sight. Thousands of ferries operated around these islands. They were of all different shapes and sizes and ages and levels of sophistication. Most shared one thing in common: they were brightly painted in glossy colors. Again, this one was entirely green. But this was no ordinary ferry. Even a dimwit like Uni could see that.

He was brought below and walked through a short passageway. Uni saw compartments where higher-paying passengers might stay for a one- or two-day trip were filled with explosives instead. On one subdeck, the rows of benches for the day riders were lined with rifles and ammunition belts. The canteen was filled with hand grenades. They reached the ferry's bottom deck. It was disguised to look like a freezer. There was a combination lock on its door. Ramosa casually spun the dial, the lock snapped, and the door swung open. A light was put on and Uni found himself looking at a wooden pallet holding a number of silver metal tubes.

Ramosa walked over to the pallet, took off the end of one of the tubes, and reached inside. He came out with a Stinger missile.

"The candles," he said to Uni with a grin. "Our birthday cake is now complete."

Uni smiled broadly. These things he recognized. He'd last seen them in the basement of Bahzi's house back in Karachi. He studied the missile Ramosa had retrieved. Nose cone, body, and fins—all in perfect condition. He counted the stash. Strangely, the count was 37, one more than the called-for 36.

"You see, the people who provided these missiles also wanted you to be sure that they work," Ramosa said, seeing Uni's confusion. "Our friend Palm Tree paid a lot of money for these gems. It is only fair that we test the merchandise for him."

Uni couldn't argue this. But how? Against who?

Again, Ramosa read his mind.

"Don't fret, my friend," he said. "We have just the target in mind. . . ."

The ride to the island of Kaagu-Tak took another two hours. It was 20 miles farther out from Manila than Gugu. The yacht arrived just before four in the morning, having parted ways with the bright green ferry just after 2:00 A.M.

Kaagu-Tak was another pinprick of rock rising up out of the deep blue water. They approached it from the north side, Uni now up on the bow with Ramosa and some of his policemen. They had both a missile and a launcher by their side. Ramosa handed Uni his night-vision binoculars and suggested he look at the coral lagoon dominating the island's north side. Beyond its rocky beach was a runway, one as basic as basic could get. Even though they were a mile out, through the night goggles Uni could see a small two-engine commuter plane was on this strip, its engines warming up. Behind it was a small aircraft shelter, a control hut, and three long barracks-type buildings.

"It's an orphanage," Ramosa told him, answering the only question Uni could possibly have. "It's run by a bunch of priests. Maryknolls, they are called. They have five camps on the islands out here. Every morning, around this time, they warm up that old plane, take off, and go island-hopping, moving orphans around, tending to their unfortunate flock. They've been doing it for years."

Uni *was* a certified simpleton, but as he watched Ramosa load the missile into the launcher, he was certain what Ramosa had in mind was nothing more than a test of the missile's aiming system, a fake firing to show that yes, if the trigger was pulled while the plane was in its sights, then it would hit the plane and the plane would go down.

The missionary plane took off. Ramosa stood on the yacht's bow pulpit, his head cocked to one side, allowing him to talk on his cell phone as he raised the loaded Stinger launcher onto his shoulder. He was getting instructions from someone on the other end; that was obvious. But who?

Ramosa proved very agile, trying to converse and line up the weapon at the same time. Finally he was heard to say: "Yes . . . it is a lock. I think it is a lock."

The voice on the other end became so loud, everyone on the yacht heard it say: "Fire, my friend. . . . Fire!"

And so Ramosa did. The missile went off its rail with a whoosh of smoke and corkscrewed itself into the air. It quickly caught the scent of the slowly rising airplane and in an instant made a beeline for it.

It was strange that it had *still* not registered on Uni that this was a live fire test—not until the missile actually hit the plane. There was an immediate puff of white smoke, then an orange ball of flame. The noise reached them a second later, a loud *pop!* followed by a sharp, guttural roar. The plane emerged from the fireball, or at least what was left of it. Its slow ascent indicated it was probably at full weight when it took off, meaning it had a dozen or so passengers onboard and that most of those passengers were probably orphans.

Uni could actually see bodies falling out of the sky now, each one hitting the sea with a splash, sometimes colliding with pieces of flaming wreckage on the way down. Uni was too dumb to be shocked. He *was* surprised, though.

Ramosa looked back at him, just as reality was settling in. He flashed his gold-plated smile. "Worried about the authorities, are you? I can tell by your face. Well, I assure you, my friend, this matter *will* be investigated by local law enforcement. Which, of course, is *me.*"

He looked out on the surface of the water broken only by the smoke and the sinking wreckage of the missionary plane. He never lost the 24K grin.

"And I have now fully investigated this matter," Ramosa went on after just a few seconds, as the crew and the female servants laughed around him, "and I have concluded that the poor orphans' plane crashed due to mechanical problems."

More laughter.

"They were orphans when they awoke this morning," Ramosa concluded. "But certainly, they are orphans no more."

The yacht ride back was indeed very pleasant. Smooth seas, more champagne, more cherries.

Uni was not smart enough to feel remorse, at least, not for total strangers. Orphans? What does the world miss if there are a few less orphans in it?

He sat at the back of the yacht, again enjoying the wind blowing over his bald head. The sea air smelled great. They were back in the bay, the lights of Manila now just 20 miles away.

The plan was unfolding like a lotus flower. He'd seen the launchers. He'd been reunited with the missiles. He'd seen them put together and doing their deadly work. It was now a simple matter of packing them and sending them on their way. If all went just as smoothly later that day, the Stingers would be inside the United States in less than a week. Then Uni would play his final part and activate the *sharfa* and the Second Time of Falling Sparrows, as Kazeel had christened it, would be at hand.

All this brought a question to Uni's mind: If the world knew Kazeel as the first superterrorist, simply because he planned and executed things like this, did that mean that he, Abdul Abu Uni, was now the world's *second* superterrorist? Shouldn't his face be on the magazine covers next? He ate more cherries and watched more bubbles. Perhaps Palm Tree was right: Maybe he *was* the most important person in the world right now. A true hero. Someone who had to be reckoned with. Someone who—

Suddenly a disturbing sound filled his ears. It was so loud, Uni felt his eyeballs shake. *What could this be?* He heard someone at the front of the yacht cry out. One of the female servants screamed. People were pointing to something off the stern. Uni finally turned and saw a huge black wall looming right behind him. It covered everything in darkness: the lights onshore, the moon, the stars. That's when he realized what was happening: a very large ship was bearing down on them.

Uni relieved himself on the spot. This frightening thing, coming out of nowhere, was about to rip him in two. Something hit him a moment later. It felt like a load of bricks. Actually, it was the bow wash of the ship crashing into the yacht. The man up front cried out again. Ramosa was at the yacht's wheel—and he wasn't smiling anymore. This immense vessel seemed determined to sail right over them.

There was a blackness now that Uni had never experienced. And the noise was beyond deafening. He kept repeating the name of the prophet over and over, but the horror seemed to go on forever.

"Hang on!" Ramosa was yelling at him. "Just hang on!"

Uni was hit with another wall of water. The yacht went up, very quickly, at least 25 feet in the air, and came back down even faster. Its nose was pushed 45 degrees to port as the side wake of the ship began to overtake them. Everything from the bridge on up was torn away by the concussion. Another tall wave hit the yacht, another crash back down to the surface. The ship blew its trouble horn. It was so intense, Uni's ears began to bleed.

The ship was passing not 10 feet away from them now and the yacht was being tossed about like a toy. Uni tried to shut his eyes, but he was too frightened to look away. He was hit by another wave and thrown violently to the deck, cutting his scalp on the broken bowl of cherries on the way down. He looked up from his prone position and saw the overhang of the huge vessel going right over his head. Engines rumbling, metal screeching. Such a horrible sound!

It was a containership; that much Uni could tell. But even with blood pouring into his eyes he knew this vessel was lucky to be afloat. True, it was enormous, but it was also very old, very rusty, and seemed to be full of holes. And there were pieces of branches and trees hanging off of it. How crazy was that?

And then just as suddenly it was gone, disappearing into the night. But not before Uni could read the words painted on its rear end.

Ocean Voyager. . . .

Uni ran his hand over his bloody bald head. Where had he heard that name before?

Chapter 16

It was six in the morning by the time Uni returned to the Xagat.

He was battered, soaking wet, his hands still trembling since nearly being killed by the ghostly ship.

The yacht barely made it back to Pier 55. No sooner was it docked than Ramosa and his gang went one way and Uni went the other. All were shaken by the close encounter. Uni found a foot taxi somehow and managed to tell the driver to bring him to the hotel. He was broke, though. He had to bum money from the sour doorman to pay the fare.

The doorman then brought him around back and in through the kitchen entrance, Uni being too waterlogged to appreciate the irony. They took the service elevator up to his suite, the doorman insisting that he call a doctor for Uni, as his head wound was still bleeding. But the *shuka* was adamantly against that idea. The doorman managed to get Uni into his room without being seen. He left him sitting on the edge of the bed, with a small first-aid kit in his lap.

"Please fix yourself," the doorman advised him.

Uni sat there alone, not moving, not thinking. The sun was coming up, and even though he was exhausted, sleep was not an option. Whenever he closed his eyes, he saw the black water of Manila Bay enveloping him, freezing him, dragging him down. It was an image he couldn't shake. How could he ever go to sleep again?

He took his Nokia phone from his suitcoat pocket. Was it waterproof? He pushed the power button, and the internal displays slowly came on. But they were dim, and condensation fogged the screen. Uni started to cry. He felt very alone.

He stared at the phone for a long time. These things worked both ways, didn't they? But he'd never placed a call to Palm Tree; the *judus* had always called him. Uni wasn't sure if he even knew how to contact his guardian angel. Was it just a case of pushing buttons? Or were there special ones? Uni didn't know. He wasn't good with numbers; more than three in a row tended to confuse him. And even if he knew how to enter it, he didn't have Palm Tree's number. Or did he? He went into the bathroom and, standing in front of the huge mirror, examined the underside of his tongue.

But he found no answers there either.

Day broke. On the streets below, Manila was coming back to life, having survived another night.

Uni sat in the small chair in the corner of the suite, once again wrapped in towels, wondering if every day was going to be like this now. Was this really how a superterrorist lived? There came a knock at the door. Uni froze. He couldn't imagine this being anything good, so he decided to ignore it. More knocking came; it was insistent now. Still he did not move. Pounding now, so loud, it hurt his saturated eardrums. He finally got up and answered the door.

He found the young woman from downstairs, the one who had thrown him out of this place and then brought him back in and since had treated him like royalty.

What was her name again? Something like Tiffany?

"I'm sorry to disturb you," she said.

Uni managed a smile and ushered her inside. She saw his head wound, his wet clothes, the tracks of his tears, but he waved her concerns away.

"I think I have good news for you," she managed to tell him. Uni's spirits suddenly brightened. Women were foreign to him. Especially Western women. But suddenly she seemed beautiful in his eyes, even though she'd been less than gracious when they first met.

A friend at last? he dared to think.

She reached into her purse and pulled out a huge envelope.

"Another package came for you," she said.

Uni nearly passed out. He stared at her—and she stared right back. She handed him the envelope, convinced this was a happy occasion. But feet back on Planet Earth, Uni practically pushed her out of the room. He placed the envelope on the bed and stared at it for a very long time. He was terrified of what it might contain. He scanned the two addresses. Like the first one he'd received, it had been sent to a blind postal box in Yemen first and then forwarded on to Manila. He picked it up, placed it up to his ear, and listened. He heard no ticking. He finally unwrapped it to find, to his horror, that it held two videotapes. A note stuck to one tape indicated it should be opened first. With one loud gulp, he pushed it into the VCR and hit play.

This tape began where the last one had left off. In the desert, at sunrise. Now all five soldiers were staring into the camera, masks off and grinning. Their hands were covered in blood. Uni recognized them all. They were the same five men who had burst in on the mud fight. *Am'reekan Maganeen.* The Crazy Americans. In front of them was a shallow grave. Kazeel's filleted body lay at the bottom. One soldier suddenly produced a small pig. He held it up to the camera, took out his knife, and in one sickening motion slashed its throat. The soldier threw it, still squealing, into the grave on top of Kazeel. Uni was horrified. To place swine inside a Muslim's grave was to guarantee he would never see Paradise.

The five soldiers threw dirt into the hole, but just enough to cover the corpse and suffocate the dying pig. Then they all spit on the grave and turned back to the camera.

"This is what *you've* got to look forward to, Cue Ball," the maniac named Hunn said. "You remember the last tape we sent you? We were about twenty-four hours behind you then. Well, by the time you see this, that will be down to three."

"Can you even count that high?" one of the other soldiers taunted Uni.

Hunn went on: "You must know by now that we are people who mean what we say. So if you know what's good for you, follow the instructions written on that second tape."

With that, the screen abruptly went to black.

Uni felt another tremor go through him. He became nauseous, dizzy. He could not stop shaking. He unwrapped the second tape with his teeth. It had a piece of Kazeel's mufti tied around it, along with a note, written in simple Arabic, that said: *Do not leave your room. Do not view this tape for one hour.*

Uni read those words over and over again. What did they mean? That he should remain here and let an hour go by? What else *could* they mean? He didn't know, and again, sometimes it hurt to think so deeply. He collapsed to the floor holding the tape in one hand and the night table clock in the other. He started watching the second hand sweep around the dial. It moved with excruciating slowness.

The events of the last few days began playing back before his eyes. Everything from being thrown out of the Xagat to becoming its most prominent guest, from being treated like a king with a limo to his frightening encounter out at sea. The weapons. The orphans. Kazeel being murdered.

What happened? Why the sudden curse? It dawned on Uni that he hadn't prayed very much in all that time. Maybe this was a case of simple problem, simple solution. He went down on all fours, facing the direction that he hoped pointed toward Mecca, and started praying up a storm. Not asking for forgiveness or grace or luck, or damnation of his enemies. Just praying and praying and praying . . .

He did not move off the floor until exactly one hour had gone by. Again with shaking hands he put the second tape into the VCR and pushed the play button. He'd done just as he'd been instructed. What now would this one contain?

The tape opened with the same scene as the one he'd just watched. The five soldiers still out in the desert, still staring into the camera, sun rising behind them. But now they were all laughing.

Hunn stepped forward once again. He said into the camera: "Thanks, Cue Ball—now we are only *two* hours behind you. You stupid shit."

The streets around Makak Beach were jammed with people, ankle-deep in dirty water, when Uni arrived.

It was now past noon. Neither the limo nor the limo driver was to be found when Uni left the hotel. He had the doorman hail him a three-wheel cab instead. It was a 30-minute trip to the poor part of Manila, but as they drew closer there was so much traffic and bustle, the cab could only get Uni within three blocks of the shore before he got stuck in the mud. He would have to walk from here.

Uni sloshed through the water, soaking his Guccis, and turned the corner to the main avenue to find the roadway was filled not just with citizens but with police also. Not Ramosa's secret police, these were regular Manila street cops. Uni's heart went to his throat. The center of all the police activity was the same place as his destination: the Buddha shop.

This was not good. Uni was tired, hungry, hungover, and scared. He also looked bad; he'd washed his suit in the bathtub again and noticed it was beginning to fray at the edges. But he was here for one reason only: he was following the plan. The weapons had to be moved out of Manila tonight. Uni was here to see if the Buddha man had shipped the 2,000 statues to the address Uni had given him. If so, Uni was to pay him.

The crowd around the old hut parted for Uni as he waded down the alley. Despite his state of disarray, he was still better-dressed than anyone else down here. Even the cops outside let him pass. He walked into the shop to find it crowded with more police, photographers, and TV media types—but curiously, no Buddhas. The shop was clean of them.

In the middle of the floor was the Buddha man himself—and now Uni knew the reason for all the commotion. The man was tied to a chair with tape and wire. His eyes were wide open. His nose was full of snot. He had two bullet holes in the middle of his forehead.

Uni took a step closer. Something was stuffed into the Buddha man's mouth. It was an American flag. . . .

Uni almost wet himself. *The Crazy Americans* . . . Their boasting on the tape was not a bluff. They were here, in Manila, already. . . .

He tried to hold down his rising panic. What should he do? What excuse did he have for being here? A policeman noticed him and approached. He assumed Uni was a mobster and so was best treated well. He asked Uni, "Are you a customer?" Uni held up two fingers just an inch apart. *A small one,* he was trying to say.

The policeman remained as polite as possible.

"Check the office," the cop told Uni. "There's a cash register in there. If he owed you money, help yourself. He won't be needing it anymore."

Though Uni understood few of his words, he did as the cop suggested, stealing $200 American and also lifting a manifest receipt that showed the Buddhas indeed had been shipped to the right address.

Uni sloshed back out to the avenue, the crowd once

again making way for him. He found the same taxi, still mired in the traffic jam and the mud. He flashed $50 in the driver's face. The taxi was quickly extricated.

Uni then handed him a wet index card with an address on it.

The cabbie was somehow able to interpret the runny ink.

"Ghost Town?" he said. "That will be double the fare, sir."

Much to Uni's displeasure, they took the long way across town. Whether the cabdriver was trying to jack him for an even higher fare or became legitimately lost, a 20-minute ride took nearly an hour.

Then, when they were finally two blocks from Ghost Town they ran into . . . another traffic jam. Uni couldn't believe it. Once again, cars and people were blocking the main road. The place of cemeteries was now a frenzy of activity. The cabbie leaned on the horn and the motor-trike eventually made its way through. But Uni's stomach did another flip. Up the hill of gravestones and wooden crosses he could see the woodworker's shop was surrounded by police cars.

As before, anyone who looked into the cab pegged Uni as a Mafioso and gladly gave way. He wished he had a card telling the driver to turn around, but it was already too late for that. They'd climbed to the top of the hill by now, and even the police were waving him through. No wonder this Armani guy was so popular, Uni thought.

He was all but royally escorted into the workshop. Like the Buddha store, it was overflowing with police and reporters. Inside the small office, the same place where Uni had sat not very long before, the woodworker could be seen, like the Buddha man, eyes open, fluids falling from mouth and nose, two large holes in his skull—and an American flag stuck in his mouth. The police here looked as baffled as the ones down on Makak Beach. But Uni knew who had done this.

He looked around the rest of the workshop. He saw lots of wood waste on the floor, discarded pieces that looked like mirror images of some very big caskets. This was as close as Uni could get to confirmation that the three big crates he'd ordered had been built and delivered.

The police treated him as deferentially as they had done on the beach. From their point of view, he might be a gangster who had ordered this hit, therefore had to be handled with kid gloves. However, Uni knew it was time to slip away. But where was he going to go? The Crazy Americans were so obviously close to his trail, they'd knocked off the only two people in Manila that he'd done business with, somehow knowing that they were scum of the earth, too.

So he couldn't go back to the Xagat. The Crazy Americans were probably hiding under his bed, with their hand axes, just waiting for him to return. Someone tapped him on the shoulder. He turned, not surprised to find it was a policeman. But this was not just any policeman. It was the *same* policeman he'd just spoken to back at the Buddha factory.

He was looking at Uni very queerly. "Good sir," he said in broken English. "What are *you* doing here?"

Uni was so frightened, he was at loss for a good reply.

"You were down on the beach," the policeman went

on, his eyes suddenly showing doubt of Uni's legitimacy as a mobster. "And you are now at this location. Do you know anything about these strange murders?"

Again, Uni was tongue-tied, for more than one reason. Other policemen began to close in on him. Camera lights suddenly blinded him. A microphone was pushed in his face. Outside, a siren screamed. Directly above, the sound of thunder.

His skull felt like it was going to explode.

So Uni did the only thing he could think to do.

He ran. . . .

It was pouring outside.

In just a minute's time, the fields of the dead around the woodshop had turned to mud.

Uni was in full panic. He knocked over a squad of police going out the door, slipping near the deceased man's Jaguar, unintentionally sliding across the hood of the taxi, then finding himself riding a torrent of mud and dirty water down the hill into one of Ghost Town's largest cemeteries. He began falling, slipping, sliding out of control, colliding with brittle gravestones and old wooden crosses. He could hear people screaming, ordering him to stop. He heard sizzling noises, a series of pops—even through the sheets of rain, the police were shooting at him! He smashed into the side of an earthen tomb, tumbling right over it and losing both his Guccis in the process.

He slid across one road and through the gates of yet another graveyard. He saw nothing but wooden crosses everywhere—a nightmare for a Muslim if there ever was one. He continued his flight, trying to dodge as many graves as he could but crashing into many as well.

It seemed to take forever, but he finally slid to the bottom of the hill, landing in a clump in a drainage culvert. He hit his head on impact and for a few moments was only aware of the dirty water running over him. Somehow he lifted himself up, expecting to see an army of police charging down the hill after him. But all he saw was the gravestones and crucifixes.

No one was chasing him. Perhaps no one had been at all. He lay back down in the stream and let the water flow over him again.

Even if this kills me, he thought, *at least here I'll get some sleep.*

Chapter 17

Night fell.

The rain stopped.

Manila's nightlife began heating up. Downtown certainly, but most especially in the War Zone. The neighborhood of iniquity was crowded early, strange for a weeknight. But there was a buzz all over the city, like something big was about to happen. Those who knew how to recognize such things could smell it in the air.

The Impatient Parrot was busy early, too. The bar out front was three deep at the rail. The *poon-tang* rooms upstairs had a three-hour wait. The mud fights out back were already playing to overflowing crowds.

The brothel's owner, the man named Marcos, had woken at his usual time: 4:00 P.M. He'd finished dinner by five and was walking the floor by six. He spoke quietly with a handful of underworld associates, discussing various deals that would be going down in and around his establishment this night. Business done, he was about to enjoy his first drink of the evening when he was informed that he had a long-distance phone call, which he took in his private office.

It was Palm Tree.

The conversation was stern and one-sided. Marcos did all the listening. The Stingers were being assembled, packed, and moved tonight, Palm Tree told him. But a crucial component was suddenly missing: Kazeel's *shuka* hadn't been seen since that morning. Moving the missiles was one thing; activating the *sharfa* was another. That could not be done without the dim-witted Uni, as only he held the last secret of the dearly departed Kazeel. The plan all along was to move Uni around like a chess piece, attracting attention in his mobster suit, so anyone on their trail would sniff him out first—and buy them the time they needed. But completely losing track of the *shuka* was never in the cards, and now his disappearance had the entire operation in jeopardy.

Like Ramosa, Marcos was being handsomely paid by Palm Tree's government, he was reminded. If this mission was not completed, then not only would the whole affair be an expensive, embarrassing failure, but anyone connected with it would have to be eliminated, Marcos and Ramosa included. If things did not change for the better quickly, they would both find themselves on a hit list to be carried out by the well-known and ruthless intelligence service of Palm Tree's home government.

Marcos was highly troubled hearing all this. He knew Palm Tree did not issue threats lightly. But as they were conversing, Marcos was scanning his crowded establishment on a bank of video monitoring screens next to his desk. And like a gift from God he saw someone sitting deep in the shadows of the mud fight room. Bald, with many cuts and abrasions on his head and neck, trying to stay in the background, but watching the mud fight with a certain amount of glee. It was Uni, the *shuka*.

And he appeared to be *very* drunk.

The change came for Uni after he woke up in the ditch.

Bleeding, battered, chilled again to the bone, he'd looked up the hill, back toward Ghost Town. The last rays of the sunset were creating weird patterns of shadows and light in the graveyards, especially streaming through the crucifixes. The silhouette of a huge cross fell upon him as he raised himself from the stream. It would have been too poetic for this to be a conversion, but the vision, plus his nap, definitely gave him a different perspective on things.

He no longer wanted anything to do with Stingers, or Ramosa, or yachts or minibars. He wanted to remove himself from history, from any involvement in the Second Time of Falling Sparrows, from the ways of Allah. He wanted himself rid of Kazeel's ghost. In fact, Uni was interested in doing just one thing: resuming his search for the Impatient Parrot.

And this time he found it, just after the evening's shower drenched him again, washing his clothes in the process. Clearheaded or with a clear conscience, he found the War Zone, turned this corner, then that corner, and *boom!* there it was, that psychedelic neon sign that to Uni meant "the place where girls fought in the mud." Why here? Because it was here that he'd last felt really safe— before the Crazy Americans broke in and started all this new trouble.

Getting into the brothel wet was no problem. *Everyone*

was wet in Manila tonight. He'd made his way through the crowd, using money stolen from the Buddha man to buy a glass not of champagne but of whiskey—the taste he'd acquired in the limo the night before. He found a seat in the rear of the back room and settled down to forget everything else.

He watched many mud fights, staring over the smaller people in front, laughing as they leered, drinking whiskey like it was milk. He could live here, he decided. Just drink whiskey, sit in the back, and watch girls wrestle in the mud.

That was *his* Paradise. He would have to eat, though, eventually—that might be a problem. Did this place even serve food? he wondered.

It was as if the devil himself had heard Uni, for at that moment he saw two more girls making their way across the back room. One of them was holding a huge frying pan with something smoking and crackling inside.

The girls stepped over and around the businessmen who were close to the mud pit, eyeing Uni while trying to keep the huge pan level. He was hungry—back when things were normal he used to eat as many as six meals a day. The girls indicated that they were indeed heading his way—they were moving in a dreamlike fashion, almost as if they were in slow motion. Maybe as a newcomer he was entitled to a free dinner here? Uni didn't know, but the combination of the whiskey and his long ordeal in the past 24 hours had his stomach aching for food.

The two girls finally reached him. They were even prettier than the two rolling around in the mud—and that was a milestone for Uni, brought on, he was sure, by the alcohol, because he'd never graded women before in his life, simply because they'd never interested him. But these two girls were raven-haired beauties, wearing short white dresses and smiles a mile wide, almost like angels. And the frying pan was not only hot; it was absolutely sizzling. He sat up straight, hoping this might be lamb curry and cabbage, his favorite dish. The two girls never stopped smiling.

Uni drunkenly pointed to himself with both thumbs, as if to ask: "For me?"

Both girls nodded. "It sure is," one replied. "Big-time, Joe."

With that, she lifted the large red-hot skillet and with a form rivaling a MLB player gave it a mighty swing and hit Uni square in the face.

Airplanes . . .

Buzzing around inside Uni's head, like a swarm of bees. They were so noisy. And painful. And they were *stinging him all over*. . . .

He woke with a scream only he could hear. His mouth was full of mucus; blood was dripping from his ears. He tried to open his eyes, but the lids would barely move. Everything from his toes to his collarbone felt broken. But most especially, his head was immersed in pain. His face, shattered. . . .

He was lying nose-down on a very oily floor. Through those bleary eyes he could see tiny pools of blood, *his* blood, mixing with a rainbow of gasoline and hydraulic fluid. His ears never stopping buzzing—but these weren't bees in his head. These were the sounds of *real* airplanes, taking off nearby.

Where am I? he thought. Certainly not the back room of the Impatient Parrot. There was no mud.

No . . . it was . . . *Manila Airport*. The two words just popped into his head. The noise. The smell. He recognized them.

He managed to open his eyes just a little more. His vision was still blurry—but considering all the whiskey he'd consumed, and the mighty whack to his head from the frying pan, he was lucky he could see at all.

He was in an aircraft hangar, big, old, and dreary. Four ceiling-mounted halogen lamps provided the only illumination. Two huge letters that meant nothing to Uni adorned one wall: *UN*. The place reeked of cigarette smoke and spilled coffee.

Twenty feet from where he lay Uni saw three packing crates. He knew right away they were the work of the graveyard carpenter. They looked like three monstrous caskets. The stack of Stinger missile tubes was just behind the crates; the launchers were piled next to them. Two huge cardboard boxes containing the red and yellow Buddhas were close by, too, along with an enormous plastic bag filled with foam packing peanuts, four big rolls of bubble wrap, and a spool of duct tape the size of a truck tire.

He heard footsteps now. Two boots appeared next to his bloody nose. Uni moved his head a little and saw Marcos, the brothel owner, standing over him.

He'd been waiting for Uni to wake up. Now Marcos snapped his fingers and two armed Filipino men arrived. They were wearing blue jumpsuits with those two letters—*UN*—on the sleeves. They were among the thirteen gunmen in the hangar dressed this way. These two roughly lifted Uni to his feet, dragged him across the floor, and threw him against the far wall, hurling an overflowing trash barrel at him for good measure.

Facedown again, Uni found himself lying in a pile of smelly rags and discarded Styrofoam coffee cups. He managed to lift his fingers to his face and wipe the crap from his eyes. The next thing he saw was the razor blade.

Marcos was leaning over him, holding an old-fashioned straight razor just an inch from his throat.

"Why did you think you could run away from us, my friend?" he asked the *shuka* cruelly. "I thought we were all in this together?"

Uni could barely hear his words. But the message the razor was sending was very clear.

"I'll make it easy on you," Marcos went on. "We only want one thing—the *sharfa*. Tell it to me now and I will kill you quickly. If not, I'll cut your throat out, one piece at a time. I assure you, that is a very painful way to go."

To prove his point, Marcos slid the blade across the soft skin just below Uni's right ear and began to slice into it slowly. Uni was horrified—and very confused. He thought the brothel owner was his friend.

Another guy in a blue UN jumpsuit suddenly appeared. He was holding a Nokia cell phone.

"It's him," was all the man said to Marcos.

Even Uni knew what that meant. Palm Tree was on the phone. Marcos withdrew his blade and grabbed the cell. Uni gasped for breath as even more blood flowed down his neck

What followed was an intense conversation between Marcos and Palm Tree on how the weapons were to be packed and shipped. Marcos did all the talking at first. He explained to Palm Tree that he had followed his previous instructions to the letter. The crates had been clearly marked 1, 2, and 3 on their inside panels. The missiles and launchers were about to be packed in all three, using layers of Buddhas to surround them. This way, the crates could pass, at least by a cursory inspection, as nothing more than a shipment of chintzy religious statues heading for the United States.

But then Palm Tree started talking, and clearly there had been a change in plans. Marcos's men were now to pack all the Buddhas into Crate 1, and all of the weapons into Crate 2. Crate 3 would be left empty. Furthermore, Crates 1 and 2 would be the only ones shipped. Crate 3 was to be dumped on a beach nearby.

Uni could tell Marcos was hearing all this for the first time. The Filipino hoodlum actually questioned Palm Tree as to why they went through all the trouble of getting the 2,000 Buddhas if they weren't going to be used as camouflage for the weapons during shipment. "I thought the *whole idea* was to move the weapons disguised as a load of statues," Uni heard Marcos say. It was impossible to hear Palm Tree's reply, but it was short, curt, and Marcos got the point right away. Things had changed.

Palm Tree hung up and Marcos began shouting out the new orders. Just as mystified as their boss, the men in the blue UN jumpsuits got to work nevertheless. A flurry of activity ensued as the Buddhas were taken from their cardboard boxes and put into one crate, with the missiles and launchers put into another. The bubble wrap was unfurled, the bag of packing peanuts cut open. The sound of duct tape being torn and applied fill the air. The entire packing operation took less than five minutes.

Then Marcos turned back to Uni. Slamming him against the wall once more, Marcos began screaming at the *shuka,* telling him how stupid he was, how he'd been manipulated, how everyone from Palm Tree to Kazeel had used him as a dupe. Marcos even held the phone to Uni's ear and let him hear a saved message from Palm Tree ordering Marcos to eliminate Uni whether he came across with the *sharfa* or not. Either way, the *shuka* had to go.

Uni's eyes went wide. His jaw dropped open. Marcos saw this and started to laugh. But Uni was not reacting to what he'd just heard the *judus* say. The reason for his sudden amazement was that he saw something apparently no one else in the hangar could see. Straight up, past the suspended ceiling, on the dirty skylight directly above his head, a heavily armed masked man was looking right down at him.

The man had his finger to his lips, telling Uni, *Don't make a sound.*

Uni's mind began to move—albeit slowly. *What should he do?* Palm Tree had all but ordered him killed. The sadistic Marcos had his razor blade back out to do the job. Yet Uni was more fearful of the ghost looking down at him than what his former friends had in store for him.

Several things happened in the next two seconds. Marcos began to draw the blade across Uni's throat again. But at the precise moment the razor touched the *shuka's* skin, there was a mighty *crash!* above them. It startled Marcos so, he dropped the straight razor, grazing Uni's ear and opening yet another cut. Suddenly four heavily armed people were rappelling from the ceiling, firing their guns wildly. All four were wearing masks and, incredibly, had American flags tied around their necks as capes.

The hangar was instantly ablaze in gunfire. More figures crashed through the skylight. Some were dressed like the first four—in black combat suits. But others were wearing sailors' uniforms, and still others were in very tattered Hawaiian shirts. All of them were firing M16s. The zing and sizzle of bullets became deafening. The electrical system was hit and all the lights went out. But the sudden darkness was quickly relit by the illuminating rounds of tracer fire. People were screaming, grunting, crying out in pain. There were 15 people inside the warehouse, including Uni and Marcos. Within 10 seconds, 13 of them were dead, riddled with bullets by the crazy men dropping from the night sky.

Uni was petrified, absolutely frozen with fear. So was Marcos, who was now standing straight up, his hands raised over his head, pleading with the masked soldiers not to kill him. One of the soldiers came out of the dark, pushed Marcos aside, and grabbed Uni around his throat. He slammed the *shuka* up against the wall again and jammed a small American flag in his mouth. Then he took off his mask.

It was Dave Hunn.

He growled at Uni: "Hey, Mr. Clean . . . *remember me?*"

Ozzi had lost his helmet on the way down into the hangar. His wrist felt broken on landing and the sudden descent had turned his stomach inside out.

He was the 5-Guy, as in the fifth guy down the rope. Hunn, Curry, Puglisi, and McMahon had been the Crashers. Ozzi and Bingo and two Spooks were the second team down. After that, Bingo's guys just started jumping into the place. Though Ozzi had been with the rogue American team for what seemed like forever now, he was still trying to get the hang of this superhero stuff. He knew losing one's helmet during a crash-and-smash was not considered good form.

It had all been a whirl for him these past few days. First the trip from Manila to the mysterious *Ocean Voyager,* by way of a stolen high-speed drug-running junk. Then the long flight to Pakistan (stealing aviation fuel along the way), getting on the trail of the real Dragos (an adventure in itself), icing them, fooling Kazeel with fake ambushes and bombing attacks until they knew every step he'd made, and then icing *him.* Bahzi, the Paki intelligence men, and Kazeel's seven dwarves came next, all leading to the team finally picking up the *shuka*'s scent. The bright yellow Sing One TV chopper nearly crashed on its way back to *Ocean Voyager.* (They'd used too much fuel diverting to a suburb of Rangoon to mail the videotapes to the *shuka.*) The spy ship set sail just before the Vietnamese government finally got wise that it had been hiding in their waters for weeks. It met the copter at sea.

From there, the American team had been able to keep track of the *shuka* the same way they'd first got on Kazeel's tail—because he'd stupidly kept using his cell phone. By remotely accessing his DSA computer back in Washington, Ozzi had tapped into the NSA's top-secret ECHELON eavesdropping system and marked Uni's phone for movement updates once every hour or so. All they had to do after that was follow the electronic footprints. At the same time, they'd dissected the phone used by Kazeel, and from this became privy to at least the basics of the supermook's Big Plan. They knew Kazeel had somehow come upon the Stinger launchers and had paid Bahzi handsomely for the accompanying missiles. They knew the weapons were to be assembled somewhere in the Philippines and then shipped to the United States. They also knew once the missiles were en route, the *shuka,* having survived his boyfriend Kazeel, was supposed to activate the so-called *sharfa,* signaling the Al Qaeda sleeper cells inside the United States to spring into action. Just about the only piece of information the team hadn't uncovered yet was the *sharfa* itself. Kazeel died because they couldn't beat it out of him. It was only after they busted into Kazeel's phone did they discover the *shuka* held the secret key too. That's why they had to get back to the 'Peens *chop-chop*—and that's why they were here, crashing through the ceiling.

The hangar was nearly pitch-black by the time Ozzi came flying in. He could see only gun flashes during his short ride down the Zorro rope. He'd hit the floor hard, hurting his wrist and separating himself from his helmet, which also contained his night-vision goggles. While reaching around for his flashlight, he unwittingly squeezed the trigger on his M16, unleashing a stream of tracers that further lit up the hangar with an intense blinding flash.

The glow from his bullets helped him spot the waylaid helmet though. He dived for it, shoving it back over his head as if it were an oxygen mask and he needed the air. He cranked the night goggles to full power and everything slowly coalesced into the reassuring green underworld of night vision.

Of course, by that time, the battle was over.

. . .

Someone got the lights back on and Ozzi thought he'd died and gone to special ops heaven. Everything they'd worked for in the last few hectic days was now before them: the Stingers, the launchers, the *shuka,* and a key bad guy who was already trying to plea bargain with Bingham and Curry. The only thing missing was a big bow to wrap it all up.

Ozzi fell to the seat of his pants, burning his hands on the muzzle of his still-hot M16. He was both exhausted and exuberant. Curry came up to him and delivered a low five so powerful, it almost broke Ozzi's other wrist. There was much hooting and hollering among the Americans as they checked the bodies of the dead. None of the gunmen had ID or any kind of anything that might tell them who they were or who was paying them. No matter. The Americans were already using their switchblades to cut the letters *UN* out of the girly-blue uniforms. Every battle gives birth to trophies. This one was no different.

Both Puglisi and McMahon slid down next to Ozzi now and delivered simultaneous bear hugs to him, so glad were they that their long ordeal was finally over. He just laughed and pushed them away. They're endured so much over the past week and a half: brutal heat, biting cold, long rides over water, and low-altitude dashes through perilous skies. Slippery mountain roads, raging Afghan blizzards, narrow escapes, gunfights, fistfights, bombings, stabbings—all on little food, no sleep, and lots of stress. Yet, in the end, they'd won somehow. They'd stopped Kazeel for good and had captured his weapons cache intact. Hundreds if not thousands of American lives had been saved. And Ozzi had been a small part of it.

All kinds of images began flashing through his head now. The triumphant trip home. A good meal. A few drinks. Maybe meet some girls . . . *Maybe they'll give me a bigger office,* he thought. *With a TV this time.*

And then, strangely, a name popped into his head: *Yogi Berra.*

Why?

An instant later came a great crash—another one. Suddenly armed men were pouring through just about every orifice in the hangar. Ozzi's first thought was: *Hey, it's the 82nd Airborne!*

But he couldn't have been more wrong. It was Ramosa's secret police instead. Lots of them.

And Yogi Berra?

Of course . . . *déjà vu* all over again.

But this wasn't an exact re-creation of the bust-up in the Impatient Parrot the week before. This time there was a gunfight. A big one.

The lights went out in the hangar a second time—a moment later everyone in the room who had a weapon opened up. The pyrotechnics when the American team first crashed in on Marcos were a sparkler compared to these fireworks. Stretched out flat on the floor now, Ozzi started firing wildly in the direction of the doors the secret police were streaming through. They all did. Ozzi was astonished that he could actually see the armed men, never mind hit some of them. That's when he realized this time he was looking through his night goggles.

It got very weird, very quickly, from there. The big

hangar was again awash in fluorescent gunfire, a single round of which could obliterate a heart or explode a skull. In the sudden murk of gunsmoke Ozzi could only see faces—just faces amid the bullet streaks—eyes wild, heading right for him, firing their weapons in his direction.

Then, just a few seconds into this thing, someone grabbed hold of Ozzi's feet and started pulling him backward. He was dragged across the floor for 20 feet or more. He never stopped firing, though—he couldn't. Not with a tidal wave of bad guys who wanted to kill him just a few meters away. His finger was melded to his trigger.

It was Puglisi who was pulling him along the oily floor. As soon as the first shot was fired, the American team had assembled into a defensive formation known as "Zulu 2." Everyone but Ozzi, that is. Puglisi had yanked him back into the fold. Finally Ozzi took a half-second to look around him. The team was set up three deep. Some were lying on the floor next to him; some were on bent knee; the rest were standing up. Their weapons raised, they formed three ranks of continuous fire. It was a brilliant tactic, quick and ballsy, but it reminded Ozzi too much of Custer's Last Stand.

The attackers were advancing with fanatical drive. The Americans were dropping them like flies, but they kept on coming anyway. The bad guys didn't have night goggles, and for the first 30 seconds that made all the difference in the world. The Americans were mowing them down, like a grisly shooting gallery.

The fusillade coming from the three-deep formation *was* frightening—but it was also costly in ammunition, which is why the battle lasted barely a minute. The Americans had crashed the place with only enough ammo to take the hangar—not fight a small war. The team ran out of bullets all at once. Suddenly the firing stopped. The floor was littered with dead mooks and empty shell casings. Incredibly, no one on the American side had been killed or even wounded.

But surely, they were dead ducks now.

A surreal moment passed. More than half of Ramosa's guys had been popped. But those that had survived quickly disarmed the Americans. Ramosa appeared from nowhere and made sure every prisoner was aggressively frisked.

When it came to Hunn's turn, he just looked at Ramosa and said: "How?"

The police captain displayed his sinister 24K grin.

"Same way as last time," he said. "We've had this place surrounded for hours, just waiting for you." Ramosa was speaking in a surprisingly sophisticated manner.

"You would have known that had you chosen to come in through the front door this time," he went on, looking up at the smashed skylights overhead. "And not by the roof. I'm afraid you've destroyed a lot of UN property, my friends. Too bad you won't be around the pay the bill."

Hunn tried to spit at him. "What do you think—you're in a James Bond movie?"

Ramosa was clearly embarrassed. He knew his last comment had been a little too melodramatic.

"No matter," he snapped right back again. "One way or the other, you're all about to die."

He directed his men to line up the Americans in a row. Each was made to kneel, facing the wall, hands behind his head. The classic position for a gangland execution. . . .

Ozzi was on the end of this sad line. *I'll be either the first to go or the last,* he thought grimly, knees starting to shake. Ramosa handed his pistol and extra ammunition to Marcos; the Filipino thug, saved in the nick of time, was practically drooling with anticipation now. There were 16 American team members in all, including the sailors and the Spooks. Marcos took Ramosa's pistol but said to him: "I will use my razor on some of them, too. If you don't mind?"

Ramosa wasn't listening, though. He was bent over the *shuka* who'd collapsed back into a heap against the wall. Marcos joined him.

Ramosa said: "I'm here not so much to save your ass as I am to get the *sharfa*. It might very well be the most valuable thing in the world right now."

Marcos lifted Uni's bloody chin. He was a distant cousin of the people who used to run the Philippines. As such, he'd inherited their penchant for violence and violation.

"But how do we get it, my friend?" Marcos asked Ramosa. "This one's too stupid to bleed it out of him. I was about to try—and so would have they, if you hadn't arrived."

Ramosa studied the bloody pulp of Uni's face. The *shuka* appeared to be clinging to life by the barest of threads, his eyes teary with confusion, horror.

"Yes, it seems strange that Kazeel would entrust something so important to such an imbecile," Ramosa said. "But the sheikh wasn't stupid. He must have imparted the *sharfa* to him in such a way that this clown could not take it with him to the grave. That means something about him should give us a clue to its whereabouts. But what could it be?"

Suddenly it was as if a lightbulb went off over Marcos's head. He turned to Ramosa.

"Have you ever heard this dimwit speak?" Marcos asked him. "Beyond a few grunts, I mean?"

Ramosa had to think a moment. "No," he answered. "I don't think I have. Not really. Has anyone?"

Marcos smiled demonically. His razor was back in Uni's face in a flash. He forced the *shuka's* mouth open and pulled out his tongue.

"Well, look at this!" Marcos cried.

He turned Uni's tongue upside down to reveal that a set of tiny numbers, 14 in all, had been tattooed there. Ramosa bent down and studied them. They seemed distorted and unreadable.

"But they are backward," he said. "Why?"

Marcos thought another moment. Then, another lightbulb.

"So this idiot can see them in a mirror," he declared. To make his point, he held his very shiny razor blade against Uni's tongue. Sure enough, only in its reflection did the numbers make sense.

"Yes, I see it now," Ramosa said. "It's a phone number. Country code, area code, and the rest. *That's* the *sharfa*. Call this number and let it ring—no one will ever pick it up probably. They won't have to. The sleepers will know to go into action simply upon hearing it."

Marcos laughed like a girl. "And the sheikh must have told this moron to keep his mouth shut—and he has. Until now."

Ramosa looked at the numbers again and winced.

"But the pain of putting them there must have been incredible."

"Nothing like he is about to feel," Marcos replied. In one swift motion, he lifted his razor and lopped off the end of Uni's tongue, the part containing the numbers. Uni howled. The spurt of blood was sickening. But Marcos simply smiled.

"Now at last, we have the unholy grail," he said to Ramosa, dropping Uni back to the floor. "And the idiot is an idiot once more."

There came a commotion at the hangar's main door. One of Ramosa's men peeked outside, then gave a hand signal. Ramosa nodded in reply. The doors opened, and a bizarre-looking airplane taxied its way into the hangar, followed by two nondescript freight trucks.

The noise inside was suddenly overpowering. Ramosa and Marcos had a shouted conversation, most of which only they could hear. It had to do with the crates, what was supposed to be in which crate, and where each crate was supposed to go after being repacked.

"It's another switch in plans!" some of the Americans heard Ramosa yell over the plane's whining engine.

"Are you sure?" Marcos was heard shouting back. *"Another* switch?"

"Absolutely!" Ramosa yelled in reply. "I got it straight from Palm Tree. . . ."

Now it was Ramosa's small army of men who went into action, repacking the crates according to the latest orders. The crates themselves were actually moved around the hangar floor to the extent that it would have been just about impossible for a casual observer to know which was crate 1, 2, or 3. Finally, though, Ramosa ordered them sealed and loaded onto their predetermined modes of transport.

This done, Ramosa turned to Marcos and started yelling at him again, still straining to be heard over the racket.

"After you take care of them," some heard Ramosa tell Marcos, indicating the captured Americans, "meet me at the you-know-where."

With that, Ramosa took the piece of tongue, put it in his pocket, and left.

Ozzi was surprised. The bubble of fear from just minutes before had dissipated. He wasn't scared anymore, just the opposite in fact.

"I'm dying for my country," he kept whispering over and over. "I'm dying . . . for my country."

A strange peace had come over the rest of the team, too, even though a grisly death was just seconds away. Sure the tables had suddenly turned on them. But they were still Patriots all, still Ozzi's heroes. He'd been privileged to know them. And *that's* why he was so suddenly calm.

Even still, Ozzi was doing his job, trying to remember everything he had heard. As he was one of the closest to the crates, he'd kept track of the packing process as best he could, taking mental notes as it proceeded at a fast and furious pace. Others along the line of captured Americans were doing the same thing. Even above the racket of the airplane and the trucks' engines, they could hear the sound of more packing peanuts being dumped, more bubble wrap being snapped, more duct tape being torn and applied. They each caught fleeting glimpses of the crates being loaded, being sealed, and finally put on their means of transport. But still, because of all the movement and confusion, Ozzi and the others could not quite tell which crate held what and which crate was going where.

In any case, the two vehicles and the airplane soon departed. One last glance over Ozzi's shoulder confirmed only a few strands of duct tape and some packing peanuts remained.

He turned his head slightly to the right now and could see Marcos out of the corner of his eye. The hoodlum had a huge .357 Magnum in hand and was fiddling with the safety button. He began walking down the line of prisoners, pressing the gun barrel against the neck of each American, sometimes yelling, "Boom!" to frighten one into thinking he would be the first to die.

It didn't work. The Americans weren't scared. In fact, Curry was laughing at him, *daring* Marcos to shoot him first. Puglisi and McMahon began taunting him as well. Soon most of the others were, too. Hunn alone stayed in his private place. He'd come up with another American flag and was quietly holding it in his hands as someone might hold a rosary.

Ramosa had left 10 men behind to cover Marcos while he performed the executions. They were gathered around the prisoners now, like lions waiting for the kill. Marcos went back down the line, muttering angrily, "I decide who will go first!" This as the Americans continued to mock him. Strangely, though, he ended not on one of the raiders but on Uni, the *shuka*. He'd been made to kneel up against the wall with the rest of them.

"I shall do the world a favor, I think," Marcos declared.

"Getting rid of a stupid freak first makes us all a little bit better, don't you think?"

Ramosa's men laughed on cue. "Do him good!" one of them called out.

"And you *are* a fucking imbecile, you know," Marcos hissed at the eunuch in broken English. "What ever gave you the idea that *you* would wind up making the headlines with this thing? That *you* of all people would come out on top? I guess idiots have no choice but to dream idiots' dreams."

Marcos then took a step back. Ozzi tensed himself for the gunshot. He could see everything now: Uni, Marcos, the ravenous secret police—it was all happening just a few feet away from him. This was going to be nasty, he thought. But he could not turn away.

Marcos smiled at the cops around him, pointed the gun at the back of Uni's shiny bald head . . . and pulled the trigger.

The sound of a gunshot exploded throughout the hangar. Ozzi saw the fire and smoke spew from Marcos's weapon. And it really did seem like the round hit Uni's skull. But whether the gun misfired or it was divine intervention or because Uni's head really *was* made of concrete, incredibly, the bullet ricocheted backward . . . and hit Marcos right between the eyes.

Silence . . . cold and eerie. Marcos stood there for the longest time, absolute bewilderment on his face. He even reached up and felt the hole in his skull. Hunn was the closest American to him. Marcos turned to him and said one word: "How?"

Hunn was so shocked by what he'd just seen, he couldn't speak. He could only shrug.

Marcos went over in a heap a second later.

Ramosa's men panicked. This was a little too freaky for them. Half began to run; the other half knew it would be wise to finish off the Americans first before they fled— Captain Ramosa did not forgive unfulfilled orders lightly.

But just as these men raised their weapons to fire, one of them was shot through the left eye. He, too, went over with a *thump!* His comrades were aghast. *Now* what was happening? Did this man somehow shoot himself, too? But then the guy beside him got a bullet through the throat and another to the forehead. The cop beside *him* instinctively ducked, but not before he caught a round right between the eyes.

All of the policemen panicked now. This was strange on top of strange, their comrades being shot down by ghosts. But the American prisoners knew what was going on. Ramosa's evil policemen were getting tap-shot.

And that could only mean one thing. . . .

The top of the hangar disappeared a moment later. Suddenly it was just gone, in a blinding explosion, cheap aluminum reduced to metallic cinders. A second after that, a huge airplane roared over the top of the building. Huge . . . *and* noisy. With a fuselage that looked like the bottom of a boat.

A second after that, six men in barely opened parachutes dropped down through the gigantic hole in the roof, guns blazing. They all hit the floor at the same time.

"We're Americans!" one of them screamed. *"Team Ninety-Nine—U.S. Navy. Get down on the floor . . . now!"*

Ozzi was stunned. They all were.

Team Ninety-Nine? he thought. *The SEAL assassins? What the fuck were they doing here?*

The American prisoners hit the deck as told and the hangar saw its third gunfight in less than 10 minutes. This one was as one-sided as the last one, though. Ramosa's men weren't combat troops; they were barely cops. They were no match for the SEALs.

As soon as the first six intruders hit the floor, another handful of armed men descended through the roof. These guys weren't SEALs. Just the opposite, they were dressed like they'd just walked out of a J. Crew catalog. Following them were more huge soldiers—as big as Hunn and his guys—wearing the same jet-black combat suits with the infamous 9/11 patch. They came down on ropes, leaving no doubt they were the ethereal tap-shooters.

The invaders dispersed expertly throughout the warehouse, hunting down and brutally eliminating the last of Ramosa's men. It took less than a minute. Then the shooting died down again.

Meanwhile the SEALs came along the row of the suddenly liberated Americans and by procedure frisked each one. By the time they got to Hunn, the SEALs were gloating mightily.

"Got in a bit of a jam, Delta?" one SEAL asked Hunn sarcastically. "Glad we could be of service."

Hunn just moaned. Happy to be alive, he knew the special ops community would never let him forget the day that SEALs had to rescue Delta.

Ozzi was equally relieved but felt even more embarrassed than Hunn. The Gitmo team were his heroes, yet he'd led them into not one but *two* very dangerous situations, this and the screw-up in the mud room. He was not one of them; just the opposite in fact. But he had one more surprise coming. One last guy came through the roof and landed right in front of him. He took off his helmet and mask and just stood there, smiling.

Ozzi couldn't believe it. It was his boss, Major Fox.

"Sir? What are *you* doing here?" he cried.

"Let me ask you the same thing," Fox replied. "I thought I left you back at the office."

Ozzi fell to the seat of his pants—again. "It's a long story," he muttered. "You must know some of it already. But how did you find me?"

Fox reached inside the young officer's breast pocket and took out his cell phone. He held it up to his eyes. "Don't you *ever* turn this thing off?" Fox asked him.

Ozzi slapped himself upside the head. He couldn't believe it. He'd committed the same stupid mistake the *shuka* had! In this Spook-versus-mook business, only an idiot left his cell phone on these days, that is, if he used the same one more than once. Powered-up cells were how the United States tracked terrorists—after all, that's how the Gitmo team had tracked first Kazeel and then the eunuch. Only a real amateur would have done this. But at least this time, Ozzie's mistake turned out to be a good thing.

Finally the two halves of the rogue American team came together in the center of the hangar. It was the first time the original team members had seen one another since the events at Hormuz. Inside 60 seconds they'd exchanged stories on exactly how they all came to be here. They rejoiced at the news of Kazeel's demise. The Kai team highly commended the Gitmo Four (or Five) for their cunning, initiative—and just plain balls in whacking the superterrorist. The Kais adventure had been of a different sort but just as down and dirty. Though mysteriously cut off from Washington after finding the B-2 spy bomber—no one ever did return Fox's phone calls—they felt they had no other choice but to continue the search for the people responsible for what happened on Fuggu Island. They did this by scouring every island, atoll, lagoon, shoal, and sandbar from the Bangtang Channel down to Manila Bay. They killed many Aboo terrorists along the way, as these places were infested with them. But they uncovered nothing connected to the events which occurred over the northern Philippines that night.

But how then did they get on Ozzi's phone trail or even know enough to start looking for him? the Gitmos asked the Kai team. What's more, how did they know about the Stingers, and the hangar and Ramosa and the *sharfa?* Did they have help—as in "inside help"? Just by body language alone, the Kai team seemed to indicate this was the case, and that it went beyond simply tapping into the NSA's ECHELON system, as the Gitmo group had done. But then the Kais warily eyed the SEALs, the SDS guys, even the DSA officers, anyone not part of the original 9/11 group and buttoned up. *"We'll tell you later,"* was all they said.

The reunion celebration was brief; everyone knew they had to get moving. It was imperative they get out of the hangar before someone else crashed in on *them*—that seemed to be the pattern these days. Plus the Stingers were gone, on their way to the United States, and the puke Ramosa had the *sharfa*. They had to try and catch up to them.

But how were the weapons being moved? That was the big question. The combined Gitmo/Spook/Navy crash team told the Kais everything they could recall hearing during the final packing and shipping process. Again, not just Ozzi had been paying attention; others had, too. But to everyone's dismay, these reports turned out to have a severe case of *rashamons*—many different versions of the same story. Some of the Americans were convinced they saw Buddhas being repacked around the missiles. Others said the bad guys had discarded the Buddhas and just packed the weapons cold. Some insisted the missiles and the Buddhas were put in a crate that went on one of the trucks. Others swore the Buddhas only went on the truck and the weapons crate was put onto the weird-looking airplane. Just about the only thing everyone agreed on was that one of the crates had been carried away empty, to be dumped on a beach nearby. But if that was the case, then why have three crates in the first place? Having an empty one didn't make sense.

"Thirty-six missiles, thirty-six launchers, two thousand Buddhas, and three crates," Fox moaned. "Who knows what it all means?"

"None of us do," Curry replied. "Because none of us could see the whole thing."

"Wait a minute," Ozzi said suddenly. "*He* knows. . . ."

He was pointing at Uni.

Ryder needed a cigarette. Actually, he needed a carton of them. Along with a couple bottles of Jack Daniel's, a pool, some sunblock, and a slew of babes.

He *was* getting too old for this. Schlepping all over Fuggu Island was one thing. But he'd trooped across so many other islands in the past week, he'd lost count. All of them darker, scarier, and with more prehistoric animals than Kong Island. Until they got the lead on the young DSA officer's cell phone, it had been a long, dirty, bloody trip. He was just happy that his feet were back on concrete again—and not stuck in the jungle muck.

But now what? They'd saved their colleagues—but the Stingers had slipped away and were heading for States, and the only guy who knew how was a certified blockhead.

But if there was one thing all of the American team members were good at, it was extricating information from people who would rather keep their mouths shut. And they were all convinced that the *shuka* knew something. The trouble was the *shuka* looked like he'd already had the shit kicked out of him—twice. He was battered and bleeding in many places; half his tongue had been cut out. His clothes were soiled and covered with many unidentifiable substances. Though he was somehow able to pull himself up to his knees, he didn't seem to be in any shape to be "persuaded" about anything.

That's why they were all so surprised when the *shuka* indicated he wanted to make a deal.

It took Uni a while to make this understandable to the Americans, for he was now a simpleton without a tongue. He first tried waving a rag as a white flag. Then he kissed Hunn's American flag, the same one the Delta soldier had stuffed into his mouth just minutes before. Only when he pantomimed pledging allegiance to it did he get his point across. Yes, he wanted to "talk."

He had a simple proposition for them. *I'll tell you anything you want to know,* he indicated. *Just don't kill me.* It was only because Uni looked half-dead already that the Americans agreed.

But then began 10 long minutes of excruciating confusion. The translation gap was not just wide; it was a chasm. No one could really understand what the hell the tongue-less, beaten Uni was trying to tell them. He was gesturing weakly, trying to use crude sign language to get his point across. He even wrote down some things in fractured, unreadable Arabic. But it was sheer torture trying to follow along.

The Americans managed to get some of it. Uni's two trips to Manila. Palm Tree. Ramosa. Marcos. The frightening ride in the yacht. The weapons themselves and the three different sets of orders on how to pack them. Of course, half the rogue team knew some of this already. But it was a road they all had to take, for the *shuka* didn't know any other way to tell a story except from the beginning, and whenever he felt stymied in his rendition, he went right back to square one and started all over again.

Finally, though, he approached some sort of climax: Why were three crates built instead of just two? they asked him. Or even just one? Had they and the Buddhas been part of a diversion all along?

Uni seemed to confirm this deflating possibility. The Gitmo contingent hadn't been subtle in announcing their impending arrival in Manila, nor had they laid low once their boots were on the ground. If Palm Tree *knew* the Crazy Americans were coming all along, just as Uni, Ramosa, *et al.*, had, that meant time was of the essence. While the American team was off killing the Buddha man and the coffin maker, the bad guys were sewing up loose ends. By the time the Americans finally zeroed in on Uni, the bad guys had bought just enough time to send the missiles on their way, making the narrowest of escapes.

This news didn't sit well with the Americans; shooting first and asking questions later was almost an occupational hazard of the 9/11 team, most especially Hunn's men. They'd blown opportunities in the past simply by being too trigger-happy while moving about as gracefully as a herd of elephants. It had happened right before Hormuz and now it had apparently happened again.

Finally Curry spoke up: "OK—so we were duped. Misdirected, outright fooled, or whatever. And we still don't know what went where or how. But why in God's name were they pulling all those switcheroos with the crates?"

They besieged Uni to spill this one last piece of information—and it was something that he knew, something he *wanted* to tell them. But there was just no way he could communicate it to them. Words failed him, as always, and he could not speak with his hands to any satisfaction or write it out in any legible way.

Desperate, as he was sure the Crazy Americans would indeed kill him if he didn't please them, he scrambled around the floor gathering up the remnants from the overturned trash can. Locating three Styrofoam coffee cups, he set them upside down on the dirty floor. Then he painfully rifled through his pockets, finally coming out with an American half dollar—a favorite in the Impatient Parrot—and two Pepsi bottle caps he'd saved from his days at the Xagat.

As the Americans watched, totally mystified, Uni put the coin underneath one cup and the bottle caps underneath the other two—then began moving the cups around crazily. After a few seconds he stopped and lifted one cup to reveal a bottle cap. He moved the cups again, then stopped again, lifting a cup to reveal another bottle cap. He did all this a third time—but this time he lifted the third cup to reveal the coin.

Gathered tightly around him, the Americans were convinced he'd gone completely mad.

But then Ryder got it.

"It's a shell game," he said, out of the blue. "That's what he's trying to tell us."

The *shuka* jumped back to his feet and staggered toward Ryder, arms outstretched as if to kiss him. Two dozen raised weapons prevented such a thing. But the meaning now was clear for all to see.

"A freaking shell game?" Puglisi cried. "*That's* what they're playing here?"

"Changing the rules right up to the last minute?" Bingo said. "Not that bad an idea, especially if you think people are looking in on you—or hot on your trail. They knew we were just hours, then minutes behind them. They knew if they kept switching the crates around, the chances were good we'd pick the wrong one to chase once we—or someone else—finally got this close to them."

"The bastards," Curry swore. He was a native New Yorker. He'd seen hustlers on 42nd Street play shell games hundreds of times while growing up. They were the ultimate suckers' bet.

"So how will we ever figure out which shell is the prize, then?" Hunn asked. "Which crate has the weapons? Which ones have the duds?"

They went over the many different versions of the packing episode again, trying to track the logic. If the crucial crate was being shipped by air, were the two trucks on hand then just to carry the "empty" shells? Or, if the weapons crate was being sent by sea and one of the trucks was just a way to get it to a ship, was the airplane just another diversion?

Ryder tried to noodle it out. "If Curly here is right and it's a shell game, then there has to be a diversion of some kind," he said. "So, maybe they put the weapons crate on the airplane and put a dud crate on one truck to be driven to a ship. Then the third crate was put on the second truck, to be dumped on the beach."

"Or, they could have put two crates on the airplane," Curry said. "One a fake, one that was real. Then they used one truck to dump the bogus crate on the beach. And the second truck was a backup."

"Or maybe the airplane is the diversion," Bingham offered. "They put the weapons crate on a slow boat, while making it seem the real delivery is going airborne."

"Well, *however* they did it," Fox said, with no little frustration, "the question remains, how in hell are we ever going to track them from here?"

Ozzi stepped up again. He was on fire now, angry that the bad guys were winning again.

"How about we go to the airport manager here and find out if any unusual flights took off in the past twenty minutes," he said. "He must know *something* weird has been going on. And if he doesn't want to cooperate, we beat his ass until he does. Same thing goes for the Manila harbormaster. Let's haul his ass out of bed and see if any suspicious ships were due to leave in the same time frame. They surely ain't driving the missiles to the states. So air and sea are the only ways to go."

Everyone was paying attention to him now. "Are you

saying what I think you're saying, Lieutenant?" Fox asked.

Ozzi was checking the clip in his M16 magazine.

"Yes, sir, I am," he replied. "It means we've got to split up. Again."

Chapter 18

It was an odd plane with an odd name.

The F-10 "Babuska" was a German-designed aircraft built in Slovakia by a Hungarian airplane manufacturer. It was just about the size of the venerable C-47 but looked more like a boxcar with wings. Its landing gear was fixed to its undercarriage, and struts held up the large rear stabilizer. It was powered by only one propeller, strange for an aircraft of its girth. The prop was stuck on the aircraft's nose like someone's idea of a practical joke. But while the plane looked ugly, and flew the same way, it could lift more than 20 tons of cargo, outrageous for an aircraft with only one engine. That engine was a powerhouse, though, a big 20,000 horsepower CAD/CAM vision of Prussian efficiency. In many ways it was more sophisticated than some jet turbines.

The plane's wings were thick and gangly, which only added to its quirky appearance. But they also allowed the plane to make short takeoffs and landings. Amazingly short. Under the right conditions, the F-10 could set down on a small runway, a road, or even a dirt path just a few hundred feet long. It could also carry a lot of fuel on-board, and with just that one engine it could fly forever.

Simple, strong, fuel-efficient, expert at getting in and out of tight spots. It was the perfect smuggling plane.

This one was being flown by an outfit called Trans-Pacific Air. After leaving the dirty, noisy hangar, the plane had taken off from Manila Airport's lone auxiliary runway, an airstrip usually reserved for diplomatic aircraft. In its hold was one of Palm Tree's three crates.

The three-man crew had worked for him before. They were legitimate cargo haulers out of Brisbane. One crewman was even an American. But when Palm Tree called, they made sure to answer. There was no limit to funding when Palm Tree wanted something done. He'd made their living a very good one.

They weren't sure where they were flying to this night, not exactly anyway. That was another Palm Tree trade-mark. As a way of maintaining security, he would fre-quently give them their orders piecemeal. They were going across the Pacific; that much they knew. To do this, the plane would have to make two refueling stops, the first being Mili Atoll in the Marshall Islands. Further in-structions would be waiting for them there, most likely the go-ahead to proceed to their second fuel stop, Ducie Island, 600 miles east of Tahiti and more than halfway to South America. If that was the case, then they were sure their third and final stop would be Medelín, Colombia.

While other people in Palm Tree's employ would han-dle the cargo from there, the crew of the Babuska knew whatever they dropped off in Colombia would be inside the United States in just a matter of hours.

Free of any scrutiny, it would enter the States under the cloak of diplomatic immunity. This courtesy of Palm Tree's country of origin.

It was a clear night for flying and the stars were in their full glory. Leaving Philippines airspace was no problem. No flight plan had to be filed; their radio call sign was of the same type used by the Filipino military. The F-10 had a great autopilot. Not unlike the B-2 Spirit bomber, on extra-long flights the crew could just sit back and let the computer fly the plane. Occasionally they played cutthroat poker to pass the time. Mostly, though, two of the crew napped while the third kept an eye on things.

They had no idea what was inside the crate strapped into their cargo bay. It was not their business to know— and the crew was smart enough not to hazard a peek. You didn't screw around with a guy like Palm Tree; he could make people like them disappear. Suffice to say whatever was inside was red-hot and they were better off not knowing anything more than that.

They started playing cards once they reached their cruising altitude of 13,000 feet, but the copilot quickly ran out of funds and the game ended abruptly. He was delegated to take the first watch. While the other two lay down on cots set up right next to the crate, the copilot strapped into his seat and ran a check of the instruments. Everything came back green. He sat back and stared out at the heavens above and the ocean below. He'd have to endure all this beauty for at least another three hours, for him a dreadfully boring prospect.

He cursed himself for not bringing more money.

. . .

It was strange how it happened. The copilot was no big fan
of viewing the sights on these long nights over water, but
about one hour into the flight he'd noticed a very odd cloud
formation about a mile below and two miles back to starboard. They were just passing over the Philippine Sea; the
weather around them was crystal clear, all except this mass
of condensation behind them. It looked like a lone thunder-
cloud, suspended in this night of fair weather. Weird. . . .

But then, as he was looking back at this strange formation, he saw a light moving inside it. Yellowish, pulsating,
getting stronger. He turned around completely in his seat
now; the light grew and grew, its beam becoming very intense. *What the fuck was this?*

The F-10 had only a rudimentary radar, certainly nothing along the lines of an air defense suite. So there was no
way they could get a sweep on this thing. Certainly they'd
seen a lot of strange shit flying around at night, especially
over this part of the South Pacific, which some people
thought of as the Asian version of the Bermuda Triangle.
But he'd never seen anything like this.

The copilot was about to wake his crewmates when
suddenly the light burst out of cloud. It was just a mile
behind them now and climbing very fast. The light was
almost blinding. It was as intense as a searchlight used by
SAR aircraft to look for downed or missing aircraft, but
such things weren't used at these altitudes.

Instinct told the copilot to knock the plane off auto-
matic, which he did. At the same time, he yelled for his
cohorts to wake up. By the time he looked back at the
light, it was right on their tail.

A second later, it went right over them.

The copilot slammed the F-10 into a steep dive, this as he watched an enormous shadow go over the top of their nose. Whatever this thing was, it was so big, it was creating a powerful wake. The turbulence began shaking the F-10's tail wing even as it was dropping in altitude.

The sudden dive put the two groggy crew members into fast motion. They scrambled up to their positions and hastily strapped in. At this point the huge object was seen to be climbing and turning, no light coming from it now.

The copilot tried to explain to the others what had happened, but his words were cut short, as he had to help the pilot regain control of the aircraft. They leveled off at 6,000 feet, after plunging more than a mile. When they looked up, the Phantom was coming down at them again.

The pilot was now flying the plane—but he didn't know what to do. This big black thing was dropping so fast, he thought it was going to crash into them. He froze at the controls; the crate groaned in the back. The object went screaming past their nose a moment later. The three cargo haulers watched it go by with a mix of horror and befuddlement. Suddenly it was gone again, leaving behind a wake that tossed them around for another few terrifying seconds. Only when both the pilot and the copilot were able to right the F-10 did they look at each other and say the same thing: *"Was that a seaplane?"*

Before either could answer, it went by them again, unexpectedly, right off their left wing. It was so close and its engines so loud, the K-10 shuddered from its spinning prop all the way back to its big booty tail. That's when the three men aboard saw that this was indeed a seaplane—or better put, a flying boat.

A Kai flying boat. Easily twice the size of the F-10.

And it was turning toward them again.

The pilot dived once more; there was nothing else he could do. He had no idea why the huge amphib was acting like this. A stray thought came to him, that the plane was somehow out of control, that the men in its cockpit were dead and that's why it was gyrating all over the sky. But just as quickly he knew this was impossible. Someone was flying the huge aircraft, wildly, recklessly, very dangerously.

And for some reason, they wanted to scare the shit out of the F-10 crew. And were doing a great job of it.

The big airplane went by their nose again, and once more the turbulence rolled over them like a tsunami. It rocked the F-10 right down to its German-engineered nuts. They all bent a little in protest.

Then the engine started to kick, and God damn! the prop began to flutter. The pilot and copilot both grabbed the controls now and turned them violently to the right. The plane was going into a stall, the curse of any single-engine aircraft, and would soon leave the flight envelope completely. After that, they wouldn't be able to control it at all.

Below them was the island of Talua, the scene of a small but bloody battle during World War II. It was isolated and uninhabited. It had no runway, never mind one that would work at night. At this point, though, the flying boat was intentionally preventing the smugglers from flying any farther. So the only place they could go was down.

Talua was actually a lagoon with a large half moon of heavy jungle bordering it. The beach on the inside of the lagoon was flat, or as flat as it was ever going to get. It was the F-10 crew's only chance. Their plane was not an amphibious aircraft. But because of its wide wings and boxy air-filled compartment it could float, maybe long enough for them to get out, if they went down in shallow water, or they could land on the beach itself. In any case, the pilot vented all their fuel. They would not be making Ducie Island tonight, or ever. . . .

"Hang on," he yelled. "This could get ugly."

They hit the beach 20 seconds later, not 10 feet from the roiling surf. The engine let out a high-pitched screech as the big propeller dug itself into the sand at 3,600 RPM. The plane bounced once, then twice. Only after the third time did it stay down for good. It skidded for another 500 feet, swerving wildly and nearly tipping over. Finally it came to rest right at the water's edge.

Some remaining fuel vapors in the left wing ignited, lighting up the dark night for miles around. The crew somehow kicked open the cockpit hatch and each man fell out into the shallow water. A wave came along and smashed into all three of them. Somehow they dragged themselves up onto shore.

From this unpleasant vantage point they saw the Kai land just off the beach. The flying boat gunned its engines and crawled up onto the shore just 50 yards away. Soldiers in black uniforms jumped from the plane even before it came to a halt. Five of them ran directly to the three floundering cargo haulers, who were still too dazed to contemplate what was happening. The rest headed for the wrecked F-10.

The left side of the plane's fuselage had been torn away and the crate was hanging halfway out. A little muscle power from the soldiers and it came crashing down to the surf. Its wood splintered and, after being hit by an-other wave it came apart completely, spilling its contents into the water.

"Damn!" someone cried out.

The soldiers couldn't believe it. The Babuska crew was astonished as well. Rolling in the heavy surf were hun-dreds of red and yellow Buddha statues.

Suddenly all the soldiers were standing over the F-10 crew. One picked up the copilot with his bare hands and held him three feet above the sand. The copilot began choking even as he became aware of this man's shoulder patch. It was red, white, and blue with a silhouette of the New York Twin Towers on it.

"Oh, crap . . ." the copilot coughed. He knew of the Crazy Americans.

It was Dave Hunn holding him up. And he was as an-gry as ever.

"Where are the missiles?" he screamed at the copilot.

But the copilot couldn't really speak, as his voice box was being crushed. He tried to mumble something, but it was not quick enough or clear enough for Hunn. He tossed the copilot way out into the surf; the man hit the top of a wave like a broken doll. Hunn then turned his at-tention to the pilot—he was the American, ex–Army Avi-ation, in fact. Hunn bellowed the same question at him, this while pushing the man's face into the wet sand with his boot. But the pilot couldn't breathe, never mind talk. Hunn finally picked him up and let him catch a breath.

The pilot kept shaking his head. "I have no idea what you're talking about," he gasped. "We just got paid to move a big box. That's all we know. . . ."

By this time, Ozzi had run up to them. Still buzzing

from the heart-stopping aerial pursuit, he'd inspected the broken airplane and the plastic statues bobbing in the waves.

"These guys are just mules," Ozzi said to Hunn now. "They probably *don't* know what the fuck is going on here."

He looked back at the dozens of Buddhas washing up on the beach. "*We're* the real suckers here," he said. "We just looked under the wrong shell."

Hunn reluctantly agreed. He dropped the pilot back into the sand, kicking him in the nuts for good measure. Then he started barking orders. A few of the statues were gathered up and loaded onto the Kai. Then the American soldiers themselves climbed aboard the flying boat. Soon the big airplane was backing out into the growing tide.

It turned quickly and, with a great burst of power, took off in a great watery ascent, leaving the three F-10 crewmen stranded on the deserted island below.

The crew of the tramp steamer *Sea Demon* was made up of escaped prisoners from the worst of China's prisons. Cutthroats, murderers, child kidnappers all, they were also international arms smugglers.

Their ship was out of Shanghai, where it was known as one of the best in the business and its crew as one of the most ruthless. It sailed to the United States an average of once a month, carrying anything from drugs, to illegal combat weapons, to explosives. Everything was unloaded at a certain pier in Los Angeles where nothing, absolutely *nothing,* was inspected by customs or any other law enforcement agency, just as long as it arrived late at night and the right people were on duty.

So the *Sea Demon* crew members were experts at this. They knew, from the captain down to the scrub boys, that a successful smuggling operation always began with a clean getaway from the port of origin. That's why the *Sea Demon* had a secret. It looked like a regular tramp steamer on the outside, appropriately rusty and grubby. But inside it was simply a cored-out hull, with very few compartments, very little plumbing, and lots of exposed wiring. The crew didn't even have cabins; they slept out on the deck. All this translated into less weight, several dozen tons of it. Stripped down as it was, once out on the open sea, this bucket of bolts could really push the waves.

Leaving Manila Harbor proved no problem this night. It was dark and the bay was in its usual state of confusion, ships coming and going, big and small. No one hailed them on the radio. The harbormaster knew better than to ask where they were going. After a short trip south, they turned toward the San Bernardino Strait, heading for the deeper waters of Pacific. Once there, they would sail due east, toward America.

Even the captain didn't know what lay in the belly of the speedy smuggling ship. It did no good for him or the rest of the crew (10 others in all) to know anything more than a crate had to get to the United States quickly. But certainly they suspected something very hot was stored in their voluminous cargo hatch.

This was not the first time they'd worked for Palm Tree, either.

Besides its quickness the *Sea Demon* also had some advanced radar on its bridge, all the better to make sure no one was following you. Or, if they were, it told you it was time to pour on the coals. This was why there was such surprise when the radar operator, who was also the cook, spotted a large surface object about ten miles in back of them. It had appeared on-screen very quickly—that was the weird thing. One second the radar field was clear; the next it was showing this enormous blip coming up on their tail.

The cook called the captain and they both stared at the screen a moment. Even in that short time frame, the blip had gained another mile on them. This didn't make sense. Nothing that big could move that fast.

They called for the first officer. He knew a bit about things nautical. By the time he looked at the radar screen, the blip was just eight miles away and moving as if the *Sea Demon* were standing still.

The first officer, a drunk and an addict, actually looked worried. He had no idea what this thing could be.

"Secret navy ship, maybe?" was his only guess.

At that moment, they got a radio call. It was from the man on stern watch. He'd spotted running lights out at 11,000 yards. They were getting bigger even as he was speaking.

This was getting scary. The three men at the radar set looked back down at the screen. The blip was now just five miles out.

"It could be a very fast-moving yacht," the cook said. "And it might be distorting our read-out for some reason."

The captain turned to the first officer and said: "Break out the personal weapons and the fifty-caliber. Whoever the hell this is, we don't want anyone to know what we've got below. You understand?"

The first officer drew a finger across his throat. He understood.

. . .

The *Sea Demon* actually had a formidable arsenal on-board. These men were veteran arms smugglers, and as such they were not above picking off a few of the larder when it suited them. Each man was issued an AK-47 or an M16, leftovers from Vietnam. Each would also get a .45 pistol and a machete.

The big fifty-caliber was also a ghost of Vietnam, a powerful one. Mounted on a capson pod attached to the stern point, it fired a round so large, just one could take off a head, blow a hole clear through a stomach, or tear into the side of a tank. Or a ship. They had plenty of ammunition onboard as well. Toe to toe they could take a military patrol boat, maybe even a small frigate. A fast yacht they would blow out of the water.

The crew was cranked now as word went through the ranks that this was some kind of sports boat gaining on them. The night was dark here, stars and moon hidden by a very low overcast. At 5,000 yards, the crew could only make out the fast-moving light, and nothing of the shape around it. Still they were hungry for a kill.

Weapons were checked. The big 50 test-fired. The captain left only the helmsmen up on the bridge. The *Sea Demon* was still plowing along at full speed, so the orders to the helm were simple: don't stop for anything less than a direct order.

The captain himself carried a slightly newer model M16, one equipped with a removable and very rudimentary "star scope." It gave him a limited capability to see in the dark, a version of night vision from 30 years ago. He was standing now on the stern railing, fiddling with this scope. The wind was up and they were taking some spray. He finally got the device to blink on, this just as he heard the first officer call out: "One thousand yards . . ."

This was convenient, as the old star scope had a range of about that far. The captain put the rifle up on the rail, aimed it at the light, and finally looked through the scope.

The next thing he knew, the first officer was picking him up off the deck.

"What's the problem?" the first officer asked him harshly.

The captain could not speak. He simply pointed to the night scope now lying on the deck nearby, then pointed to his eye. Then he started to crawl away.

The first officer picked up the scope, took one look, and then wanted to join the captain. What he saw in the hazy light of night vision wasn't possible. It looked like something from a bad dream.

What was gaining so rapidly on them was not a top-secret military vessel or a sporting yacht. It was an enormous, old, and very ugly containership, much uglier than the *Sea Demon*. And it was making at least 50 knots.

Before the first officer could say anything, the big ship was just 300 yards off their starboard.

So the first officer shouted one word: "*Fire!*"

The resulting fusillade was five seconds long and only served to light up the night. Now the crew could see what the captain and his first officer had seen.

The enormous ship. Moving impossibly fast.

Everyone aboard the smuggling ship was highly superstitious; they all believed in spirits and devils. The crew fired again because now they just assumed this ship was actually from hell and was here to take them down to the depths with it. But before they could end the second volley the ghost ship was right beside them, not 100 yards away. It was actually *slowing down* to keep pace with the swiftly moving cargo freighter. Up close, it looked like a monster. It was at least five times the size of the smuggling ship in length and width and more than six decks higher.

Foolishly the crew started firing their weapons again. The first officer became coherent enough to shout orders to the 50-caliber-machine-gun crew; they started firing furiously as well. Their huge rounds just bounced off the side of the containership, though—literally *bounced off* and back toward the *Sea Demon*.

The huge ship then moved in even closer. Suddenly one of the containers on its bow dropped its walls. Inside was a weird igloolike object, with a long barrel sticking out of it. Officially this was known as a CIWS—for close-in weapons system. In reality it was a Gatling gun. Computer controlled, aimed, and driven, it could fire 600 rounds *a second*.

Gatling guns made a very strange sound when they were fired. A sort of electrical burping. That's what the *Sea Demon's* crew heard now as the CIWS gun opened up and, in a single two-second barrage, took out the freighter's mast, all of its antennas, and half the flying bridge. As this was happening, another container down on the ghost ship's stern dropped its walls, too. It also contained a CIWS. This gun opened up on the freighter's rear quarters, its barrage going over the crew's heads, snapping metal stanchions and running hooks and walking right down the rear end to where the ship's turnscrews lay. It continued its massive fusillade until something somewhere below the waterline was heard to *crack!*

The smuggling ship shook from one end to the other. Below the waterline, both its propellers had been blown away.

Those who dared to look up from the deck of the smuggler in the next few seconds saw the strangest sight of all. The huge containership had come up right next to the freighter and, still moving at 25 knots, brutally side-swiped them. The noise of the collision was deafening, the sparks blinding. Then in the midst of this, the smugglers saw armed men swinging over on ropes, as if this were a Ship of the Main being taken over by pirates. What was wrong with this picture? It was the men cowering on the deck who were supposed to be the buccaneers.

The first two soldiers to reach the smuggling ship fired a long stream of tracers over the heads of the frightened crew. Again no translation was needed here. Every crewman threw his weapon as far as he could. The two raiders were then joined by two more. Then two more. Then four. Then eight. Most were wearing some version of the same combat uniform: black, with a huge helmet and many weapon posts. Many wore a patch on the left shoulder showing the New York City Twin Towers with the Stars and Stripes behind. Upon seeing this, the crew of the smuggling ship moaned as one. They knew they were doomed now. These were the Crazy Americans.

And *they* were the real demons of the sea.

Fox and Bingham both hurt their backs swinging over from the *Ocean Voyager* to the smuggling ship.

"We're too old for this shit, Bingo!" Fox yelled, catching his breath after a slippery landing around middecks. Meanwhile the younger Navy guys and even a few of the

Spooks were swinging between the two ships with moves smoother than Zorro.

Bingham yelled back in agreement but then straightened himself out. The deck was chaotic. The bridge of the smuggler had been blown away by both Gatling guns. The noise being made by the two ships slamming into each other was earsplitting. Back on the stern, the Navy guys were solving the problem of POWs. There wouldn't be any. They cut the *Sea Demon's* only lifeboat loose from its mooring and then one by one threw the members of the smuggling crew over the side. It would be up to them to sink or swim after that.

Both ships had just about come to a stop by now. The *Sea Demon's* captain was the last guy to get tossed over the railing; then Fox, Bingo, and a squad of sailors and SDS guards bounded below decks.

They soon found themselves in the very large, nearly empty cargo hold. The *Sea Demon* really *was* little more than a hull with engines. "Is this the same as hollowing out your wheel well to move some grass into Laredo?" Fox asked enigmatically.

"Absolutely," Bingo replied, spraying his flashlight all over the darkened chamber.

There was only one piece of cargo in the hold—it was the second crate.

The Americans swarmed all over it, yanking nails out with their trench knives, small crowbars, and, in at least one instance, teeth.

There was no rhyme or reason to it, but enough nails were removed at the right time for the four walls of the big coffin to fall down simultaneously.

"God damn!" Fox cursed. "Did *we* chase the wrong horse . . ."

The crate was empty.

It was called Katang Bay.

One of many dirty inlet beaches found south of Manila Airport, it was about a mile from the seaside slums of Makak. Katang Bay was bordered on three sides by enormous debris-strewn sand dunes. Windswept and foreboding, these dunes seemed as tall as skyscrapers in the darkness.

This was where Ryder found himself now, atop of one of these monsters. Looking over the edge, it seemed like a mile down to the bottom and the beach below. Small waves were lapping up against the shore nearby. Rodents scurried about as the water splashed in, then retreated back into the bay. A torch was burning atop a small jetty that extended out into the water. A few boats were bobbing nearby.

And the third crate was there, too, sitting in the oily sand about twenty feet from the water's edge. Just as they had been told, it had been dumped here on the beach closest to the airport, or, more accurately, thrown off the back of a truck without ever stopping. An obstacle course of refuse and filth stood between the crate and the dunes. The beach was a disposal ground for several shantytowns nearby, a kind of combination junkyard and garbage dump. If the smugglers wanted to put the crate someplace where it would never be found, they'd dumped it in the right spot.

Martinez and the B-2 pilot John "Atlas" were with him. Ryder knew this was a bit of a fool's errand, coming here to look for the insignificant third box. But he felt it was necessary for reasons other than the mission. Martinez's mental condition had deteriorated badly over the past week or so. Sure, he'd popped Aboos with the rest of them during their island-hopping campaign to Manila. But at the same time he'd become more remote than ever, at times almost catatonic. Ryder had to get him home, back to the United States to his family and proper psychological care, before he slipped any further into the abyss. So this was his solution: take Martinez here, giving him a sense that he was helping out but at the same time keeping him out of the line of fire.

It was the same for Atlas. He, too, had fought aggressively against the Aboos, but the ordeal of his plane crash and the horrific imprisonment that followed had also taken its toll. Plus, he was a pilot, not a special-ops guy, and it was just a matter of time before he got hurt or even killed. So Ryder had suggested he come with him, too. They'd been up here for about ten minutes. All they had to do now was sit and wait for the others to call.

Ryder shifted over Atlas and slid up next to Martinez. No surprise the Army officer had been silent since arriving here.

"What do you think, Colonel?" Ryder asked him. "All quiet on the Western Front?"

Martinez just looked out on the beach. Though there was a lot of hustle and bustle happening nearby, the beach itself was very much away from it all, isolated on the edge of the sprawling dirty, grungy metropolis of Manila. Martinez said nothing.

"Don't worry, Marty," Ryder told him. "We'll be going home soon. We've done everything these people expected us to do and more. No matter how this ends, we fulfilled our promise, so they have to fulfill theirs. I think we could all use a few burgers and some good hooch, don't you?"

Finally Martinez smiled, probably for the the first time since the events at Hormuz. Maybe burgers and beer was all that the shell-shocked Delta officer needed, Ryder thought. He patted Martinez on the shoulder. "And when we get back," he said, "I'll even let you buy the first round."

Martinez began to reply . . . but the words wouldn't come out. And he wasn't smiling anymore. Suddenly he was pointing frantically down to the beach.

"What is it?" Atlas asked, right next to him.

Ryder slipped on his night-vision goggles again. He saw first one, then two, then three human images on the scope. They seemed to have marched right out of the water. Ryder relayed all this to the other two.

"Could be pearl divers," Atlas said. "That's a big business around here."

Ryder tried to focus in on the figures, but the glare of the city lights nearby made them look ghostly and indefinable on the night scope. At least one of them was carrying a combat rifle, though.

"Diving for pearls—or shooting clams?" he murmured.

At that moment, their cell phone rang. Ryder answered it. It was Ozzi.

"Did the guys on *Ocean Voyager* call you?" the DSA officer asked him urgently.

"Not yet," was Ryder's reply.

"Well, they called us," Ozzi told him excitedly, "and they came up negative with the cargo ship."

Ryder had to take a moment to let this sink in. Just as they had suspected, a mysterious plane had left Manila Airport shortly before the Kai team burst into the warehouse. An equally mysterious freighter had left Manila Bay earlier in the same time frame. The split American teams had taken off in hot pursuit.

"You mean they got the Buddhas?" Ryder finally asked Ozzi.

"No," Ozzi replied hastily. "*We* got the Buddhas; that's all the airplane was carrying. The crate aboard the cargo ship was empty. . . ."

Ryder looked over at Martinez and Atlas. They could hear Ozzi's voice because he was yelling so loudly into the phone. Atlas started to say: "But if the Kai got the Buddhas, and the cargo ship's crate was empty . . ."

Then he stopped. They all looked back at the crate on the dirty beach. The decoy that really wasn't a decoy at all. . . .

"*Sh-i-i-i-t!*" Ryder cried, dropping the phone. He yanked his weapon off his back and went over the top, rolling down the mountain of sand. Atlas and Martinez were right behind him. All three were slipping and sliding down, so out of control at one point both Martinez and Atlas overtook Ryder in the confused race to the bottom.

Just as the three landed at the foot of the dune, they saw a flare go up about fifteen hundred feet offshore. It was followed by a great *boom!* An object came flying out of the night from the same direction where the flare was launched. It was a grappling hook; they could see the reflection off its prongs as it landed with a thud on the beach. It was attached to a rope that disappeared into the dark water. No sooner had it come down than the three ghostly figures retrieved it and hooked it onto the crate.

The Americans got to their feet and began running. Helmets flying, ammo belts falling off, they were like three soldiers who'd overslept and missed the start of the battle. They'd been fooled again, the smugglers' shell game sucking them right in. And now, if they let this crate escape, the Stinger missiles would be on their way to the United States, with no way to stop them.

The crate started to move. It was on a skid made of eight pontoons, which had lain hidden under the wet sand. The crate was being pulled right into the water, the three men who'd done the attaching casually riding on top of it. It started to sink at first but then bobbed back up and leveled off. By the time the Americans reached the spot where the crate had stood, it was already disappearing into the darkness.

Ryder came to a slippery halt, pulled his weapon up, pulled his night goggles down, and started firing. His tracers lit up the night. The three men riding atop the crate had to hastily dive into the water, his bullets came so near. For the first time they realized someone had seen what they had done. They were soon swimming madly alongside the big floating box.

Meanwhile Atlas and Martinez had plunged right into the water, firing as they went, and kept on going. Ryder followed, still shooting his weapon. He did not stop firing until he was up to his neck in the water and holding the rifle over his head.

But God damn! it wasn't enough. The crate was at least a couple hundred feet away by now and was being pulled away very quickly. And he couldn't swim and shoot at the same time.

Ryder finally stopped and looked around. Atlas was beside him. But where was Martinez?

Then came a throaty roar from behind. Ryder and Atlas turned to see a motorboat heading for them at high speed. Was it here to run them over and drown them? No—Martinez was at the wheel!

He stopped in a great whoosh of dirty water, and Ryder and Atlas quickly climbed aboard. Where did Martinez find the boat? How was he able to start it up and get it going so quickly? There was no time to ask and at the moment it didn't matter. In seconds they were in hot pursuit of the disappearing crate.

Now it was water flying, tracers disappearing into the night. Ryder was shooting wildly, but what was he shooting at? He didn't know. He was confused. Things were happening fast, yet they were unfolding like a dream.

Martinez was driving the boat like a madman. Atlas was firing his M16 wildly as well. Ryder flipped his night-vision goggles down again. He was surprised they still worked after being soaked. The boat was a dilapidated 12-footer, its engine sputtering and laying down an unintentional smoke screen behind them. They roared out of the inlet and were nearly blinded by the lights of Manila now. The brightness above just made for more darkness below, turning the water especially black. Now they couldn't see anything more than 20 feet in front of them. Atlas was still propped up against the windshield, though, firing round after round into the murk. Occasionally they caught a brief glimpse of the crate and the pontoon raft bouncing in the waves. It didn't seem to be moving any faster than they were. How could it stay ahead of them for so long? It didn't make sense.

Martinez gunned the motorboat's engine, but instead of responding it began coughing badly. Ryder looked back at it. Not only was it smoking heavily, but licks of flames were shooting from under the outboard cover. No doubt it was going to crap out in a matter of seconds. Doomed again. . . .

That's when he heard Atlas shout: *"There they are!"*

Ryder was back at the windshield in a flash, M16 up, night scope leveled. Atlas was really cranked—cranked *and* angry. He had a right to be a little nuts, though. To his mind, anyone who came within the sights of his rifle at that moment was just as bad as the person who had pushed the button that launched the SAM that killed the guys in the tanker and shot him down that night. He took it all very personally.

"See them!" he was yelling in Ryder's ear. And suddenly Ryder saw what Atlas saw.

In the green glow of night vision about a half-mile ahead was what at first looked to be nothing more than a diving platform, something that might be found floating in the old swimming hole back home, just a lot bigger. There were six more scuba divers standing on top of it. They had an electric winch, and with it were reeling in the crate and its pontoon float. Ryder had seen one of these things before. It was an SLP-I, for surface loading platform, inflatable. It was a kind of temporary docking place used by waterborne special ops soldiers to tie up small raiding boats, store fuel, set up communications. SLPs had been used a lot in the Persian Gulf over the years, especially during the secret war against Iran.

The crate was quickly up on this platform and indeed frogmen were unloading the Stingers within. Other people on the inflatable platform were in the process of stacking the weapons. The speedboat was only about 1,200 feet away by this time, but then the engine really started chugging. At the worst possible moment, they began slowing down.

"Son of a bitch!" Ryder and Atlas screamed in unison.

The engine died completely a few seconds later. They were still 1,000 feet away from the floating platform and their forward momentum carried them another 100 feet or so. But then they stopped for good. Atlas went nuts. He pushed a new clip into his M16, sighted through the night scope, and let loose another volley. Meanwhile Ryder and Martinez were looking at the engine to see if anything could be done.

Suddenly Atlas cried out: "Jesus Christmas! I got one of the bastards."

Ryder leaped back up to the front of the motorboat. He didn't need his night scope to see that indeed, Atlas had shot one of the men on the platform and he had fallen into the water. He was struggling even as he was caught in a current pushing him away from the float and toward the motorboat. He appeared to be gravely wounded. Atlas was not satisfied, though. He kept firing at the man, sending ripples of bullets all around him. Soon enough the man stopped struggling. Then he stopped moving altogether.

Atlas was quickly hanging over the side; Ryder was right beside him. Together they reached down and grabbed the body. They had pulled him halfway into the boat . . . when suddenly Atlas let out a chilling scream.

"This is fucking impossible!" he cried.

He looked at Ryder as if he'd seen a ghost, which in a

way he had. The body was that of Atlas's former flight partner, the guy they called Teddy Ballgame.

At that moment, before Atlas could utter one more word of exclamation, Ryder felt the motor boat suddenly rising below his feet. One moment they were on the surface of the water; the next they were 15 feet above it. Then 20, then 25.

What was happening? All of them grabbed for something to hold on to, startled for their lives. Somehow Ryder was able to look down and see a large black mass had surfaced right below them. It had come up so sharply, it was carrying them up with it.

The first thought through his head—crazy, as he knew it could be his last—was: *Is this a fucking whale?*

The motorboat was shattered by the impact from below. Ryder, Atlas, and Martinez were thrown into the air; it was like they were weightless. The boat's motor blew apart, sending burning gasoline everywhere. In his last conscious memory, as he was falling into the water surrounded by flaming debris, Ryder saw that this was not some great black whale sent by the devil to kill them.

It was a submarine.

A big one.

The Kai found them the next morning, floating 20 miles out in the South China Sea.

Ryder, Martinez, and Atlas were all clinging to the coffin-shaped packing crate, barely alive. Their encounter with the huge submarine had nearly killed them. The discarded crate was the only piece of debris large enough to save their lives; it had floated right up to them in the hell that followed the sub's sudden appearance. As they drifted away, half-drowned, they saw the weapons being loaded into the sub by men in dark naval uniforms. Once done, the divers on the floating platform climbed onto the sub themselves. Then it disappeared, vanishing beneath the waves.

Ryder remembered little after that. He'd been hit on the head by something after crashing back down into the water. He barely recalled Martinez pulling him up to the top of the crate. But then sometime during the long night he'd pulled Martinez back up after *he'd* fallen over.

Throughout this, Atlas just held on, blank look on his face, never quite recovering from finding his ex-partner floating in the water, torn apart by his bullets. Why would Teddy be in league with the people stealing the missiles? How could he possibly be involved? There was no way to tell. But now Atlas had the same haunted look in his eyes as Martinez.

The sun had just come up when the Kai appeared overhead. Ryder had emerged from his haziness by this time. The big flying boat was a welcome sight as it orbited them once before coming in for a landing.

The coffin-shaped crate rode the swells over to it, and soon helping hands were pulling the three men aboard. Ryder went first, glad to get off the crate. But both Atlas and Martinez seemed reluctant to go. Finally they, too, were hauled aboard the big Kai. The empty box, their strange lifeboat, was then allowed to drift away.

It was only when the plane's door was closed and Ryder's eyes adjusted to the faint light inside the Kai's cabin that he saw the other members of the American team were aboard. Both the group who'd pursued the F-10 cargo plane and those who'd chased down the smuggling ship the *Sea Demon*.

But the Americans were not flying the plane. The people at the controls were members of the Japanese Maritime Forces, its original owners. The Americans were sitting in rows inside the cargo compartment. All of them were in handcuffs.

Watching over them were several squads of heavily armed, rock-jawed Green Berets. Standing on the flight deck above everyone else, dressed in brand-new, never-been-worn combat camos, was General James Rushton, presidential advisor for special operations.

He did not look happy.

Chapter 19

Ozzi's stomach was tied in knots. His palms were sweating. His eyes were burning. He was tired and nervous and aching all over. To make matters worse, everything around him was swaying with the movement of the sea.

He was sitting inside a small, damp, dimly lit compartment. It was painted entirely in U.S. Navy gray and was just big enough for a desk and four chairs. The tiny room reminded him of his office back at the Pentagon. *Oh, to be crammed inside that little cubbyhole right now,* he thought. That would be heaven. He'd never leave it again. But the way things looked, he seemed destined to spend time in a space even smaller than his dear old cube, one surrounded by metal bars and razor wire.

It was the height of irony that the American team was now being held aboard the carrier USS *Abraham Lincoln*, the same ship the original 9/11 unit had saved almost two months before. The supercarrier had rotated out of the Persian Gulf earlier that week and was on its way to a new station off the coast of North Korea when it was diverted to the Philippine Sea. After picking up Ryder, Martinez, and Atlas, the Kai had flown east, toward the Pacific and the hastily arranged rendezvous with the carrier. Once the big flying boat landed next to the *Lincoln,* the entire 9/11 unit, plus the SEALs, the SDS guys, Atlas, and the two DSA officers, were transferred to the carrier via rescue rafts. Curiously, Atlas was immediately flown off the ship, destination unknown. The remaining detainees were put in isolated cabins scattered throughout the huge ship. These cabins were then designated as "temporary brigs" and made off-limits to the rest of the crew.

As it turned out, a quadruple whammy had been in play all along. While the two American teams were off doing their various things, General Rushton had organized yet *another* special ops team to track them down; this one was made up entirely of Green Berets. Their tip-off? When the Kai contingent turned over the prisoners they'd rescued from the Aboos to a passing cruise ship, the freed hostages went directly to the U.S. embassy in Manila to spin their tale of the mysterious American unit that had saved their lives and was still out there, skulking around in a Japanese flying boat. Rushton and his search-and-arrest team left the United States soon afterward.

They'd arrived in Manila about the same time the *Ocean Voyager* was intercepting the *Sea Demon.* Traveling in a top-secret KC-135 surveillance plane known as *Compass Point,* they'd followed both the *Ocean Voyager*'s activities plus the Kai's forcing-down of the F-10 cargo plane by using an NRO real-time TV satellite, the kind of eye in the sky that could count the number of but-

tons on your shirt. Both the Kai team and the crew of
Ocean Voyager were contacted by the *Compass Point*
plane and told to surrender. Navy jets flying in the area
gave them little choice but to comply.

The containership and the flying boat were seized soon
after that.

The cabin Ozzi was sitting in now was located on the
middle deck of the *Lincoln,* a space used by the ship's
chaplain to hear confessions. Directly across the desk
from him were two special prosecutors attached to the
National Security Council. Both were civilians; both
were wearing suitcoats and ties. They'd accompanied
Rushton on the quick trip over from Washington, apparently forgetting to pack their tropic-wear in the haste.
Rushton himself was sitting in the corner off to Ozzi's
left, arms folded, bulldog face in place. The tightly
pressed creases on his new camouflage suit had yet to
show any signs of relaxing. Ozzi could smell his cheap
cologne from across the room.

The men from the NSC did all the talking at first. They
were here to compile evidence for a criminal case against
the rogue team. They told Ozzi up front that the main
9/11 guys, the SEALs, the State Department guards, and
Major Fox had already been interrogated—everyone had
been grilled but him. *Last in line again,* Ozzi thought. It
took them nearly 15 minutes just to read him the charges
facing those involved in the Manila affair. The list was a
long one: disobeying direct orders, destruction of government property, desertion, breaking into government-
restricted cyberspace, all on top of dozens of national
security violations. Adding to the misery, the prosecutors

told Ozzi he was facing additional charges, including issuing false orders and aiding and abetting the unlawful release of the Gitmo Four. Their conclusion: he was looking at more than 500 years in jail.

While Ozzi couldn't deny that he and the others had broken a number of military laws, he also told the prosecutors that to a man, the entire team felt it had been in the country's best interests to do so. But the NSC men reminded him, just as Fox had so long ago, that while tales of rogue military units made for good bedtime novels, they just weren't tolerated in the real world. They couldn't be. And so it had come to this again: just like after Hormuz, the heroes had been turned into villains.

"We've already gone over everything the others told us," one prosecutor said to him now. "From the B-2 crash, to looking for these supposed missiles, to killing this Kazeel guy, double crosses and *triple* crosses and shell games and the like. The same story, over and over. But we have to be straight with you. We have a hard time believing any of it. And so will a jury."

The room started spinning for Ozzi at that moment. Sweat began dripping off his upper lip.

"But I *lived* through it," he told them. "Or half of it anyway. And I trust the people who lived through the other half. Believe me, I . . ."

But the second NSC guy held up his hand and cut him off.

"Lieutenant, if I can be blunt here for a moment, the things that you people claim you did are simply preposterous. I mean, breaking up mudfights in whorehouses? Impersonating Chechen bodyguards? Flying all over Southwest Asia in a news chopper? Tracing this imaginary weapons cache by tracking a mute eunuch? You maintain this entire scheme hinged on the actions of an idiot, for Christ's sake! We found the guy just where you said you left him, half-dead in that hangar. He can't talk, he's barely alive, and on his best day he couldn't add two and two and come out with four. Yet you make it seem like he was the ringleader, a major player in this supposed Stinger deal."

"But he was," Ozzi insisted. "We were all sure of it. . . ."

The first NSC man spoke again: "Then there's the way you all say it came to a head. That your half of this mystery team crashed in on these supposed missile smugglers in the hangar, and then another bunch of smugglers, who were part of the Philippine National Police no less, crashed in on you?"

"But *that's* the way it happened," Ozzi pleaded. "Until . . . well, until the other half of the nine-eleven team busted in on them, and . . ."

He began painfully stumbling over his own words. Suddenly they felt very foolish coming off his lips. He had to agree with the NSC guys. The whole thing did *sound* crazy . . . not to mention that had the two teams hung around the hangar long enough, Rushton's Green Berets would have busted in on *them*.

The first NSC man went on.

"You must have known none of this would check out. Your boss, Major Fox, was sent out on a simple recovery mission to look for two missing aircraft—and suddenly he falls off the map. Meanwhile you write out false orders to get some very sensitive detainees released—then you all meet up in Manila. *Then* all this nonsense takes place, and that's when the bullshit really starts to fly. You have to admit, it sounds like a plot from a bad paperback novel."

Ozzi just stared back at him. Something was beginning to smell here, and it wasn't just Rushton's Old Spice.

"OK then," Ozzi finally challenged them. "What do *you* think happened? What do *you* think we've been doing out here all this time?"

That's when Rushton rose from his seat, straightened his camo suit, and spoke for the first time. "Frankly," he began in his trademark smug tone, "all the evidence indicates that you and your merry band were indeed involved in a smuggling operation. But it was a *drug* smuggling operation. One that went horribly awry."

Ozzi couldn't believe what he was hearing. "Drugs? *Are you crazy?*"

Rushton just shrugged. "Not likely," he said, casually examining his finely manicured fingernails. "Look at the evidence. You admit having contact with this Buddha-statue man, don't you? He was a known drug smuggler, until you people killed him, that is. This woodworker— same thing, well-known by the National Police for his involvement in illegal operations, specifically making shipping crates for hiding heroin.

"That cargo plane you forced down—again, people steeped in the Southeast Asian heroin trade. And the freighter your friends stopped? It's considered the *Queen Mary* of smuggling ships around here. Plus, you admit flying to Pakistan and Afghanistan—only the poppy capitals of the world. I mean, just connect the dots: it was a large drug deal gone bad. And apparently you fellows wound up on the wrong end of the stick. You should have picked your companions more carefully out here. There's a lot of very disreputable people in this part of the world."

Ozzi wanted to go right over the desk and throttle Rushton—just beat him to a pulp. The sight of someone else's blood flowing did not bother him anymore, not after spending the last 10 days with the Gitmo crew. But it was evident now that the odorous general was playing some kind of game here, maybe for the benefit of the NSC men, but maybe not. Certainly Rushton had known about Fox's mission to find the B-2 spy bomber, as well as his plans to ask for help from the original 9/11 team members. How? Because Fox had cleared both missions with Rushton first—he would have never been able to leave Washington if he hadn't. And certainly it had been Rushton who'd set up the UPX connection between Fox and the people who he'd been talking to throughout the long night on Fuggu—before being so suddenly cut off and set adrift, that is. How else would Fox have had enough juice to call in cruise missile strikes the next morning?

And what about the bomber itself? What was it really doing flying over the Bangtang Channel that night? What was it carrying in its bomb bay? And why was it so important that all evidence of its crash site be eliminated, and then those people who'd seen it up-close be suddenly turn into nonpersons? Ozzi knew of only two people who could answer those questions. One was Atlas—and he was long gone by now. The other was his apparently traitorous partner, the guy called Teddy Ballgame. And he was dead.

And while it was no surprise that Ozzi's self-penned orders to go after Kazeel would eventually cross Rushton's desk, he still didn't have a clue who tipped off Ramosa that the Gitmo crew had flown to Manila to whack the superterrorist. Did someone in Washington make that call?

Ozzi studied Rushton up and down now. He was pompous, egomaniacal, conniving and deceitful. And he was displaying a penchant for changing history to suit his own needs. But could he really be a traitor, too?

"I don't know what your angle is here, General," he told Rushton darkly. "But I can tell you this: whatever you want to believe, or make other people think, between those two teams, a lot of Aboo terrorists wound up dead, a major plot to shoot down the spy bomber was uncovered, and the world's first superterrorist was eliminated.

"And the men who did those things aren't drug smugglers or criminals. They're heroes. *Patriots*. More than you will ever be. And they have absolutely no reason to lie."

Another deep breath for Ozzi. The two NSC men were suddenly riveted on him.

"Now the problem is those Stingers are still on the loose," Ozzi went on, "and they are most likely heading for the U.S. And the *sharfa* go-code is still in possession of this unscrupulous puke Ramosa. Stopping him, sir, is what you should be focusing on—not how you're going to punish the likes of us."

Dead silence in the room. The NSC men were speechless. Rushton, too, seemed surprised by Ozzi's verve. He began rubbing his crimson cheeks with his small, hairless hands. Ozzi could almost see the tiny wheels turning in his head.

"You claim they have no reason to lie?" Rushton finally said. "Then how do you explain the refusal of these original Nine-Eleven characters to talk about what they were doing at the Tonka Tower that day?"

"They were saving thousands of people from terrorists . . ." Ozzi shot back. "What do you think they were doing?"

"I watch TV, lieutenant," Rushton replied, voice dripping with contempt. "I saw what happened. But perhaps you should ask your friends exactly *how* they came upon the TV news chopper they were flying that morning. And how did they know the attack was going to take place—when every other intelligence service in the world had no idea it was about to happen? Your comrades didn't mind spewing out their tales of playing superheroes for the past week and a half. Why then are they so reticent about what happened in Singapore just two weeks before?"

Ozzi found his eyes darting around the room. Rushton had a point. None of the original 9/11 team members had spoken one word to Ozzi or Fox about that day in Singapore. Nor was that the only thing they were tight-lipped about. None of the Kai team ever revealed how it was that they were so suddenly tuned in to what Ozzi and the Gitmo team were doing. How did they know to cue in on Ozzi's phone or even that he was in the Manila area? Fox had been traveling with Ryder, Bingham, *et al.,* and even *he* didn't know how they did it. Ozzi had a theory, though. It boiled down to a single name, a shadow, an elusive presence that was somehow still hovering on the edges of this thing: *Bobby Murphy.*

But there was no way Ozzi was going to bring that up here.

"Look, General," he began again, his anger building

despite efforts to stay cool. "Are you looking for a fall guy here? Is that it? If so, then let it be me. I will take responsibility for *everything* that happened. If you want to pin a drug rap on me, so be it. I'll be glad to sit before an NSC board of inquiry. I'll even welcome a court-martial, if that's what you are trying to cook up.

"But don't pull the Nine-Eleven team down into the gutter with you. How many times do I have to tell you? No matter who sent them out or why, they saved *thousands* of American lives at Hormuz and *thousands more* in Singapore. And because of them, the world is rid of its first superterrorist. *And,* they've probably disrupted Al Qaeda more in the last four months than the entire U.S. intelligence community has in the last four years. It's *just not right* to punish those men after what they've done for our country."

Rushton opened his mouth—but no words would come out. He stared down at the floor instead, unable to look Ozzi in the eye. The NSC wonks were averting their gaze as well.

Ozzi took this as a sign his words were finally hitting on target.

"All these guys wanted was to get home again," he said, his voice cracking. "They just wanted to get back to America. To see their families again. To touch American soil again. You're a soldier—or at least you used to be. Don't you at least owe them that?"

Finally Rushton looked up. His face was beet red now, his lips pursed and sinister. But his eyes, they were telling a different story. Puffy, watery—they were oozing guilt.

Yes, Ozzi thought, *this is a man who is definitely hiding something.*

"Nice speech, lieutenant," Rushton said. "But on the contrary, I consider the whole lot of them security risks. Not to do so would be dereliction of duty on my part. So not only are these men not going home; they will stay in my custody until further notice. And when I return to Washington, I plan to seek a Executive Order barring them from ever entering the United States again."

Ozzi felt like he'd been hit in the stomach with a hammer. His mind began racing crazily again. A severe beating was too good for Rusthon. He wondered if the NSC men were armed. If he could somehow get a gun from one of them, he could shoot Rushton instead, put a couple bullets right between his beady eyes, then maybe blast his way out of this joint. . . .

But then, strangely, he saw Rushton's face soften a bit. The rotund officer walked past the NSC men and sat on the corner of the desk closest to Ozzi, effectively blocking the prosecutors' view. Up this close, Rushton looked oddly feminine.

"Lieutenant Ozzi," he began again. "Let's cut the BS and get to the point of your being here. I've reviewed your service record. I know you've done outstanding work for the NSC. And I know you come from a family who have served our country proudly as well. Now, you're facing several lifetimes in jail—and it will be no country club, I assure you. But I believe I can offer you a ray of hope here. A way that you can avoid disgracing your family."

What the hell is this? Ozzi thought.

"All you have to do is tell us everything," Rushton went on. "Fill in some of the holes—like where you all got the crazy notion that there were Stinger launchers being carried by that B-2, and what really happened at Singapore—and then just fall into step with the official report. It will be like a plea bargain. You help us, we help you. I'll make sure you get off."

That was it. Screw getting a gun. Ozzi decided he was going to kill Rushton with his bare hands right then and there. The mere suggestion that he could be flipped, so easily turned into a rat, filled him with a blood rage. But then, just as he was about to explode out of his chair . . . he realized something. Suddenly he knew what was *really* going on here. If Rushton was offering *him* a deal, and he was the last guy in line, it could only mean one thing: Everyone before him—Fox, the original 9/11 guys, even the SEALs and the State Department guards—*must* have turned him down. No one had cracked. No one had bought into Rushton's game.

"No other takers, is that it, General?" Ozzi asked him, still fighting mightily to keep his cool.

Rushton let his guard slip and shook his head no. "Not a smart one in the bunch," he said.

That's when Ozzi finally smiled. *God damn,* he thought. *The whole team is going down together. Including me. . . .*

And at last, at that moment, he felt like one of them. One of the team. One of the heroes. A patriot. It had been a long time coming, but when it arrived it was like getting hit by a lightning bolt. Electricity, from his head to his toes. Suddenly, he was on top of the world.

"So?" Rushton asked him. "What do you say, son? Are you willing to take my offer? Are you going to be the only one smart enough to save your own skin?"

Ozzi just leaned back in his chair and relaxed. He wasn't sweating anymore.

"General," he said proudly. "You can go to hell."

By chance, Ryder and Hunn were put into the same holding cell at the bottom of the *Lincoln*. They were both wearing prisoner suits, bright orange of course.

"How's the chow down at Gitmo?" Ryder asked Hunn dryly. They were sure that's where they were going.

"It sucks," Hunn replied.

Ryder leaned back against the damp wall, wondering if it would be possible to forget everything that had happened and just go to sleep. But he was hungry, too.

"You didn't sneak a roast beef sandwich in here with you, did you? I'll split it with you, if you did."

"Nope," Hunn replied. "But look what I do have. . . ."

He reached deep into the crotch of his prison suit and came up with a cell phone.

"I don't want to know where you've been hiding that," Ryder told Hunn wearily.

"Don't ask; don't tell," Hunn said.

Ryder repositioned himself against the wall. His head felt like it was going to burst, he had so many secrets he had to keep.

"Well, maybe we can use it to call out for pizza when we get to jail," he said to Hunn. "Do they even have pizza in Cuba?"

Hunn laughed in his angry sort of way. "It's not just an ordinary phone, Colonel," he said. "I took it off that *shuka* mook as I was stuffing the flag into his mouth. You know, just before the shit hit the fan? I figure it's got to be how he was getting his orders."

Suddenly Ryder was interested again.

"Hit the redial," he suggested. "See who picks up."

Hunn thought a moment, then did just that.

On the other side of the world, on a messy desk inside a soundproof office on the thirteenth floor of an otherwise nondescript mercantile building, a special red cell phone lit up. Just by habit, the man known to some as the *judus* went to answer it, but then hesitated, his hand hovering over it.

He'd been sitting at this desk now for the last 100 hours, managing the acquisition and shipment of the Stinger missiles to America. Despite some bumps in the road, his plan had worked beautifully. The 36 weapons would be inside the United States within hours, all the diversions and feints having been played to perfection. It was exactly the ending he wanted. So why ruin it?

Answering the ringing phone would probably do just that, he thought. He was exhausted. He needed a cigarette. He needed a drink. But most important, he needed to celebrate, just a little bit. So he let the phone ring until, finally, the person on the other end gave up. Then he picked up the cell phone, erased its memory, and disconnected the battery. Putting the phone between the heel of his shoe and the floor, he crushed it so it could never be used again. The remains he threw into his wastebasket.

He checked his watch. It was early afternoon. Yes, it was time for him to go home. He put all sensitive materials into his office safe. He also shredded a few very incriminating documents and placed them in the burn bag for disposal. Then he turned out the lights and locked the door behind him.

He walked through the outer office. There were several

dozen people here, lower in rank than he, lording over computer screens, fax machines, and banks of scramble phones, the typical landscape of a foreign intelligence office. He nodded good-bye to several of them, chatted briefly with a few more. It had been raining for the past four days, they told him, something he could not tell from his windowless office. They all remarked with humor about his staying power and dedication. They told him to go home and get a few days' sleep. He assured them that he would.

He walked to the elevator, passed his ID card through the egress security check, then placed his briefcase up to the document scanner. The machine confirmed that he was not taking any unauthorized security materials home with him. He stepped onto the elevator and rode it down to the small hidden lobby on the first floor. Another security check waited for him here: another X ray of his briefcase and a retina scan. He was cleared for the final time, and went through the unmarked door to the building's real lobby, the one that served the import-export businesses that made up about half the tenants in the unassuming building.

He stepped out onto the street, and took his first deep breath of fresh air in almost five days.

The neon sign from the restaurant next door was crackling slightly, trying to lure him in. It was a chic bistro called The Palm Tree. He'd been there many times before, but the cognac was rarely up to his standards. And a bottle of some very good stuff awaited him at home. That's where he would go.

Normally he would have taken a cab. But the rain had stopped by now, and he knew he had to stretch his tired legs. So he lit a cigarette and started walking.

He liked the way Paris looked after it rained.

Read on for an excerpt from
Mack Maloney's next book

SUPERHAWKS: STRIKE FORCE CHARLIE

Coming soon from
St. Martin's Paperbacks

Guantanamo Bay
Cuba

The storm had blown in just after sunset. The rain was coming down in sheets, lightning was crashing. Rolling across the bay, the thunder was horrendous and booming. With visibility down to zero for most of the mid-Caribbean, it was not weather for flying. Yet an unusual cargo plane was sitting on runway number 2, hard on the edge of the U.S. Navy base, its propellers churning the fierce downpour into a driving, violent spray.

Though all of the cargo plane's insignia had been painted over, this aircraft belonged to the Iranian Air Force, an unlikely visitor to this American facility hanging by its fingernails off the eastern end of Cuba. The plane was here as a result of nearly a year of top-secret negotiations between the U.S. and Iran, part of a very hush-hush diplomatic agreement. The U.S. kept several hundred Al Qaeda and Taliban fighters captured in Afghanistan after 9/11 at Guantanamo Bay. Many of these people were not Afghanis; in fact, terrorists from more than two dozen countries were being held in prisons here. Seven of them were citizens of Iran; all seven were also related to someone on the governing board of religious mullahs that ran the troublesome Persian country.

The aim of the secret negotiations between the two arch-enemies was actually very simple. Iran just happened to be holding seven top-echelon Al Qaeda members. None of them were Iranian. The seven Iranian citizens the U.S. was holding were foot soldiers, with friends in high places. The U.S. wanted the so-called Tehran 7 for questioning and prosecution; the mullahs wanted their sons back. It was a prisoner exchange then. Seven-for-seven. An even swap.

The howling storm was a complication no one wanted or foresaw. The two sides had battled each other right down to the last comma on a document so classified, it would be burned and its ashes scattered after the exchange was made. Timing was the most important element. The Tehran 7 were being held at an Iranian border crossing at that moment, ready to be pushed across into US-held Iraq as soon as word of the plane's departure from Gitmo was confirmed. Any delay—be it weather or mechanical—would be a deal breaker; the distrust between the two sides ran that deep.

That's why the cargo plane had to be loaded, had to get into the air and make the all-important confirmation call back to Tehran.

Hurricane or not, it had to take off.

Things had to go right on the ground, too. That was why the isolated section of the air base was surrounded by no less than a hundred Marines, backed up by two squads of SEALs watching the waterfront nearby, as well as a sniper unit stationed in the hills above. This small army had been in place for hours, sweating out the brutal heat of the waning day, only to be soaked through now by the driving evening rains.

A stretch van would be transporting the seven Iranian prisoners from Camp X-ray, the main Gitmo holding facility, to the runway. The van was to be escorted by two Marine LAVs, small, heavily armored tank-like vehicles. A U.S. State Department representative would also be accompanying the van, traveling in a separate car. His name was John Apple. His counterpart, a general in the Iranian Air Force, was serving as the co-pilot for the transfer plane.

Once the van reached the runway, Apple and the Iranian general would each count the seven prisoners as they got off the bus, and again as they climbed aboard the plane—this last bit of diplomatic nonsense insisted on by the Iranians. Only after both men were certain that the seven prisoners were safely aboard would the cargo plane would be cleared for take-off.

It was just one of many complicating factors in this anxious exchange that all seven of the Iranian detainees was named Khameni. In fact, five of them had the exact same name: Raset Rasanjan Khameni. To avoid confusion, it was agreed upon early in the negotiations that the detainees would be known simply as K-1 through K-7.

The plane's first destination would be Mexico, but only by necessity. When it touched down at Guantanamo, its fuel tanks were three-quarters empty. It needed gas to get home. The U.S. had steadfastly refused to refuel the plane though, just as the Iranians had steadfastly refused to allow U.S. fuel in their tanks. So, with a nudge from the U.S. the Mexican government agreed to allow the plane to refuel at a tiny military base in the Yucatan before starting its long flight westward. With another fuel stop in Fiji, and a final one in Beijing, the plane was expected to arrive in Tehran thirty-two hours later.

A huge celebration would be waiting for it in the Iranian capital, timed to lead off the government's national nightly news. The seven fighters were expected to be greeted as heroes.

The prisoners' van arrived a few minutes late as the rain grew even more torrential and the winds picked up to forty knots. The van pulled up to the back of the waiting airplane. Conversation was nearly impossible around the loading ramp, thanks to the gusting wind, whipped up further by the gyrating turbo-props. The Iranian general was waiting impatiently at the bottom of this ramp. He, too, was soaked through. He'd been nervously watching the line of wary Marines standing very close by. Both sides wanted to get this over with quickly.

Apple and the Iranian general met at the bottom of the cargo ramp. There were no handshakes. They simply stood side by side, ready to count aloud as each detainee stepped off the small bus. Per the agreement, each prisoner was still shackled by hands and feet, had a black mask pulled down over his head, and was barefoot. Each was wearing a bright orange jumpsuit adorned with his ID—K-1, K-2 and so on—painted in large black letters on the back.

Together, Apple and the Iranian general counted off seven men stepping from the van. Two Marines escorted each detainee to the bottom of the ramp where the general would check off a number corresponding to the back of his prisoner uniform. Then the detainee would be allowed to climb up into the plane and be seated. At U.S. insistence, the shackles and hoods would not be removed until the plane was airborne.

The loading process took longer than expected because the detainees came off the van out of order. They were rearranged in their seating by the plane's pilot, and only then did Apple and the Iranian general agree that the exchange was complete.

Again, there were no handshakes. The Iranian general simply climbed up the ramp and closed it himself with a push of a button. Not thirty seconds later, the plane's engines revved up once more, and it started pulling away. Apple gave the Marines a pre-arranged signal; they began to slowly withdraw from the runway. The cargo plane pilots added power, their props screeching in the tempest. There was no conversation with the base's air traffic control tower. The plane immediately went into its take-off roll.

It needed the entire length of the 6,000-foot runway. But somehow, some way, the plane finally went wheels up, and in an explosion of spray and power, slowly climbed into the very stormy night.

Apple returned to his living quarters just outside Camp X-Ray, went directly to his kitchen cabinet, and broke out a bottle of cheap Cuban scotch. He poured some over a few melting ice cubes, and with the thunder still crashing outside, drained the contents of his glass in one noisy gulp.

He was three weeks away from retirement. Full pension. House on the Chesapeake. The works. That this pain-in-the-ass deal was finally over made him very happy. All he had to do was phone in a report to his boss in Washington, then he would go to sleep for at least a week. After that, he could start thinking about packing his government bags for good.

He poured himself another healthy drink, then padded into the living room of his glorified hut. He picked up the secure scramble phone, but before he could punch in the first number, he heard a commotion outside. He could see through his picture window that a Humvee had screeched to a halt on his sandy front lawn. Six Marine guards fell out of it; two immediately ran up to his front door. They did not knock, didn't bother to ring his doorbell. They simply burst in, soaking wet, M-16s pointing everywhere. They looked scary.

"What's happened?" Apple demanded of them.

The Marines just grabbed him by the shoulders and carried him out of his hut.

"You've got to come with us!" one of them yelled at him.

The ride up to the detainee compound was the most hair-raising episode of Apple's life. The Humvee driver was a kid no more than eighteen years old, and the other Marines were screaming at him the entire way to go faster . . . faster! . . . *faster!* The kid followed orders, and drove the winding, muddy, very slippery road like a madman, nearly sending the Humvee hurtling over the cliff several times.

Somehow they made it to the main compound gate. This barrier was open—never a good sign. The Humvee roared right through, drove the length of the barbed-wire encirclement, and down another series of hills to an isolated plywood barracks. This was where the seven guys named Khameni had been kept throughout their incarceration.

There was another gaggle of Marines here, excited, soaked, and scary-looking, too. Conversation had been hopeless in the swift ride down here, the wind and torrential rain did not help it now. The Marines yanked Apple out of the Hummer and into the isolated prisoner barracks.

The interior was dark, only the beams from the Marines' flashlights broke through the fog that had seeped in here. The State Department rep, not used to all this excitement, nearly slipped three steps in. The floor was coated with something very sticky. Another young Marine beside him directed his flashlight at the floor.

"Be careful, sir," the Marine told Apple.

That's when Apple realized they were both standing in a pool of blood.

More flashlights appeared, and now they lit up the entire room. On the floor in front of him, Apple saw seven bodies lined up in a row. Each one had had his throat cut.

Apple's first thought was that these people were Marine guards—but actually the opposite was true. They were detainees, more specifically, the seven Iranian prisoners named Khameni. It took several long moments for this to sink into Apple's brain. Then, through the blood and rain and wind and chaos around him, it hit like a lightning bolt. He grabbed the young Marine next to him.

"Are these really K-One through Seven?" he asked in astonishment.

The Marine nodded blankly. "We've already ID'd them through photographs," he said. "Those are them, sir."

Apple nearly slumped to the floor. He felt like he was suddenly living inside a ghastly dream. What his eyes were telling him simply seemed inconceivable. *How? Why?*

Then another thought struck. This one even more troubling than the seven murdered prisoners.

"But if these are the Iranians," he mumbled. "Who the hell got on that plane?"

Mary Li Cho drove to the securest location she could find in a hurry, the top floor of a parking garage three blocks from the MCI Arena. She was the only car parked up here, and the other six levels below were just about empty. She was sure no one would intrude on her. The garage was so high, she could see almost all of Washington from here. The White House. The Lincoln Memorial. The Pentagon. The Potomac. All of them sparkling in the warm evening air.

She speed-dialed Nash's number more than fifty times in the next ten minutes, and each time his phone was busy. She was quickly growing annoyed. What kind of game was he playing here? Why all the mystery and intrigue? She got enough of that at her top-secret job.

It was now 8:45. She tried Nash five more times. Still busy. Seat back, she opened her moon roof and looked up at the stars. But instead, she saw the silhouettes of two fighter jets pass silently overhead. They were F-15s . . . That was strange. Fighter overflights had not been seen here in D.C. since the days immediately after 9/11. Yet these two were clearly circling the capital. Why?

She tried Nash again. Finally, she heard ringing. He picked up right away.

"It's me," she said sourly. "Your date."

"I'm sorry," he began in a hushed voice. "I'm still at work. And work just got nuts. Are you alone?"

"You're not here," she shot back. "So I must be, right?"

A short pause.

"I'll make it up to you," he said. "It's just . . ."

But she'd heard enough already. He had to work late. OK. No big deal. Certainly no need for a song and dance.

"Just call me then," she told him coolly. "When you're certain you can get away."

She started to hang up, but then heard him say, "Wait . . ."

"Yes?"

"I have something else I have to tell you," he said. "And it's disturbing news, I'm afraid. Some things that we just got in here, at work, I think you should know about."

Li felt a chill go through her. This was unexpected.

She asked, "What kind of 'things'?"

"Absolutely top-secret things," he replied, his voice low. "NSC things. Are you sure you're in a safe place?"

"I am," she insisted. "And frankly, you're scaring me."

"Well, get used to it," he said. "Because there's some scary shit going on." Another pause. Then he said, "What do you know about Hormuz and Singapore?"

Nash was referring to a pair of highly classified, highly mysterious incidents that had happened in the past few months.

What occurred at the Strait of Hormuz was nothing less than Al Qaeda trying to pull off an attack to rival 9/11 or anything since. They hijacked ten airliners and two military planes and attempted to crash them into the U.S.

Navy aircraft carrier *Abraham Lincoln* as it was moving through the narrow Persian Gulf waterway. The attack failed because a last-minute piece of intelligence delivered to the Navy allowed them to know exactly where the hijacked airliners were coming from, what their flight paths were, and their estimated time of arrival over the carrier. The advance warning came from a deeply secret special-ops team that had been skulking around the Persian Gulf for months—or at least, that was the rumor.

Then, just six weeks ago, Al Qaeda–led terrorists managed to take over the top floor of Singapore's Tonka Tower, the tallest building in the world, trapping several hundred American women and children inside. The terrorists wired the building's glass-enclosed summit with nearly sixty pounds of plastic explosive, intent on toppling the building and killing another two thousand people caught in the floors below.

Just as the terrorists were about to detonate their explosives, one of the dozen TV news helicopters circling the building suddenly landed on its top-floor balcony. Someone inside the chopper shot four of the terrorists dead. Other men from the copter and more leaping in from the roof killed the three others and defused the bombs with seconds to spare. As soon as the crisis was over, the rescuers, who were dressed in U.S. military special-ops uniforms, briefly displayed an American flag, then got back in their TV news helicopter and promptly disappeared.

The Pentagon spin on the matter was both deceitful and marvelous: The rescuers were part of an elite special-ops group, so secret neither their names nor anything about them could be revealed. Truth was, no one with any power inside the Pentagon, the White House, or anywhere else in the U.S. government had the faintest idea who these mysterious soldiers were—only that they were probably the same group who had saved the day at Hormuz.

The problem was, they were not under anyone's control. They were a rogue team operating on their own, without oversight from higher authority. This type of thing sent shivers down the spines of the top brass.

The whole Hormuz-Singapore thing hit particularly close to home for Li. She'd always suspected her missing bosses, Major Fox and Lieutenant Ozzi, had gone off to look for the mysterious unit.

So when Nash asked about Hormuz and Singapore, Li replied, "I know what happened at both places, more or less . . ."

"Okay—well, now there's a third side to the triangle," Nash said. "Something that ties in Hormuz and Singapore and here it is: There's been a jail break at the detainee compound at Guantanamo. It occurred while a prisoner exchange was taking place with, of all people, the Iranians. We were releasing seven of their citizens, Taliban types we'd caught in Afghanistan, while they were giving us seven Al Qaeda capos they'd grabbed up recently. The Iranians flew an unmarked cargo plane into Gitmo to pick up their people, and these seven characters were put aboard, still in hoods and shackles. The plane took off, but about ten minutes later, someone discovered the seven Iranians who were supposed to be on the plane were actually back in their detainee hut—with their throats cut. They were all lying on the floor, lined up in a row."

Li almost burst out laughing. "This is a joke," she told him. "And a really weird way to get out of our date—"

"It's no joke," Nash replied harshly. "And I could get shot for telling you all this. So just listen. This is where Hormuz and Singapore come in. Besides the Al Qaeda and Taliban types at Gitmo, there's also a number of so-called 'special prisoners' being held down there—and that's also highly classified, by the way. These 'special prisoners' are all Americans. There's a bunch of them. They've been deemed threats to our national security and have been locked up down there, without trial, without access to attorneys, some of them for months."

Li couldn't believe this. "Are you saying these are American citizens who were helping the terrorists?"

"No," Nash replied. "What I'm saying is that these 'special prisoners' and the guys who showed up at Hormuz and Singapore are one and the same."

Li was astonished, almost speechless. "These heroes everyone has been looking for are in jail? Who the hell is responsible for that?"

"That's a question for another time," Nash said hurriedly. "The important thing is that the way it looks now, seven of these 'special prisoners' somehow managed to take the places of the seven Iranian POWs who got their throats slit. How? No one has a clue. But even that doesn't matter anymore—in fact, it's a very moot point."

"Why?"

"Because," Nash said deliberately. "Shortly after takeoff, this plane blew up in mid-air. One second it was on the radar, the next it was gone. It went right into the sea, taking everyone with it."

She gasped. "My God . . . What happened?"

"The Iranians themselves most likely planted a bomb onboard," he told her. "You know, set to go off as soon as the plane left Gitmo? The brain trust here think the Iranian bigwigs never intended for the plane to get back home. Their POWs were all related to high government officials in Tehran, and the mullahs probably didn't want a bunch of Taliban heroes with connections inside the government to be running around loose. Iran's a pretty volatile situation these days.

"Now, you'll probably never hear word one about this ever again. We got our Al Qaeda guys as promised at a checkpoint in Iraq, and the Iranians got rid of seven troublesome relatives, one way or another. A good day all around. Everyone should be happy."

"Except for the 'special prisoners' on the plane," she said. "Who were they really?"

"Well, that's the bad news," Nash answered slowly. "That's why I felt it was important to tell you all this. That you heard it from me first—and not someone else."

A much longer pause. "They've ID'd at least two of the people who were aboard that plane."

A troubled breath.

"And it was your bosses, Li," he said. "Those guys, Fox and Ozzi. We just got the official word from Gitmo. Both are confirmed deceased."

It wasn't quite *House on Haunted Hill*, but it was close.

It sat behind a row of empty warehouses at the end of a dead-end street, near the Potomac Reservoir extension road, just over the line in Virginia. The Navy had built this place back in the 1920s as an auxiliary weather station, but the sailors back then were better at sailing ships than constructing houses. This one was ugly from the first nail, and eighty years of rain and heat had only compounded the error. It had a strange, miniature-Kremlin look to it, with a skin of faded-green shingles and two creaky turrets rising from the back. A black brick chimney, leaning 70 degrees, sprouted atop the sagging roof. Add the rickety fence, the dirty brown lawn, and the two dead apple trees out front, and what was once homely was now just plain creepy.

This was what Li called home. She lived here for one reason only: The rent was very, very low. In fact, when she first came to live in D.C., she nearly had to turn around and go back home, so few were safe living spaces for young women just starting out on the government payroll. After weeks of searching and living out of a bag, this place became available. It was convenient and it was affordable. Creepy or not, she took it.

She parked out back now, in the small turnaround. Li had lived here for almost a year, but she'd yet to go into the garage, never mind park in it. It was cold up here as usual. A fog had lifted off the reservoir and was pouring through the old chain-link fence and into her backyard. She made sure her car was as close as it could be to her back door, then grabbed her briefcase, her phone, and her unused overnight bag. It was her habit to always hurry inside.

She climbed the back steps to the porch. From here, over several very bad neighborhoods and the winding Potomac beyond, the lights of the Lincoln Memorial burned dully in the mist. The normal bustle of the city was lacking, even way up here. Li paused for a moment, trying to make some sense of it. Everything was so quiet. Even the wind was still. But then she heard a muted rumbling from the south. What was that? Not a truck on the highway nearby. Not thunder, in the clear sky.

She looked out from under the porch's roof.

Two more F-15s flew overhead.

BOOTS
ON THE
GROUND

A Month with the 82nd Airborne in the Battle for Iraq

Karl Zinsmeister

Boots on the Ground is a riveting account of the war in Iraq with the 82nd Airborne Division as it convoys north from Kuwait to Iraq's Tallil Air Base en route to night-and-day battles within the major city of Samawah and its nearby bridges across the Euphrates. Karl Zinsmeister, a frontline reporter who traveled with the 82nd, brilliantly conveys the careful planning and technical wizardry that go into today's warfare, even local firefights, and he brings to life the constant air-ground interactions that are the great innovation of modern precision combat. Readers of this vivid day-to-day diary are left with not only a flashing sequence of strong mental images, but also a notion of the sounds and smells and physical sensations that make modern military action unforgettable.

Includes photos taken by the author while with the 82nd in Kuwait and Iraq!

"A fast-moving story of courage and competence, written by an observer who offers a far different picture from what was presented by our mainstream media. A moving tribute to what free soldiers united in a common cause can accomplish."

— Victor Davis Hanson, military historian

ISBN: 0-312-99608-X

Available wherever books are sold from St. Martin's Paperbacks

BOOTS 04/04